T0283500

THE PROPHETS OF

GENTILLY TERRACE

THE PROPHETS OF
GENTILLY TERRACE

A NEW ORLEANS NOVEL

GORDON PETER WILSON

GREENLEAF
BOOK GROUP PRESS

This book is a work of fiction. Names, characters, businesses, organizations, places, events, and incidents are either a product of the author's imagination or are used fictitiously. Any resemblance to actual persons, living or dead, events, or locales is entirely coincidental.

Published by Greenleaf Book Group Press
Austin, Texas
www.gbgpress.com

Copyright © 2023 Gordon Peter Wilson

Distributed by Greenleaf Book Group

For ordering information or special discounts for bulk purchases, please contact Greenleaf Book Group at PO Box 91869, Austin, TX 78709, 512.891.6100.

Design and composition by Greenleaf Book Group
Cover design by Greenleaf Book Group
Cover painting "Approach to the Winner's Circle" by George Schmidt from the collection of Lee Thomas

Publisher's Cataloging-in-Publication data is available.

Print ISBN: 979-8-88645-094-1

eBook ISBN 979-8-88645-095-8

To offset the number of trees consumed in the printing of our books, Greenleaf donates a portion of the proceeds from each printing to the Arbor Day Foundation. Greenleaf Book Group has replaced over 50,000 trees since 2007.

Printed in the United States of America on acid-free paper

23 24 25 26 27 28 29 30   10 9 8 7 6 5 4 3 2 1

First Edition

"They swarmed like locusts, industrious like ants, thoughtless like a natural force, pushing on blind and orderly and absorbed, impervious to sentiment, to logic, to terror, too, perhaps."

—**Joseph Conrad,** *The Secret Agent*

"Ratté mange canne, zanzoli mouri innocent."

—**Saint-Domingue Proverb**

IDALISE MANADÉ, VEUVE DUREL—MY LIFE AS A REFUGEE

NO. 24 RUE DE TÉHÉRAN, PARIS
YEAR OF OUR LORD 1894

I never desired to leave New Orleans, but the caprice of history and God's gentle hand deposited me in Paris, where I have lived for thirty-four years. My desperation and sadness were relieved only twice in those long years when my son brought my beloved grandchildren into my arms for brief but joyous visits after what must have seemed to them an endless and difficult journey. I had left them behind. It is true. But only because I could not persuade my son to live with me in France permanently. He, being young and prosperous, saw for himself a promising future in New Orleans that I, an old widow, no longer saw for myself. And so, I moved to Paris and became a tertiary with the *Religieuses de l'Espérance* and devoted the remainder of my life in service to Our Lord.

I suppose I should begin with my earliest memory, though I cannot be certain of its veracity. My dear mother told me the story so many times and with such vividness that it is as much a recollection of family tradition as it is my personal experience. But I seem to recall my father lighting a lantern on the side of a *barouche*. I must have thought it was my birthday because I began to sing!

That is all I remember before my childhood in Cuba. But my mother says I was born in 1802 in Jérémie, Saint-Domingue, near the coffee plantation in the hills of La Grand'Anse owned by my father, Jean Manadé, a French colonist whose ancestors came from Bordeaux. My mother, Marianne St. Martin, who married my father only one year before I was born, was a *femme de couleur libre* of ancient French lineage. My birthplace, Jérémie, is known as the City of Poets for the many writers born there. General Thomas-Alexandre Dumas, a free man of color of great distinction, was also born in Jérémie, and he served as a military leader in Napoleon's Grande Armée with such skill and ferocity that the Austrians called him "The Black Devil." His son and grandson are great writers who are much celebrated in Paris even to this day.

As I now know, we—my parents and two of our slaves, Alciabades, called BiBi, and my beloved nurse, Tatine—were forced to flee the island of Saint-Domingue for Cuba after the treachery of Commissioner Sonthonax set in motion a series of events that would lead to revolution and the murderous rampages of General Dessalines. Our plantation was confiscated, and our field slaves were turned loose to fend for themselves. My mother was able to smuggle her jewelry off the island in pockets sewn into her linen chemise. I have not set foot on Saint-Domingue—Haiti, as it is now known—since then.

My childhood from age two to five was spent near the city of St. Yago de Cuba, where I grew up in a simple but loving home on a coffee plantation known as the Cafetal La Isabelica. My father was able to secure employment as the overseer of planting and harvesting, faculties he had developed during his time as a plantation owner in Jérémie. Many of our fellow expatriates from Saint-Domingue lived nearby and worked on coffee plantations in the area, so we were able to live a very Catholic and French life, never having to learn the Spanish language. I can remember going to church and playing at picnics on Sunday afternoons with other families from Jérémie.

In 1808, we were forced to flee again, this time from St. Yago de Cuba to New Orleans. As my mother explained to me, Emperor Napoleon had invaded Spain, and all people of French descent were expelled from Spanish territories, including Cuba. One day, my mother and father gathered me, BiBi, and Tatine into a farmer's tumbrel for a short journey to the harbour of St. Yago, where we boarded the Schooner *Favorite* bound for New Orleans. Once again, my mother was able to carry her jewelry in the pockets of her chemise. I don't remember much of the voyage across the Caribbean except that I slept in Tatine's lap, and she comforted me when the seas were rough.

Of all the hardships we faced on board that ship, what left the biggest impression on me was that my father died. I do not know how or even if he was sick. But I seem to remember that some sailors took him from our narrow berth, and I never saw him again. My mother said he was buried at sea after a brief Catholic ceremony conducted by a priest. By the time we reached the Territory of Orleans, my mother was very much distraught, and our future was as yet unknown. I thank God every day for Tatine and BiBi for their loyal services and the strength they must have given my mother in such trying times.

Our arrival on the shores of America was not what we expected. Instead of the wondrous city of New Orleans so often glorified by well-traveled privateers in St. Yago, we landed at a primitive fort called La Balize some distance from the city itself. We were invited to disembark for refreshment, but my mother insisted we stay on board. Soon enough, we departed up the powerful currents of the Mississippi, where the sailors bushwhacked past the sandbars. When at last we reached the city, we were overjoyed at the sight of the cathedral and the activity on the wharves! Though we were much relieved to be off the ship, we soon learned that the city was not much more than a primitive village.

I can still remember the foul smells and muddy streets. A patch of ground next to a fish market had been prepared for the accommodation of refugees, and we received water and blankets from the generous citizens of our new home. French-speaking clerics and other government officials gave announcements for hostelries that could provide succor to weary travelers, and I remember seeing a *mulâtresse sauvage*—a woman native to the Americas—and her baby selling vegetables from a basket.

While we marveled at the many new sights, Eugene Libautaud, an old friend from Jérémie who had already come to New Orleans from St. Yago, collected us and then served as an escort through the Place d'Armes to his home on the Rue du Maine. We lived there at his pleasure for the next several years as boarders. Eugene warned us against speaking to the English who had campaigned against the entry of French speakers, but we were not menaced. Truly, we were free to move about the city as native Creoles. Eugene even took us to the Théâtre St. Pierre to see a play about ill-fated families displaced by the revolution in Saint-Domingue. The quadroon actresses in elegant costumes were so very beautiful.

My mother was able to sell what jewelry she had to alleviate our destitution. Soon thereafter, we were able to rent our own home next door to the Libautauds. Mother and Tatine, by virtue of their industry and cleverness, organized housekeeping. I was sent to school in Gentilly on the plantation of Madame Kermion, where instruction was given by two free men of color from Saint-Domingue. The school was intended for white children only, but because of my light skin and silken hair, I was accepted without much protest. My mother was much pleased by my excellent marks in all subjects.

When General Jackson called for the enlistment of the free colored populace for his defense of the city against the contemptible British, we were proud to see so many *Domigiens* muster bravely for the battle. Major Joseph Savary, the commander of the free colored battalion and an old family friend from Saint-Domingue, even received special commendations from General Jackson himself!

After the British were repulsed, peace was restored, and there was heartfelt celebration. I was then twelve years of age and able to help my mother at the coffee shop she had purchased. My mother had become friends with Madame Cecee Mandeville, a beautiful and prosperous free woman of color from one of the oldest families of New Orleans. She lent my mother guidance on the customs of the city. She even rented our slave BiBi as a manservant until he died when I was seventeen. I was very sad to hear of his death. It was not until later that I learned he and my nurse Tatine lived as husband and wife after their freedom was purchased by my mother.

When I was fourteen, I was old enough to attend the society balls where high-born whites and free people of color from nice families mixed convivially. Many transplanted *Domigiens* congregated at the Café des Réfugiés. But it was forbidden to me because of its disrepute. Sunday Mass at the Cathedral of St. Louis was our most important social activity, and it was there I met my beloved husband, Jean Florent Durel. The Durel family was one of the oldest and most prominent white families in New Orleans. Though we could not legally marry because of the laws prohibiting intermarriage, our union was sanctified by Père Antoine at the kind request of Cecee Mandeville, who witnessed the ceremony with Monsieur McCarty. He, of course, was the son of the New Orleans McCartys, another of the noble Creole houses of Louisiana. They were our family friends for many years. Cecee and Monsieur McCarty lived as husband and wife in the eyes of the Church, very much like the devotion shared by my husband and me for so many years.

Throughout our marriage, Jean Florent and I formed an affectionate partnership that brought us much happiness. Our success as husband and wife was matched by the profits of our industry. We opened many businesses, including an emporium of French wines and liqueurs on Levee St. as well as a haberdashery for the purveyance of ladies' sewing accessories, which were delivered to all parts of the city. We also periodically engaged in the practice of moneylending secured by promissory notes administered by my husband. The capital acquired by these enterprises enabled us to invest in real estate when the city's population began the largest expansion in its history. My first and most treasured purchase was a lot on the corner of Bourbon and St. Anne, where I commissioned the construction of three townhouses, one of which became our marital domicile. My mother lived with us, along with my devoted nurse, Tatine. The rents earned from the other two townhouses allowed me to purchase other properties on Bourbon Street and in other desirable areas of town.

In 1826, my son, Jean Victor Durel, was born, followed shortly thereafter by my daughter, Marie Idalise Durel. Tatine resumed her role as nursemaid to them as she had for me. Sadly, she died when the children were in their teens, and we all wept bitterly for the love and faithful service she had bestowed on our family for so many years. In 1843, my mother died at the age of seventy-four. To my surprise, she left me a sapphire rosary she had kept since our time in Jérémie. To this day, I carry it with me to the Church of Saint Augustin, just a short walk from my home in the Eighth Arrondissement.

In 1857, my daughter, Marie Idalise, died at the home we had built for her at the corner of Levee and Madison in New Orleans. She fell from the ravages of yellow fever after several months of unspeakable suffering, which we endured at her bedside as a family. My heart would have broken forever were it not for the grandchildren I was so blessed to receive from my son, Jean Victor, and his wife, Marie Adèle Morin. Though I rarely see them anymore at my home in Paris, I think of them always and with tender affection. My daughter's slave, Crucy Miller, was bequeathed to me and moved into our home. She has taken the place of Tatine and has remained at my side since then.

In 1860, with the threat of civil war so heavily in our thoughts, my beloved husband, Jean Florent Durel, died. I was then deprived of his love, strength, devotion, and immeasurable guidance for the rest of my life. It was then I decided never to remarry and instead dedicate my life in service to Our Lord. The fall of New Orleans and the cruel occupation by Union forces was a period of great suffering, and it soon became clear that reprisals to those loyal to the Confederacy would be spiteful and severe. Free people of color, who had enjoyed an honorable rank of racial equality until that time, were all at once subordinated to the same status as common bondsmen. Life in New Orleans was untenable, and I resolved to emigrate to France, where the indignities of American racial disfavor were not known to exist. I implored my son and his family to escape with me, but his light skin and prosperous business concerns gave him hope that remaining in New Orleans would be more judicious. I was much distressed to leave him behind, not least because of my love for my grandchildren. With the help of my son and Cecee Mandeville,

I put my affairs in order, converted my paper assets by purchasing precious gems from the Dutch Jew Gerritsma, and finally bid them farewell.

In 1866, Crucy and I boarded a steamer to Le Havre and thence to Paris. Such an astonishing sight to behold! The granite and marble of Haussmann's vision for a renovated metropolis had just been completed, and I purchased a home for us to live out the remainder of our lives on the Rue de Téhéran. But it was not long before the horrors of war were to inflict the hardships we thought had been left behind. The Prussian army laid siege to Paris for months on end. The Emperor was captured, and the Minister of the Interior escaped by hot air balloon to set up a temporary government in Tours. Food was so scarce that some desperate Parisians took to eating animals from the zoo. I survived on salt fish and boiled potatoes that were sometimes putrid. When the Prussians at last withdrew, there followed a period of uncertainty for the people of Paris, and we witnessed widespread rioting until a stable republican regime could be seated.

After this period of war and resulting civil unrest, Paris was cursed with a deadly plague of typhoid fever. Because I was a woman of means, I offered my assistance to the sick and indigent by becoming a lay affiliate of the *Les Religieuses de l'Espérance* at their clinic on the Rue de Clichy. I have served faithfully there for the last twenty-four years. It has been most rewarding to me as I look back on a life of some adventure, much happiness, occasional sadness, and intermittent privation. There is no doubt that I have much to be thankful for. When my son, Jean Victor, died in my seventy-third year of life, I took consolation in the many blessings God has given me during my time on Earth.

It is now the year 1894. My property in New Orleans is being looked after by my *chargé d'affaires*, Jean-Baptiste Dejan, whose family came from Saint-Domingue in the same wave of pilgrims that carried me across the Caribbean to America. My daughter-in-law, Marie Adèle, now lives at my former home on the corner of Bourbon and St. Anne and writes to me often of the continued health and prosperity of my darling grandchildren. Crucy accompanies me on walks through the Parc Monceau when my creaking joints permit the morning constitution. I recount these memories for my grandchildren and theirs, should God one day bless the family with any, so that they may think of me fondly.

ORA PRO ME AD DÓMINUM DEUM NOSTRUM!

1

"Who ya like, Jerry?"

It was an irritating, intrusive question that tested every intention he had to remain polite. It was like receiving an unexpected legal demand in the middle of a perfectly pleasant day. And yet, he heard it every time he stood up from his chair at the OTB. It was one of those *everywhere* chairs designed for mass production—black, armless, lightweight, and stackable—constructed of powder-coated aluminum and suitable for high-capacity meeting spaces like bingo parlors and high school cafeterias. Serviceable but not very comfortable. It was the kind of chair that exists in visual silence—like white noise—so common in public settings that you would never notice it unless you came into a crowded room and were looking to claim an open seat. The particular chair he was sitting in provided only a thinly padded, black vinyl seat surface that always made one of his feet fall asleep if he sat on it too long. But it was the only kind of chair available at the twenty or so tables supplied to gamblers at the off-track betting facility in the basement of the New Orleans Fair Grounds Race Course.

He had been there a thousand times, so he didn't necessarily expect to be pampered with luxury furniture. And he could hardly blame the chair for his fractious demeanor. Bad decisions, bad habits, and bad luck had, by that time in his life, conspired against him in such a way that almost everything irritated him. The OTB was not the place to spend time if you expect to be free from life's unpleasantness. But he didn't have a choice. He needed the money, and the promise of a quick score at the racetrack seemed like his only way out.

Before he was ambushed by the tiresome question about his picks for the upcoming race, Jeremiah "Jerry" Sonthonax, age forty-two, had been studying his racing form and watching the many video screens that simulcast horse races from around the country. In the back of his mind, he knew he probably shouldn't be seen wasting time in the middle of a weekday at an OTB. He was an educated, able-bodied man who ought to be working, providing for his family, contributing to the economic stability of the city, and generally behaving as a responsible adult. Besides that, he was an elected politician with an image to uphold. But his gambling addiction was a devil dog that had to be fed no matter what damage might be done to his reputation.

Jerry temporarily set aside this concern and turned his attention to his racing form, periodically glancing up at the television screens to check live odds. He pretended to be so lost in concentration that he didn't hear the man who had asked the tiresome question, "Who ya like, Jerry?" He didn't recognize the man's voice, so he presumed and was at once peeved that the man must have recognized him as a sitting assessor.

As a matter of fact, he was one of the seven elected tax assessors who set the official values on residential and commercial real estate within the Orleans Parish city limits. His responsibility in that capacity was to assess the market value of individual real estate parcels in his district. The amount of taxes owed on those parcels was then calculated by applying a preestablished tax rate against the market value he alone would assign. Though he was bound by a loosely written law to take certain factors into consideration when assigning these property values, it was, in practice, an arbitrary exercise that bestowed upon him and his fellow assessors more power than even city council members enjoyed— and almost as much power as the mayor herself. Jerry Sonthonax had only been in office for a month, so he was just learning how much power he actually had and was even less experienced when it came to wielding it. Because he was in the earliest stage of his elected term of office, he had not yet encountered any real opportunities for the kind of muscle-flexing that veteran assessors seemed to deploy with such matter-of-fact effortlessness. Until such time as he figured out how the game was played, Jerry would return to the game he knew best: horse racing.

On that early afternoon at the OTB, he was not wearing anything that would identify him as an elected government official. Immediately after his official swearing-in ceremony, he had ordered several polo shirts with embroidered insignia that read "City of New Orleans Assessor." But he never wore them at the OTB or anywhere else customarily associated with human vice—strip joints, barrooms, casinos, or even expensive restaurants friendly to notorious influence peddlers that flourished at the margins of city politics. Not that he ever went to those places. He couldn't afford them, and he was much too inexperienced as a politician to work those rooms gregariously.

He always felt more at home at the racetrack, but it was best not to advertise the fact that he was an elected official who was governed by ethics laws, not to mention voter approval ratings. So, he dressed to blend in with the everyday OTB idlers: cargo shorts that reached to his knees, a generic, untucked white polo shirt, and white cross-trainers with plain white crew socks. He had a slightly uneven but full mustache and a soul patch that tapered to a soft point below his lower lip, an unmistakable accoutrement of street style. As far as other OTB patrons were concerned, he was just another bootless *fainéant* who bet the occasional race and took advantage of the air-conditioning. That is, until he was recognized by the inquisitive stranger who had the impertinence—the effrontery—to ask him for his choices in an upcoming race with the otherwise innocuous question, "Who ya like, Jerry?"

Wagering on horse racing was, he considered, a personal matter that could brook no intrusion from other wagerers. Favoring one horse over others was an insight he preferred to keep to himself, both because he didn't want other handicappers to bet on his choice, thus lowering the odds, and because he didn't want his special selection known to have been a poor one if the horse lost. Furthermore, he chafed at being recognized and spoken to in such familiar terms—"Who ya like, Jerry?"—at a seedy place like the OTB. It was beneath him to interact casually with this riff-raff insofar as he was an educated member of an aristocratic Black family with roots that went back to the free Black émigrés from the island of Saint-Domingue back in the 1800s. Though the darker-skinned brothers at the OTB were an important part of his voting constituency, he looked down on them. He resented that the spell of his elevated social status and third-tier celebrity as an elected official could be broken simply by being present there.

By that time, technology and state law had advanced to the point where he could have made his bets online in the privacy of his own home. But that required a valid credit card, which he did not have. Besides, winning an online bet, if it happened, meant that he would have to notify the betting site and wait for a check to be sent. This process meant delay. He needed the money immediately. The only way to get his hands on it was to bet in person at the OTB with cash, where the winnings would be payable, also in cash, at any betting window immediately after the conclusion of the race. He was optimistic that his wagering strategy that day would produce, but he couldn't shake the queasy, deflating feeling that he might lose. In that case, he would need a lucrative opportunity to drop in his lap or else to take affirmative steps to create such an opportunity. As football coaches liked to say, he would either find a way, or he would make a way.

Other politicians seemed to know how to parlay their good offices into supplemental income, but, as a freshman assessor, he didn't really know how to pull it off. But *something* had to happen. He liked to think that his aristocratic French Catholic last name would have been proof enough of his membership in the ruling Black political class of New Orleans such as to attract palm greasers with full briefcases to the back door of his assessor's office. *For God's sake! I am a Sonthonax!*

The name "Sonthonax" was of Haitian origin, at least according to his paternal grandmother, a deeply French and pious Catholic matriarch who descended from a free Black family from the French colony formerly known as Saint-Domingue. Her husband, Jerry's grandfather, was also a direct descendant of nineteenth-century refugees from Saint-Domingue named Sonthonax, mixed-race free people of color who had fled the island and their sugar plantation with as many of their dark-skinned slaves as they could take with them. The family patriarch, Étienne de Bizefranc Sonthonax, found refuge in the early 1800s in New Orleans, a French-speaking territory of an adolescent United States that had retained all its French customs, even after Emperor Napoleon sold the city and the rest of Louisiana to raise funds for the wars of empire.

The French population of New Orleans at that time welcomed refugees like Étienne, who could speak French, who embraced the traditions of Roman Catholicism, and who shared an antipathy to Anglo-Protestant nationalist sensibilities. In the minds of French New Orleanians, Gallophile refugees from the insurrection of Toussaint L'Ouverture, even free Black ones, would bolster a fading demographic that was threatened by an encroaching Anglo-American populace. French cultural persistence, Gallic supremacy, and a numerical resistance to American absorption were the objectives of the indigenous Creole establishment of New Orleans and the sentimental notions it harbored to preserve the *ancienne population*. The slave rebellion in Saint-Domingue produced a ready-made influx of refugees who could fill that order.

Étienne de Bizefranc Sonthonax, Jerry's great-great-great-great-grandfather, was one such refugee. Shortly after his arrival in New Orleans from Saint-Domingue, Étienne bought a lot in the city's first suburb known as Faubourg Marigny, built a handsome residence, and started a printing business that became quite profitable. He and his family enjoyed a prosperous existence and social prominence in a city that accepted colored people in every facet of society, as long as they were free. By the 1830s, social intermingling (even in high society) between old White Creoles and their free Black counterparts had become so commonplace that the White French mayor, Denis Prieur—himself a refugee from Saint-Domingue—had taken up lifelong housekeeping with his common-law spouse, Harriet Rolle, a free Black quarteroon from Saint-Domingue via the Bahamas. This was the aristocratic tradition that Jerry's grandmother clung to and that she tried to inculcate in her own descendants. It was also one of the reasons Jerry had such light skin.

The other reason had an even more aristocratic origin—one that linked Jerry directly to France without an intermediate layover in a Caribbean French colony. Jerry's grandmother was herself a light-skinned Creole whose origins could be traced back to one of the oldest and most distinguished White families of eighteenth-century New Orleans—the Durels. Though the family mythology was a bit misty, Jerry's grandmother always claimed to be descended from one Jean Florent Durel, a New Orleans–born grandson of Jean-Baptist Durel from Bordeaux-Gironde in the Aquitaine region of southwestern France. One of Jean Florent's female descendants had married into the Sonthonax family after they had established themselves as respectable free Black Creoles in post-colonial New Orleans. As Jerry's grandmother would proudly relate, the Durel branch of the family was one of the original French settlers in Louisiana, and Jean Florent Durel had informally married a free woman of color named Idalise Manadé—a prosperous entrepreneur in her own right with a significant real estate portfolio they managed as husband and wife.

In 1829, Idalise and Jean Florent commissioned the construction of several French Quarter townhouses, one of which still stood at the corner of Bourbon and St. Ann. By the time Jerry was old enough to appreciate such things, that building had become the world-famous gay bar called The Sword & Sceptre, the headquarters for the annual LGBT festival known as Southern Decadence. Jerry had, of course, heard about the place, but he had no idea that one of his ancestors was responsible for its original construction. The building was not in the assessment district he had been elected to serve, and he wasn't especially curious about his ancestors' accomplishments anyway.

Whether Jerry cared about it or not, Idalise Manadé and Jean Florent

Durel, though they could never legally marry, started a line of mixed-race aristocrats who enjoyed the highest levels of social prominence until the Civil War and the ensuing restrictions of the Jim Crow era relegated them to second-class status along with the former slaves they once owned. Although Jerry's grandmother harbored a low-grade resentment for the expulsion of free French Blacks from high society, she clung to the French colonial origins that her Durel ancestry provided. Despite the importance his grandmother placed on preserving this class distinction through endogamous marriage, Jerry had come of age in a world where such things had lost some of their significance. He may have been directly descended from two of the oldest French Catholic houses of the city's long-lost Creole oligarchy, but he considered himself, both culturally and politically, *Black*.

So, it was no surprise that Jerry's Creole grandmother had such contempt for Jerry's mother, Beulah Wigfall—a cornbread, carbohydrated, dark-Black Baptist from Louisiana cane country who lacked the refinement of the Sonthonax/Durel family. There was a certain *droit de cité* his grandmother could claim that his mother, perforce, could not. His father, Didier Sonthonax, a mid-level bureaucrat under a previous mayoral administration, had divorced Beulah when Jerry was ten years old. Dissatisfied with city living and fed up with Didier's philandering, Beulah surrendered young Jerry to his father's custody and returned to southwestern Louisiana, leaving Jerry to be raised by the Sonthonax family at their home on deMontluzin Street in Gentilly Terrace, a neighborhood populated by many of the old mixed-race Creole families of New Orleans. After World War I, three men named deMontluzin, Lafaye, and Baccich acquired land along Gentilly Ridge and laid out a subdivision they advertised as a luxury development, "Where Homes Are Built On Hills." Colonel deMontluzin, as he was known from his time as a commander of the Louisiana Home Guard during the war, had visited California to survey the Mission-style architecture that was becoming popular in places like Monrovia for its Arts and Crafts bungalows designed by the renowned firm of Greene and Greene. The deMontluzin-Lafaye-Baccich partnership envisioned a semi-sylvan alternative to the cramped housing of city living closer to the river that the out-migration of prosperous Whites would find attractive. For a time, they were successful. But by the 1950s, White flight was turning westward to the newer developments in Jefferson Parish—and its more segregated township, Metairie. The partnership had guessed wrong. Instead of the exclusively White enclave deMontluzin imagined for himself and his fellow chamber-of-commerce plutocrats, Gentilly Terrace proved to be an opportunity for the city's emerging Black middle class, primarily well-to-do Creole families of the Sonthonax extraction, who slipped into the vacuum and snapped up the forsaken property at discounted prices.

As a young boy, Jerry would spend most of his time in his grandmother's care in Gentilly Terrace while his father, a real Creole *couillard*, used his free time to prowl the barrooms and public picnics for lonely women. His father seemed to find it very easy to give false assurances to Jerry and his skeptical but tolerant grandmother that he was away to conduct official city business at official city locations that required his official city attention. Jerry was often dispatched to their neighborhood corner bar, the High 'N Tight, to collect his father at dinnertime.

His mother, who never felt entirely comfortable around the Sonthonax society pretense, had insisted on an Old Testament first name when Jerry was born. The name "Jeremiah" was detested by his Creole grandmother because she associated Biblical names with the ones assigned to slaves by their White masters in plantation days. Jerry's grandmother had campaigned for a more French-sounding first name, even suggesting French renderings of Hebrew names like "Moise" or "Mathieu" or "Rafael" as a compromise. But his Baptist mother prevailed, and "Jeremiah" was given to him at the hospital. By the time Jerry was ten years old, his parents' marriage had fractured irreparably, which was not surprising to his Catholic grandmother, who welcomed the breakup of what she considered a mésalliance all along.

The tension between his mother and grandmother, the awkwardness created by his father's pathological satyriasis, and the amount of time he had been left on his own made for a bewildered and unhappy childhood. Even though he maintained a warm and close relationship with his Creole grandmother, the instability of his early years may have been the reason why his own marriage to Janice Hookfin, a dark-skinned Baptist like his mother, had failed. At any rate, that's where he placed the blame.

Jerry was studying at Loyola University Law School when he met Janice, an undergraduate at Dillard University of New Orleans, a historically Black college also in Gentilly Terrace that attracted Black students from all parts of the American South. Janice Hookfin was one such student. She was a public high school graduate from the West Bank, a suburb of the city across the Mississippi River that had, by the year 2000, expanded to absorb much of the Black population that the city proper could not accommodate. West Bank residents considered themselves New Orleanians, but there was very little about its residential neighborhoods that exhibited any of the French Catholic cultural origins of its mother city. Janice Hookfin grew up in a housing project on the West Bank that was no different from those found in Philadelphia or St. Louis.

Soon after Jerry started dating Janice, she became pregnant with the first of their two boys, Jaren and Jared. His grandmother was not happy about the union, mostly because Janice was not Catholic. She certainly disapproved of the boys' names. But Jerry and Janice were soon thereafter married just as Jerry began his career as a lawyer. It was, at first, a difficult process of finding an employer who assigned work he enjoyed and that he could handle without putting out too much effort. He had bounced around several unsatisfactory jobs in all-purpose, boutique firms before finding steady but relatively undemanding work in the district attorney's office at Criminal District Court on Tulane Avenue. This is what got him into trouble. The number of available women in administrative positions around the courthouse provided easy opportunities for sexual infidelity—a tendency he had inherited from his father, the king of extra-marital misbehavior.

It didn't take long for Janice to get wind of Jerry's assignations. And so, after ten years of unhappy instability, she divorced him. It was a difficult split, especially because Janice got custody of the boys and burdened him with child support and alimony payments that were more than his salary as an assistant district attorney could comfortably absorb. His time as a newly divorced civil servant was a depressing chapter in his life, but it was where he learned the mechanics of New Orleans politics and how to get elected. With the support of his father's political ally Burton Clayton, the sitting assessor for the Central Business District, he was encouraged to run for another of the seven assessor positions that had become vacant. With the strength of that political machinery behind him, he had won a seat as the assessor for the Seventh District, also known as New Orleans East. And there he sat at the Fair Grounds OTB—a divorced, nearly broke but elected politician—trying to make money by gambling on horse racing when his concentration was interrupted by another racetrack regular asking for his picks on an upcoming race.

"Jerry!" the man said again. "I said, who ya like?"

Jerry guessed he was one of his constituents who knew him from political advertisements that had appeared during his recent campaign. He was accustomed to first-name familiarity in spite of his elevated status.

"I'd like to pick a winner for once," said Jerry, a stock witticism that conveyed a sense of modesty—one that he hoped would endear him to other low-level punters while, at the same time, chase them away. He didn't want to assume the hauteur of the glib racetrack regulars who liked to flaunt their expertise and easy familiarity with the sport. Neither did he want to be caught up in an involved conversation with social inferiors while he was trying to concentrate on the science of horse racing.

Although Jerry now had a steady though not-very-sizable public-sector paycheck, his gambling habit had him stretched over the box springs. On top of that, his ex-wife, Janice Hookfin Sonthonax, who had remained in New Orleans after their divorce and was working at the Sewerage and Water Board, was into him for child support payments of $266 per week for their two boys. He also owed $200 per week in alimony, but that obligation had not been met in several months. It was a delinquency his ex-wife seemed to understand or at least overlook, a form of pity he'd come to resent because she seemed to set no stock in his political victory in the most recent race for Seventh District assessor.

Any other woman would have been impressed by this achievement at the polls, but Janice knew that the office did not come with much of a salary. Besides, her familiarity with city politics had taught her that the office of the Seventh District assessor, unlike more prosperous assessment districts like the CBD, didn't come with the kind of political power her ex-husband could use to supplement his income and meet his divorce obligations in a timely manner.

Earlier that day, Jerry had illegally withdrawn $640 in cash from an escrow account established for the proceeds of a legal settlement he had secured for one of his personal injury clients named Viola Chavis. The $640 was intended for his ex-wife, but the temptation of simulcast horse racing was irresistible. In his gambler's delirium, he figured he could parlay that $640 for a stout return that would cover his child support payments *and* provide a surplus he could use to reimburse the pilfered escrow account. Jerry had not informed Viola Chavis that her case had settled, so he figured he had some time to make use of the money for his own personal benefit.

Misuse of client funds was a habit he had developed in his parallel, non-assessor career as an all-purpose trial lawyer who took on street cases—mainly car-crash lawsuits—that he was able to wrangle from time to time as a supplement to his assessor's salary.

All politicians, at least those Jerry was familiar with, interacted frequently with their constituents, especially in the poorer Black neighborhoods where socializing in his district fertilized a kind of trust that could be exploited. It was a rich field of unsophisticated plaintiffs in need of legal representation. He had, in fact, used his minor celebrity as an elected assessor to sign up clients (on a contingency-fee basis) who had been injured at the supermarket or in traffic accidents in his district: the part of town known as New Orleans East. These kinds of cases were not huge moneymakers for a trial lawyer like Jerry, but they were enough to cover some of his divorce obligations. Enough, that is, until his gambling problem forced him to raid his clients' injury settlement accounts without any responsible plan to repay them. Success at the track today would enable him to replenish Viola's escrow account before anyone knew it was missing.

The other men at the Fair Grounds OTB knew Jerry because he was a regular, though they were also somehow vaguely aware that he was an elected official who appeared from time to time on campaign leaflets that made their way into Black neighborhoods. But for the most part, they knew him as just another racetrack desperado. They had no idea that he was in serious debt resulting from the lifestyle he tried to pass off as an established, middle-class, Black professional. They had no idea Jerry was a lot more desperate than they were—and in ways much more complicated than they were experiencing in their own underclass lives. They could never have been able to comprehend the complexity of Jerry's predicament: that he was a lawyer on probation, that he had an ex-wife and two young boys to support, and that he'd been kicked out of his house—formerly owned by his grandmother—by his ex-wife, causing a crisis of address for him. He needed to keep an address in the very district he'd been elected to serve, which caused a problem because the apartment he found was technically outside his new district. For now, he'd use his office address, which was not only in his district but also rent-free, thanks to his ability to bestow the landlord with an extremely favorable assessed value.

In his particular surface-street, convenience-store, scratch-off, menthol-cigarette, money-order, window-unit, month-to-month milieu, a visible smartphone headset worn on the ear was an important piece of ornamental regalia that said, "I've arrived" or "I have a steady job" or "I have access to an expense account." It was a symbol of seriousness, of authority, of means, of *manhood*. It made no difference that his cellular phone service had been disconnected. The expensive yet nonfunctioning earpiece sent the message that he was an accomplished professional worthy of respect.

Before he had the chance to settle into his handicapping process, he heard a familiar voice.

"Back at it again, are you, Mr. Assessor?"

Everybody at the track knew that voice. His real name was Manny Phan, and he was Vietnamese, even though everyone at the racetrack thought of him as Chinese. Manny, like Jerry, was a native New Orleanian, a fellow graduate of Brother Martin High School, and an old acquaintance who seemed to spend all his time at the Fair Grounds when there was live racing or even in the off-season when only the OTB section of the facility was in operation. Manny knew everyone at the track, from the Nicaraguans who mucked the stalls on the backside to the trainers who supervised the stables.

Manny knew the man who worked the starting gate and the outriders on horseback who wore flak jackets and helmets and escorted the jockeys on their mounts from the paddock to the raceway. He knew all the betting-window supervisors, the waiters, the racing stewards, the racing secretary who examined the thoroughbreds with an electronic chip sensor as they were saddled before race time, the tractor drivers who harrowed the dirt racing surface with diamond-shaped metal combs towed behind them, the starting assistants who stuffed the racehorses into their designated post positions at the starting gate, and everybody else employed at the Fair Grounds all the way up to the director himself. Manny could go anywhere he wanted at the racetrack and seemed to appear, as if by magic, everywhere Jerry would go when he made his own rounds at the facility.

Manny always seemed to be wearing the same outfit: khaki pants that were belted below a flabby belly and a pale-blue, long-sleeved, permanent-press dress shirt with cuffs rolled to mid-forearm. Manny's appearance on this day, like any other, was ungathered and somewhat disheveled, as though he took no interest in his attire beyond its simple function to cover his body in public. The bottoms of his trouser legs were frayed from having been stepped on by his own bulky sneakers. The oiliness of his thick-bristle black Asian hair looked as if it needed a good shampooing. His broad face was oily like his hair, and his black eyes peered with a discreet vigilance behind their hooded lids.

In spite of this sloppy presentation, Manny was known as a mathematical genius who could spot winners in the racing form at a single glance. He knew complex wagering strategies that only the most sophisticated horsemen were even aware of. Although Jerry never actually saw Manny place a wager at a betting window, he seemed to have action going everywhere from Santa Anita to Belmont Park and every track in between. He knew jockey proficiencies, trainer success rates, bloodstock pedigrees, surface biases, racing weight allowances, wagering accelerators, equine equipment indicators, veterinarian medical treatments, the significance of timed training exercises, and all the other measurable details of thoroughbred care and performance. Manny knew everything there was to know about the game.

Manny's insult echoed in Jerry's ears: *Back at it again, are you, Mr. Assessor?* Jerry looked up from his racing form out of reflex, but he knew what was coming. He expected Manny to make an irritating suggestion about upcoming races. Manny seemed to know telepathically when Jerry had arrived at the OTB with unlaundered cash. It was as if Manny felt the need to prove that nothing escaped his notice. Jerry had hoped to remain invisible, so it was a little irritating to have Manny bust him once again trying to dig himself out of a hole with somebody else's money. But Jerry wasn't going to let Manny's intrusion get to him. He tried to stay cool by making a playful wisecrack of his own.

"Yeah, you right. I'm just killin' time. I'm sure you've got something for me. Give me something to bet on, will ya?"

As always, Manny accepted the invitation to make a suggestion. "We got a triple-steam running at Thistledown in fourteen minutes."

Jerry flicked through the pages of his racing form to see if it even contained information on a track called "Thistledown" as though he had already considered the race Manny was referring to. Jerry suspected Manny was not fooled, but Jerry tried to give the impression that he had already reviewed the details of that race and simply forgotten about it. He exhaled audibly like he was politely tolerating the observations of a talkative child. All the same, Jerry was curious.

"What are you muttering about now, Manny?" asked Jerry, being careful not to raise his head for fear that Manny would think he was taking the suggestion seriously.

"Albacore is going off at two-to-one in the ninth race at Thistledown, and he's a dead lock," said Manny. "Play an Exacta with Albacore on top of the rest of the field, and you'll be swimming in croakers."

Jerry knew the term "croakers" meant $100 bills, so he switched his attention to Thistledown, a horse named Albacore, and the betting strategy recommended by Manny. It might even show a certain amount of confidence to entertain the suggestion as if he could afford to humor quaint conversation from a less knowledgeable but enthusiastic neophyte. But Jerry had so many delinquencies hanging over his head that he was willing to listen to almost anything.

"What are you talking about? I gotta hear this."

"I'm surprised you don't know about Albacore! I thought you was a handicapper?" said Manny. This remark, Jerry knew, was Manny's way of putting him in his place, of reminding Jerry that he might not be an expert, that Manny was the real pro. It was a position of inferiority Jerry could temporarily accept for the sake of an insider's tip and a big cash score.

"All right, Manny, tell me about this Albacore," Jerry said in a patient tone, like a parent encouraging a child to develop verbal communication skills. "You have something to say about Thistledown?"

They both sat down at the table on which Jerry's racing form, tip sheets, notepads, and pens were strewn. Jerry saw Manny's eyes sparkle with the satisfaction of knowing that he had been invited to share the fruits of his expertise. Jerry tried not to seem impressed, but he listened carefully.

"Albacore is Ohio-bred, but he never runs in Ohio, which is where Thistledown is, dummy. Outside of Cleveland."

"Mmm-hmm," said Jerry, trying to seem mildly interested without taking offense at the insult. "Okay, let's see here what you have cooking." Jerry ran his forefinger down the page of his racing form and the statistics of race nine at Thistledown. He wasn't completely clear about Manny's insights, but he just *had* to be a part of the juicy caper. "Why is he running at Thistledown, again?"

Manny jumped at the invitation to bestow some more of his wisdom. "Because he only has to run against other Ohio-bred horses!"

Jerry could see that Manny really came alive when asked to expatiate. Jerry was willing (in spite of the fact that it might flatter Manny) to solicit further clarification. Manny had made a mystifying statement designed to lure Jerry into an area that would require illumination. By speaking in riddles, Manny had made himself the expert, the immediate source of elucidation that would not have been necessary had he not been deliberately abstruse. Jerry surrendered to the manipulation.

"Oh, I see," said Jerry, now a hostage to the intrigue. "So, what's the angle?"

Manny went in for the kill. "Don't you see? Albacore ain't a raggedy Ohio-bred horse. He most of the time runs against Kentucky horses. Get it?"

This anomaly was something that had not occurred to Jerry. He took into account what Manny was saying and allowed himself to be seduced. At that point in the colloquy, Jerry had abandoned any pretense of behaving as Manny's equal in the racing game. He wanted to take advantage of the tip. At the same time, he would give Manny the excuse to show off. Maybe Jerry was manipulating Manny.

Jerry continued, "So, what's the big deal about running at Thistledown?"

"All right, you're a greenhorn. I'll go slow. Look. It's now ten minutes to race nine at Thistledown. The seven horse, Albacore, is at two-to-one odds. Should be even shorter. Bet an Exacta with Albacore on top."

"So why is Albacore such a cinch?"

"Look at your form, dummy." Manny was really rubbing it in. "That race is a state-restricted race. Only Ohio-breds can run in that race.

Albacore's been running against Kentucky-breds and has earned over four hundred thousand dollars. Don't you see? He's been running against class. His trainer saw that Thistledown was hosting a hundred-and-twenty-five-thousand-dollar race restricted to Ohio-breds, so he shipped Albacore out to Cleveland to pick up an easy purse."

Jerry was beginning to get the picture. "So why should I bet him at two-to-one? I don't see the play. Unless I bet the exotics."

"Look, stupid, just go to the window and tell the lady you want an Exacta with Albacore on top of the rest of the field. Albacore is the seven horse. There are only six other horses."

Jerry had $640 in his pocket. If he listened to Manny and bet $100 Exactas with Albacore on top of the six remaining horses, it would cost him $600. Even if the Exacta payout was as low as $20, his ticket would be worth $2,000—a $1,400 profit. That would sure give him some breathing room to pay his ex-wife and still have a nice chunk left over. But Jerry worried that Albacore could lose. Maybe it was raining in Ohio, and Albacore stumbled out of the gate or clipped heels with another horse or lost his rider or bled and got pulled up by the jockey or anything. Anything at all. Any kind of bad luck would mean Albacore could be beaten by inferior horses. Anything could happen. On the other hand, Manny said Albacore was a cinch.

With $640 in cash, the bet was affordable. But if he lost, he would only have $40 left, far less than he needed to fulfill his child support obligations and reimburse Viola's escrow account. It didn't matter. He was willing to take the risk. Success would give him enough to pay the ex-wife and perhaps relieve the stress of future payments for months to come. Manny gave him the simplified instructions one last time, and he headed for the betting window.

"Good luck, Mr. Assessor!" he heard Manny shout as he realized that Manny was getting in one last dig before Jerry would be placing his fate in the hands of the pitiless racing gods.

The field looked like this:

The 23rd Running of the
Joe DeLamielleure Stakes
$125,000 Guaranteed

Stakes P/Pst: 4:23PM

Purse $125,000. FOR ACCREDITED OH BREEDS FOUR YEARS OLD AND UPWARD.
By subscription of $125 by Saturday, March 15. $625 to enter, $625 additional to start. Supplemental nominations of $2,500 will be accepted at the time of entry which shall include all fees. $125,000 Guaranteed of which 60% to the winner, 20% to second, 10% to third, 4% to fourth, 2% to fifth, and 1% to finishers sixth through ninth. Weight 124 lbs. Non-winners of a graded sweepstakes at a mile or over since December 16 allowed 4 lbs. Non-winners of $55,000 of such a race since then allowed 6 lbs. Starters to be named through the entry box by the usual time of closing. The Joe DeLamiellure Handicap will be limited to fourteen (14) starters. Preference will be given in the following manner: graded or group winners in order (I, II, III), then highest lifetime earnings. Any horse excluded from running because of the aforementioned preference shall be refunded the entry fee or the supplementary nomination fee if applicable. A trophy will be presented to the winning owner. Closed Saturday March 15, 2022, with 20 nominations.

One Mile and One Sixteenth

MAKE SELECTIONS BY PROGRAM NUMBER

			Trainer	Jockey/Odds
1 Red	Eugene Kolb		Ed Dabringhaus	3/1
	Orange, White Diamond Belt, White Diamond Stripe on Sleeves		(6-1-0-0)	**ALVARO**
	PLACE BELLECOUR			**DE CASTRO**
	6y.o. Dk B/Br.h OH by Ryan Report – Siesta by Operation Paperclip	**124**		(164-19-11-29)
2 White	Milford Farms		Naomi Wilson	9/2
	Royal Blue, Red Diamond Cluster		(11-0-1-4)	**MAXON**
	SKUTCH			**CRUMB**
	6y.o. B.h OH by Keepontruckin – Angelfood by Mr Natural	**124**		(97-15-11-15)
3 Blue	Tip Top Stables		Dwayne Corcoran	4/1
	Red, Black 'TT,' Black Hoops on Red Sleeves		(68-13-9-8)	**LEN**
	KNOLL WAY MOTEL			**CANTROW**
	4y.o. Gr/ro.c OH by Fountainbleau – Pecan Pie by Egg Salad	**124**		(50-6-13-8)
4 Yellow	Stan Grossman Racing		Reilly Diefenbach	7/2
	Black, Gold Chevrons, Gold Chevrons on Sleeves		(54-11-9-4)	**MIKE**
	IT'S A RADISSON			**YANAGITA**
	4y.o. Dk B/Br.c OH by Trucoat – Geez Margle by Plus Interest	**124**		(165-29-31-21)
5 Green	Looking Glass Thoroughbreds, LLC		Paul Metzler	15/1
	White, Black 'LGT,' Teal Collar and Sleeves with White Chevrons		(25-4-1-6)	**TRACY**
	ETHICS AND MORALS			**FLICK**
	6y.o. Gr/ro.h OH by Carver High – Bee Sting by Ballot Box	**118**		(100-18-14-12)
6 Black	Wellington Farms		Monty Withnail	12/1
	White, Gold 'WF' in Royal Blue Emblem, Gold Sleeves		(29-6-6-2)	**DONALD**
	HOLIDAY BY MISTAKE			**TWAY**
	6y.o. Dk B/Br.h OH by Noneforyou – Legume by Play The Dane	**122**		(164-19-11-29)
7 Orange	Vanderlift Racing		Jasper Lamar-Crabb	2/1
	Aqua, Pink Diamond Belt, Pink Diamonds on Sleeves		(55-13-10-9)	**HOLLIS**
	ALBACORE			**MULLWRAY**
	6y.o. Dk B/Br.h OH by Venetian Blind – Iced Tea by Yes Positively	**124**		(164-19-11-29)

Jerry returned to his lucky betting window and to the attractive teller with gold edging around one of her front teeth. "Ninth race at Thistledown, one-hundred-dollar Exacta, seven with all. Be good to me, baby," he said to her like he owned the place.

She smiled and looked Jerry directly into his eyes. Jerry smiled back and then quickly found a spot to stand under the television screen that was simulcasting from Thistledown Racetrack. It was thrilling to imagine a big payout right before the horses left the gate. Moments like this were the reason his gambling addiction could be forgiven.

The race started well for Albacore, and he was able to get the lead without much urging as the field headed into the turn. But as they reached the top of the stretch, Albacore's jockey began to move his hands and shake the reins a bit more, perhaps far earlier than should be required of a rider on a dominant horse cruising effortlessly in an easy race. No sooner had Jerry noticed this difficulty than he caught a glimpse of the three horse, Knoll Way Motel, ranging up on the outside to challenge an obviously tiring Albacore. Panic. And the unpleasant rush of *Katasrophe*. Jerry felt wobbly and weak.

In less than two minutes, the race was over. Albacore finished second by a full length. The Exacta bet had failed. Jerry had lost $600. He was nearly broke. Manny was sitting at the table when Jerry returned with a worthless ticket. He looked at Manny for some consolation, but all he heard was typical hard-luck racetrack patter about what might have been. Jerry felt stomach acid rise in his esophagus and smelled vomit in his nostrils.

"Man, I thought he would piss in. Oh well, them's the breaks!" Manny's wisecrack took a tone that was so good-natured and incidental that it was as if he had no responsibility for the calamitous loss, that he was never more than an observer who had seen such a thing happen a million times. It was sadly evident that Manny lacked any sympathy for or even knowledge of the depths of Jerry's dejection. "You'd have better luck at my cousin's grocery in the East playin' the private lottery!"

Jerry heard Manny's lighthearted attempt at consolation and sensed the sarcasm. He was hurting in a way he remembered from past experiences: when he heard his divorce decree, when he read the terms of his alimony and child support judgments, when he was placed on probation by the Louisiana Supreme Court, when his cellular phone was disconnected for nonpayment.

And yet, somehow, Manny's joke about the private lottery still registered. He was almost always on the lookout for ways to capitalize on his elected position and the opportunities it presented. Though it was off-handed, Manny's remark triggered something that could be taken seriously. Jerry's district included the Vietnamese neighborhoods in New Orleans East, and he was aware that Vietnamese businesses in that district conducted all sorts of side hustles that municipal regulatory authorities knew nothing about.

But a private lottery? That angle was a revelation to Jerry. It occurred to him that the buildings occupied by those Vietnamese grocery stores were subject to real estate taxation based on their assessed value. He was, he reminded himself, the assessor for those buildings and could, all by himself, officially declare their value on the tax rolls.

Although most of the buildings in New Orleans East had very little actual inherent value as real property, it vaguely occurred to him that a grocery store running a private lottery might present an opportunity for a targeted reassessment and a lightweight shakedown.

He began to feel some relief from his depressed state. The teeth of the gears in his head started to engage, and he could almost hear something like the turning of a crank. He lifted his heavy head and stiffened his flaccid neck to speak: "What's this about a private lottery?"

Jerry saw that Manny was no longer smirking or chattering or cracking wise with his customary racetrack breeziness. Manny may have inadvertently disclosed a secret known only to the Vietnamese community. Jerry had become the beneficiary of a cultural and possibly familial betrayal. He hoped Manny would provide just the slightest bit more information, if only to camouflage that he had revealed to Jerry, an elected city official, something more serious. But Manny would not be sucked into further discussion on the topic.

"Well, gotta go. Good luck and good racing!" shouted Manny over his shoulder as he vanished into the throngs of feckless dreamers madding in the off-track betting section of the Fair Grounds Race Course.

"Thanks for the info, pal." Jerry's rejoinder was audible only to himself but loud enough to give him some satisfaction. But his real satisfaction lay in the fact that he had come upon information that presented the possibility of something more profitable than a lousy Exacta bet, the kind of capital enterprise that only politicians could conceive.

If, Jerry pondered, the Vietnamese grocery in New Orleans East was running a private lottery, the owners of that property would not be surprised by or perhaps even concerned that their building might be vulnerable to an assessment that was higher in value than the physical structure at that location would otherwise indicate. If he could somehow communicate to those owners that the threat of reassessment was possible, they might be persuaded to make an arrangement with him to prevent a significant, and certainly painful, tax hit.

The other assessors around town, whose districts were home to more valuable commercial real estate, routinely put the squeeze on owners who were only too happy to contribute to the campaign funds of their assessors and prevent a heavy tax increase. Burton Clayton, Jerry's political mentor and the assessor for New Orleans's Central Business District, engaged in that sort of thing on a routine basis. But Burton—who was also an old friend of Jerry's father—controlled the CBD, where office buildings were far more valuable than the sheds and shanties that pocked the commercial strip malls of his miserable New Orleanss East waste bunker of a district. It wasn't the CBD, but maybe the information about the private lottery put Jerry in a position that Burton, also a powerful Black politician who'd worked his way up the local ladder, could at least understand.

Burton Clayton drove a Mercedes-Benz and ate at Eberhard Garrison's Steak House. Jerry had, many times throughout his political apprenticeship, met with Burton at his mid-century modern, glass box, Walter Gropius–inspired, horizontal rambler on Bancroft Drive overlooking Bayou St. John to discuss political enemies and dependable loyalists.

Burton Clayton would know precisely the mechanics of kickbacks that might suddenly come available when the unspoken threat of property-value reassessment loomed. Yes, Jerry thought, a meeting with Burton Clayton would have to be scheduled immediately.

As Jerry began his exit from the Fair Grounds Race Course OTB basement facility, his eyes caught an accidental glimpse of the glass-enclosed display case the Fair Grounds had installed to honor members of its Hall of Fame. Old black-and-white photographs from the track's more elegant era—when men wore hats and Black spectators milled about in segregated corrals—were pasted at irregular angles above silk racing programs and other period memorabilia. Jerry sniffed at those pictures because he knew them only as vestiges of a repellent age when Black subjects were deliberately avoided by cameramen who knew very well what was expected of them. The only Black people who seemed to make it into these promotional photographs were jockeys and grooms.

Jerry exited the OTB with nothing but a lousy forty bucks in his pockets. In spite of his betting losses, he finally felt some optimism about his financial prospects because he had an alternative plan that didn't involve gambling. And Burton Clayton, who was a master at the gentle art of political extortion, was the man who could help him put it in place. He'd have to schedule an in-person meeting because his cellular phone service had been disconnected. He only hoped his car would start.

2

The very next day, just three blocks away from the Fair Grounds Race Course, on a street called Grand Route St. John, Glenn Hornacek stood before the mirror over his bathroom sink, where he was shaving and combing and plucking and anointing himself with a variety of replenishing lotions.

Naked to the waist, he had an extra-large white towel tucked just above his deep navel and above the symmetrical slabs of adipose flesh fat that had accumulated above his hips like a 1960s Cypress Gardens ski belt. He had a wheat field of hair across his flabby chest that had spread to his shoulders and covered his beach-ball stomach. He had once waxed the hair on his dorsocervical fat pads, but it had grown back so quickly that he had come to accept his body fur by telling himself it had the effect of cuddly masculinity.

He tapped the beard stubble from his razor on the curved porcelain surface of the sink and ran the palm of his fur-backed hand around the bowl so that the whisker-flecked dollops of excess shaving foam would drain completely under the running hot water.

It was pleasing to start his day on Grand Route St. John, in a neighborhood known as Gentilly, which he'd deliberately chosen when he moved to New Orleans, as a testament to his political sympathies and one that could place him in close association with a specific segment of the

New Orleans community. Known for its quaint, polyethnic shabbiness and working-class grit, Gentilly had begun as a bedroom community of Arts and Crafts bungalows for middle-class professionals seeking a more modern suburban lifestyle back in the 1920s.

But its promise of peaceful, community neighborliness had given way to the creeping cancer of urban decay, though much of its well-built architecture still stood in defiance of the dashed hopes for upward mobility the area once entertained. It retained, somewhat, its reputation as a place for homeownership and family wholesomeness, though it was no longer the utopia promised by its developers. Over time, middle- and lower-middle-class Blacks had moved in and eventually claimed Gentilly as their own. But by the turn of the twenty-first century, there just weren't enough of them to maintain the insularity privileged classes use to keep crime from interrupting their daily lives. It was less dangerous than the slums of the inner city, but carjackings and home burglaries had become increasingly common.

More recently, Gentilly had become a neighborhood adopted by enlightened and romantic White interlopers keen to cultivate a certain romantic identity: an open rejection of the bourgeois predictability of the bland way of life that prevailed in the exclusively White suburbs of Jefferson Parish. Gentilly was home to the New Orleans Fair Grounds Race Course, where the New Orleans Jazz & Heritage Festival was held and where the artistic and the avant-garde flocked to express their contempt for the dullard and the doctrinaire, the boring and the banal, the milquetoast and the marionette, simply by living there. It was frontier living, to be sure, inasmuch as it was close to some of the more dangerous ghettoes of the city, but there was enough residential stability for White progressives to make a statement about tolerance and race-mixing.

By far, the most important part about living in Gentilly was its geopolitical relationship with the Jazz Fest, a yearly event where free-thinking hemp-and-cork earth worshipers gathered in the hundreds of thousands to stroll around, listen to live music, eat ethnic cuisine, and generally express their appreciation of folk dignity. It was a religious pilgrimage for its devotees who took their places in the swarm of like-minded gypsy hairballs. For them, it was the Hajj in Mecca, a grunge-rock concert at Filmore West, a Dust Bowl migrant encampment, and a Red Cross evacuation shelter all rolled into one. Though Glenn never really listened to music as a young man, apart from whatever his classmates played on their high school car stereos, he found that a New Orleans identity could be acquired simply by living near the sacred site.

Glenn was not a native, so his idea of what a native New Orleanian should look like, how he should behave, and the particular elements of the culture he should embrace had to be adopted in a way that looked . . . *authentic*. He learned quickly to dismiss the silly, romanticized elements of the city—like naughty-boy Bourbon Street quaintness and candy-stripe Dixieland clarinetists with straw boaters and arm garters—that had, for years, been promoted in 1950s tourist brochures. It was the *real stuff* only insiders knew about that he would slather all over himself to prove that he belonged.

Like Alexander's generals in Egypt, he was going native. If Glenn were to be truly authentic—a simon-pure denizen of a back-a-town *borghetto*— he would have to affect an easy familiarity with installation art shows in Tremé, experimental theater in St. Roch, and late-night Yaka-mein bowlfuls in the Bywater (things only people like Bob Dylan and Anthony Bourdain would discover in their deepest chthonic expeditions). He had heard one sarcastic businessman refer to people like him as "Big Easians." The insult didn't soften his resolve. Nor did the fact that one local historian had, in a more scientific analysis of New Orleans's gentrification patterns, coined the term "super-natives" to classify his ilk: a network of out-of-town settlers in search of historic, even neglected, housing stock where they could renovate dilapidated property, set up housekeeping, and enjoy the conveniences of urban living without paying the premium prices fetched in the already-established areas of town. It might be a little risky taking up residence in these high-crime precincts, but "super-natives" like Glenn had faith. They could show the world that there was nothing to be afraid of. Even better, they could prove their commitment by joining in

the traditional Black social gatherings those neighborhoods were struggling to keep alive. For too long, aloof White New Orleans had failed
to appreciate the cultural pricelessness of the Afro-Caribbean ancestral spontaneity such gatherings evinced. Glenn wanted very much to be
known, particularly by Burton Clayton, as an enthusiastic participant in
the campaign to preserve the rituals of authentic Black self-expression.
His desire to ingratiate himself to Burton was transparent, to be sure, but
the sincerity of his racial sensitivity could never be gainsaid.

Soon enough, the grandfather of them all—the Jazz Fest in Gentilly—
would be upon him. Glenn would be discussing the big performers who
were considering surprise appearances, the food vendors who had secured
the most coveted booth space, the exclusiveness of his access passes, the
number of days he planned to attend, and his strategy for making his way
around festival grounds to catch certain key acts. When the time came,
he would find himself under a straw hat in full festival regalia among all
the other middle-aged, sandalwood weed-spleefs as a dusty Roquefort
churned in the grimy crevices of his sweaty flesh folds.

The Jazz Fest was an easy way to show that he could stand in battle formation with like-minded folks who would abjure the drudgery of
office-hour regimentation, zombie consumerism, Presbyterian rigidity,
philistine complacency, soul-crushing conformity, Rotarian boosterism,
and the American mediocrity of every odorless, uncurious Babbitt who
ever spent a Pleasant Valley Sunday reciting the Pledge of Allegiance. The
older he got, the more difficult it had become to endure the harsh physical conditions of a massive, open-air event with its long lines for stinking,
portable toilets, and hot beer. But he had to do it.

Furthermore, living on Grand Route St. John was an open statement
that he intended to live up to the image he was trying to project—proof
positive that he did not fear mixed-income, socio-racial intermingling. It
was an investment in the political nature of his career, an advertisement
that he would serve the interests of minority voters, specifically Black
ones, even if he happened to be a White man.

His official title was president of Parallax Consulting, ostensibly a real estate and property development consulting firm that assisted and advised commercial investors from outside of New Orleans who inevitably encountered the impediments of permitting, taxation, and minority set-aside regulations that City Hall imposed. He had acquired this niche expertise when he first arrived from St. Louis as the regional director of the large real estate consulting firm hired by the New Orleans Convention Center to handle day-to-day construction details. When the final phase of the convention center expansion was completed and the contract fulfilled, he decided to stay in New Orleans and establish his own firm built upon his experience navigating the arcane channels of municipal bureaucracy through which all public-private enterprises must travel.

In reality, Parallax Consulting was a one-man shop that liaised with a variety of elected city officials for a fee—one that would be passed on, in part, to the very politicians whose approval could be bought. Disguised payola was distasteful and perhaps illegal, but it was an impurity unsmeltable from the system it contaminated. It was realpolitik at its most venal.

Glenn Hornacek would never admit the service he provided was a shady one, and he certainly didn't like thinking of it that way. In his mind, it was perfectly legitimate insofar as he provided a necessary service to commercial developers whose projects were a benefit to the city at large. Nothing wrong with that. Just a cost of doing business. It was like that song that said something like, "If I'm not the one who does it, somebody else will." Parallax Consulting was a one-stop clearinghouse for fast-track bureaucratic approval for commercial interests in search of regulatory latitude. And that wasn't free.

Through the years, his business had become even more specialized, one that turned on the peculiar manner in which the city collected property taxes. It was a system that had become—in spite of its egalitarian origins—particularly susceptible to corruption. There were seven tax assessment districts and seven elected assessors to serve those districts, where the fair market value of real property determined the property owner's tax liability. Each piece of real estate, subject to certain exceptions, was burdened with a millage rate that carried a tax obligation of

$51 for every $10,000 in value a particular piece of property enjoyed. Under that system, the more value a particular property was assigned by the assessor in whose district the property sat, the more tax was owed. The most valuable property, and, so, the higher the tax liability, was situated in the Central Business District—also known as the CBD—whose sitting assessor was a man named Burton Clayton. Owners and developers of office buildings in the CBD were constantly wrestling with Clayton to have their assessments kept in check in order to keep their tax liability as low as possible. Though they were perfectly willing to compensate Clayton for his favorable treatment, open bribery was out of the question.

This is where the services of Parallax Consulting and the expertise of Glenn Hornacek were so valuable.

It worked this way: commercial property owners and developers in the CBD would appeal to Burton Clayton for assessment mercy, always in person and usually at a downtown restaurant. Clayton would politely listen to these overtures, glance perfunctorily at glossy pamphlets, spreadsheets, and market surveys, drink a few bourbon and Cokes, eat a thick steak, and then, sufficiently lubricated, recommend that they hire a consultant to present their appeals to him in terms he could understand and that were more easily adaptable to the formula he used in his assessment calculation. When asked if he had a particular liaison in mind for such a service, Clayton would promptly recommend Parallax Consulting through its principal, Glenn Hornacek. And when, as suggested, the consultation meeting took place later, Glenn would give assurances that Clayton's assessments would be kept at a tolerable level and a fee for his consulting services would be paid. Parallax Consulting had nestled itself very comfortably, indeed.

The final component of this public-private transaction was easy to predict. Parallax Consulting would then make the proceeds of the consulting service available to Burton Clayton through various means, including campaign contributions to Clayton and his political allies, investments in shell corporations controlled by Clayton, gifts to Clayton family members, luxury car lease payments for vehicles to be used by Clayton as he saw fit, and donations to any other pet projects Clayton supervised in his quasi-public empire.

Glenn Hornacek understood and accepted what might be considered odious to polite society—that is to say, White society—but he had forsworn their approval long ago when they rejected him from their gardens and salons. Membership in the impermeable social amnion of White New Orleans was utterly out of his reach, in spite of the fact that he had money. Any other Southern city would welcome a resourceful entrepreneur like him into prominent social circles, but not here. It took decades, or even centuries, to overcome the stigma of New Wealth.

And so, he would get even by ingratiating himself with powerful Black city officials like Burton Clayton. It may not have been his first choice, but he took to his role as the adopted mascot of the Black political class with great gusto. It was a delicious reprisal: Clayton would first gig rich White businessmen with predatory assessments on their real estate, and Glenn would then swoop in with promises that those assessments could be reconsidered if a reasonable consulting fee were paid. The two were conjoined parts of an extortion racket that brought a certain spiteful satisfaction as well as a steady income to both men.

Right from the beginning of this confederacy, Glenn understood that his political sympathies, which were already adaptable to opportunity, would have to be tailored to serve the interests of Clayton's continued reelection. Even in his spare time, Glenn stayed in character by stumping for Clayton's Black political allies, appearing conspicuously at Black-culture community rallies, and choking down oversalted soul food. He also found time to show his belief in the political movements that Burton supported and the progressive causes Burton's constituency responded to—things like sleeping under the overpass to raise awareness for the homeless, keeping a compost heap outside his kitchen window, fighting against the evils of fracking and fossil fuels, shopping at the Saturday morning locavore farmer's market, plunking souvenir tambourines alongside ethno-activists at outdoor Afro-Cuban music concerts, picketing for safer bicycle lanes, and generally adopting every righteous appeal to philodemic virtue he could sign up for.

Though none of these gatherings ever made direct demands for increased taxes or expanded governmental administration of the funds those taxes would generate, the socialistic messaging was clear enough for Burton's voters to understand. They might be indifferent to the environmental benefits of electric cars and solar panels, but they definitely supported . . . *benefits*. Glenn's open participation in this kind of social protesting, therefore, endeared him to a politician like Burton Clayton, whose incumbency as First District assessor was the key to Glenn's income. When Glenn first arrived in town to work on the convention center, he didn't necessarily have any partisan political leanings one way or another. But as he gradually slipped into his niche as Burton Clayton's facilitator, he came to understand that a strong political ideology would be a prerequisite.

Like most entrepreneurs who profit off the redistributive populism of majority-minority cities, he was politically flexible. So, he shape-shifted into a righteous egalitarian and champion of bohemian values, if for no other reason than to please his benefactor, Burton Clayton. The transformation was made all the more appealing by the aura of Fabian erudition enjoyed by those who could claim, however tenuously, an association with soulful, sensitive, art-guard culturati—those who could count themselves in the company of great men of letters like Upton Sinclair and Gertrude Stein. Glenn was to be a contemnor of the philistine and songbird of Parnassus! It was a backstage pass to a colloquium of the giants of the literary clerisy! He might be part of a criminal conspiracy, but he could take comfort in the fact that his venality was in service to the underprivileged and culturally underappreciated citizens of New Orleans. He slept well at night knowing that the machinery of his graft could grind away under the protective cover of a festival-tent orthodoxy that cared, *truly cared*, for the Common Man.

As Glenn reflected on his position in all of this with some satisfaction, he turned his attention to the day's wardrobe. At age sixty-two, he had become what you might call portly and what you would certainly call bald. He had a forty-six-inch waist and two symmetrical patches of hair on each side of his padded head. Several years before, he had begun experimenting with facial hair to distract from his shiny pate and the expanding surface area of his visible skull. He once tried a full beard, but that made him look like a truck driver.

Plus, it was itchy. Not to say . . . well, *rebarbative*. A mustache alone made him look like a mariachi guitarist. A beard with no mustache made him look like a Salafist Muslim staffer at a Staten Island community job center. A Van Dyke beard made him look like an actor in an MGM costume musical from the 1950s. All of those options were rejected.

But some years before, the goatee had become fashionable. Leading men in popular movies, millionaire entrepreneurs, and even some lawyers were wearing goatees, and not necessarily to offset hair loss. To those who were suspicious that his facial hair was worn merely to distract from his baldness, he could make a strong case that the goatee was simply an element of modern style. Even still, it had its drawbacks. It had to be regularly trimmed to prevent his looking like a tattoo artist, but that maintenance became an easy part of his morning routine. He liked to think *his* goatee made him look like Rod Steiger in *Dr. Zhivago*.

Another source of anxiety was his height. He was not quite five foot, eight inches, and it always made him feel inadequate in business meetings. He had considered lifts and even bought a pair of cowboy boots for the inch-and-three-quarter boost they provided. But lifts were uncomfortable, and he couldn't really pull off cowboy boots without being able to claim a past association with actual ranch life. Ex-fraternity boys from state colleges could wear cowboy boots, but Glenn had graduated from a commuter college in St. Louis. He would have to raise his stature by other means: by driving an expensive car, speaking loudly, laughing conspicuously when he knew he was being watched, and lodging his heels on baseboard moldings when posing for photographs.

The tippy-toe stances he had relied on throughout his life did, however, produce one feature of his physique that gave him something to be proud of: his calves. His mighty calves! They were well-defined and rock-hard. He often admired them on mornings like this when he came out of the shower and could flex them in private under the flattering overhead lights of his bathroom. If only they could be displayed more often and under such conditions! He would have to settle for weekend occasions when short pants were acceptable. Too bad.

His girth, on the other hand, was a bit more complicated. The problem was that he had to decide how and where, exactly, his trouser waistline would be placed. The choice was between wearing pants with a smaller waistline that would be belted under his protruding stomach—which required yards of shirt fabric for complete skin coverage—or wearing pants with a forty-six-inch waistline that would be belted across his posthole navel. A beneath-the-stomach waistline made him look like a warehouse loading dock supervisor who chewed cigars. On the other hand, an above-the-navel waistline made him look like Burl Ives. After much experimentation, he had decided on the high-waisted profile because it could be disguised by a suit jacket or sport coat on the weekdays and a guayabera or untucked festival tunic on the weekends.

Besides the goatee, there were other methods of counteracting the effect of his glaring baldness. Men, of course, no longer wore hats in business settings ever since JFK rakishly strolled hatless at his 1961 inauguration parade. But casual social occasions and holiday gatherings were hatwear free-for-alls. He had a collection of baseball caps, berets, porkpie hats, fedoras, knitted skull covers, veranda Panamas, bunted campaign boaters, and colored bandannas for every occasion. Costume parties and art gallery openings were lighthearted occasions where almost any kind of wacky headgear was acceptable. He would even snow-ski, ride a zip line, or go on safari just for the opportunity to wear a helmet.

On that morning, he would wear a blue worsted-wool suit (the sleeves had been shortened to account for the size 50 suit coat required to accommodate a man of his weight) and a robin's-egg-blue pinpoint cotton shirt with contrasting white collar and French cuffs. His necktie was Lamborghini-red silk with a woven hexagonal pattern. His shoes were oxblood brogues with decorative toe perforations. His leather belt matched his shoes, and his cufflinks were aggressive, half-inch bronze ovals bearing his monogram. He surveyed this symphony of fabric and tack in front of a full-length mirror before making his way to the breakfast table where his wife, Strickland, was already seated.

She was concentrating on an electronic computer tablet, which she held very close to her face with her left hand and swiped periodically with the index finger of her right. She appeared to be put out by its contents.

"Good morning, honey. Full calendar today?" He was always congenial to her in the morning because she seemed to take her career very seriously, even though she didn't earn much money.

"Mmmmm," she managed to push out, never looking up from the computer tablet.

"My schedule is not too bad if you wanted to meet for lunch, perhaps?" he suggested, mainly to seem cheerful. He didn't really have time to meet her for lunch, but he knew she would decline the invitation. She would never let him think her crowded schedule allowed for such frivolousness.

"Today's impossible," she said. "I'm going all the way uptown for lunch with our architectural coordinator at Tulane. Then meetings all day after that."

"All right, but we're still on for five thirty for Lucinda's soft opening?" He was referring to a cocktail reception for Lucinda Valcour, a Belgian expatriate who chose New Orleans for the restaurant, Grimod, she was opening with proceeds from her minor European inheritance.

"Oh, yes," she said with agreeability but not enthusiasm. Her focus was on the computer tablet.

"Okay, then. I'll meet you there and then. I guess it'll just be a tasting menu. I hope it'll be enough for a meal. Heavy hors d'oeuvres, at a minimum."

She did not respond. He was only trying to make conversation by mentioning *heavy hors d'oeuvres*, but he could tell she didn't really care about the dinner menu. He, on the other hand, always kept such things in mind because of his concern for his weight. Any food that was passed around at parties or served in bite-sized portions in lieu of a proper meal sounded fattening. All the same, he didn't want to go to a restaurant and leave hungry. He hoped she hadn't sensed his reservations about the prospect of finger food.

He continued the conversation she seemed to feel no need to conduct: "Okay, well, I'll see you there, sweetie. Be gentle with the Tulane academics. They're not accustomed to the way the real world works!" He wanted to laugh a little to convey to her that they shared a serious professional advantage over the impractical, visionary professors at Tulane, but she did not seem to be in the mood to conspire. Before Glenn could sit down to his cottage cheese and fresh fruit breakfast, Strickland had collected her purse and charged out the front door without any further discussion. It didn't bother him that she seemed abrupt. He loved the fact that she was preoccupied with her career, whether it warranted her serious attitude or not.

She was, to his bursting bosom, his beloved Strickland Hornacek (née Butterworth) of Fairfax, Virginia. Although born in hunt country, Strickland was raised from age five in the Adams Morgan section of Washington, DC, where her father worked at the Department of the Interior in the Carter administration. When Jimmy Carter left office, her father got a job with the Brookings Institute so the family could stay in the DC area. She went to high school at The Madeira School as a day student and then graduated from Mary Baldwin University with a degree in social and community relations. She had all the credentials and sensibilities Glenn Hornacek wanted in a companion, and together they formed a political (as much as romantic) union that suited both of their careers.

She had relocated to New Orleans for a job at the Herschel and Miriam Ziskind Center for Housing Justice, a nonprofit partnership with Tulane University established to combat the affordable housing crisis with which New Orleans was afflicted after Hurricane Katrina. They had met ten years before at a fundraiser for one of Burton Clayton's political protégés, Jerry Sonthonax. Strickland was ten years younger and had a refined and aristocratic nose, green eyes, perfect teeth, and a pronounced bust, but she had inherited a broad bottom and tractor-pull thighs. Those unfortunate features, however, placed her in his range of acquisition. They were both, he had to admit, overweight. But, after a short courtship, they were able to relieve one another of unwed loneliness at a private, secular ceremony in the British Virgin Islands.

The Herschel and Miriam Ziskind Center for Housing Justice, where Strickland worked, was set up to find affordable housing for low-income Black residents of the city who had been displaced by Hurricane Katrina and others who, sometime after the storm, had been squeezed out by rising residential property values in their old neighborhoods. This displacement was heart-wrenching to sympathetic activists from all parts of the country who could only conclude that the diaspora of Black residents had been caused by federal government insensitivity and the pitilessness of capitalism. The gargantuan shrug of an unchecked market economy had cast poor people to the worst, crime-ridden neighborhoods of the city's periphery.

It was still more distressing to Black politicians who saw a diluted Black population as an erosion of their voting majority. Organizations like the Ziskind Center, funded almost exclusively by Tulane (in fact, Strickland Butterworth Hornacek's paychecks were actually issued by Tulane University), were the first line of defense against Black voter diminution. Strickland and Glenn together lamented the injustice taking place under those circumstances, and Glenn was only too willing to condemn openly the demographic trend, especially when Burton Clayton's reelection depended upon a Black voting majority. Should Clayton get voted out of office, Glenn would—in one stroke—lose his sole source of income.

But the Ziskind Center was doing its darnedest to maintain the status quo. Its faculty was impressive: a distinguished colloquium of activist-scholars from every corner of the nation's academic establishment. The center's website and official brochure included a picture of each faculty member above an ornamental riband of his or her gem-strung post-graduate degrees (e.g., Nathan Rudman, PhD from Columbia, SScD from Oberlin, MLS from Occidental), and a strategically placed roster of younger Black staffers with similar, but perhaps less prestigious, credentials (e.g., Tamaiyra Lumpkin, MSoS from Jackson State, BLS from Western Kentucky–Owensboro). According to these glossy publications, the mission of the Ziskind Center was to organize and implement a variety of community projects that would, if successful, preserve the residential security of the city's poorer Black residents and repatriate those who had been displaced back into the city limits. These projects were likewise set forth in the center's glossy marketing materials: green spaces to promote "wholesome and accessible park use," neighborhood facilities to provide "day care and healthy living alternatives," solar-powered charging ports to foster climate consciousness, leadership training programs to champion housing justice, farmer's market distribution hubs to dispense sustainably sourced nutrition, and several other programs joined in battle to engage what was termed "Tactical Urbanism." The objectives of these and other similar efforts were, to Glenn and Strickland, irreproachable. To embrace them was a noble sentiment. To take action was jihad.

Meanwhile, the city council was doing what little it could to combat the sinister forces behind Black displacement. At first, it tried raising property taxes to generate funds for city agencies formed or temporarily deputized for the purpose of assisting poorer residents struggling to remain in what was becoming an expensive place to live. This method had proved effective in the past because homes owned by the poorer residents of the city were never assessed at a value that imposed an impossible tax burden on them.

But more recently, raising property taxes had backfired because the homes once immune from elevated assessments had become more valuable, and their owners were being hit with taxes they had never before had to bear. In addition, landlords of low-income housing units were simply passing on the increased tax burden to their tenants in the form of higher rental rates. So, that solution only made the problem worse.

On another front, the city council enacted new laws targeting the luxury apartment buildings that were popping up to meet the demand of professionals in search of the downtown living experience. Those laws imposed a requirement that a certain percentage of the proposed units be set aside for affordable housing, which met with such resistance from prospective developers that they threatened to cancel their projects altogether. Black residential displacement was truly becoming a crisis. Glenn and Strickland were all too aware of this exigency and would bemoan the inequity whenever they got the chance.

With all this in the back of his mind, Glenn Hornacek finished his breakfast and set off for his weekly meeting with Burton Clayton. He draped his suit coat carefully on a wooden hanger hooked to the assistance handle of the driver's-side rear seat of his blue BMW X6 SUV. As he slid behind the wheel and started the powerful engine, he took a moment to enjoy the comfort of the seat's leather upholstery and how perfectly the lumbar and tilt adjustments could be made to accommodate his forty-six-inch belly and still account for his short legs. *Ahh, the genius of German engineering!* The commanding power of the luxury vehicle seemed to flow right up through the tufted, hand-stitched leather to his spinal column until it reached the part of his brain that produces dopamine.

In this chemically exhilarated condition, he backed out of his driveway and drove from his Gentilly neighborhood toward Clayton's office downtown. He turned onto Esplanade Avenue toward the river and then into the French Quarter via Dauphine Street all the way to the CBD. The morning drive gave him some time to reflect on his stable and satisfying home life. Glenn reminisced about the early days of his marriage and how he and his wife went about converting his Gentilly bachelor pad into a workable marital domicile.

He had, three years before his marriage, purchased the house from the owner of a lumber importing business. It was a somewhat unprepossessing Carpenter Gothic cottage built around 1913 in what was then a working-class neighborhood. There was a small porch with turned balusters, which originally served as the home's entrance up front, but the former owner had sealed off that door and moved the formal entrance to the side of the house just beyond the off-street, one-car driveway. In spite of the modest appearance of the home's exterior, Hornacek had maintained the lumber magnate's original renovation and fashioned, in his own way, an interior of contemporary luxury. The walls and countertops and cabinetry were all paneled in the sumptuous and exotic hardwoods of Central and South America imported by his predecessor's lumber company: Brazilian cherry, Patagonian rosewood, Santos mahogany, Amazonian bloodwood, Spanish cedar, satinwood, and eucalyptus. The living and dining areas downstairs were not carpeted, so Glenn had chosen simple but expertly loomed rugs of beige and other neutral colors to complement the scumbled warmth of the wood-grain confines. The furniture and fixed elements were all refurbished from local architectural salvage emporia to express his acquired appreciation for New Orleans traditions as well as his natural penchant for a more rustic aesthetic. He adorned the walls with regional art and artifact: limited edition Jazz Fest posters, naïve folk art from Black artists throughout the regional South, junk sculptures cobbled by public school children, concert memorabilia from traditional jazz and blues performances—all intended to signify his connection to the soul of the American common people. None of this would have been evident to the car burglar or home-invasion junkie prowling the neighborhood for luxury items that could be easily pawned.

He had deliberately allowed the exterior of the house to patinate and project a certain level of degeneration—not so much to appear abandoned but enough to look casually ramshackle, a sly suggestion of solidarity with his less affluent neighbors without surrendering the comfortable living space inside. It was his hidden sanctuary, an auxiliary chapel decorated with smudged wood-block prints and street-scrap iconography.

"I love it. I love it all," Strickland had said on her first visit to her future home. "I can even see places where parts of my collection would fit nicely. I have an old pharmaceutical cabinet, a wooden one, I got in Greenwood, Mississippi. And if you wanted to replace that old Home Depot commode in the powder room, I have an old box-and-chain contraption, all antique porcelain, I saved from my grandparents' old house in Virginia."

"Whatever you want, wherever you want. It's your house now. Go crazy. I suppose it could use a woman's touch anyway."

"I'm dying to see the bedroom upstairs. Should I be scared of the closet situation? I don't want to impose too much, but I do need closet space."

These recollections of his first moments of their marriage were fond ones. Truth was, he and Strickland got along quite well then and thenceforth. They had no children and were not planning on any, so the most treacherous aspect of homemaking would be sidestepped at the outset of the relationship. There was plenty of money for eating out, vacations, and other recreation when their career schedules permitted, and neither of them had personal habits or idiosyncrasies that seemed to be irritating to the other.

Sex was another matter. At this stage, ten years in, sex was not a regular occurrence, let alone a requirement. He didn't demand it, and she didn't expect it. It was enough that they had mutual interests when it came to socializing and entertainment, to say nothing of their dedication to the same social causes. Besides, there was internet pornography available to him almost anywhere at any time. He wondered whether she resorted to the same kind of sexual satisfaction.

At the end of his introspective morning commute, he pulled into the reserved parking spot at Burton Clayton's downtown office building and began to review the mental catalogue of items he wanted to discuss. They were, for the most part, routine matters: confirming assessment reductions for particular office buildings, receiving instructions on the disbursement of funds, discussing rumored real estate transactions that would present opportunities for regulatory intercession, and, naturally, the shakedowns that accompanied them. Waiting around for and then pouncing on such exchanges was their stock-in-trade.

Out of the elevator and through the frosted glass doors of the office entrance, he was greeted by Clayton's receptionist, Lynette: "Good morning, Glenn. We're sending out for coffee if you want some."

"Thank you, no. Had plenty already at home."

Glenn passed easily through the receptionist checkpoint and into Clayton's office as if it were his own. In a way, it was, inasmuch as he had brokered the assessment value of the entire office building. After the reduced tax liability had been established, Clayton's office was provided to him rent-free. The office space was, therefore, the direct result of his efforts, so he had no reservations about freely entering a domain that was just as much his as it was Clayton's. The two of them were roped together like mountaineers, and from Burton's twenty-first-floor office, the two of them could look down upon the surrounding buildings of the Central Business District and the as yet undeveloped surface parking lots where future projects might be built. All of it was theirs to harvest.

Soon after Burton had been elected to the plum position of CBD assessor, he had come to depend on Glenn to help capitalize on his puissant taxing authority. Glenn was an indispensable lieutenant, to be sure, but Burton never considered Glenn to be anything more than a dutiful adjutant—efficient and productive but subordinate nevertheless. Glenn, on the other hand, liked to think of himself rather more an Agrippa than a Maecenas. In that capacity, he felt entitled to a blue gumball police light like the one provided to Clayton by his friends on the force. Glenn often wondered why a tax assessor would qualify for such a thing in the first place. And yet, the upholstered mahogany visitors' chairs that were arranged to face Burton across his tubular steel and tempered glass desk seemed to be lower than the carbon-fiber mesh captain's chair that the boss sat in. The futuristic desk chair that Burton sat in had been engineered to swivel and roll and recline, whereas the visitors' chairs were stationary and rigid and . . . *puny*. This was no accident. When Glenn took a seat, he tried to look comfortable in the hierarchal seating arrangement by leaning back, placing his interlaced fingers on the top of his head, and crossing his legs. The pose proved impossible because the chairs were too small for a man of Glenn's size to complete the contortion and because his hefty thighs prevented any such make-yourself-at-home nonchalance. He would have to break right in with ordinary business discussions to keep what was left of his composure.

"I spoke to McMillan yesterday, and he's griping about the Valerius Capital Tower arrangement we made for the building next door to his," Glenn said without any desultory prefacing. "I reminded him that his property'd be up for review soon enough. The Valerius Capital deal is totally different than his, anyway, so he shouldn't be looking for like treatment."

"Don't worry about McMillan," said Clayton dismissively. "We kept him at the same number that he's been at since the end of last cycle. In spite of the brand-new twenty-four-story that was put up right next door."

"I'm not necessarily worried. He just keeps calling all the time, asking for a face-to-face. Driving me nuts. Startin' to think he's not making his loan payments, and maybe he's looking to sell if he doesn't get relief from us." After all these years, Glenn was comfortable enough to act irritated around Clayton, or at least commiserate like they were equals put out by the same troublesome client.

"Good. I hope he defaults. We don't get enough out of him to keep making forbearances. If he sells, the new owners will be faced with reassessment and, just like that, we've got a new customer. Just like the sun in that old song, we are perched in the sapphire sky."

Both Glenn and Clayton snickered at the thought of fresh meat. It was the perfect moment for Glenn to rise from his chair and stroll toward the window as though he were taking stock of the CBD inventory. Moving freely about Clayton's office with casual confidence was Glenn's way of showing he did not consider himself in any way Clayton's subordinate. Just as he was about to bring up the next item for discussion, Clayton's phone rang.

"Hold on." Clayton glanced at the liquid quartz caller identification panel on his office phone. "Hold that thought. I gotta take this."

Glenn listened to the only side of the conversation he could hear.

"Jerry! What's up, old buddy?" Clayton placed the speaker end of the phone into the palm of one hand and whispered to Glenn, "It's Jerry Sonthonax." Glenn knew Jerry as the newly elected assessor for the New Orleans East district.

Clayton's half of the phone conversation continued: "Yeah, I've been out to the East. I've seen those ratty strip malls. Nothing but grocery stores and nail salons and such. They might make money, but that doesn't mean those buildings are worth anything."

Glenn guessed Jerry was asking for Burton's advice about how to assess a profitable business, but one that was housed in a worthless building in a bad neighborhood. *Poor Jerry. He gets elected to the office of assessor only to be stuck in a district that has no commercial real estate of any value.*

The telephone conversation resumed: "Oh, really." Clayton's mouth formed an expression of mild surprise as if to say, "I didn't know that."

Glenn listened with curiosity as Clayton continued the phone conversation: "I'll tell you what. We can meet for lunch tomorrow to discuss. I might have some ideas. Are they being looked at by the Feds?" Clayton stared at Glenn even though he still had the phone to his ear. "Listen, we'll talk about this later. I have somebody in my office right now. All right. I know. All right. I gotta go. We'll talk tomorrow."

Clayton returned the receiver to its plastic base and spoke directly to Glenn: "Seems that a Vietnamese family has an illegal lottery or something going on in their grocery store. Wants to know what kind of valuation he can place on that kind of operation. I was thinking maybe you could do some diggin' and come up with some ideas."

Glenn knew Clayton depended on him for his creativity, not to say cunning. Glenn's first reaction was to demur, to blanch, to shy away from anything that might involve the interest of or, even worse, surveillance by federal law enforcement. He stated as much: "I wouldn't go messin' around with that kind of stuff. It's small potatoes anyway. Too risky for me. It's certainly not worth *your* time."

"I know. But I'm his mentor. I got him elected. I knew his daddy pre-Katrina. They used to call him 'Delicate Jerry' in high school because he had a magic touch with the girls. Anyway, it's only a lunch meeting. You can come if you want, but I at least gotta talk to him—like I would family. Anyway, you're welcome to come. But I don't suppose he'll be paying for lunch. He's in no position to spring for steaks. He couldn't afford to throw a taffy pull in a telephone booth, if you get my meaning."

"I'll let you know. Me and the wife are going out tonight, and I gotta limit the rich meals. Counting on heavy hors d'oeuvres, even though that sounds rich enough already."

"Heavy hors d'oevures," said Burton. "Never could understand that expression. Reminds me of 'business casual' or 'posh nibbles.' I can understand why the French hate Americans. On the other hand, the French for 'baseball bat' is '*batte de baisbol*,' so I suppose we both have room to complain."

"You're right," said Glenn, in complete agreement with Burton, as he was on all things. "Okay, I'll let you get on with the rest of your day. Let me know what you want me to do about Jerry and the Vietnamese thing." He saw no point in prolonging the morning meeting with nothing too important to discuss or that couldn't wait. He waved goodbye and headed for the parking garage as Clayton took another phone call.

But there was another reason for his early departure: it freed up just enough time for him to make it to an Alcoholics Anonymous meeting. Glenn's substance abuse, mostly under control since his wedding, was percolating inside him, and he was starting to feel the cravings that had plagued him before his marriage. He had managed to give up the cocaine and the booze and the late nights and the dangerous habitués of Davy Jones's Locker Bar, where he was once well-known. Stimulants of every kind were available there, twenty-four hours a day, and it was a constant struggle to resist visiting that French Quarter dive. It was an easy place to score blow.

The AA meetings were never really enough to extinguish the urges of chemical dependency, but they were enough to distract him from temptation long enough to attend to business matters and, more importantly, the mundations of married life. Strickland was aware that he attended such meetings from time to time, but he had informed her that he only attended on a voluntary basis, just enough to stave off a mild reliance on alcohol that he had conquered, mainly with willpower, years before.

She did not know the full extent of his substance-abuse problem or that his alcoholism was more than just mild. Nor did she know that there was a cocaine addiction on top of that. At this point in his life, with a happy marriage and a lucrative career cruising along smoothly, an AA meeting would be just the thing.

3

Alexander "Lecky" Calloway, forty-five, a pink-white lawyer with a translucent, whiskerless face the color of uncooked veal, looked out of one of the living room windows of his Duffossat Street mansion and considered the position he had reached on the Uptown social scaffolding. He could not complain, but the best he could muster was a slightly uneasy feeling of satisfaction.

Up to that point in his life, every decision he'd made had been calculated to secure an elevated level of wealth and social distinction. The big house in the exclusive 70115 zip code off St. Charles Avenue was an essential element of that plan, but the people keeping score—the people that *mattered*—demanded more than just lavish displays of disposable cash, even if executed in good taste. Anybody with enough money to throw at architects sensitive to historical restoration and preservation could do that.

What he wanted was to be one of those people who seemed to *know* one another without ever actually being introduced, one of those people that others were *supposed* to know. Lecky was amazed that, having married well, he was no longer invisible. He had instantly become an accredited member of a special echelon of elitist Whites who somehow magically acquired the ability to recognize one another on sight.

Yet, maintaining his credentials required vigilance. Intramural friendships had constantly to be cultivated, and solicitousness to ranking institutions had to be made at attention. This, in spite of his luxury home on Duffossat Street, was the reason for his feelings of insecurity.

The home, which he owned with his wife Hildegard "Hildy" Calloway (née Thompson), was classified by puzzled but dauntless experts as "Colonial Revival." Lecky was delighted that the architectural style of his home had been given such a grand title, and he would repeat it to anyone who asked.

In fact, the home was a hodge-podge of Doric columns, Italianate balustrades, Federal-style dormer windows, Mediterranean roof tiles, a semicircular Georgian portico of obnoxious magnitude, and, to complete the Richard Morris Hunt Marble House effect, a glass-roofed conservatory. Now known as the Greishaber-Calloway House, it was designed in 1904 by the architects Soulé and MacDonnell, one of several New Orleans firms in service to untaxed industrialists of the Gilded Age with more cash than hereditary refinement.

Alois Grieshaber, who originally commissioned the grand manor, was one such tycoon, the second-generation son of a German émigré who made his fortune selling spirits, cordials, and liqueurs after the Civil War. The house, which Hildy and Lecky offered up for inspection and approbation by their peer group whenever they got the chance, had something of a scandalous history. Three years after it was completed, Alois had quietly sold the house when his own son, Grieshaber, Jr., was charged under the old Mann White Slave Act for spiriting his low-born fifteen-year-old girlfriend to Mississippi for, as the law proscribed in those days, "immoral purposes." Mr. and Mrs. Grieshaber, already anxious about their tenuous immigrant social status, ratted him out and later shunned him, even when the lovesick colt married the object of his misadventure. His parents had warned him against mixing with scullery maids and Cinderellas who would seduce him to madness. The young couple eloped anyway, but the Grieshabers could not abide the scandal and so took the rather drastic step of notifying the United States Marshals. It was a rash decision insofar as it enflamed Victorian sensibilities to a greater degree than the

Edwardian peccadillo would have warranted if left alone. The boy was ultimately convicted, and the Grieshaber escutcheon, such as it was, clung temporarily to its damaged cabinet, only to be splintered when the details of the sad affair were published in the newspaper.

The Grieshabers sold the house in 1907, and it changed hands several times until, in 1984, it was on the market again at a staggering price. Hildy Thompson Calloway and Lecky Calloway were able to acquire the home with cash from the dowry her father, Elliott Thompson, vouchsafed to any suitable candidate willing to marry his slightly masculine, less-than-prepossessing daughter. Lecky was from a respectable family and evidently sincere, even if suspiciously effeminate.

But the field of prospective husbands, once the usual con men and four-flushers had been disqualified, was meager. When Lecky at last proposed, the wedding was celebrated with a welcomed degree of relief. Elliott Thompson had, at last, married off his linebacker daughter and was therefore glad to disburse the money necessary for her to set up respectable housekeeping. Hildy had fantasized since childhood that the Grieshaber House would one day be hers, always confident that a comprehensive renovation would return it to its former grandeur. She was confident the Thompson dowry would be enough to overcome the Grieshaber scandal that seemed to attach itself to the foundations of the house itself.

The interior décor, once in the hands of Hildy Thompson Calloway, was decidedly English. She had, in spite of the prevailing distaste for brown furniture, maintained her allegiance to her grandmother's treasured heirlooms. Pembroke tables, Davenport chairs with pierced splats and trifid feet, Hogarth credenzas, Carlton House cellarets, and Royal Dalton porcelains were everywhere on display. Against one wall of the formal drawing room was a hunter-green three-seat Bridgewater sofa with brown bullion fringe and crimson velvet throw pillows. On either end of the sofa were satinwood Chippendale candlestands. The furniture stood imperiously on an enormous olive-green Axminster carpet with a cream-colored center medallion of woven swans and cornucopias. The coffee table was of Chinese lacquer with blackened, fluted legs. On the periphery of the grand room were lowboys, break-front cabinets, and other pieces with horizontal surface space surmounted by famille verte and gilt-mounted lamps with their oyster-white pleated silk lampshades.

The walls were a buff egg-yolk yellow. The hung family portraits, in glaring incongruity, were not as old as the furniture. They were rendered in the style of 1950s advertising illustrations that emerged from the Famous Artists School of Westport, Connecticut—a style popular with country club past presidents, board room executives, and Junior League docents of mid-century America.

The entire ball-and-claw effect of the formal living areas seemed to be taken from Ogden Codman and Edith Wharton in their seminal, tidewater monograph, *The Decoration of Houses*, or one of Nancy Lancaster's Colefax & Fowler showrooms. As far as Lecky was concerned, it was a crypt of overstacked artifacts that had outlived any utilitarian purpose they might have once served. Nevertheless, Hildy kept a team of terrified Nicaraguan housekeepers on a regular schedule of dusting and polishing just in case any of the elders from Trinity Episcopal Church happened to drop by for a snap inspection.

On that ordinary morning, Lecky felt confident enough to pose a question that, in any other family, would have been an innocuous one, but one that he knew, in his family, would give his wife heartburn.

"Did you speak to your father yesterday?" he asked after summoning the courage required to be impertinent.

"Of course. He doesn't think it's going to be a problem. Everything seems to have quieted down." His wife, Hildy, age forty-six, was in constant contact with her father for the obvious reason that he was the source of the money—which also meant that he was the source of their social standing. Hildy and Lecky depended on him for everything they cherished most. So, therefore, his words of guidance were given a great deal of deference. Lecky accepted this position willingly for the sole reason that money and social standing were the reasons he courted and married Hildy in the first place. But he would soon learn that he had married the daughter of a foreign god.

At the time of their wedding, a standard Episcopalian muster, Hildy carried significantly more flesh weight than the average debutante. But Lecky didn't marry her for her pulchritude. He married her for her purse. And for that, he consented to a life of permanent subordination. Hildy's wedding gown, he now understood, was a harbinger of what was to be the style of her wardrobe from that point forward: a thick brocade contraption with padded pauldrons riveted securely about her industrial-strength torso. Lecky could remember standing at the altar as Hildy barreled up the aisle at the beginning of their wedding ceremony. She looked to him like Holbein's portrait of Henry VIII, and just as forbidding. A human battleship in search of an enemy.

Since then, her everyday dresses were all very similar in effect: sleeveless, knee-length, silk-lined shift dresses, usually green gold with cream-colored floral embroidery, rendered inwrought and stiff by Tyrian needles—a shapeless profile for a woman who had given up on her figure. When seen from a distance, the brocade cladding against her formidable profile resembled the fenestrated sterncastle of a Dutch frigate. Or maybe a dented traffic bollard.

She still wore stockings but never heels any higher or slenderer than alphabet blocks, even though they might have been by Chanel. Her overall appearance was intimidating, and on that particular morning in the overstuffed living room of the Duffossat Street home, he was reluctant to discuss anything that might displease her or might be considered a prickly matter.

But there was an important family problem that required their attention as parents of two girls. Lecky loved them both immeasurably, but they carried an unhappiness and an insecurity belied by names given to them at birth—names Lecky and Hildy thought were acceptable to the Episcopalian sensibilities of their social set. Their oldest was named Caroline after a family friend who was president of the local chapter of the Garden Club, a judgmental matron who monitored such things in accordance with an inviolable social catechism. Their youngest was named Ainsley, not so much to honor an ancestral tradition, but because it was common among those who did. The name "Caroline" carried an inherent Hanoverian majesty to which Lecky and Hildy believed they were entitled. Imposing on a child the burden of her parents' inadequacies was an unfair assignment of responsibility, a cruelty of expectation that Caroline would, simply by bearing a distinguished first name, secure the family's rightful place in the ranks of social nobility—the kind of encumbrance, also unfair, often forced upon innocent Little Leaguers by frustrated dads chasing sports glory by proxy.

Later on, Lecky feared that the name "Caroline" was being given by parents who only aspired to aristocratic distinction without the concomitant birthright to do so. In fact, the mimicry had started to cheapen its subject. Lecky had come to the conclusion that people in New Orleans who named their daughters "Caroline" were usually running from something—trying to disassociate themselves from an embarrassing immigrant background—some heirloom in the attic that they hoped no one would ever be nosy enough to uncover: the Jewish peddler's burlap sack, the Arkansas hayseed's poultry hutch, or the Sicilian *contadino's* wobbly-wheeled fruit stand. Lecky wasn't altogether sure what he was running from, but naming their daughters Caroline and Ainsley was an open declaration that they would conform, nihil obstat, to the accepted heraldry of the social arbiters they solicited. That sense of insecurity, he feared, was bound to show up negatively in the character development of children as they reach young adulthood.

The current crisis—and this was the most serious one they had faced as a family—involved their older daughter's substance-abuse problem. Caroline, age twenty-five and a recent college graduate, had descended into cocaine addiction and had been sent off by them to North Carolina for treatment at Longleaf State College in a program administered by Dr. Jefferson Caldwell, an expensive specialist known for his success with even the most intractable drug abusers. Dr. Caldwell happened to be a personal friend of Hildy's father from his days at Washington & Lee, so Caroline had been accepted into the exclusive program as a personal favor—and a check for $75,000.

They had tried to be good parents to their two daughters, Caroline and Ainsley, born three years apart, but Lecky could not be altogether sure their efforts had been successful. The girls had problems, but nothing that couldn't be dealt with quietly within the family unit. Or so it was hoped. As they got older, the girls began to exhibit the side effects of growing up with parents beholden to a social status they revered above all else. Caroline and Ainsley always fulfilled their duties as children of class-conscious slaves, but there was to be an emotional reckoning. Teens and young adults, Lecky understood, always wrestled with some degree of rebelliousness, but his girls—especially Caroline—were acting out in ways almost pathological. The family had always been successful in keeping the embarrassing matter hidden from their Uptown social set, but recent rumors about Caroline were threatening, *tribu movere aliquem*, to compromise their designs for Ainsley's prospects for a seat on the court of The Lancaster Club's annual Hesperus Ball held every year on the Wednesday before Shrove Tuesday.

Hildy's father, a former king of that ball and prominent senior member of The Lancaster Club, had managed to suppress the rumors, factual though they may have been, at least long enough to install Ainsley as a maid in the Hesperus Court in spite of her sister's drug problem. Lecky was also a member of The Lancaster Club and had done his best to ease concern among the members that the Caroline Situation would put a stain on that year's court. The board of The Lancaster Club had been kind enough to overlook Caroline's hospitalization and to decide that Ainsley should not be penalized for the sins of her junkie sister. These were drastic matters in the Calloway household even as the rest of the world carried on in complete oblivion.

Hildy delivered the instructions to her trembling husband on how to proceed in light of these complications: "You're going to have to spend more time at The Lancaster Club if we're gonna get through this. The new member party is one week away. But not so far off that we shouldn't plan ahead. You'll have to leave work early to come home and change so we can get to the club no later than six thirty."

Hildy knew The Lancaster Club schedule better than he did, so Lecky listened closely. For she alone determined their social schedule. He was a dutiful, though grateful, husband. She had the money and the unquestionable authority. He knew he was being led around by his nose, but he accepted it. He was in every sense her handbag, playing Baciocchi to her Elisa Bonaparte.

"It's weeks away, dear, but I'll be ready," he said. "What's the dress?"

"It says cocktail casual. But you should wear a tie. You can always take it off if we feel overdressed." He noticed she said *we*. Lecky was just an extension of her, an accessory, a minstrel in her retinue.

He managed to ratchet up some gentle defiance. "I'm not going to run to the bathroom and take off my tie in the middle of the party. That's worse than showing up underdressed."

"Wear the tie anyway. We can say you just came from work. Here's the invitation."

She handed him a printout of the email from the club secretary to the membership. It had been sent to his email address, but Hildy had access to all of his computer accounts. And why shouldn't she? She paid for them.

The invitation looked like this:

> *The Board of Governors of The Lancaster Club cordially*
> *invites you to attend the New Member Party*
> *6 o'clock Cocktails and Heavy Hors d'Oeuvres*
> *7 o'clock dancing to*
> *Boogie Flex—Atlanta's hottest new Dance Band*
> *Members and their Ladies only*
> *Dress is cocktail casual*
> *(jeans are never permitted on club premises)*
> *Validated parking available at the Valerius Capital*
> *Tower, Poydras Street entrance*

Lecky got a knot in his stomach every time he read "heavy hors d'oeuvres." He couldn't imagine a more unappetizing description of banquet fare. The British expression "posh nibbles" might have been more appropriate at a place like The Lancaster Club, but "heavy hors d'oeuvres" had become accepted through assuefaction—a misshapen phrase, crafted to convey that a substantial meal would be provided, but nothing as formal as a full buffet or seated dinner. Everyone knew what it meant. Lecky thought it was a crude expression, dressed up in French finery, used to assure the typical clubman, conditioned to expect the sturdy foodstuffs of his hunting camp, that his stomach would be safely larded for the heavy drinking to follow. Yet it was delicate and palatable enough for frightened female guests with already low expectations.

As a member of The Lancaster Club, Lecky was expected to join in the hunting/fishing/golfing braggadocio and rucksack anecdote that the members so often resorted to for stimulating conversation on club premises. Perhaps, Lecky reasoned, the mostly forced but always reliable raillery was necessary to offset the effete costumes that members wore with corresponding gusto at the Hesperus Ball: talcum-white hosiery, pointed shoes with Tudor cinches, bejeweled tunics, and silver wigs. These men, boorishly disposed to rattle off the coarsest and most scatological jokes when gathered in their off-stage dressing rooms, would parade around in these outfits on canvas-covered flooring like the cast members of an Austro-Hungarian opera. As incongruous as it seemed, Lecky enjoyed the pantomime and the feel of the stockings against his pink-white loins.

It was somewhat less ironic for Lecky, who, at age forty-five with two grown daughters, had begun to loosen the restraints of his suppressed homosexuality. He knew very well he was gay. His father always used to tell him he was born with a pleat in his trousers. He had, in fact, experimented with a Japanese exchange student in a game of mutual masturbation while in high school. Yet, he was careful to camouflage those tendencies as he navigated college fraternity life, law firm office interaction, and the Uptown social scene. But by this time in his life, with two daughters who were pretty much adults, Lecky felt comfortable enough to explore, ever so slightly, the world of gay living, eventually going so far as to buy a secret smartphone at his own expense that could not be monitored by Hildy, her father, or anyone at his law firm.

He often daydreamed of an openly gay life surrounded by the wash-board stomachs of Olympic divers and the Apollo lines of perspiring firemen. Although he would never forsake the status he enjoyed as a member of The Lancaster Club or as the husband of an old-family heir-ess, his fantasies had possibilities, especially because homosexuality, once considered a degenerate aberration, had come to be viewed by an amused but increasingly demure bourgeois establishment as a benign variant with its own space in society. As a matter of fact, polite society had come to accept that certain married men, who were mostly respon-sible providers for their families, were enjoying a bit of gay recreation on the side, as long as it didn't interfere with their community or pro-fessional obligations.

He was familiar with an expression used to describe such men: they were known as "New Orleans Straight." It was a special subspecies of homosex-uality unique to New Orleans, and everyone seemed to be aware of it to some degree. Lecky often wondered whether his fellow members of The Lancaster Club or others in his social milieu presumed that he was part of that para-culture. He had his own suspicions about particular side-saddle husbands he and Hildy socialized with, but he had no firsthand knowledge of it. He couldn't very well ask around without exposing himself or embar-rassing someone else, though he wanted to know how to pull off something like that. But first, he needed to somehow get in the game, to make himself available, to find out what was available to him personally. He needed to, as they say, *meet* someone.

"I'm going upstairs," Hildy announced, "to make sure Caroline gets to her AA meeting on time. Don't forget to call my father and thank him when you get to the office. And tonight, we have the art gallery thing, so be home in time to get ready. We might want to get there a little early to see the exhibit before it gets too crowded."

"I know, I know. Believe it or not, I'm looking forward to seeing some of the art. Stuart has some of her stuff in his office. It's getting to be pretty expensive." He was referring to Stuart Whitcomb, the senior partner at his law firm, and the feminist artist Rigoberta Palenque, whose paintings were becoming very popular among wealthy art collectors and their interior decorators.

"Yeah, well, we're not going to buy anything," she admonished. "We have enough artwork in the house already."

"No, I was thinking of something for my office," he replied, trying to assert himself slightly.

"I know, you like to copy Stuart. It's getting a little obvious."

"I'm not trying to copy Stuart. He has one small piece. And it's an old one. Her style has changed quite a bit since Stuart bought his. I'd be looking for something a little more, uh, daring." He wanted to say "bigger," but he thought he'd try to use a little terminology from the artspeak handbook. It came out all wrong. She didn't notice.

"Lecky," Hildy said, "we're not buying any more artwork. And I don't have time to discuss this. I've got to get Caroline off, and you have to get to the office."

Ugh. The office. The drudgery—the prosaic suffocation—of practicing law. Lecky was a shareholder at his firm, but only because of his tenure there and his loyalty to the firm. Well, that was not altogether true. He had been offered the position of shareholder mainly because Stuart Whitcomb wanted to cement a relationship with Lecky's father-in-law, Elliott Thompson, and secure the firm's image as a fixture in the blue-blooded institutions of the city. In that mascot capacity, Lecky's responsibilities as a lawyer were minimal, and his paycheck reflected that.

Not that he cared. He didn't need the money, and he didn't want the burden of high-stakes litigation anyway. Defending car-crash cases for old-line insurance companies that had been clients of the firm for decades was his simple specialty. The work was predictable and unchallenging, but it allowed him the time needed to fulfill the social obligations imposed on him by his wife. That is not to say that he resented those obligations, but they were obligations, nonetheless.

On this morning of his somewhat predictable life, he'd become more distressed about his eldest daughter, Caroline, than his wife seemed to be. He had not, up to that point, allowed his concern for Caroline to disrupt the usual pattern of social engagements and dinner plans, posing for society page photographs on the charity event circuit, entertaining foreign dignitaries at his Duffossat Street home, and supporting architectural preservation organizations—all on top of the routine responsibilities of a mid-level lawyer—but the Caroline Situation had become more serious.

She had only recently returned from those three months of isolation, detoxification, and therapy for the cocaine addiction she had acquired in college or shortly after graduation. Though he was aware that almost all college students experimented with drugs, Lecky was always confident that Caroline was smart enough to avoid full-blown dependency. But she had not. He could not ignore the possibility that he and his wife had failed as parents. When it became an undeniable reality that Caroline's addiction was severe, he felt guilty and wondered what had gone wrong.

It was necessary, then, to relieve himself of that guilt by placing blame on the other people in Caroline's life and, perhaps, factors beyond his control. Sure enough, her mother—Hildy—had put too much pressure on her. This had forced him, as a counterbalance, to spoil her and excuse her shortcomings without providing even mild discipline. But it was too late for blame placing. Now that Caroline had returned home from treatment, he wanted to provide the love and support that he must have selfishly withheld when her slide into addiction began.

Such was his conviction when Hildy came down from Caroline's upstairs bedroom and joined him in the formal parlor. It was the first he had dared sit in that room for a long time, and it was more uncomfortable than he imagined it would be.

"She's crying." Hildy made this announcement while stuffing random articles into her purse in a violent manner that he recognized as frustration.

"What's wrong? I thought we had gotten past all of that?"

"I don't know," Hildy snapped. "She won't tell me exactly. Maybe she just wants attention. She's being selfish again, and I don't know how much more of this I can take."

"She must have told you something." Lecky tried to shift the focus of the crisis away from Hildy's frustration and over to Caroline's unhappiness. "What did she say was bothering her? You must have some idea."

"I don't know. Why don't you ask her? She's coming down now."

At that moment, Caroline walked slowly into the living room, sat down on the silk dupioni sofa, and crossed her legs Indian-style. She was wearing gray sweatpants, thick cotton socks, and a sorority jersey. Her eyes were swollen and red from crying. Lecky moved toward the sofa and sat beside her. He wanted to put his arm around her but saw that Hildy's glare warned against any physical comfort that might show his toleration or, worst of all, sympathy for Caroline's distress.

"What's wrong, sweetheart?" he asked, risking a display of tenderness that would surely be viewed disapprovingly by his wife. "You can tell us. We're your parents."

Hildy exhaled in contempt of the melodrama and headed for the kitchen. Lecky felt safe enough to put his arm around Caroline, though he would speak softly now to ensure their privacy.

"Whatever it is, it can't be that bad. You're doing so well with your recovery. Did someone say something to you in group?"

Caroline sniffled and whimpered but kept her head down and stayed silent.

Lecky pressed on: "Has there been a setback? Is this a boy thing? Tell me, sweetie. We can work through this."

Just then, Hildy emerged from the kitchen and sat down on one of the opposing Hogarth chairs, crossed her fat legs, folded her arms, and began a kicking motion with her suspended foot. She spoke impatiently: "Just tell your father what the problem is. We can't keep having these meltdowns."

Hildy's callousness seemed unhelpful, but Lecky dared not challenge her. He might have had better luck getting Caroline to confide in him had Hildy remained in the kitchen, but he was in no position to ask her to leave the room.

"It's best that we talk about it," he said to Caroline. "Your mother and I want to help you." Lecky wanted to sound soothing without undercutting Hildy's demands for an explanation. He tried to be constructive while remaining gentle and sympathetic: "Would it help if you talked to Dr. Caldwell? You really opened up to him when you were in North Carolina. It might make it easier for you. He always seems to know just what to do when you're feeling bad."

At last, Caroline's mouth opened slightly, indicating she was ready to speak through the last of her tears: "No. I don't want to talk to him. I don't want to talk to any more doctors. I don't want to talk to anybody."

"Then just tell us what the problem is, and we can move on. It doesn't do any good to keep it bottled up. We have a right to know, at least for now, so we can get you back to being a functional person," said Hildy, in a clinical and administrative tone.

Lecky interceded to soften the sudden harshness of Hildy's continuing demand for answers. "What she means is that, well, you've made so much progress and showed such promise. We don't want you to get off course. It's always better just to get it all out. It'll make you feel much better, and God knows it'll make me feel better knowing that you can trust me." Lecky looked at Hildy to show that he knew he had overstepped his authority. He looked back at Caroline and corrected himself: "I mean, trust us."

"If she doesn't want to talk, Lecky, then don't make her." Hildy spoke as if Caroline wasn't even in the room. "We're not trying to make ourselves feel better here. She can tell us when she's ready. Maybe after this morning's group session she'll feel more comfortable talking to us. Or to Dr. Caldwell. Either way, she'll have a better attitude than she has now."

"For heaven's sake, Hildy, try to be a little more understanding." Lecky was being careful not to raise his voice. "I think she needs to open up to us. We are her parents." Lecky turned directly to Caroline while his arm remained around her shoulders. "Holding it in just makes it worse. I'm sure there are private things you talk about with Dr. Caldwell, and others you talk about in AA. But this might be something it's best to discuss with us, here, with your mom and dad. There's nothing so bad that we can't . . ."

Caroline appeared to be fed up with the interrogation and exploded. "I got an abortion. I got pregnant, and I got an abortion. I paid for it with my own money, and I don't need to talk about it with anyone."

The temperature of the room dropped.

Hildy uncrossed her legs and sat forward in her chair with her knees together at an angle from her massive torso. Lecky removed his arm from Caroline's shoulders and fell back on the cushions of the sofa. There followed a brief silence, but there seemed to be some electric static in Lecky's ears.

He spoke first to fill the vacuum and to demonstrate to Caroline that the disclosure was not as jarring to him as she might have thought: "Well, all right. That can happen. You're not the first to be faced with that decision. As long as you're healthy. I assume you went to a doctor—I mean, a safe doctor. These things are a lot safer now than they used to be. I mean, there can be some medical complications, you know, that can crop up." Lecky was stumbling through a topic he knew nothing about while trying to reorganize an unwieldy and now raw confrontation. "It was surely a routine procedure. It's really nothing you should be worried—or ashamed—about. I know plenty of people who—"

"I didn't even know you had a boyfriend," Hildy interjected with disgust. "When did this happen? Do you mind telling us when this happened? Or where? Do you mind telling us who's responsible for this? Do we know him?"

"It's Dr. Caldwell, okay? You're the one who sent me to him. You're the one who wanted me to go to North Carolina." Caroline was incensed. "It was your idea."

Lecky felt the static in his ears grow to a scalding sensation that traveled across his scalp. He glanced at his wife, but she was staring at Caroline. Lecky involuntarily, or perhaps deliberately, cleared his throat. He knew that it sounded, to his wife at least, like a pitiful bleat, a nervous tic that betrayed weakness. Caroline rose from the sofa and walked slowly toward the stairs to return to her room.

It was at that point that Hildy turned to Lecky. His first impulse was to follow his daughter upstairs, but his wife's gaze kept him pinned to the sofa. After a few moments of silence and immobility, Lecky found the strength to rise from the cushions and walk across the parlor directly in front of his wife. He could feel Hildy staring at him. It felt like a retreat, but it seemed like he had no option but to proceed to his law office.

"Where are you going?" she asked.

"I've got to get to work." He could barely hear himself speak, so he spoke again in an effort to satisfy Hildy and, at the same time, deliver parting words that would excuse his departure. But it sounded cowardly and fragmented, as though he didn't really know where he was going. "You'll have to, you know, deal with this. I can't . . . I've got . . . She needs some time to . . . I've gotta go."

"What are you talking about? Well, whatever. Just go."

With that, Lecky removed his keys from his front pocket and walked through the living room toward the kitchen. From there, he opened the back door of the house and descended the stairs that led to the rear carport. His mind was racing, and he felt dizzy. He didn't hear it, but he assumed Hildy would lock the door behind him.

—

As he drove to his downtown office, Lecky set aside thoughts of his poor daughter and her predicament—something that had already taken up time and created an even greater rift between him and Hildy.

Instead, he allowed himself to think back to the clandestine sortie he'd made some months before in the French Quarter of New Orleans—a reminiscence he didn't enjoy while in the presence of his joyless wife.

Curious to survey the gay landscape, he had decided to visit a celebrated gay bar on the weekend of Southern Decadence, New Orleans's annual celebration of gay culture that lasted four days and was, for the gay men's world, a traveling carnival of gay-themed events, amusements, musical skits, merchandise, and all things gay. On that occasion, he purchased, by means of his secret smartphone, a VIP ticket for the opening ceremony and set out on his mission at twilight wearing an understated but bespoke ensemble—subdued enough to look casual but smart enough to look stylish, or at least style-conscious. *Oh, how his pink-white loins had tingled with expectation!*

But he was almost immediately disappointed. The most celebrated gay bar in the French Quarter was not what he had imagined. It had the reputation as a glamorous supermarket for the para-coital dilettante, but after he had parked his Lexus in a Chartres Street surface lot and walked toward the corner of Bourbon and St. Ann, he encountered noisy crowds of drunken gay men disporting in leather motorcycle gear, horseshoe mustaches, shaved heads, and sadomasochist tattoos.

It was an unsettling scene, but Lecky soldiered on to the address listed on his secretly purchased VIP ticket. As he approached his destination, he looked up to the elevated gallery that wrapped around the corner structure. There he saw a shirtless man in silver-studded bandito cross-straps and a matching leather codpiece administering a vigorous, reach-around tube tug to a younger man, also shirtless, wearing a shoulder harness with a leather underbust belt and white angel wings.

No one else on the crowded gallery seemed to be put off by this display of homosexual intimacy and, in fact, carried on drinking and chatting within touching distance of the couple as if it was an expected part of the Southern Decadence experience. Though this interaction was jarring, Lecky was not going to be disheartened. In fact, he steeled himself by taking a moment to admire the architecture of the building that housed the Bourbon Street club, and to read the sidewalk plaque describing its history.

The building, an old Creole townhouse triplex on Bourbon Street, had its own relationship to scandal, which was not uncommon in old New Orleans. It was built in 1829 for Idalise Manadé, a prosperous free woman of color, originally from Saint-Domingue, now known as Haiti, whose mixed-raced descendants, of varying degrees of African dilution, were still prominent members of the Black political establishment. Idalise was a successful investor in real estate in and around the Vieux

Carre with a nice dowry when she married—informally because mixed-race marriages were illegal in those days—a scion of an old White Creole family, a man named Jean Florent Durel. They had two mixed-race children, Jean Victor Durel and Marie Durel, for whom she bought homes nearby. Having outlived her husband and her daughter, Idalise eventually moved to Paris some time after the American Civil War, where she took her vows and became a tertiary with the *Religieuses de l'Espérance*. When she died in 1896 at her home on Paris's Rue de Téhéran, she bequeathed part of her fortune—1,000 French francs—to the indigent hospital run by that order of nuns in Paris's Eighth Arrondissement. Her son, Jean Victor Durel, had remained in New Orleans and started his own family.

Lecky was not aware of this colorful history when he arrived at the club that evening, but he would not have been surprised to learn that descendants of Idalise were now members of the Black political power structure who controlled the city council, the local elected judiciary, and the notoriously corrupt panel of tax assessors led by Burton Clayton, Jerry Sonthonax, and others. The gateway that was to be Lecky's introduction to gay life bore the tinges of scandal in more ways than one.

As he got closer to what appeared to be the entrance checkpoint of the club, Lecky was able to appreciate even more the simple elegance of the architectural design. As he had already observed on his approach by foot, the building had a wraparound gallery and multiple ground-level bays that opened to the street. He was soon able to determine that it was really two separate but related parts of one business. The first floor housed a saloon called The Sword & Sceptre, a name that suggested the wood-paneled coziness of an English village pub. The second floor was known, but not advertised, as Swordplay, an expansive discotheque open only after dark and designed for the throbbing-dance-beat hedonists who could participate in more advanced homosexual behavior under the anonymity provided by strobe lights and machine-generated smoke that smelled of marshmallows. As things turned out, Lecky would not be going upstairs to Swordplay.

Nevertheless, Lecky entered The Sword & Sceptre hoping that the downstairs atmosphere would be mercifully tamer than what he had witnessed from the street. He produced his laminated VIP identification card hanging from its attached lavender lariat when confronted by a shirtless, muscular doorman coated in a thin film of shimmering musk oil. Lecky was eye-level with the bouncer's nipples, but he tried not to stare at the man's anatomy for fear of coming off as a wide-eyed newcomer. After a brief verification process, Lecky was granted admission without so much as a smile.

Once inside, he beheld a scene that reminded him of the men's room at the Port Authority bus station in Midtown Manhattan: pudgy, middle-aged men wearing ill-fitting, knee-length denim shorts, white crew socks, white Reebok tennis shoes, crusty yellowed undershirts with deep neck scoops and floral-print department-store blouses unbuttoned to the waist—clothing combinations they apparently believed were de rigueur at any gay men's function. These men looked like reincarnations of Truman Capote or Whittaker Chambers who had lost their luggage and then were forced to buy replacement clothes at the gift shop of a Florida tourist court. He felt out of place in his hound's-tooth blazer, silk Countess Mara tie, and creased serge trousers.

Lecky observed these men milling about and chatting with their co-sexualists from Arkansas, Arizona, and anywhere you might find a truck stop. They chatted intermittently with scrawny young waiters with Xerxes beards who carried trays of complimentary Jell-O shots. These waiters were clad only in leopard-print bikini briefs and leather workboots with lug soles. Occasionally, and what seemed to be matter-of-factly, the middle-aged rubes would fondle the waiters' genitals as they got acquainted, sometimes *over* the Lycra bikini fabric and sometimes *inside*.

After these casual encounters, the waiters would resume their primary responsibilities as bar-top dancers, where they crouched on their haunches like pond frogs. Seated patrons could then enjoy an eye-level view of the dangling Lycra goody bags offered for their examination. In this counterposed arrangement, more creative ways to fondle the bikini-clad dancers could be tried, and erections could sometimes be produced.

This was not at all what Lecky imagined openly gay life would look like. Where was the Moroccan plumage? When was the Eyelash Cotillion supposed to begin? Any idea that he would be enjoying the refined and comely decadence of Magdalene College Ganymedes with flat nipples, laurel wreaths, and Zephyr-kissed curls quickly vanished. He had miscalculated his readiness for the experience.

So, he unceremoniously bolted from the discouraging scene with a much clearer understanding that a more gradual entrance onto the homosexual proscenium would better suit a novice like him. The expedition had been unsuccessful, but he'd learned a lot. He'd find the right time to try again.

For the time being, he had to shake off this memory and collect himself for his drive to the office. He had abandoned Caroline at home with Hildy, and God knows what kind of torture his confused daughter would be subjected to. He felt guilty, but the situation at home was more than he could handle. Procrastination, he knew, was a form of cowardice, but he had not yet found the footing to assert himself. Not yet.

4

FBI Agent Margot Hoang supposed, or maybe even hoped, that something serious could come from the chance meeting at the hotel ballroom seminar. She hadn't been on a date for some time, and the most recent ones had been with conceited loudmouths born without the embarrassment gene who took her to wise-guy restaurants or interminable rock concerts so far from her apartment that she felt like an unransomed hostage.

That is why Margot—whose original Vietnamese name was Thuy Hoang (pronounced "Twee HH-Wong")—insisted that their first date take place at a restaurant in Metairie, the New Orleans suburb just minutes from where she lived. She floated the condition with such deftness that her date would know, right from the start, that she would not be at his mercy, yet could still feel she was game for the outing. She was relieved that he got the message and agreed.

It was a popular spot, safely lit in a heavily trafficked shopping mall, and only a ten-minute drive from her condominium on Lake Marina Drive. The Corsair Towers complex where she lived was on the bulkhead shoreline of Lake Pontchartrain, within the city limits of New Orleans but several miles west of the CBD. The twelve-story apartment building was part of an upscale, fenced-in living community contiguous with the

Jefferson Parish suburb of Metairie at the foot of its main thoroughfare, Veterans Memorial Boulevard.

A restaurant close to her home was convenient and, above all, easy to escape from should this first date, for some reason, go sour. She did not expect a clunker, but it was in her nature to have an evacuation plan in place ahead of time. The art of the tactical retreat was part of her training at the academy in Quantico, Virginia, where her career with the Federal Bureau of Investigation began. Reliance on hornbook law enforcement procedure might not be the most romantic predisposition for a first date turkey shoot, but it was, by that stage of her career, such a scientifically engineered part of her personality that it would have been dishonest to try and disguise it. In addition, it was in her nature to give off clear signals to prospective suitors that she was self-sufficient, capable of handling things herself, and invulnerable to predatory Lotharios. On the other hand, a detectable aura of vigilance might not be such a bad feature of a first-date attitude, especially when that date was with a New Orleans police officer whose law enforcement experience matched, to some degree, her own.

She was glad they had *not* met on a dating website or been set up on a blind date by a mutual friend. They had met professionally, or so she liked to think, at a training seminar in a downtown New Orleans hotel. The seminar was convened to foster cooperation between federal and local law enforcement agencies. It was an accidental valentine that deposited them at the same table in the designated event space of the hotel that day.

Margot had not expected anything special to happen at the seminar. It was an obligatory part of her ongoing FBI discipline. When she arrived at the registration desk just outside the Remoulade Ballroom on the hotel's second floor, she could appreciate the gigantic scale of the 1970s-era facility and the efforts made by the hotel's convention coordinators to convert the expanse into a somewhat more intimate lecture theater. The seminar tables had been arranged banquet-style in long, horizontal rows and covered in shiny gold, easy-care, poly-cotton tablecloths. The rows were separated symmetrically to create a long center aisle down which attendees could walk to reach their assigned seats. This regimented arrangement rested on acres of duraplast, event-space carpeting that bore repeating French Baroque medallion patterns. The carpeting was sumptuous and professionally installed, no doubt the kind requisitioned in bulk from corporate hotel headquarters for use in their franchised empires. It was the kind, she concluded, that had been designed to appeal to the industrial tastes of ballroom decorators. She had seen these design motifs before in other large-occupancy hotel event spaces—ornamental floor textiles promoted with stately European names like "Belvedere," "Sans Souci," and "Malmaison"—each variety woven with exuberant undulations and curvilinear flourishes in brown and caramel that had the primary purpose of hiding dirt. Stackable utility chairs were placed on one side of each table row facing the speaker's dais, and each seminar guest was provided with a notepad bearing a faint hotel watermark, a tiny, eraserless pencil stub, and a clear plastic water cup.

The speaker's table was similarly appointed, except that the chairs had been placed on the opposite side so that the seminar moderators faced the audience. In the center of the speaker's table was a tabletop lectern fitted with a gooseneck microphone. Ferocious air-conditioning gales and windowless lighting contributed to the artificial atmosphere. Yet, veterans of these job-training symposia seemed to accept the corporate/commercial surroundings as the minimum standard for such events.

But Margot Hoang, serious as she was about her continuing education, could not completely concentrate on the seminar subject matter. For, just as the first speaker began his slide show, a young man in his NOPD uniform—the one who would soon be her first real date in years—took the seat beside her. It was a coup de foudre. She had been struck immediately by the fact that he was wearing the long-sleeve version of his NOPD patrolman blues. Clean and sharp. Throughout the lecture sessions, she did her best to resist glancing his way. But when she got caught peeking, she made certain to smile. He seemed a little bashful himself. She tried to reacquire her professional attitude by scribbling assiduously on her notepad. He had no wedding ring. She hoped he had no tattoos.

Near the end of the day-long seminar, her attention span had become compromised, partly from fatigue but mostly from the handsome police officer who had remained in the seat beside her for the seminar's duration. She sat back in her banquet chair and considered a staged yawn, thought better of it, uncrossed her legs, recrossed them, and gently placed her forearms on her thighs in a playful display of exhaustion. The little performance felt natural enough to engage her target, so she looked directly at him and said, "I think I've got the idea." She meant it to sound pleasant and humorous without the sourness that sarcasm often conveys.

He seemed receptive to her guarded flirtation when he responded by saying something like "No kidding!" or "Oof!" That one brief moment, that tiny exchange, was enough to pierce the invisible force field between them.

When completing the enrollment forms for the seminar weeks earlier, she specified that her nametag read "Margot Hoang," the same Americanized name she had adopted when her Vietnamese parents enrolled her in grammar school as a child. She had chosen that name from a list prepared by a deacon at her church, Mary Queen of Vietnam, who spoke both French and English and who understood the younger generation's desire to assimilate. She liked the name because an older girl in her neighborhood had chosen it from the same list, and it seemed like a dreamy name for a freshly scrubbed American girl. His nametag read "Francis Ernst."

She continued the playful colloquy by saying something like, "Oof is right!" She immediately regretted parroting his cartoon patter but then considered that it might have been accidentally funny.

"I could sure use a cup of coffee," he said, not quite asking for her to join him but, she sensed, suggesting that she might consider it.

"I'll join you. Shall we proceed, officer?" She had taken the pressure off his meek invitation by offering one of her own. Margot and Francis set off to the self-serve coffee station behind them.

At the back of the Remoulade Ballroom, the seminar administrators had placed another long table that served as the refreshment station for the attendees. It was covered by a white poly-cotton tablecloth similar to the ones covering the audience tables, but this one had gold bunting that reached to the carpeted floor. Neatly stacked towers of upside-down coffee cups and saucers stood beside silver, spigoted urns with folded paper labels that read "Regular" and "Decaf." Margot noticed none of this because the matter at hand was making the acquaintance of Francis Ernst, the handsome policeman with the clean uniform.

Desultory conversation could be heard in the refreshment area as they emptied packets of artificial sweetener into their creamed coffee. Margot tried to think of witty remarks that would blend smoothly with the insubstantial but affable conversation they had started back at their assigned seats. While she would never admit doing so intentionally, she allowed a long wisp of her licorice-black hair to fall over one eye. It may have even become tangled in her eyelashes.

As they stood before each other—Margot and Francis, Francis and Margot—she saw him swallow nervously. It was an involuntary reflex that she had been trained to notice in suspects under interrogation. But it was not guilt that she sensed in Francis. It was, she allowed herself to conclude, evidence that he might be attracted to her feminine aspect and her eyes. Margot blinked once as she lowered her chin and tried to hide a swallow of her own.

A week later, he called her at home and asked her to dinner.

On the night of their first date, Francis arrived promptly at her condominium gate and even held open the passenger door of his compact Toyota for her.

"Why, thank you, sir. That's something I'm not used to!"

"Not at all," he answered. "I'm looking forward to trying this place. I've never been here before." Francis walked around to the driver's side, folded his six-foot frame behind the wheel, and smiled at his date before setting off on the short drive to Metairie. Margot smiled back with more than just polite acknowledgement. It was a smile of optimism and, well, happiness.

The restaurant, which she had led him to accept by the power of suggestion, was called "Mardi Gras Mambo!," a name designed to capitalize on the holiday festivity of travel-guide Noo Orleenz and attract middle-class White suburbanites who would prefer to avoid the city's interior. The restaurant's name had a tagline that read "Keep the Party Goin' Year Round!" Even though it wasn't a restaurant franchise, the interior décor seemed to mimic the contemporary casual dining chains of middle America: tiered platforms with tufted booths, chrome railings, varnished blonde wood surfaces, cylindrical chrome light fixtures, a sine-curve cocktail bar with embedded strip lighting, and yards of purple carpeting with random but repeating images of trumpets, confetti, streamers, and stylized comedy/tragedy masks woven into it.

The teenage hostess who greeted them lacked as much confidence in her job as she had in her short black dress and high heels, which Margot regarded with a flush of faint jealousy and hands-off-my-man possessiveness. The girl was unaccustomed to the lift and angle produced by the outrageous height of the heels, but she managed to escort Margot and Francis through the dining room on gangly legs and growth-spurt knees. She led them to a booth on a platform that was one step up from the carpeted main floor.

Margot slid into one side of the padded scallop, and Francis slid into the other so that they were apart when seated but not so far from each other to prevent a respectful intimacy. The booth's padding was more comfortable than she expected, especially because her feet, with the added length of her high heels, could reach the floor without dangling like a child's.

For this, their first date, Margot had chosen a blue pleather cocktail dress with a placqueted back zipper that stretched from the top of her cervical spine to a spot below her coccyx bone. The dress was hemmed at mid-thigh, and it fit tightly around her athletic figure, a feminine shapeliness acquired on Quantico obstacle courses and maintained at the FBI gymnasium. On her small Vietnamese feet, she wore matching blue Pleaser-brand pumps with four-and-a-quarter-inch heels, hidden platforms, and rounded toes (but no stockings). The heels caused her calves to constrict into little muscle rocks. The pleated bust was designed to accommodate her surgically augmented breasts, and the whole effect was Miami Beach nightclub sexy. If the ensemble did not befit a licensed FBI agent, who cared? It was meant for him. Margot wanted him to see that she was as feminine as she was professional, as flirtatious as she was serious, as available as she was formidable. Somewhat incongruous with the outfit was a thin gold necklace bearing a small crucifix. It was a First Communion gift from her grandmother. She never took it off.

Francis Ernst, she had already observed, had himself taken great care to dress smartly on their first date even though he seemed only to inhabit his clothes instead of wearing them. They had a brand-new, right-off-the-rack stiffness, and it occurred to her that Francis may have neglected to remove all the sales tags from the individual pieces of his outfit before putting them on. Indeed, Francis did not know enough to snip the temporary shipment threads lightly sewn by the manufacturer on the rear vents of his sports jacket.

These minor signs of awkwardness confirmed for her that his bashfulness at the seminar was sincere. He was at least six feet tall, muscular without bulging steroid artifice, with short brown hair, blue eyes, and a masculinity combined with the bewildered clumsiness of an infant discovering the external world for the first time. He was what you might call . . . cute. No. More than that. He was . . . exquisite.

Underneath his blue moleskin jacket, he wore an aubergine cotton shirt with contrasting inner collar that was open to the second button. It had an irregular pattern of green and gold geometric shapes that almost matched the restaurant carpeting. His jeans were dark-washed denim, and he wore dark brown, square-toed loafers but no socks. The stiffened cuffs of his patterned purple shirt extended well past the sleeves of his jacket because a larger shirt size, with its proportionate sleeve length, was tailored to accommodate his muscular chest. Once again, Margot thought to herself, more diffidence and more . . . cuteness. The hostess handed them their oversized menus. Francis, it seemed to Margot, felt an obligation to speak.

"I heard about this place from my captain. He told me the food here is real good. And Capt. Roussell really knows. He travels a lot, so he's been to a lot of restaurants."

"They sure have a wide variety here. The menu is eight pages long!"

"No, I know," Francis said. "Do you want to start with a drink first, or maybe some wine?"

"Sure," she said, showing only mild enthusiasm. Margot didn't really drink alcohol very often but could muscle it down for an occasion such as this. "Maybe one of these champagne specialties or even just plain old champagne."

"I don't really drink that much, you know, with being on duty and all," Francis said. "Never really did, since college. You kinda hafta drink at the fraternity house," he continued, leaving out that he had graduated from Nicholls State University in Thibodaux, Louisiana. "I drank when I *had* to but never a whole lot."

"Me neither," Margot agreed, relieved that she would not be expected to get sloshed. Margot took her job very seriously, even though she did not want to seem too prudish. "I'll have champagne or wine every now and then, but the FBI keeps close tabs."

"I'm glad you told me," said Francis. "I've often considered applying, you know, if I ever felt like I was, you know, stuck in a rut with the NOPD. Not that I do. I actually like my job, but I wouldn't mind having options if I thought I needed them."

"Oh, you should. I applied when I was in my twenties, and it's worked out well. I had to train at the academy in Virginia but was lucky to get an assignment here in my hometown. They needed me here because of the large Vietnamese population."

Margot was Vietnamese American, but she had no accent, and her eyes were a bit rounder, perhaps because her mother was a mixed-race descendant of a Vietnamese great-great-grandmother and a French government official from years back in colonial Saigon. It gave her, she liked to think, the perfect mixture of the Orient and the Occident. She hoped Francis found her physical aspect pleasing enough to pursue the romance.

"Oh, I know. I work out of the Seventh District, which includes New Orleans East, where most of the Vietnamese live. I don't know why I'm telling *you* that."

"That's where I grew up!" Margot said, trying to put him at ease and disclosing, ever so gently, that she was not ashamed of her Vietnamese background.

"I actually spend a lot of time there, as you might imagine, and I've gotten to know the people at Mary Queen of Vietnam pretty well." Francis was referring to the Catholic church on Dwyer Boulevard that served as the fulcrum of the Vietnamese community in New Orleans East.

"You might have met a lot of my relatives. I still have family there. My family spent most of our time, when we were together as a, you know, family at Mary Queen of Vietnam." Margot was glad to have this in common with Francis. "Where do you go to Mass?" She deliberately used the term "Mass," hoping that Francis was Catholic. Her parents didn't care whom she dated or married as long as he was Catholic.

"Oh, I go to St. Angela Merici in Metairie, out here where I live. The NOPD no longer requires that officers live in Orleans Parish, so I like being near my parents. Plus, I went to Archbishop Rummel High School, so it feels more like home."

Margot liked his lack of pretense and the natural, almost childlike way he revealed a dutiful affection for his parents. She looked at him across the table, examining his face to determine if what she sensed was indeed sincere. She was pleased to see him hiding behind his giant menu as if he were embarrassed to have disclosed too much of his wholesomeness, as if he regretted revealing a distaste for fast living and hard partying. He was looking better and better by the minute. And he was Catholic. And for some reason, he did not shorten his name to "Frank" or "Frankie" or some other version of his first name that another man might adopt over the more feminine-sounding "Francis." His decision to stick with the original was a sign of unassuming confidence. Margot's fantasies began to expand.

"Let's see what they've got here," said Francis, changing the subject as he ducked behind the massive menu again. Margot was satisfied that her evaluation of Francis was accurate. After all, she had received extensive FBI training in character profiling. But this might be something more personal—maybe even the beginning of . . . oh, she didn't want to get ahead of herself. She turned her attention to the menu with continued and even increasing optimism. As they both read in silence, a waitress appeared at the table and introduced herself.

"Hi, I'm Brooklyn, and I'll be taking care of you tonight. Would you like to start with a cocktail or something from the bar while you're looking over the menus?"

"Maybe a Bellini or one of these champagne drinks," Francis said. "You want to try one?"

"Sure, a Bellini sounds great. I think I can have at least one. The FBI won't mind."

"Two Bellinis," said Brooklyn. "Would you like to hear the specials before I get your drinks?"

Margot was not interested, but she listened anyway. She mainly wanted Brooklyn to disappear so she could be left alone with Francis. Brooklyn rattled off the memorized offerings while the couple took the opportunity to smile at each other like they were enjoying an inside joke. It was a stolen moment of playtime.

The menu selections were extensive. The eight-page menu offered every type of cuisine hungry American diners, who might nevertheless be familiar with regional Louisiana food traditions, could imagine. At the top of the first page was a loosely rectangular section circumscribed by Mardi Gras beads that read "Start Off with Our Wild Magnolia Bloody Mary Bar" and a list of self-service ingredients patrons could use to mix their own custom-made concoctions.

There was a salad section with the usual, unchallenging choices of Caesar, mixed-green, Greek, fresh beet, etc., to which chicken could be added at an additional charge, along with a choice of seven different dressings. The appetizer section contained a multitude of choices, including a lobster ravioli, fresh-water buffalo mozzarella, chicken wings with a choice of five different sauces, a California sushi roll, alligator sausage, fried and char-grilled oysters, and fried calamari. Set apart in a separate menu box was a section entitled "Build Your Own

Second Line Seafood Pail," which listed a choice of raw oysters, steamed clams, lobster tails, boiled crabs, Alaskan king crab claws, and boiled crawfish. The entrées were divided into separate sections spread out over several pages: First was a "From the Grill" selection of steaks and chops (pork, beef, veal, alligator), one of which was promoted with the title "Try Our Laissez Le Bon Temps Filet." There was a section called "Bottomless Pasta Plates—All-You-Can-Mangia!" of seven different pastas with a choice of five different tomato and cream-based Italian sauces. Next was a "Seafood Delicacies" section of flounder, trout, red snapper, redfish, catfish, swordfish—available fried, grilled, or blackened—soft-shell crab, tuna steak, salmon, and back-fin lump crab cakes and a house specialty called "Pompano Fee-Na-Nay." The next section was entitled "Like Ya Mama's," with a list containing rosemary-roasted chicken, red beans and rice with a choice of smoked sausage or pork chop, meat loaf, hamburger steak, stuffed peppers, stuffed eggplant, grilled chicken breast, chicken-fried steak with white gravy, and corned beef with cabbage. Another special section was entitled "Try Our Aged Prime Rib." At the end of all this was a children's menu for those "12 and Under" followed, at last, by a list of beverages, sides, and a "Make Sure You Save Room For . . ." list of desserts. It was so overwhelming that Margot struggled to find something that she could choke down and still seem tempted by the restaurant's astonishing miscellany.

By the time Brooklyn returned with their Bellinis, Margot and Francis had managed to work through the menu and order quickly. Margot avoided the seafood and sushi. There was no need to emphasize an already obvious association between Vietnamese immigrants and raw fish. So she ordered rosemary-roasted chicken with popcorn rice. He ordered a medium-well filet mignon.

"So, tell me some more about the FBI. What kind of cases are you working?" he asked, trying to distract her from the embarrassing fact that he preferred, like a fussy ten-year-old, his steak cooked medium-well. She let it pass. The love-crush can brook almost any shortcoming in the darling of its fancy.

"I love it," Margot said. "All the same, I'd like to get out in the field a little more, though. There's a lot more office work than I expected. Especially considering the amount of physical training we went through. Lately, I've been chained to my desk filling out report forms and—" She stopped herself from mentioning the surveillance tapes she was reviewing after a tip-off about possible financial crimes at a Vietnamese grocery store.

"I know what you mean. Even though I'm on the streets most of the time, as soon as I see some action, like a chase or an arrest—drug busts and that sort of thing—I'm back at my desk filling out paperwork. I don't like that part, but I gotta do it to make the district attorney happy. Most guys cut corners on the paperwork part. I mean, girls too. We have female officers too." Francis corrected himself as a courtesy to Margot, or so she sensed. "Some of our best officers are females . . . I mean women. When I was in the Second District, my captain was actually a woman."

Margot smiled at him as if to forgive his fumbling. She wanted to relieve his embarrassment. She didn't want Francis to get spooked by feminist righteousness, if any she had. She was wearing four-and-a-quarter-inch heels, for heaven's sake. She said, "At least I get to take my frustrations out at the firing range."

Francis smiled and leaned toward her. "I go to the firing range myself for the same reason. Do you train with your service sidearm? I've heard the standard-issue FBI pistol is a Sig Sauer p226. Or a 9mm anyway."

"Actually, the bureau now authorizes the Glock 17, but I carry a 19. I like the control it gives me." Margot was careful to explain her choice of firepower. The Glock 19 was smaller than a 17, but she didn't want Francis to think that it was too heavy for a female officer, just that it was more functional. Or efficient. Or something. Like the shortstop who prefers a smaller glove for better control. Or like Napoleon preferred a smaller horse for its maneuverability on the battlefield. "I think it gives me an advantage in close-quarters combat. So that's what I mostly train with at the range, although occasionally, there is compulsory work with an M4. We all have to qualify with an M4."

"Maybe we could go to the range together? I'm there all the time, even beyond our once-a-month mandatories. We should go!"

Margot jumped at the nonspecific, nonbinding invitation for another date, indefinite though it was. "I'd love to. The FBI range is closed to outsiders without special dispensation, but I'm sure I could get clearance for the NOPD range." Margot was concerned she might have been scornful to the local police agency that some of her fellow FBI officers considered inferior. But she wanted to make the outing happen. She tried to soften the presumption: "I think the FBI already has standing clearance at the NOPD range."

"Yes, I think so," said Francis. "I'll ask my sergeant. He likes to encourage extra work at the range from all his officers. Plus, he knows I'm trying to get from officer II to officer III. Then I can take my test for sergeant. Which is my goal. For the short-term, anyway."

As Margot listened to his plans for advancement, Francis reached for the cracker basket. But the extended sleeve of Francis's shirt brushed against his Bellini flute and knocked it over. The drink spilled onto the table, ran toward the edge closest to Margot, and then dripped onto her lap.

She instinctively flinched in her seat and began wiping the mess with her napkin, starting with her dress and upper thigh, then to the table, where Francis was moving items around to help with the cleanup. The table was covered with all sorts of dishware, flatware, salt and pepper shakers, stainless-steel display stems holding laminated advertisements for specialty drinks, and promotional bottles of cheap wine. Brooklyn miraculously appeared to help with the catastrophe.

"My God, I'm so sorry," Francis pleaded, trying to rise from his seat at the booth to get a better angle.

"It's all right," Margot said soothingly. "It's just a little champagne." Margot wondered whether the accident was his clumsy way of avoiding alcohol consumption. Margot had not touched her Bellini either.

"I have to apologize for my shirtsleeves. For my whole outfit, actually. I'm not very good about clothes. Outside of my police uniform, the only things I really ever wear are sweatpants and workout clothes. A buddy of mine had to take me to the mall just to put this outfit together. It's all very embarrassing."

"I think you look great," said Margot, trying to provide Francis with a soft landing spot. "I spend most of my time in my uniform too. I know how you feel. It doesn't matter. I'd rather hear about your police work in New Orleans East, especially since I grew up there." She was being kind by dismissing the Bellini accident and returning to their first-date conversation as though the interruption was too minor to dwell on. Francis seemed grateful for her mercy.

"Well, working in the East is definitely a challenge. I hafta remind myself that the district covers over eighty-five thousand acres." Francis seemed happy to move on from the embarrassment: "It's considered the Badlands. Especially the areas farthest from town. Like in Little Woods and those areas. There aren't really any homeowners outside of the Vietnamese families, so there's a lot of turnover. The people who live out there pretty much let it go to seed." Margot understood that Francis was being careful not to say *Black people.* "The criminals from Central City, even the West Bank, use it as a refuge. It's easy to hole up there. Nobody talks to the police. The address numbers have all been ripped off the houses, and a lot of the streetlights have been shot out. If you're involved in a stolen car pursuit, you can be sure you'll end up in the East. When I first got transferred to the Seventh District, I wasn't too happy. But now I kind of like the action."

"It's not as bad where I grew up," Margot said, "Village De L'Est, out on Dwyer Boulevard—"

"Oh, no. I wasn't referring to that area. The Vietnamese area near Mary Queen of Vietnam Church is nice and quiet. Well-lit, freshly painted fences, nicely landscaped. It's hard to believe it's even part of that same district. You should be proud of your old neighborhood."

Margot knew much of the background of the old neighborhood, New Orleans East, and the Vietnamese enclave at its edge, though it had a depressing history. It was never really a part of the city because of its topography: marshes and swamplands adjacent to the Lake Pontchartrain estuary.

Back in the 1900s, it had been acquired by one Colonel deMontluzin, an early real estate speculator, who had had some success with an earlier development in Gentilly Terrace, so much so that he believed he could invest safely in the vast area farther east. Once again, deMontluzin had guessed wrong. He tried at various times to sell off twenty-five-acre parcels as country retreats from the sweltering New Orleans city limits, but nobody wanted to take a chance on the remote expanse with no electricity or running water.

Another group led by a man named Rosenberg tried something similar in 1914 with a proposed development he called "Flowerdale," but it never got past the planning stages. In the 1930s or 40s, some local New Orleans businessmen snatched up some of the acreage, but they didn't have any luck as developers either, even after they laid paved street grids as an enticement. The main thoroughfares of New Orleans East still bear the names of those ambitious but failed developers: Reed Boulevard, Downman Road, Hayne Boulevard, and Morrison Road.

Some of that real estate was eventually acquired by Samuel Zemurray, the legendary New Orleans tycoon who skippered the United Fruit Company and ultimately donated his St. Charles Avenue mansion to Tulane University, where it is still used as the president's residence. In 1954, Zemurray sold his tract in New Orleans East to Joe W. Brown, a Las Vegas real estate mogul whose widow, in turn, unloaded it on a New York investor named Marvin Kratta in the early 1960s. Kratta's company, the LaKratt Corporation, hired an urban development planning company to design a futuristic suburb like the ones that had been successful in St. Louis and elsewhere.

The idea was part of a 1960s American trend that attempted to capitalize on White dissatisfaction with urban decay by luring middle-class Whites tired of inner-city congestion into preplanned, wonderland living communities. The *Ville Radieuse* concept (which had failed over and over again in places like Chandigarh, India, and Brasilia, Brazil) was still being copied by late twentieth-century American architects and developers who remained bewitched by the legendary reputations of Le Corbusier and his adherents. There was no need, the developers preached, to live in drafty wooden houses in cramped neighborhoods when modern brick-on-slab housing was available in the suburbs. Exponents of this migration and the immediate rewards of contemporary, utopian living initially met with some success.

The same was true for New Orleans East or, as part of the area was imaginatively rechristened, Lake Forest. As it happened, the LaKratt Corporation's parent company, National Equities, was based in Chicago, and its principals insisted that the development and its subdivisions be given names that evoked suburban success stories from areas in and around their hometown. Francis often wondered why a neighborhood in his Seventh District patrol was called "Kenilworth."

But the Vietnamese neighborhood where Margot grew up was a different story. At the fall of Saigon in 1975, the United States government evacuated many South Vietnamese refugees who feared political or religious (specifically Catholic) persecution. One of the stateside refugee camps was at Fort Chaffee, Arkansas. A short time after their arrival, the refugees at Fort Chaffee were visited by New Orleans Archbishop Philip Hannan, who arranged for their resettlement in New Orleans East. Most of those refugees were Catholic themselves, remnants of religious proselytizing that took place under the French colonial occupation of Vietnam. The refugees at Fort Chaffee were only too happy to leave military barracks for the promise of private homes and a piece of the American Dream.

Whether New Orleans East was ever part of the American Dream was debatable, but Margot had been able to graduate from college and join the FBI in a matter of one generation.

Margot was enjoying the dinner table conversation, and she wanted to know more about Francis's family. "Do you have brothers and sisters?"

"Oh, no. I'm an only child," he answered. "I don't really know why. Most of my parents' friends have big families. They all lived in the Irish Channel long ago, but we moved out to Metairie when I was little. From what they've told me, the Irish Channel was a family-oriented area, a lot like the Mary Queen of Vietnam community where you grew up. Only, their church was St. Mary's Assumption. German Catholic. There's none of us left there anymore. We all moved to Metairie."

"Oh, I know the pattern," she said, trying to welcome the comparison. "Actually, a lot of our family friends, especially the younger generation, are moving away from Mary Queen of Vietnam. Like my sister. She's a doctor in Nashville." She was worried that reeling off her sister's success story came across as bragging, so she qualified the statement by pointing out the similarities between her family and his. "My brother still lives here, in Metairie, I mean. And my parents still live in Mary Queen of Vietnam Parish."

As they talked, neither seemed to be too interested in eating. Margot was becoming more and more comfortable that her immigrant background was something Francis would consider less unusual, less foreign. Not that she was embarrassed about it, but she was glad it would not be something that Francis would be turned off by.

After the awkward Bellini incident, she noticed that Francis had relaxed. The remainder of their dinner conversation was easy—that is to say, natural and unforced. The food was disgusting, and Margot was not at all concerned that setting her fork down would be construed by Francis as a sign that she was dissatisfied with the dinner date. Francis hadn't seemed to enjoy the food much either, and he put his fork down in like manner, as though they were sharing yet another inside joke that no one else knew was being told. It was an indescribable sense of becoming suddenly aware that gears were meshing. It was thrilling.

"I can't eat another bite! It was yummy, but more food than I'm used to having for dinner!" Margot regretted saying "yummy," but it was a girlish expression she thought might have sent the right message—a message to him that she was letting her guard down.

"Oh, neither can I. My captain was right, though. This place is great. I could stay for dessert, but I'm sure you have to be home soon. I don't wanna keep you out too late. I mean, I could stay out as long as you want, but I don't wanna get you into trouble with your job or your boss. With the bureau, I mean."

"Oh no, not at all." She was letting him off the hook. He was fumbling, and she wanted to be agreeable. She was careful not to ruin her chances for another date. "We'll just pick up where we left off next time!"

"Oh, absolutely! You pick the restaurant. You probably know more places than I do, anyway." His naïve deference continued to appeal to her.

"I'm sure I can think of something," she answered as she placed her napkin on the side of her unfinished plate. Francis signaled for the bill.

When supper was ended, they completed the scootch-slide out of the booth in opposite directions and walked to his car in the parking lot. At that point, Margot began to fret the uncertainty of the evening's finalé: Would he walk her to her door? Would she invite him in? Would he try to kiss her in the car? Would she take him to bed on their first date? As she made these calculations in her head during the ride home, Francis tried to continue their dinner table conversation.

"We didn't have time to hear more about your career. I'm sure FBI work is more exciting than a beat cop in the Seventh District."

"I suppose it's really a lot like yours," she demurred. "Only, I guess there's more interstate coordination, out-of-state fugitives, and that sort of thing." It was against regulation for Margot to discuss ongoing casework. She was sure Francis was aware of that restriction. "Pretty routine stuff as FBI work goes."

Upon their arrival at The Corsair Towers condominium complex, Margot opened her own door so that it would not appear to test Francis's knowledge of etiquette. At the locked gate outside of the complex, she was prepared to allow him to walk her to the front door of her unit, but Francis gave no indication that he presumed an invitation upstairs would be made. She didn't press the issue.

"I really had a nice time," said Francis. "I hope we can do it again. At least I can call you to go to the shooting range together, okay?"

"Definitely. Call me later this week, and we'll coordinate our schedules."

Without threatening to pass through the outer gate, Francis leaned toward her politely and kissed her on her cheek. Decisions about further sexual interaction would be postponed, at least until their next date. It was an appropriate and satisfying way to end the first one, and Margot felt just as much romantic excitement, if not more, than she would have felt had they ripped each other's clothes off and rolled around on the floor. As Francis returned to his car, they said their goodbyes and until-next-times with satisfied smiles.

The date had gone well. It was an evening filled with gold and goodness, so Margot felt the natural inclination to call someone and report. But she didn't really have a close friend to confide in. She considered calling her mother or her sister-in-law, but she made a point to avoid giggly girl-talk where her family was concerned. It was important for them to think that she was too serious about her career for such silliness. Besides, she preferred to disclose as little of her personal life as possible to anyone.

—

Back in her apartment that night, Margot felt the excitement of her first-date romance still shimmering when she plopped down on the couch and reached for the FBI case file assigned to her only two days before. She didn't usually take work home, but this case was an interesting and exciting one—which she made sure not to mention at dinner.

A grocery store in New Orleans East was under FBI surveillance for operating an illegal lottery. The operation had caught the attention of the federal government because a preliminary investigation had determined it had become so lucrative that a serious tax evasion question had been raised. The IRS Criminal Investigation division had enlisted the cooperation of the FBI to provide linguists and investigating agents for the suspected malfeasance.

Margot had been aware all her life that illegal gambling was taking place in the Vietnamese community, but she never asked her parents for precise details. She didn't want to embarrass them. Besides, she could figure it out on her own. As far as she knew, her father did not engage in such things, and gambling was certainly condemned by their family's parish priest at Mary Queen of Vietnam. Apparently, the IRS suspected that ordinary Vietnamese villagers were buying crude lottery contracts from the proprietors of the Phuoc Tho Duong grocery store, which was located in a strip mall on Chef Menteur Highway, only blocks from the church.

Margot had been tapped by her supervisor to review documents seized from the grocery store by various state and local agencies and to translate wiretapped conversations. Because she could speak Vietnamese fluently, she was a natural choice for an investigation of this type. As with all FBI investigations, there was the possibility that other related criminal transgressions could come to light. It would be Margot's responsibility to assemble all the evidence in a digestible way for use by the United States attorney's office.

The local branch of the IRS had come to the preliminary conclusion, without staff linguists capable of understanding the Vietnamese language, that the grocery store lottery would be drawn once a week, and the winning three-number combination would be determined by the last three numerals of the dollar value of the Sunday offering collected by Mary Queen of Vietnam Church. According to the IRS referral, these kinds of homespun enterprises were not uncommon in immigrant neighborhoods. The IRS suspected, and the FBI had been asked to confirm, that winning tickets were somehow determined by the total sum collected at all five Sunday masses and then published on the church website every Monday morning. Margot knew that a cottage gambling industry driven unwittingly by the charitable efforts of Mary Queen of Vietnam Parish would be scandalous, but she was determined to fulfill the assignment with complete objectivity.

She put the case file down for the evening, resigned to resume her police work in the morning. She would sleep well that night knowing that, if nothing else, Francis was in her future.

5

And so, Jerry Sonthonax—elected Seventh District assessor, opportunistic lawyer on probation, hard-luck horse race handicapper, light-skinned Black Catholic, divorced father of two, urban desperado, delinquent consumer credit risk, prospective emoluments felon—drove his leased phantom-gray metallic Chevrolet Impala toward Central City for an appointment with Burton Clayton, his political mentor and fellow property assessor, to pay tribute and discuss his options.

The car's air conditioner was off, and the windows were rolled down to save gas, so it was a struggle to affix his wireless Bluetooth headset to the side of his sweat-slicked face. Though he knew Burton Clayton would be wearing a tight silk suit, Sonthonax could only manage gray trousers and a maroon cotton polo shirt because he could no longer fit into any of the suits he had purchased online long before the divorce. He was comfortable, but his breathing was shallow, and he had coffee heartburn.

Clayton had insisted they meet in Central City at the Herschel and Miriam Ziskind Center for Housing Justice, a private nonprofit organization that occupied sleek air-conditioned offices on Oretha Castle Haley Memorial Boulevard (formerly Dryades Street), one of the several community development programs incorporated (with funding from the Department of Housing and Urban Development and sustained by Tulane University) to combat the residential displacement of Black voters from the city limits of New Orleans. Burton Clayton had free use of the Ziskind Center's facilities for any purpose, public or otherwise, because its administrators, and those of several other community-service centers around town, maintained a close association with public figures like Clayton, whose political objectives and goodwill were in line with theirs.

Jerry Sonthonax hoped that he could cultivate a similar relationship with the Ziskind Center, though it wasn't in his district, by making an appearance there on the arm of Burton Clayton himself. When he arrived, Jerry was met by an olive-skinned girl in her mid-twenties. She introduced herself.

"Mr. Sonthonax! Hi, I'm Hannah. Welcome to the center." She extended both her arms sideways and parallel to the ground, with upturned palms, like a vaudeville emcee asking the audience to behold a fabulous stage set. "Burton—uh, Mr. Clayton—said for you to wait in the conference room next to the Action Center. I've got you all set up in there. We have some students from Duronsolet Middle School here for an awareness class, but they shouldn't disturb you. They're pretty well-behaved!"

It struck him that she referred to Burton Clayton as "Burton"—a familiarity that betrayed a suspiciously close alliance with the Ziskind staff. He wondered how Burton Clayton managed to get money out of or into this organization. He was certain there was *some* kind of financial refluence taking place, and it was exactly this sort of peculation Jerry wanted to learn about when he requested the meeting. Why couldn't he pasture in Gilead as well?

Hannah escorted him into the conference room furnished with a sleek brushed-aluminum table and ten futuristic chairs with black-mesh carbon-fiber seats and flared chairbacks. The room was separated from the Action Center by a picture window through which Jerry could see the middle school children fidgeting and largely ignoring the calls-to-order of their facilitators—another young, olive-skinned White woman in jeans and a middle-aged Black woman wearing a custard-yellow maxi dress and a matching dashiki headdress. Miniature chairs with primary-colored polyethylene shells and steel legs had been pushed to the walls of the Action Center to allow for an open playspace for the children to interact with one another. There was a slightly older White man with a closely cropped beard and black cargo pants who seemed to be some kind of supervisor. He hovered over the proceedings in the Action Center by leaning against the wall with his arms folded and one leg bent at the knee with the rubber sole of his electric-blue running shoe flat against the wall surface.

The man was only a silent observer, a ranking chaperone who might have had the authority to intervene and guide the proceedings but who forbore to assert that authority in front of the children. His presence and posture would have made him seem like a plantation overseer, except that the way he crossed his arms—as if he were wearing an invisible straightjacket instead of Charles Atlas–style with one fist tucked into the crook of the other arm—made him look less imperious, more respectful of and sympathetic to the solemn teaching ceremony taking place under his benevolent scrutiny. The children were receiving instructions on how to play a large board game that was spread on the floor.

Jerry paced restlessly around the conference room table and was relieved to find an arranged assortment of folded promotional fliers that he could read as he awaited Burton's arrival. The pamphlets were neatly stacked on a smaller brushed-aluminum table in the corner of the conference room. They were sleek promotional materials, professionally printed and obviously expensive to produce. Jerry flipped through them with his coffee-colored fingers and tried to guess how they had found their way into the Ziskind Center's offices on Oretha Castle Haley Memorial Boulevard.

This stretch of town was in a very poor neighborhood, but some of its buildings had been renovated with the help of federal urban-renewal grants. The street on which the Ziskind Center sat was once known as Dryades Street, where immigrant Eastern European Jews had established a flourishing commercial district in the 1920s and 30s known as Little Warsaw. But by mid-century, the resourceful shopkeepers of that era had long since abandoned the area, leaving behind only the architectural vestiges of their prosperity. The Ziskind Center and other subsidized institutions on the same street were doing their best to breathe life into the forsaken slum.

The infusion of federal dollars had, indeed, brought a certain cosmetic optimism to the neighborhood, but Jerry had seen the results of these urban-renewal programs before and knew that they never really took root. From what he could tell, the initial infusion of federal dollars would always be sucked up by well-connected private contractors and administrative salaries, after which the gleaming new buildings inevitably fell into disrepair. These artificial revitalization projects certainly provided politicians with proof that they could deliver the goods for their constituencies, but those results never seemed to last longer than the next voting cycle.

Under the strain of his present circumstances, Jerry didn't give a shit about neighborhood revitalization. He wanted some of that money.

The pamphlets Jerry browsed as he waited for Burton were the standard politically motivated literature he expected to see at a housing justice command post, all of which looked like organizations he would gladly support because their formal names intimated a concern for the maintenance and support of the urban poor. Some were even familiar to him as potential sources of campaign donations that he had approached, at the recommendation of Burton Clayton, when he ran for office:

> *The National Fair Housing Law Project*
> *The National Low-Income Housing Coalition*
> *The National Fair Housing Alliance*
> *The Alliance for Housing Justice*
> *Americans for Financial Reform*
> *Prosperity Now!*
> *The Lawyers' Committee for Civil Rights Under Law*
> *The National Community Reinvestment Coalition*
> *The Art Into Housing Initiative*
> *The Poverty and Race Research Action Council*
> *The Feinbaum Center on Poverty Law*
> *The Louisiana Fair Housing Action Center*
> *The Neighborhood Development Foundation*

The Sustainable Housing Initiative
The Tulane University Civil Rights and Federal
Practice Clinic
The Loyola Law Clinic
People for Places Preservation Consortium

Jerry had not received any money from these organizations but was certain that Burton was on the boards of some of them, providing political legitimacy and bureaucratic stroke in return for an honorary stipend. It was a game Jerry was only just learning to play. His visit to the Ziskind Center, under Burton's auspices, was a chance to see this kind of logrolling in person. He wanted in.

On the wall opposite the picture windows that looked out on the Action Center was a chart approximately six feet wide and four feet tall that appeared to set forth individual staff responsibilities in furtherance of the Ziskind Center's missions and objectives. Across the top were the names of the individual staff members, and running vertically down the left-hand side was a list of responsibilities each member would be expected to manage. The roster of names read like the tribal genealogy in the Book of Genesis his grandmother read aloud to him when he was a small boy. The vertical list of tasks assigned to each staff member was expressed in quasi-military terms that stressed the urgency of the housing crisis faced by the Ziskind Center. The chart looked like this:

	Hannah	Aaron	Rachael	Caleb	Shoshanna	Yael	Aiayah
Action Plans							
Chokepoints							
Encroachment Zones							
Tactical Touchstones							
Sector Bruising							
Pushback Threats							

The squares created by the chart's crosshatching contained an impressive variety of handwritten notations and color-coded symbols. Jerry briefly considered the advantages of such a chronocard for his own assessor's office, but he wasn't entirely sure he could match the creativity of the mission categories adopted by the Ziskind Center. Plus, he had no staff.

Resting beside the stacks of pamphlets and below the chart was a laminated paperback children's book entitled *Sundyata's Sweet Stand* illustrated by Folami Fulton-Delpit and published by the Ziskind Center. Jerry picked it up and began to read. The book was about a Black second-grade girl who lived with her single mother. From time to time, little Sundyata would set up a lemonade stand on the sidewalk in front of their house. Her young friends from the neighborhood would often assist Sundyata in her fledgling business and delight in the camaraderie of unsupervised child's play. The group of friends included a White boy, a Black boy, a Vietnamese girl, a brown-skinned Semitic girl who wore a purple hijab, and a White girl with blonde hair confined to a wheelchair. They enjoyed one another's company working at this sidewalk stand and generally accepted their cultural and ethnic differences with perfect, childlike innocence.

But, as the storyline unfolded, the neighborhood idyll was under threat. Sundyata and her mother faced eviction from their rented apartment. Sundyata's mother had been searching desperately for an alternate residence in the same area for the same rent, but the available properties advertised in the newspaper were either too expensive or too far away from the neighborhood they had enjoyed for so many years. But, in the tradition of most children's literature, Sundyata hit upon a solution that her mother had overlooked. Across the street from her sweet stand and only a block away from their threatened residence was an apartment house with a "For Rent" sign in the front yard!

When Sundyata and her mother, as the story continued, made polite inquiries with the prospective landlord—a White man named Kurt—they were told the apartment was no longer available, and they were summarily turned away. A short time later, Sundyata observed from her perch at the sweet stand that a White single mother and her own daughter had made identical inquiries and were then granted the lease. The omniscient narrator of the book then went on to explain the inherent unfairness of Kurt the Landlord, his unpublished rental policies, and the illegal race-based discrimination that had taken place. In the end, Sundyata and her mother enlisted the services of the Ziskind Center and its friendly staff, who were able to intervene on their behalf and secure the desired housing. The sweet stand had been saved, and the children were able to reacquire their innocence in the face of the unchecked marketplace and its insidious cruelty. On the last page of the book were "Talking Points for Parents" that offered guidance on how to overcome housing inequities and a list of government agencies to whom reports could be made. The last page also explained that a children's board game was available at local public libraries and certain schools to illuminate the deplorable realities faced by the urban ethnic poor in need of decent housing.

Jerry looked up from the book through the conference room picture windows and saw that the children from Duronsolet Middle School were playing the actual board game advertised on the last page of *Sundyata's Sweet Stand*. To get a better look at the board game, Jerry opened the door of the conference room and moved discreetly to the back wall of the Action Center. The laminated gameboard was spread across the tiled floor of the Action Center, and the children, who appeared to be ten or eleven years old and all of them Black, knelt along the edges of the playing surface and spiritedly argued over the game's progress, as children do.

The colorful gameboard graphics were like any other children's game, like *Candyland, Sorry!,* and *Go to the Head of the Class*, only quite a bit larger. The outer edges contained spaces for the players to move their game pieces around the board pathway according to the roll of a single die. The inner area of the gameboard contained depictions of various housing alternatives: On one end were the desirable apartments near simple drawings of parks, schools, hospitals, libraries, and retail shopping. At the other end were the less desirable housing options that were situated across a simple set of railroad tracks in an obviously less desirable area near smoke-belching industrial plants, smelly garbage dumps, and liquor stores with meretricious neon signage. As the players moved around the board, they would periodically draw from piles of "Situation Cards" or "Self-Esteem Cards." Each card contained a random directive based on the ethnic or racial makeup of each player's game persona. For example, one card might read "If you are African-American, move back 5 spaces" or "If you are Movement Restricted, move back 2 spaces." Each player had been assigned a specific character at random. The player pieces matched the ethnically diverse characters from the accompanying book: a White boy, a Black boy, a handicapped girl, etc. The game was obviously rigged so that the White player enjoyed every advantage delivered by the cards, while the remaining players, burdened with their racial, ethnic, or disability status, would never be able to secure residence in the desirable game neighborhood. From what Jerry could gather, the objective of the game was for each player to travel successfully through the pitfalls of the playtime housing market. The winner of the game would be determined by the player who could complete the journey first and secure rental housing in the gamescape area with the most wholesome amenities.

As Jerry quietly observed from the sidelines, the "Situation Cards" would introduce a shift in circumstances for the participants to manage. One card read: "Federal income tax cuts: Non-White and Disabled players go back 2 spaces." Another card from the "Self-Esteem" pile read: "Funding for public television slashed: Non-White and Disabled players go back 3 spaces." There was also a row of game board squares superimposed by an express-lane arrow labeled "White Slide" that allowed the White player-character (there was only one without a disability) to proceed in accelerated fashion across six game spaces and advance toward housing satisfaction and ultimate victory. Jerry concluded that the game was designed to teach children the disparity of treatment received by non-Whites and the disabled by rigging the contest against them. By suffering through the challenges presented by the game's thematic format, the children could experience a simplified simulation of real-world housing discrimination. But the children didn't seem to be interested in this important life lesson. They were more concerned with winning the game. In spite of the facilitators' best efforts, the children clamored over who would get to be the White boy in the game, the character they knew would ultimately be the winner.

"I was Maddie last time!"

"It's my turn to be Christopher!"

"Miss Rachael, I don't want to be Abdul again!"

"Mr. Caleb, she's always Christopher! She wins every time!"

This was not at all the result the facilitators had expected.

"Children, children!" Rachael the facilitator implored. "Don't worry about who the winner will be! You need to talk about *why* Christopher always wins. If it's unfair, then you need to discuss with each other *why* it's unfair. Donnell, don't throw the die at her!"

The scene was erupting into a fight over the fairness of the game. The Ziskind Center faculty and the game's designers were hoping to teach the children about the *un*fairness of the exclusionary housing crisis. That didn't seem to be happening. The efforts of Rachael and Caleb notwithstanding, the children were behaving like children. Jerry could tell that Caleb, the supervising administrator, was getting restless. The children had gone from frustrated to hostile, and the lesson-play facilitators had lost control of the lesson plan. It was a cardinal rule of grant-mission, community outreach protocol for supervisors like Caleb to remain disinterested observers, even when their field-level operatives stumbled through their maneuvers. Correction of subordinates was never to take place in front of the children, no matter how disastrously circumstances might degenerate. But Caleb could no longer be restrained by departmental policy. Jerry moved in closer to see how he intended to intervene. The scientific training Caleb had received in the completion of his doctorate in social work gave way to a kind of kitchen-pantry pragmatism: "Kids! Kids!" he admonished, clapping his hands and raising his voice above the shrieking cacophony. "You know what? Let's take a snack-pouch break! Who's ready for a snack pouch?"

One by one, the children set aside their hostilities for the possibility of an approved treat. The beleaguered facilitators seemed relieved that Caleb had jumped into the fracas. Maybe, Jerry thought, the facilitators needed a snack pouch break as well. Come to think of it, Jerry could have used a snack pouch himself, whatever it was. On second thought, it was probably some sort of organic-oat-flake-dried-fruit health mix that would scratch the roof of his mouth. Perhaps he didn't want one after all. Just then, it occurred to him that the White landlord antagonists of the Sundyata story and the accompanying board game deserved to be gouged by assessors like him. Those revenues could then be passed on to the city's general fund for social programs that benefited his voting constituency. An act of political heroism! A populist redistribution of wealth! A deliverance to the hand-to-mouth proles of New Orleans! This fantasy of Spartacist intervention was broken when he remembered that his personal situation was much worse.

Just then, Burton Clayton walked into the Action Center and motioned for Jerry to join him in the conference room. Burton breezed through the premises with the confidence and familiarity of a chef through his kitchen. Jerry fully appreciated that he was on Burton's turf, but he was prepared, in his desperate state, to put Burton on the spot. He intended to assume the role of political equal demanding attention to a mutually troubling problem. What was bad for Jerry was bad for Burton. Jerry needed money, and Burton would know how to get it.

Burton closed the conference room door behind them and spoke: "Before you start, I'm not gonna sit here for an hour, not even fifteen minutes, listening to a sob story about Wally Woebegone and his child support problems. I haven't got the time." Burton was establishing at the onset of the meeting that he would be generally unwilling to do the younger politician any favors. "This is your mess, and I don't have the time, let alone the inclination, to clean it up."

Jerry had already briefed Burton on the assessment discrepancy/ opportunity presented by the Vietnamese grocery and its illegal lottery, but he did not expect Burton to sense that he was in financial distress. On the other hand, it was not surprising that Burton had made the obvious deduction. Burton was an experienced political operator and, in spite of his tight suits, was still a man of the streets.

"No, I have no time for that either," answered Jerry, surrendering to Burton's skip-the-preliminaries frankness. "I'm only here for technical advice. I'm really only here to ask a mathematical question."

"A mathematical question? I doubt you'd ask for a face-to-face meeting to ask a mathematical question."

"Well, it's a property assessment question, so it's not exactly mathematical. I've got a building in the Seventh District that has no precedent as far as property value."

"Yeah, yeah. You already told me. The Vietnamese grocery. Commercial property in the East is all worth the same on the tax rolls unless you're talking about an amusement park or garbage dump. The city has not seen those values fluctuate in the last thirty years. I don't see that you have a lot of leeway there."

"Well, as I told you, this is a small grocery store in Little Vietnam, way out on the Chef, out there by Dwyer," Jerry responded, referring to Chef Menteur Highway, the main artery through New Orleans East that once carried passengers and commercial cargo to Mississippi, Alabama, and Florida before the construction of Interstate 10. "It's an ordinary cinderblock corner store."

"So, it's a Vietnamese convenience store. Slap it with a two-hundred-fifty-K assessment like every other convenience store. You're not gonna squeeze much more out of that property."

"It's not that simple," Jerry answered, gently sliding into the real reason for the meeting. "It's a real nice business they got going there, throwin' off lots of cash."

"Mmm-hmm. So, you think they're selling more than cigarettes out there, do you?"

"Well, they sell the usual convenience store merchandise, plus some crazy Vietnamese food and hard liquor. But that doesn't account for the real cash it's throwin' off."

"All right. I know what you're talking about. You told me some of it. Some kind of illegal lottery?"

Jerry could see that he had stimulated Burton's guarded curiosity. "It's bigger than you might think. Those people have a lot of disposable cash in that area, and a lot of it seems to be flowing through that store. It's a major enterprise, just like it was back in Vietnam."

"I see. How did you come upon this information? Those people have a very closed culture. Especially first-generation. They're still sellin' live ducks and chickens, as far as I know. Somebody feedin' you information?"

"I've got a friend from high school," Jerry answered. "He's Vietnamese. He knows the owners. He goes to that store sometimes. That's why I trust him."

"Not Manny from the racetrack? *Now* I know what this is about. As the song says about the will and the won't—the first is strong, the other weak," said Burton to gain his point with an apothegm he had, it seemed obvious to Jerry, held in reserve for just such a moment. "You've been hangin' out at the track, and Manny's put you on another quick score. You're not supposed to be going to the track while you're on probation. A lawyer on probation has restrictions. Why are you foolin' with Manny?"

Jerry knew ahead of time that Burton would smell Manny at the bottom of all this. He would have preferred to leave Manny out of the discussion, but he needed to drop Manny's name to paint a believable picture. "I'm not talking about a racetrack tout sheet. It's a private lottery."

"Louisiana already has a lottery. Convenience stores, even Vietnamese ones, sell Louisiana lottery tickets all over town. Why would they be selling private lottery tickets?"

"From what I can gather, the Vietnamese don't trust the government. They want their own lottery. They keep it within the community. That way, they control the whole operation. They don't have to pay the state for the lottery tickets, they don't have to pay lottery fees, they don't have to report their lottery sales, they don't have to maintain the machines, and they don't have to pay taxes. It's a cash business. They like it that way."

"I see. So, how does this work? What did Manny say about how this works?"

"It's pretty simple, really. They come in with their own contracts—that's what he calls them. They come into the store with their own number combinations and buy the special tickets for a dollar apiece. Just like they used to do in the Irish Channel."

Jerry was reminding Burton about the illegal lottery operated by German, Italian, and Irish immigrants from corner stores in the area close to the Mississippi River that was, from 1900 to 1950, the residential neighborhood of dockworkers. Burton had grown up around that neighborhood and often told stories of purchasing Irish Channel lottery tickets for his grandmother through a hole in a fence from a White man whose face he never saw.

As Burton was certainly aware, the winning lottery combination would unwittingly be published in the newspaper's sports page. Every morning after a racing day, the New Orleans Fair Grounds Race Course would submit the day's handle, or total dollars wagered, and the last three digits of that statistic determined the winning lottery numbers. Jerry knew that Burton knew the simple workings of a private lottery because Burton had himself been part of one as a child.

"So how do they get the winning lottery combination?" Burton asked. "The Fair Grounds doesn't publish its daily handle in the newspapers anymore."

At this point in the conversation, Jerry was forced to lie a little. He didn't really know the mechanics of the Vietnamese lottery. After speaking to Manny, he had tried to verify some of the rumors going around. It was all supposition, but he had to provide Burton with some hard-sounding facts that Burton would be convinced by. "From the Mary Queen of Vietnam newsletter. Every Monday, the Catholic church out there reports the Sunday collection. It's the same thing. The last three digits of the Sunday collection are the winning numbers. It's all printed in Vietnamese, so nobody else really knows what's going on. It's perfect. The Vietnamese old-timers go to a Vietnamese store to buy Vietnamese private lottery contracts and check the Mary Queen of Vietnam newsletter on Monday for the winning combination. It's foolproof. Nobody ever knows what the hell is going on out there."

"So, you think because of this off-the-books industry, the building ought to be assessed at a higher rate?" Burton asked.

Jerry could see that Burton's mind was beginning to put together a shakedown plan. It was time for Jerry to pick up the pace. "I think if I went out there—or someone went out there—and told them their building was up for reassessment, they might be willing to make arrangements," Jerry said. He was signaling to Burton that he was aware of the extortion scam Burton was running downtown. In essence, Jerry was putting on the gentle squeeze.

"That doesn't sound right," Burton said. "Tellin' people they got a tough assessment comin' is like tellin' 'em they're already screwed."

Jerry knew that he was making some headway. Burton was playing stupid, feigning naïveté about assessment shakedowns when he well knew property owners were willing to pay assessors to avoid increased assessments—especially in the Central Business District, Burton's sinecure, where the value of office buildings carried a significant potential tax liability. And so, Jerry smiled when Burton showed the first signs that he might be willing to help.

"Well, I might know someone who could deliver your message if that's the way you wanna go," said Burton. "He could, I suppose, impress upon your Vietnamese property owners that they might be facing a steep increase. But I'll need to know exactly what your situation is. I know your cell phone's been disconnected. You've got a car lease that hasn't been paid. Your campaign fund is almost tapped out. We might be able to help with those, but we're not payin' bookies or child support. And I damn sure ain't gonna help you if you can't stay away from the racetrack."

Jerry had made a breakthrough. He was willing to eat shit about his gambling problem and his difficult family circumstances if it meant Burton would supply the apparatus for the oblique blackmail of a Vietnamese grocery store.

So, he pressed on: "Maybe your friend, Glenn, could pass that way and offer his services." By mentioning Glenn Hornacek, Jerry was signaling to Burton that his alter ego, Hornacek, was his well-known plenipotentiary.

Burton shifted slightly in his chair and averted his eyes. Jerry took those involuntary movements to mean that Burton was ready to do business. Burton's voice became softer and more serious: "I'll talk to Hornacek. I'll see if he's interested. He doesn't do much business out in the East, but it wouldn't hurt him to be seen in a district other than mine. But I don't think he knows you, Jerry."

"Oh, he knows me. He'll know me if you tell him he *should* know me. Hornacek ain't stupid."

"Okay, I'll feel him out," said Burton, trying to bring what had become an unsettling conversation to a close. "I'll let you know if something can be done."

Burton rose from his chair, indicating to Jerry that the meeting was over. Jerry rose from his chair, showing his respect, gratitude, and satisfaction that the meeting had been successful. Jerry expressed this relief by asking an unrelated question designed to flatter a political mentor who would soon be his financial salvation.

"This is a nice office. What's your involvement with the Ziskind Center?"

"I'm on the board. Chairman of the board. Their work is very important to me. And it should be to you. They're in my district even though a nonprofit doesn't pay property tax."

It was a joke intended to conclude the meeting on a more informal, happier note. Jerry smiled in appreciation and almost put his arm around Burton to express a chummy confidence in their association, but he thought better of it and simply offered a respectful handshake.

On the way out of the conference room and into the Action Center, Burton spoke casually with members of the Ziskind staff, as if he were part of the family. Jerry remained one respectful step behind Burton and smiled at the pleasantries, even though they did not include him. Back out on the street, Jerry and Burton went their separate ways on Oretha Castle Haley Memorial Boulevard. Jerry suppressed another satisfied smile.

—

Ten minutes later, Glenn Hornacek heard his phone ring on the speakers of his BMW and saw on his dashboard touch screen that the call was from Burton Clayton.

"Burton! I'm in my car on speakerphone, but I'm alone." Glenn was always careful to establish phone security so that the subject matter of their conversations could be framed accordingly. "I'm on my way to my wife's office, but we can talk as I drive."

"Listen, Glenn, I need you to take a job for a friend out in the East. I don't know everything, but it doesn't sound like much. I can explain everything later. In the meantime, I just need to know your availability. It could be nice for you."

Glenn Hornacek immediately recognized the coded language. Anytime Burton was arranging a shakedown, the initial proposal was always made in a familiar code. Glenn was somewhat mystified that it involved property in New Orleans East because that was outside of Burton's assessment district. Besides, there weren't any commercial properties of significant value in that area, and the East was not known as especially fertile ground for political extortion. It was a vast area, a marshy tract originally drained by some Chicago developers with fringe connections to organized crime who envisioned the project as a semi-sylvan suburb within the city limits of New Orleans. The ambitious dream had failed, and New Orleans East was now a deteriorating slum where fugitives went to ground and dead bodies were dumped. He had never before conducted appraisal services in that area and certainly never at the behest of Burton Clayton. But the history of their relationship was such that he could not ignore Burton's overtures. Glenn was therefore obliged to listen.

"Are you familiar with Little Vietnam?" Burton asked over the unsecure speakerphone.

"Not really. I know it's on the outer edges of the East. They have a Catholic church out there, maybe?"

"Exactly. A Catholic church and some family-owned businesses. Look into it, and we'll talk later."

"Will do," Glenn said. "I'll be in my office this afternoon and later this week."

"Excellent. We'll talk then."

Glenn had been curious about this business opportunity since he overheard the phone conversation back in Burton's office. The Vietnamese section of New Orleans East was the only safe area of the East, and it was known to be peaceful and law-abiding. They were an industrious people who saved their money and assimilated faster than most ethnic immigrants, but their numbers did not carry much political significance, or, at any rate, enough that could challenge or even threaten Black political hegemony.

There must be some other aspect of Vietnamese civic significance that would trigger the interest of Burton Clayton, a politician who traded almost exclusively in Black demographic currency. Glenn had never before dealt with the Vietnamese, either commercially or personally, but he was always willing to trust the instincts of a political savant like Burton Clayton. Without Burton, Glenn was out of business. Perhaps Burton wanted to explore a new frontier.

Then it dawned on him: *Bango!* Like a thunderbolt! Burton was on the board that oversaw Joe W. Brown Park, a seldom-used greenspace and playground that had been built and maintained with grants from the federal government and yearly appropriations from the city council. In fact, he remembered that one of Burton's relatives had been awarded a no-bid personal service contract to cut the grass and provide other custodial services at the park. Burton was planning to make a bigger move out in the East now that he had installed a friendly assessor, Jerry Sonthonax, whom he could control. New Orleans East was an area ripe for exploitation, and Burton intended to expand his operations. If that were the case, it was an opportunity for Glenn as well.

This was good news. Glenn was uplifted by the prospect that Burton would include him in the new venture. As he drove his BMW toward downtown, he wondered why there would be a well-funded park named after somebody whose name he knew only from racetrack mythology.

6

Glenn Hornacek had not told Burton Clayton the truth. He was not, in fact, going to his wife's office that day. He was going instead to an AA meeting to keep a promise to his wife that he would continue his commitment to sobriety.

His primary addiction was to powdered cocaine, but there were derivative addictions to alcohol (vodka, in particular) and opiate painkillers (ground into powder and often mixed with cocaine). In recent years, he had come to embrace his commitment to The Program, as recovering addicts referred to the AA fellowship, by speaking openly about his descent into dependency without embarrassment and by becoming an unofficial ambassador for the organization.

Every chance he got, he would offer up for public inspection the ten-year AA recovery medallion he kept on his keychain. At airports, government buildings, and sports arenas, he would toss his keychain with casual conspicuousness into the bowls provided at the metal-detector checkpoints hoping someone would notice. Most people, he had learned, were sympathetically predisposed to bestow their congratulations for and even draw inspiration from his Augustinian *confessiones*. So why not take advantage? He could recast himself as a flawed mortal who had got religion. Weakness, yes. But, in the end, virtue.

After years of rehearsing, he could, on command, recite this parable of the dissipated son: Once upon a time, he had hit rock bottom, recklessly abusing cocaine and alcohol as an unavoidable consequence of a dependency on painkillers prescribed by a doctor for a serious back injury. Alas and forsooth, he had fallen from a ladder while volunteering to help rebuild houses in the Lower Ninth Ward after Hurricane Katrina. His convalescence was an arduous process that tested faith and fortitude, but it was made bearable with the help of aggressive pain treatment from well-meaning doctors. At the time, accepted medical protocol sanctioned the administration of powerful synthetic opioids that have, since then, proved to be a scourge of their own.

Treating physicians, as it turned out, were themselves victims of an avaricious pharmaceutical industry, and Glenn was merely an end-user waste product of Big Pharma profiteering. He could not, therefore, be blamed for turning to alcohol and cocaine once his resistance to habit-forming narcotics had been breached. The slide into an even more malignant addiction came as no surprise to the public at large, so immediate forgiveness for the weakness was axiomatic. He could, under the cover of that old chestnut, righteously proclaim that he was an addict qua hero worthy of universal sympathy, if not outright veneration. A sentimental world all too ready to celebrate his courageous battle against a pernicious enemy was happy to oblige.

It was the same ruse perfected by upper-middle-class White men who explain away strictly cosmetic nose jobs as secondary procedures incident to minor car accidents that require hospitalization. *Sorry I've been away! Can you believe it? Some woman slammed into me on Elm Street, and I had to get my nose reset! Plus, I had a deviated septum anyway. So, I'm like, while you're at it . . . heh, heh. But I'm feeling much better now!*

When an underlying condition, especially one that can be attributed to other careless agents, can be used as a pretext to indulge a vanity or repudiate responsibility for drug addiction, forgiveness and understanding magically become obligations of the captious skeptic. Glenn relied on society's chumps to fall for the canard in order to resume his life as a penitent but inspirational sinner.

But he did not have time to explain all of this to Burton Clayton. Instead, he lied and told Burton that he was going to his wife's office when he was, in fact, going to an AA meeting in another part of town.

With all this in the back of his mind, he drove his BMW X6 down Claiborne Avenue upriver to the corner of Jefferson Avenue, where the meeting was scheduled. He had not previously attended an AA meeting at this location, but it was typical of the venues where such convocations were held around town. The church building on that corner was the most recent location of the First Unitarian Universalist Church. He had never heard of that denomination before, but it seemed welcoming enough.

The church structure was actually a quasi-Gothic version of ordinary church architecture favored in the 1950s. It was not cruciform, but it had a nave and an apse and an entrance portal with pointed archivolts beneath a large stained-glass rosette. Across the lintel was carved "First Evangelical Church."

The building, he surmised, had been acquired by the Unitarian Universalists from a previous congregation that had disbanded or moved somewhere else. Vertical canvas banners were hung on either side of the entrance portal, one of which read "Everywhere in Chains" (above a clenched fist and the broken pieces of metal shackles) and the other "It's All Relative" (above a stylized figure of a faceless human head and halo).

A religion that advertised such sympathies could be useful to Glenn Hornacek, who saw himself as a bulwark against the heartlessness and intolerance of the petty bourgeois. His professional existence, after all, depended on his ability to align himself with Burton Clayton's political platform. It was essential that Burton remain convinced that they shared a commitment to the same social causes—the ones that guaranteed Burton's continued reelection. He thought of posing for a picture in front of these banners, but there was no one around to take the publicity shot.

He entered the church through an open side door, but the building appeared to be unoccupied. Glancing at his watch, he realized he was thirty minutes early for the meeting and would have to kill some time. He walked into the open space of the nave, where rows of high-backed wooden pews had been removed so that only the first four rows closest to the chancel remained. A middle-aged White woman with gray hair wearing a long denim skirt that reached mid-calf, a simple cotton blouse, and tan sandals appeared out of nowhere to greet him.

She looked like a milkmaid. "Are you here for the meeting?" she asked in a friendly tone.

"Yes, thank you. I guess I'm a little early."

"Not a problem. Make yourself at home. Group members should be arriving soon. Meantime, have a look around and take in some of the great work we're doing. There's a lot of healing going on inside here."

"Thank you. I will."

The rear area where the pews had been removed was now an open space where stackable chrome chairs with black vinyl seats and seatbacks had been arranged in a circle. The floor of this space, though perhaps once wooden, was covered in vinyl tiles in a large hexagonal maze pattern, similar to the meditation labyrinths that were laid in contemplation gardens and parks across New Orleans. Toward the front of the nave was a two-stepped chancel, but there was no altar—only an acrylic lectern with a metal, goose-necked microphone stem. Draped on the front of the lectern was a large felt banner with the image of a flaming chalice inside the thin borders of a large circle. On the rear wall of the chancel facing the congregation were images of religious icons printed on a series of vertically hung cloth banners: crosses, ankhs, Buddhist vectors, a Yin Yang swirlicue, a Muslim Star and Crescent, a sinusoidal map of the world that resembled the 1950s Pan Am Airlines logo, a human hand with a circle set in its palm, an emblem that looked like a biohazard warning, a sailing ship's helm, a compass design that might have been the Seattle Mariners team logo, and other symbols of faith or American pop culture Glenn did not recognize. The banners reminded him of the official NFL bedsheets he slept on as a boy. The motley collection of religious iconography seemed to signal that the church was multidenominational or at least open to all faiths—a clearinghouse for passport ecumenism. There were also LGBT rainbow flags and multicolored African Nationalist textiles hung at intervals on the perimeter walls of the church.

On a long table off to the side of the space where pews had been removed was a display area where stacks of leaflets and other reading material were offered to the congregation or other visitors who might want to learn more about the ministry. The literature was extensive, but he had thirty minutes to occupy himself before the meeting—and no vending machine in sight. These publications seemed to have a political as much as a religious emphasis, and he soon realized that this "Church Without Creeds" was an open garage for any rattletrap theological jalopy looking for a place to park—a religion that made a nonbinding belief system out of every behavioral aberration American relativism could generate, a featherbed for fallen Christians like Glenn. He was starting to like it.

As far as Glenn could discern from the pamphlets, the thrust of Unitarian Universalism was to "Look Within Not Without"—an emphasis on the Enlightenment, rationalism, scientific certitude, and diversity built on evolution, with a sprinkling of the Judeo-Christian ethic on the surface of an essentially secular corpus. Suggested reading included Henry David Thoreau, Thomas Jefferson, Thomas Hobbes, John Locke, Jean-Jacques Rousseau, Theodor Adorno, Max Horkheimer, Jürgen Habermas, the Frankfurt School, the Institute for Social Research, Zarathustra, Gilgamesh, Confucius, Noam Chomsky, and Sigmund Freud. As he moved from left to right across the display table, the literature became more and more political. Code words were everywhere in evidence: commodification, commodity fetishism, exploitation, paternalism, hetero-patriarchy, oppression, suppression, the tyranny of the family, unconscious bias, hermeneutics, epistemological imperatives, anarcho-syndicalism, immiserating colonialism, gender fluidity, secular humanism, progressivism, non-species humanism, postmodernism, paganism, cultural hegemony, pantheism, Gaian transcendentalism, prehistoric naturalism, and Wiccan mysticism. Glenn was not completely sure what all of these words meant, but he knew what was going on.

And then there were the materials concerned with housing displacement: the Louisiana Fair Housing Action Center, The Herschel
and Miriam Ziskind Center for Housing Justice, HousingNOLA, the
City of New Orleans Office of Human Rights and Equity, The Choice
Neighborhood Initiative, the Greater New Orleans Housing Alliance and
its "Fit for a King" housing summit, The Alliance for Housing Justice,
The Affordable Housing Crisis Center, ActionNola, City of Yes, and the
NIMBY Deterrence Consortium. These flyers were placed, for reasons
apparently intended to frame comparisons, adjacent to similar ones published by the Gaza Emergency Relief Fund, The United Palestinian Appeal,
Pencils for Palestine, the United Nations Relief and Works Agency for
Palestinian Refugees, The Maia Project for Palestinian Children, and a
children's primer called Bedtime for Bedouins. One pamphlet was entitled "Jainism: The Dharmachakra and the Resolve to Halt the Samsara
through the Relentless Pursuit of Ahimsa." Glenn guessed that the sovereignty of Israel was not recognized by the Unitarian Universalists. This
would explain why there was no Star of David among the religious icons
displayed on the premises.

As he moved farther down the line, he saw publications by groups such
as European Dissent, which decried the pathologies of home ownership
and the "brain parasite" that was influencing Black residents to sell their
homes at a profit to White speculators. The group declared that "Whiteness
Isn't Real" and that "Whiteness Is Patronizing." Another group called
Showing Up for Racial Justice (or SURJ) introduced a Black, queer feminist lens to the cause of universal emancipation. Other groups represented
were The Congress of Day Laborers/Congreso de Jornaleros, 13th Night,
Stop Jail Expansion, The Congress of Racial Equality, and an organization
called Food Justice that encouraged strict adherence to what was called
a "co-opivor diet." And then there were the organizations battling Black
criminal incarceration: The Innocence Project, The Exoneration Initiative,
Challenging E-Carceration, and The Exculpation Enterprise.

And still, there were more pamphlets. The next group of brochures
was more overtly political in nature—if that was possible—published

by groups such as Stop Fascism Now, The People's Resistance Front, Collectivists Against Regional Fascism, Fascism for Dummies, and Fascism Shmacism. He could not resist investigating a little further, so he picked up a brochure entitled "Chalcolithic Gnosticism in the Age of Suppressed Pre-Socialized Memory." On the cover was an illustration of a Reubenesque earth mother (as she might have been rendered by Paul Cadmus) wearing a ceremonial sash that read "Madonna Fecundita" and a bonnet that read "Isis Lactans." She was depicted busting terra cotta pots over the fragile skulls of her acorn-belching husbands, who whimpered beneath her apron strings. The table of contents listed chapter headings such as "Numenism in the Temple of the Spirit," "Capnomancy and Cleromancy: A Practical Introduction," "Bréhémont Cheese-Hole Reading and Tyromancy in the Pharmaceutria of Theocritus," "Neanderthal Palingenesis and You: A Daily Affirmation," "The American Nuclear Fallacy: Debunking the Primacy of the Family Unit," "The Soothing Psalteries of Gautama," "Understanding the Demiurge," "Lactose Intolerance and the Bigotry of Nutrition: A Holistic Solution," "The Avenging Climate: This Time It's Global," "The Delusion of Cisgender Normativity," and "Jonathan Livingston She-Goat: The Emancipation of the Clitoris." Wow. None of this was entirely comprehensible to Glenn Hornacek, an old altar boy from Our Lady of the Pillar Parish in St. Louis, Missouri. But it sure seemed interesting, certainly provocative, and positively disestablishment.

And finally, at a separate table devoted to one subject, were materials related to a religious denomination known as *Theosophy*. According to one brochure, Theosophy was a belief in an astral plane of overarching ether, closer to a science than a religious faith, that recognized a secret doctrine of universal precepts shared by all men regardless of race, caste, sex, creed, or color. It looked intriguing to Glenn in its blending of Orientalism, Rosicrucianism, and Neoplatonism with elements of Judeo-Christian mysticism and Martin Luther King. The source text for this Gnostic, mongrel spirit-science was a book entitled *The Secret Doctrine* by Madame Helena Petrovna Blavatsky, a name he had never seen before. Also on the Theosophy table was a stack of stapled papers bearing the heading "The Catasterism of Koot Hoomi: An Adept in the Firmament," a subject that seemed to fit nicely with the pantheistic cosmology of the Unitarian Universalists. Right next to that stack was a single copy of an art monograph entitled *The Triumph of American Painting* by Irving Sandler. The cover of this book contained an image of one of Rothko's yellow-and-orange color-field paintings with the challenging title "Orange and Yellow, 1956." On the wall above the table was a poster of the Guggenheim Museum with the caption "Frank Lloyd Wright's Temple for the Spirit." The Unitarian Universalists sure had their hands full.

For the most part, these reading materials thrashed and roared against the fatalisms of Western orthodoxy, but they were too obscure to be the stuff of lunch-counter discussion—except, that is, the complaints about prison incarceration rates of racial minorities. In a city that was 58 percent Black, no aspiring politician could expect to be elected without a campaign promise to implement criminal justice reform. Politicians at every level emphasized sentencing alternatives like supplemental job training, increased mental health services, and mandatory drug rehabilitation to combat the racial disparity within the local prison population. Glenn understood the political value of these sentiments and would often vaporize on the subject with his wife or, most especially, in the presence of Burton Clayton when a spontaneous demonstration of political fealty was called for. It occurred to him that an affiliation with the Unitarian Universalist Church should be placed prominently on his résumé. It also occurred to him that he could secure a place for himself within the Church by offering up his services to the cause. After all, his stock-in-trade was the political exploitation of racial injustices—he kept a shoebox full of scratch-pad ideas for the benefit of any of Burton Clayton's causes. He could just as easily make that arsenal available to the Unitarian Universalists as a demonstration of his goodwill.

The ideas kept coming. The Orleans Parish Criminal Court complex was only minutes from the First Unitarian Universalist Church, yet none of its social-justice literature seemed directed specifically that way. Maybe he could call attention to that massive edifice and the brazen symbolism of its, as yet, unchallenged authority. It seemed to Glenn that the UU policymakers had overlooked the New Orleans Criminal Courthouse as a perfect target for their political outrage.

Glenn had not researched the matter, but he suspected the history of the Orleans Parish Criminal Courthouse, constructed in 1931 of gray granite, might bear closer examination. Surely a fortress like that was the product of a less-progressive age when the administration of harsh punishment was considered the one and only way to curtail criminal behavior. Given the time to investigate the matter, he would have discovered that he was right.

The building was designed by the German American Max A. Orlopp, Jr. The friezes and metopes were adorned with bas-reliefs of allegorical White-male athletes in various poses so common in the authoritarian, state-sponsored art of 1930s Germany. The life models used by the sculptor, Angela Gregory, were the heroes of Tulane University football from that era, Jerry Dalrymple and Adolph Jastrup. The glamorized male physique in any context, but particularly on the face of a criminal courthouse, was bound to be offensive to Black defendants and those who decried the disproportionate rate of Black prosecution and incarceration.

At the side entrance of the building, unknown to the Unitarian Universalists and their allied pamphleteers, were carved pilasters surmounted by the words "Law" and "Order." Those pilasters on either side of the portal were, in fact, stylized reliefs of wooden-rod bundles capped by protruding axe heads, also carved in granite. These symbols, themselves allusions to the Roman and Etruscan values of civil stability, were known as *fasces*, from which the word "fascist" was derived. These symbols of tribal order, completely unnoticed by the Unitarian Universalists or anyone else, once represented the unity of ancient societies (bundles of wooden rods bound by leather straps) and the authority (axe heads) they assumed. It might be supposed that in 1931, the year the building and its ornaments were designed, the terms "fascist" and the political term "fascism" had not yet acquired their odious connotations. And yet, there they stood, invisible to the Unitarian Universalists, the fair housing activists, the Palestinian sympathizers, and the social-justice evangelists of New Orleans. Those groups complained with great vehemence about other monuments to bygone priories and value systems, but here was an even more flagrant Mnemosyne to fascistic repression, complete with a decidedly German pedigree, unaffronted and unassailed.

There was a kind of irony built into a sturdy granite fortress of punishment that had been decorated with neofascist figurative allegories—an irony that was completely lost on the Unitarian Universalists. If the sloganeering contained in their reading materials was any indication, they were falling all over themselves to condemn any public installation commissioned before 1965. And yet, here was the criminal courthouse, of all things, trumpeting its fascistic message for all to hear. But nobody was listening.

As he continued his brain-racking for ways to ingratiate himself with the Unitarian Universalists, Glenn saw that other members of the AA group were arriving at the meeting, and he should take a seat with them. The milkmaid appeared again as if by magic and welcomed the new arrivals. It was clear at the outset that she would be presiding over the meeting of addicts in The Program. A mixture of a dozen people of all ages, races, and income brackets arrived and took their seats in the circle of prearranged group-therapy meeting chairs.

The milkmaid called the meeting to order. She began solemnly. "We meet here today in humility to admit our weaknesses and shortcomings, to declare our commitment to sobriety, and to strive for meaningful recovery. So, welcome all."

The group members responded in turn with happy purring and smiling, a communion in which Glenn Hornacek agreeably joined.

The milkmaid spoke again: "Who would like to begin this morning's meeting either with an affirmation or a testimonial?"

A middle-aged Black man with an untucked shirt and a festival-style straw hat spoke first: "My name's Derrell, and I'm an alcoholic . . ."

But just as he was beginning his testimonial, a new arrival interrupted the proceedings. He was a young White man, probably in his thirties, wearing tan trousers and a wrinkled blue cotton oxford shirt with a buttoned-down collar. It looked as if he had miscalculated the alignment of the front buttons of his shirt and pushed them through buttonholes that were one level lower than their corresponding mates. The asymmetry created by his carelessness forced one side of his collar up to his right earlobe and made him look off balance. He was obviously intoxicated, and he smelled of alcohol mixed with body odor. He had greasy dark hair that he tucked behind each of his filthy ears. It was clear he had not slept the night before or bathed anytime recently, and he spoke in a loud voice as drunks often do.

The group members looked at the milkmaid and at each other, uncertain what they should do. The milkmaid attempted to provide some sense of calm to the awkward situation by speaking with patience to the noisome and obnoxious interloper. "Felix, Felix, we welcome you as we welcome all, but we prefer that you take a seat and lower your voice . . ."

The drunk, apparently named Felix, was having none of it as he circled in large steps around the gathering, screaming and pointing in a great demonstration of his Dutch courage: "I know you and you and you and you. I know all your parents and all your relatives. I'm not impressed with your social status or your money or fancy cars or your Carnival organizations. I know what you've been up to. You bunch of cows!"

Glenn was not sure to whom or what he was referring, inasmuch as the mixed-race group was not exactly high society, and he wondered whether the milkmaid would be able to maintain order. The rest of the group also looked perplexed, and some of the younger women even seemed frightened. The milkmaid rose from her seat and attempted to ease the tension by approaching Felix for a more intimate discussion.

"Felix. Maybe it's better if you came to another meeting when you are ready to be better served by the process. Our group members are here to—"

"I don't give a shit what's best! I don't give a shit what you people think. You all know these meetings are a complete waste of time."

The milkmaid put her hand on Felix's elbow and tried to escort him to the side of the church toward the door.

"Get your hands off me. I'm leaving. Fuck you, and fuck all of you!"

The milkmaid made a show of rolling her eyes and sighing in exasperation before returning to her seat in the circle of addicts. "Sorry for the interruption. I don't think Felix is quite ready for a meeting at this stage of his illness. As we proceed, we are reminded from his behavior the damage that substance abuse can inflict. Derrell, you were saying?"

The meeting continued with unguarded confessions and anecdotes of successful resistance to temptation, interpersonal difficulties, and family crises. Last to speak was a younger woman, approximately twenty-five years of age, who had shoulder-length blonde hair and blue eyes swollen from recent crying. She wore stylishly tattered blue jeans and a tight cotton T-shirt that read "WHATEVER" across her chest. One leg was crossed underneath the other on the chair seat, and she slumped as she looked down at the tiled floor and spoke: "My name's Caroline, and I'm an alcoholic."

The milkmaid took command: "You look distressed, Caroline. Why don't you relate your feelings at this moment?"

"Well, I don't know where to start, I've just returned from North Carolina. From treatment. At a rehab center at some college my parents made me go to."

"That's great, Caroline. Was the treatment successful? Why don't you tell us about your experience?" The milkmaid had a soothing way of speaking.

"The doctor at the treatment facility is an old friend of my parents. I met him when I was much younger. But I hadn't seen him for a while. He seemed nice at first. But then he became angry with me."

"Why did he become angry with you? Can you share that with us, Caroline?"

"I got sick of being there. It's at some North Carolina college campus in the middle of nowhere. Most of the people were older. After dinner, there was nothing to do. I had a one-on-one session with him in the morning and a group session in the afternoon, but at night we were left to ourselves. In the stupid dorm room. There was no TV. And no computer. All I had was my phone. After a while, I was up there for a month, I just got bored. I couldn't call any of my friends because I didn't want them to know where I was. I couldn't call my parents because they would rat me out for using my phone during treatment. I just didn't know what to do."

"Was phone use prohibited by the program?"

"Yes, and I couldn't use my phone, even if I wanted to, because I didn't have a charger for when the phone went dead, so I didn't want to use up the battery. Anyway, the only time I really used it was to call my source for a hookup."

"A hookup? Were you arranging for outside deliveries?"

"Yes. I was able to get stuff from the outside, and I got caught. The doctor found out about it and called me in for a disciplinary intervention. That's what he called it."

"And what was said at the disciplinary intervention?" the milkmaid was pressing hard, perhaps too hard, as Glenn saw it.

"Oh, the usual. He threatened to tell my parents. But I asked him not to." The young woman's voice was getting softer and softer as she got deeper into her depressing story. "What I mean is, I was weak." Caroline tucked the hair that had fallen on one side of her face behind her ear. Glenn could see that she had a tiny gold-bead earring and a small tattoo of a pink-and-blue bear cub on the upper part of her slender neck.

"Sometimes, even oftentimes, we feel at a disadvantage when speaking to a program director. Especially when we are under the influence, as you obviously were." The milkmaid was trying to instill in Caroline some degree of stability so that she could continue her story.

"Anyway, he promised not to tell my parents, but he told me to return the next day for another disciplinary follow-up. Which I did." At this point, Caroline began to weep openly. "That's when we had sex. Well, not really sex. I didn't really know what I was doing. I was so coked up. He was having sex. But I wasn't having sex. I was just trying to get through my month in North Carolina and get the hell out of there. But we had sex a couple more times after that, and I finally left the program."

Glenn could hardly believe what he'd just heard. A doctor forced his patient to have sex with him? What kind of pervert would do that? The poor girl . . .

He realized that his own recovery involved far fewer pitfalls than many of the other group members were going through and certainly nothing approaching the difficulties faced by poor Caroline. It also occurred to him that Caroline had one hell of a lawsuit against the doctor, and against the treatment facility, for sure. And its insurance company. And the state of North Carolina, for that matter. His mind raced to think of ways in which he could make money off of Caroline's misfortune. He had no reason to feel guilty or greedy for this reflection, which, for the moment, was all it was.

The milkmaid pressed on: "Were you discharged by the doctor? I mean, were you released from the program with any kind of certification? I gather the substance-abuse aspect of the treatment was less than successful."

Caroline continued: "When I got home, I realized I was pregnant. He's a seventy-year-old man. I was pregnant by a seventy-year-old man. And he's a friend of my family. What was I supposed to do? I had to get an abortion."

"Well, I think what's important is that you are physically healthy. I know the emotional trauma was difficult, and the distress might continue for a longer period, but for now, you are physically safe. I mean, your overall health has not been compromised. But the doctor crossed a lot of boundaries. And you should remember that your boundaries are just that: your boundaries. You have no reason to feel at fault when someone violates those boundaries."

"I had an abortion. I don't know whether that means my boundaries have been violated or not. I already told my parents. They're terrified I might mention this to someone. They don't want any of it to get out. I hate that guy."

Glenn wondered whether Caroline was referring to her doctor or to her father. It didn't matter because he was preoccupied with the potential lawsuit and how he could wrangle a finder's fee out of Caroline's tragedy. If he could somehow present her and her potential lawsuit to a suitable attorney, he figured there was a referral fee for the taking. In his experience with such lawsuits, this was a $2 million case. Minimum.

"I think Caroline deserves the empathy and collective strength of the group. She showed a lot of courage and continues to show a lot of courage, dealing with her situation. Keep her in your thoughts and prayers. We'll be meeting next in one week for those of you committed to the program. So, let's end this meeting with a brief affirmation of gratitude for any strength we've gained from her honesty."

Glenn was surprised that the meeting was being terminated after such a short period, but he guessed that the interruption by Felix and the shock of Caroline's disclosures had led the milkmaid to think that things were spinning dangerously out of her control. He was, nevertheless, relieved that he could take credit for another attended meeting without ever having to give out the details of his own recovery. Glenn could turn his attention to Caroline's possible lawsuit and his plans to profit, personally, from it.

At the completion of the meeting, the members began to disperse, except for Caroline, who remained seated in her chair. Glenn remained seated as well, hoping for an opportunity to speak privately with her and perhaps propose a further course of action. It would be a delicate operation, but he could always say he was looking out for her best interests, regardless of how it might benefit him personally.

The milkmaid approached Caroline and put her arm around her. They spoke inaudibly as Glenn waited patiently in the now vacant circle of recovery. The milkmaid offered to escort Caroline to her car, at which point Glenn saw an opportunity to lend his assistance and secure a moment alone with her. It worked perfectly because the milkmaid peeled off and entrusted Caroline to Glenn, who thereupon assumed the responsibility for her safety.

As they reached Caroline's car, a late-model blue Japanese compact, Glenn explained that he understood her unfortunate experience and that he knew lawyers who could advise her on the advantages of a well-pleaded lawsuit.

"You don't have to decide right now," he said. "Just think about it. There may have even been a criminal violation here, or in North Carolina, rather, and people should be held accountable. Here is my card. I can help you if you think it's the right thing to do. No need to mention this to anyone else, and I certainly feel no need to mention it to anyone else myself. It's just a question of right and wrong. You're a victim here. You should know your rights, whether you choose to do anything or not. I don't have anything to gain here. I just don't want to see a fellow member of The Program left without an ally. Just think about it and call me if there's anything I can do."

"Okay. Thanks for that. I'm not sure where I stand with my parents or if I should even care what they think. I'm kinda mixed up right now. I'm gonna have to let you know."

"That's perfectly fine! It's a decision only you can make. Just remember I'm here to help."

"I know. I'll call you." Caroline dropped her head and ran the fingers of her right hand across the side of her face, collected a wisp of soft, blonde hair, and secured it behind her right ear so that it wouldn't adhere to her glossed lips. "Just so you know, the drunk guy Felix who just barged into the meeting?" She ended the sentence with a rising inflection to indicate it was a question, one which sought confirmation from Glenn that he remembered Felix, the obnoxious man who had been so disruptive only minutes before.

"Hard not to notice a guy like that," said Glenn. "He came flapping in like a waterfowl. He was claiming to know something about everybody at the meeting. Like he was ready to blackmail somebody."

"Well, he knows something about me. He's my dealer. I haven't bought from him lately, but he is my source in town."

Glenn tried not to look surprised. He wanted to maintain his reassuring demeanor. "Oh, well, we all have one of those who manages to show up at the worst possible time."

"I just thought you should know. I hate the guy, anyway."

With further words of reassurance, he put Caroline in her car and sent her off to consider her options. He gave no further thought to the fact that some guy named Felix was her coke dealer.

As he walked to his parked BMW X6 SUV, Glenn's fantasy about the possible lawsuit expanded. This wasn't a $2 million case, it was a $7 million case. A 10 percent referral fee could amount to as much as $700,000. It would be the easiest lawsuit ever filed.

Maybe an actual civil filing would not even be necessary. A demand letter from a lawyer on legal stationery might be enough for the college or the treatment center or both to write a check just to avoid the publicity. If, indeed, Caroline's doctor had provided treatment under the auspices of the college, the liability would certainly extend to the school and its institutional affiliates. The statutory medical malpractice limits that might be applicable in the state of North Carolina would have no bearing on monetary recovery. And the potential range of defendants was not limited to the college or its employee physician. Who knows what other entities could be put in the crosshairs?

Glenn had stumbled upon a bonanza. All he needed was the right lawyer to write the letter. Burton Clayton was not a lawyer, but he would know exactly the right man for the job. Burton Clayton was a master of discretion and creative blackmail.

Glenn Hornacek had a phone call to make as soon as he got in his car.

———

Back at his office downtown, Lecky Calloway called his wife at the family home on Duffossat Street to carefully measure her mood and to receive instructions on how *he* should act in the face of the Caroline Situation.

She was, for the moment, unaccounted for, running around with explosive information that could threaten family stability or, what was worse, a personal situation that could expose the family to extreme embarrassment. Lecky had, by that stage of their marriage, accepted subordination to his wife's authority and was forever awaiting orders from her in all matters.

Even though Lecky earned a respectable salary at his law firm, Hildy controlled the real money, their social rank, and their overall status in the community. He had always been slightly disgusted with himself for sacrificing his independence for the benefits the marriage brought, but this most recent exigency had awakened something dormant in him. This incipient courage did not, as yet, embolden him to challenge his wife's authority on such things as parental supervision, let alone a criminal prosecution related to their daughter's drug treatment and possible rape.

Nevertheless, his concern for Caroline suggested to him that steps should be taken strictly in her interest regardless of what his wife might think. It was almost a feeling of masculinity in its primordial sense. That is to say, it was a fatherly reflex to protect Caroline in any manner he saw fit and at any cost.

He felt more confident broaching the issue over the telephone: "We're gonna have to report this. If not to the authorities, then at least to the college. I suspect it's not the first time Dr. Caldwell has engaged in this sort of behavior. It seems like we have an obligation to other patients. He could be preying on other young girls at this very moment."

"Dr. Caldwell is a friend of mine. And a friend of my father's. Given her behavior these last few years, I don't think we can be entirely sure that he's the only one at fault."

"For God's sake, Hildy, she was a patient in his care. She trusted him. We entrusted her to him. It's possible we have a legal obligation to report this."

"That is out of the question. At least until we have all the information. She may have gotten pregnant from someone else, another patient at the facility. She might not even have gotten pregnant at all. She's been lying about everything else, why wouldn't she lie about this?"

"Let's not accuse her of anything right off the bat. Let's find out how the group meeting went. Try not to jump down her throat, Hildy."

"Hold the phone. She just pulled into the driveway." Lecky could hear his wife step to a window in the kitchen overlooking the driveway. Caroline would be getting out of her car and climbing the back stairway.

Lecky heard his wife begin the interrogation over the open phone: "You're back! How was group? Were you able to get any direction or at least some understanding from them? I beg your pardon? Sue Dr. Caldwell? Where did you get an idea like that?"

Lecky could only hear one side of the conversation. But he was dumbstruck. He guessed that Caroline was barging past her mother through the kitchen and up the stairs to her bedroom.

"She's gone upstairs," Hildy said, back on the phone. "She's talking about a lawsuit. She's been talking to someone. Get home immediately."

The direct order seemed harsh, even for Hildy. She was usually careful to avoid open, especially verbal, displays of her authority, so the blunt command to *get home immediately* was jarring. It brought out something in Lecky that he didn't recognize. For a split second, he considered a refusal that matched her tone in bluntness, but the blood pressure required for the sedition subsided as quickly as it had risen. He placed the handset back in its preformed plastic console and left the office for the drive home as instructed.

7

When Lecky pulled into the driveway of his house on Duffossat Street, he was in a dejected state. He spent a brief moment behind the wheel of his car and prepared for the rough confrontation ahead of him. He had been *sent for*. And that meant his wife was displeased, possibly with him, but more probably with the immediate crisis swelling up around his daughter Caroline's abortion.

Anytime Hildegard Thompson Calloway summoned him home from work, there was unpleasantness ahead. He felt like Ehrlichman getting summoned by Nixon to the Oval Office after the Watergate break-in hit the papers: he knew she was really going to take the bark off. There were going to be questions, most of which he could not answer, followed by rage and then unmistakable suggestions that he, Lecky, was somehow to blame. In short, he was going to have to *eat shit*.

After spending a few moments alone in the driveway preparing for the remonstrance, he gathered himself together with every intention of discussing the Caroline Situation on even terms. In other words, he resolved to stand a little taller than usual and stiffen against the expected indictment. But each step he took up the back stairs seemed to chip away at the confidence he had cobbled together in the car.

The very instant he stepped over the kitchen threshold, she started into him. "I'm beginning to think that these AA group meetings are becoming counterproductive," Hildy said. "I think we should pull her out of there."

He reached down deep and began the defense he had mapped out with such conviction. He tried to assert himself: "What? And send her back to Dr. Caldwell in North Carolina? Ship her off to another exclusive specialist in California or some other remote location? Don't you think she'd be better off at home, where we can keep a closer eye?"

Hildy's first reaction to his mild resistance was to withdraw from the kitchen and head for the living room. It was a silent message that Lecky was to follow her there for further instructions. Attendance at a Living Room Summit was not optional. It was a subpoena to appear for the reading of an *Edictum Praetoris Familia*. Nevertheless, today he was more phlegmatic than he had been on previous occasions, perhaps because his alternative suggestions were perfectly defensible, if not preferable. He followed her into the living room and took a seat on one end of the Bridgewater sofa with the brown bouillon fringe.

She opened the proceedings from her seat on one of the Hogarth chairs closest to him: "I spoke to my father, and he thinks it's probably best to put her in the care of a professional. At least for a couple of months. Just for now. While the situation is acute."

"The situation? I agree that Caroline's condition is acute, but I would like to know what situation he's referring to." He tried to soften the tone of his protest. "What I mean is that Caroline should be our main concern here and that we are in the best position to help her. Especially if she has a lawsuit on her mind. She's an adult. Technically, she doesn't need our consent. If that is what we want to prevent, we might want to keep her as close to us as possible. I think we can say that treatment facilities in far away places have not gone well."

"We're not going to keep her here. There are too many distractions both for her and for us at this time of year. It's out of the question."

Lecky took advantage of a short pause: "Before we make a decision, we might at least take her feelings into consideration. Don't you think?"

Whereupon, she jumped down his throat: "I *am* taking her feelings into consideration! I think she should take *our* feelings into consideration! I think *you* should take *my* feelings into consideration!"

"Please, Hildy. Let's not be too emotional," he responded in a voice of diplomacy designed to lower the temperature. It also gave him the feeling that he was taking some control, like he was the voice of reason: "We'll get through this."

"Shit!" she said out loud, letting off some steam and trying to bring the discussion to an end. Lecky sensed that she was prepared to act unilaterally but that she was willing to wait. For his part, he was willing to give her some time to digest his uncharacteristic assertiveness, minimal though it may have been.

Lecky understood perfectly well his wife's *real* concern: Caroline's younger sister, Ainsley, was poised to become Queen of the upcoming Hesperus Ball. His father-in-law, Elliott Thompson, a ranking member of The Lancaster Club and former King of Hesperus himself, had been unsuccessful in his campaign to install Caroline as Queen several years before. At that time, Cecil Richardson, by virtue of his superior wealth and family history as Hesperus royalty, superseded Elliott Thompson's claim to the throne for his granddaughter Caroline. This meant that he and Hildy would have to wait until Ainsley came of age before the Thompson/Calloway family could receive the honor of having a daughter crowned Queen.

But a family embarrassment or some other social distraction—such as drug addiction, sexual molestation by a treating physician, an unwarranted pregnancy, and emergency abortion—could very well jeopardize a Carnival entitlement that had been so carefully and patiently earned. Only three years earlier, Lecky would have understood this priority. He may well have participated in such a cover-up himself for the sake of coveted social recognition.

But more recently, it seemed, he felt less willing to do so. Something in his personality or wherewithal was beginning to change. His love for his daughter Caroline, combined with the fact that he had grown weary of his wife's officiousness, had steeled him to challenge her authority.

Although this particular moment was, perhaps, not the time to announce his departure from the *belle estate*, he could sense that the courage to do so was growing inside of him.

And so, he spoke: "I know you think that this is Ainsley's year. And I know it's understood that she will be named. But there might be more important things to consider." He wanted to say "more important things in life," but that seemed too serious or perhaps too much of a criticism of his wife's superficial social priorities. Lecky was trying to introduce the idea that securing the throne for Ainsley should not be their most pressing concern—without a doubt, a prickly concept for Hildy to understand.

"What good would it do to file suit, to expose Caroline to the ridicule?" Hildy responded. "What good would it do to reopen the wound? All it would do is punish Ainsley! And it's *her* year!" Hildy paused and then stood assertively from her seat with the alphabet-block heels of her Chanel pumps smashed into the deep pile of the Axminster carpet. "It's *my* year!"

Lecky took some satisfaction in knowing that he had lured his wife into blurting out the real reason behind her rejection of any plan that had the smallest chance of family humiliation. It was enough for him to end the conversation.

"I think you should think about Caroline. We can discuss this more when we've had time to reflect. But I've got to get back to the office. I had hoped this conversation would have included Caroline when you asked me to rush home in the middle of my workday." He chose the word "asked" as if he had a choice. Hildy must have sensed the polite recharacterization of her demand because she offered no response.

Lecky stood from his chair without looking directly at his wife and watched the tops of his tasseled shell-cordovan loafers cover the distance from the living room carpet to the marble floor of the kitchen, where the back door led to the driveway carport. Hildy remained silent throughout his ceremonious departure, even though there was ample time for her to throw out a final cutting remark. That's the way he wanted it.

The ten-minute drive to work would give Lecky time to reflect on his daring challenge to his wife's authority. It was a victorious feeling that gave him room to daydream a little about his own homosexual liberation. He knew he was gay, and he had, at last, come to expect that he would eventually give in to his natural, irrepressible desires. The cruel restrictions of puritanical American convention had loosened considerably since the time that his children were babies. Though his twilight visits to French Quarter gay bars had proved disappointing, he had not abandoned his interest in the possibility of gay life. Maybe, just maybe, the time had come for a discreet encounter if the conditions were right. This most recent act of marital defiance had given him a taste of his own reclaimed sovereignty—a shrug of independence that could, at last, make self-fulfillment a reality. His house on Duffossat Street got smaller in his rearview mirror as he drove away.

He had, in other private moments, browsed the wide variety of Internet offerings for gay men, everything from dating websites that were not necessarily gay-specific (Craigslist, Tinder, and OKCupid) to the more exclusively gay hookup sites (Adam4Adam, Grindr, and Whisper), and even the raunchier gonzo à la carte fetish emporia (SquirmAndDrang, HustleAndMuscle, and Warmwipe). They all seemed tawdry and desperate, completely lacking in romantic wholesomeness. On the other hand, he was not looking to come completely out of the closet, forswear his family life, and land a new lifetime partner. At least, not yet. What he longed for was male intimacy with someone he could care about—a certain tenderness that would include an erotic component. Neither the bar scene nor the semi-anonymous web marketplace offered what he considered to be ideal.

What he wanted was to be known as "New Orleans Straight," that peculiar strain of amphibious creature he knew, or at least suspected, dwelt in the highest social circles of the city. He was convinced that such creatures were members of The Lancaster Club or even his own law firm—married men with children in exclusive private schools, men who kept up appearances but whose effete mannerisms would become more pronounced after a couple of drinks. It was a way of life that would allow for a hidden gay-male relationship undisruptive to a customary, even aristocratic, heterosexual family and business existence. It would be, he imagined, a kind of gay way station—an interim quiescent stage of transformation free from any dramatic disclosure that he was a twink, a bottom, or a camp-pink (on the one hand), or a butch, masc, or gladiator fag (on the other). People could gradually become accustomed to the idea that he was gay so as to avoid the shock of a lurid exposé. It seemed like a prudent way to spare his daughters the scandal of secret extramural behavior that he had reason to believe would be considered shameful by the public at large. If his sexual preferences could in some way be introduced gradually, then he might be able to preempt the snickering enjoyed by society spectators who traded in the misfortune of their member-competitors.

There were, of course, other gay men who had employed this stratagem successfully. In fact, many had become smart-set mascots: the ones who squired rich divorceés to black-tie galas, composed breathless guest-column dispatches from the cotillion circuit, served on charity fundraising committees for unassailable nonprofit causes, attended top-agent residential sales awards banquets, and generally participated in high-society frivolity without ever having to face questions about the actual mechanics of male homosexual coitus. Lecky envied those who had carved out and then occupied that special, spot-duty niche. But he had some questions of his own.

Though he sometimes fantasized about anal sex, he dreaded the thought of India-rubber bulb douching, high-fiber dieting, and disinfectant enemas that would be required, especially if he were to be on his knees *in flagrante euryproktos*. It wasn't that these preparations were necessarily objectionable—in fact, they were simply hygienic and sensible. It's just that they reminded him that a secret gay relationship could be messy in more ways than one. And the last thing he wanted was to find himself chasing down rent boys on the street with cries of "Give me back my photographs!" He would have to find another way.

By the time he arrived downtown, it was past noon, and his law office was on its lunch hour. He decided to use the time to go shopping for some new clothes. He felt entitled to the luxury now that he had set in motion the overthrow of a tyrannical regime back at home. Buying a new suit or slightly dressy ensemble was an indulgence he could undertake without his wife's approval inasmuch as it required only a minimal cash outlay drawn from his own personal salary as a lawyer. Major cash expenditures, such as new cars, school tuitions, real estate purchases, and luxury vacations, were his wife's exclusive province. The real money was hers, or, rather, hers at the pleasure of her father, and she alone made those kinds of decisions. He accepted that arrangement in return for the social cachet and material comforts that the marriage brought. At least, that is, until recently. He was beginning to draw away from the security of a closeted gay existence. The recent suffering experienced by his daughter Caroline and the callousness of his wife's reaction to it, insistent as she was to preserve the family's claim to a Carnival throne, had caused him to reconsider his submission to social niceties. Buying himself a new suit would, at least in some small way, serve as an expression of independence.

Nowak's At Canal, the upscale, national department store near his downtown office, had recently acquired the trade name and assets of a luxury men's boutique known as "Cinch." The boutique had not survived the market shift to internet sales. But it had found new life as an affiliate of Nowak's, if in name only. The internal boutique installed in the men's department at Nowak's was open for business as Cinch at Nowak's. Only the most prestigious and bespoke labels were offered there, so Lecky Calloway was excited to see the latest collections. A new suit, or maybe even a new pair of trousers and complementary sport coat, would brighten his mood and boost his resolve. He intended, after all, to insist that Caroline remain close to home, contrary to—indeed, in spite of—his wife's expressed desires. He needed some battle armor to face the challenge.

As he made his way up the escalators to the third floor of Nowak's, where the men's department was located, he searched for and soon found the boutique he came to see. The sign on the lintel read "Cinch" above the open shop front that had been built out and painted a light purple, or amethyst, to distinguish the space from the rest of the retail expanse on that floor. It reminded him of the mint-colored Prada enclaves in Saks Fifth Avenue.

Almost immediately, he was met by an attractive and energetic sales-man in a tight Air Force–blue suit with very high armholes, a pinpoint white cotton shirt with a fashion spread collar, and a tangerine-orange silk tie. He was a ruddy White man in his mid-thirties, about six feet tall, with dark brown hair cropped closely on the back and sides but tufted and wavy on top. He wore hand-cobbled black leather shoes with a monk strap and no socks. A heavy gold watch adorned his left wrist, and his black belt had a matching gold buckle. He was muscular without being bulky. He was beautiful.

"May I help you find something, sir?" the slender salesman asked.

"Why, yes. I guess I'm looking for a new suit. Or a coat-and-tie combo, anyway. I guess I would need pants with that, too." Lecky tried to laugh without giggling, but it came out as a titter. The handsome salesman did not giggle back, but he did smile. That was something, if not reassuring, but it did not make Lecky any less nervous.

"Well, we have some exciting new things from our designer exclusives I could show you. I'm guessing you're about a 42 regular?"

"Yes. Right on the first try. The pants never fit right when I buy a 42 suit, but the jacket always fits me perfectly."

"Oh, no worries, we can tailor the pants. You're right, though, getting the jacket to fit off the rack is the most important thing. Any particular color you had in mind?"

Lecky wanted to seem relaxed. He avoided direct eye contact. He tried to concentrate on the racks of suits, their cut, their color, and their fabric, but his mind was racing too fast to appreciate the clothing. He pretended that he was accustomed to designer labels and fine tailoring by dismissively fingering one suit after another. An uninterested shopper, or so he thought, gave the impression that he was familiar with luxury merchandise. The pantomime continued as the salesman followed behind from an attentive, but not intrusive, distance.

"My name's Felix, by the way. How did you hear about our new boutique?"

"Nice to meet you. My name's Alexander Calloway. I heard about the store from a friend. I've actually been to Cinch in New York, before it got picked up by Nowak's, of course." It was a clumsy name-drop, but he wanted to convey some sense of worldliness. And wealth. He wanted to separate himself from the ordinary sightseers who stumbled into the boutique while their wives got pampered at the prescriptive counters two floors below.

"Oh! I started with Cinch at the New York store. They asked me to move down here to open this boutique. I've only been in New Orleans for about a year. But I've enjoyed it. I live in the Quarter, so I can walk to work. Just like New York, but smaller and cheaper."

The conversation continued without much real substance, except that he learned the salesman's full name was Felix Peterbilt, and he was from Cincinnati or the Chicago suburbs—it didn't much matter to Lecky. But it was instantly clear that Felix was gay.

From a very young age, Lecky could determine instantly whether a man, or even less readily a woman, was homosexual and whether that man could sense that he himself was a lavender comrade. Up until recently, Lecky would attempt to camouflage his predilection, if only to make clear that circumstances did not permit an open acknowledgement. Sometimes, after a few drinks, Lecky could sense that his voice would acquire a higher pitch and that his fricative consonants would become sharper in their sibilance. The more he drank, the more he sounded like Truman Capote or even Oscar Wilde (if contemporary descriptions of his conversational tone were accurate). But he had not had any drinks by that time of day, and he was closely monitoring his speech patterns. This circumspection, however transparent it might have been, was always honored by other gay men who well knew the dangers of overt effeminacy and who also understood the obligations of gay politesse.

But, on this occasion, Lecky's clay was cracking, and his duplicity was giving way to opportunity. This, he had almost forgotten, was what romance felt like. So, he allowed himself to prance slightly as he began, perhaps more delicately, to riffle through the elegant fabrics on display.

Soon enough, he had selected a suit very similar to the one Felix was wearing and repaired to the dressing room to try it on. Felix followed him into the chamber of six individual fitting rooms, each with a louvered wooden door that did not occupy the entire space of the doorframe—like the doors on airport bathroom stalls. He took off his trousers and was pleased, and a little relieved, to notice that the boxer briefs he had chosen that morning were pastel colored and clean. They also had a snug fit around his crotch, and that made him feel gathered up.

When his new suit pants were secure with the white shirt he was wearing tucked snugly inside the waistband, he opened the dressing room door to ask Felix his opinion. He made a point to stand toward the back of the cubicle so that the space invited another occupant. Felix slipped into the dressing room and closed the semi-door behind him. He placed his hand on the placqueted fly of the new trousers and stared into Lecky's reddening face. Lecky allowed himself to drift close enough to kiss Felix, but the salesman demurred, averted his eyes downward, and sat on the thinly padded bench that stretched on the side wall of the dressing room, perpendicular to the courtesy mirror.

Lecky felt he may have violated some rule of casual dressing-room encounters by offering mouth-to-mouth contact. He was embarrassed about his clumsiness but was relieved when Felix began to unclasp the waistband of Lecky's trousers. Felix slowly unzipped Lecky's fly and began fellating him. It all happened in a dizzying instant, and not a word was spoken.

At first, Lecky cursed himself for giving off the signal that he was available for, or even desirous of, homosexual congress. But it was welcome, nonetheless. As the transaction was underway, Lecky noticed a small shaved area on the top of Felix's head, across which stretched a small white butterfly bandage. It appeared Felix had been struck on the head and had sustained a minor injury that did not require stitches.

The wound might have concerned Lecky had not the buccal onanism brought such pleasure. Standing in the dressing room on the receiving end of oral copulation was, in some sense, hierarchal. He imagined himself as King James I, administering House-of-Stuart prerogatives to the Duc de Boucquingham and other random courtiers. *Rex fuit Hildy, Nunc est regina Lecky.* It validated his tentative bid for authority over his wife, or at least over himself. He was becoming, or so he hoped, his own man.

The matter was over quickly, and Lecky swooned in labefaction. It was a flash-bang episode, but Lecky presumed that incidental, anonymous sex coupling was the way things were done in the gay community, or perhaps the gay underworld. He supposed he would have to get used to the procedure if this lifestyle was to become his own.

The two lovers gathered themselves after some perfunctory but happy remarks. Lecky removed his new suit and draped it over Felix's arm. They left the changing area together and walked to the checkout counter without ever having pin-fitted the suit for tailoring.

Lecky presented his credit card, and Felix zipped the garment into a travel bag. The two men smiled at one another as if to confirm that the sex act had been a minor, delightful, and unregretted bit of playtime fun and that they might meet again. At any rate, Lecky certainly felt that way. But he wondered whether Felix was only securing the sale. For the time being, the experience was enough for Lecky.

Back at his desk that afternoon in his office overlooking the French Quarter, Lecky Calloway—the distracted lawyer, frustrated husband, and tingling lover—began his social media research for information about Felix Peterbilt, the salesman/manager/retail coordinator of Cinch at Nowak's. He was not able to find much information about his background, only some digital photographs of Felix's social life away from work. Pictures of birthday gatherings and vacation candor made it clear that Felix was out of the closet. Lecky was anxious to determine if Felix was in an exclusive relationship. There were men that appeared more than once in the informal photographs, but conclusive evidence was not apparent. No matter what, there was enough information available on the Internet to allow Lecky to contact him in the future if he wanted or if there was a suitable pretext to do so.

The web surfing was interrupted by the bleeping of his office phone. The receptionist announced over the internal line that there was a phone call from Dale Dutton, the account manager at The Wellspring Group, a gigantic insurance company that wrote automobile, homeowner, and business liability policies all over the Southeastern United States. Wellspring was one of the firm's steadiest and most lucrative clients, the bread and butter of the firm's litigation section. The account was the primary asset of managing partner Stuart Whitcomb's portfolio, and Lecky was one of the five or six lawyers who handled lawsuits filed against Wellspring and its policyholders.

"Alex. Dale Dutton here." They had never actually met in person, so Dale did not call him by his nickname. "How are you, sir? We've got a new claim against one of the old Voelker policies issued to a business called 'Phuoc Tho Duong Enterprises d/b/a Phuoc Tho Duong Grocery.' Ever heard of it?"

"No, not off the top of my head. Where is it located?"

"Somewhere in New Orleans East, according to Google Maps. It looks like it's probably some kind of convenience store. Some guy drove into an outdoor sign, and it fell on top of his car. It caused minor damage to his roof, but a week later, when I talked to him, he started complaining of a sore neck and back. Typical car crash, soft tissue injury claim. But it's a one-car accident with a building, or part of the building. It's a big metal sign in the parking lot that he says was not very stable. Anyway, it fell on his car, and he hurt his neck. Or so he says. He also says he sustained a gash on top of his head. Like from when the sign fell on the roof of the car."

"Are we talking policy limits here? I presume it's bigger than a little ten-twenty automobile policy."

"No, it's a commercial general liability policy with three-hundred-thousand-dollar limits. Gonna require more attention than a stupid traffic accident. I've already asked him to sign releases so I can get medical records, but that's still in the works. No suit has been filed yet, but I need you to go out there and take pictures of the premises and find any witnesses. They may have security cameras with some good footage. Can you go check it out?"

"I surely can. Where is it exactly, or what's the address?"

"A street called Chef Menteur Highway. The address is fourteen-two-oh-one. It looks like some kind of industrial area. Doesn't look like a very nice neighborhood. A lot of Vietnamese immigrants living there, I guess."

"No, I know the area somewhat. I don't really have any reason to go out there much, but I know about the Vietnamese community in the East. Hardworking people who emigrated here after the war. A lot of them are Catholics." It was a gratuitous statement, the remark about the Catholics, but it was an Episcopalian reflex he had learned from his wife.

Dale didn't seem to notice or find it relevant.

"Well, whatever it is," Dale said, "it sounds like they might have security cameras. Just go out there and survey the property. Maybe the manager saw the accident. I told them not to fix the sign, so it still should be down. Take some pictures. Meantime, I'll round up the medical reports and tell the injured fella that a resolution is in the works. I'd like to get this resolved before suit is filed."

"No, I understand. I'll head out there first thing tomorrow morning and start the process. I'll call you when I get back and email you the photographs. How does that sound?"

"That sounds just about right. He didn't give me the impression he was hurt too badly or that he was disabled. But, you know how these things go. As time goes on, the injuries get worse and worse. And if they end up talking to a lawyer, then surgery is right around the corner."

"I know the routine," said Lecky, chumming around with his insurance adjuster like a couple of refinery workers on their lunch break. "What's this guy's name, anyway?"

"White male, thirty-nine years old. Works in retail. His name is . . .

uh . . . Peterbilt. Felix Peterbilt. I'll send you his information, but don't call him yet."

Lecky felt the blood rush up his neck and across his scalp. There was no way this could be anybody other than the salesman from the dressing room. He quickly rounded off his conversation with Dale Dutton and shut the door to his office.

8

Agent Margot Hoang was always stiffened with purpose when she arrived at the FBI field offices on any particular workday, especially whenever a new investigation had been assigned to her. But on this morning, she felt an added sense of diligence that could not be attributed to the freshness of a new case. There was a layer of private optimism on top of, or mixed in with, the happy dedication she brought to her official workload.

The bureau had poured a significant part of its academic budget to train cadets like her against the dangers of after-hours seduction. Compromised agents under task were a threat to the entire organization. She had a sworn duty to comply with the code of ethics contained in the FBI regulations and was aware that violations were grounds for reprimand and even dismissal. Margot would never put at risk the career she had worked so hard to construct. And yet, she allowed herself the buoyancy that a new romance always brings. It couldn't hurt, she reasoned, to fortify her professional attitude with an injection of private happiness. Besides, she couldn't help it. She was in love.

Francis Ernst, the New Orleans police officer she had been dating for the past several weeks, was not constantly in her thoughts, but she could always summon the image of him in his dress blues when she wanted to and when it would not interfere with work. Impressions of their ongoing courtship were always with her, but never in a way that compromised her law enforcement duties. On the contrary, those feelings, even when they only lingered in the background, gave her a sense of confidence that made an already productive mindset even more so.

As she steered her car into the FBI field office parking lot off Leon C. Simon Drive, she made a final check of her uniform and service equipment: black Merrell Yokota mid-ankle trail shoes with lug soles, Prussian blue cargo pants and matching cotton polo shirt with an embroidered FBI insignia, black tactical wristwatch (men's version), black gear-duty rig belt with its modular equipment pouches, supple leather holster and a loaded 9mm Glock 19 service pistol. Although FBI regulations did not require her to wear anything more than the undefined "business casual" attire while conducting work at the office, she preferred to wear clothes and carry equipment that made her look more like a federal marshal than an FBI special agent.

It was permissible for her to do so, and she was unburdened from the need to plan fashionable civilian outfits every single day of her office career—not to mention the dry-cleaning bills and the impracticality of heels. Other agents may have snickered at her habit of showing up day after day in combat gear, but they seemed to accept it as a personal preference that did not detract from her ability to complete assignments—even though most of her work was conducted from an office chair in a low-paneled eight-by-six cubicle. She was, after all, dressed for tactical field operations, and there was no scoffing at that. In any case, it was easier to wear a uniform of some sort because she could wear it every day. Wearing a uniform was her way of protesting the bureau's relaxed business-casual dress code, which she considered undisciplined. Worst of all, she detested the fact that the only concession the bureau had made to the virtues of group discipline was the requirement that agents wear the official FBI windbreaker when conducting raids or making arrests. The windbreaker—made of 100 percent machine-washable nylon taffeta with snaps and elastic cuffs—did not, in her estimation, engender the necessary esprit de corps any effective law enforcement agency should cultivate. Furthermore, the windbreaker was not available in a size that fit her tiny frame.

Leon C. Simon Drive, where the FBI headquarters was located, had been named for a prominent New Orleans business executive in the years leading up to the First World War. Leon would have been surprised that a street named in his honor would one day become the address of a federal government building, let alone an FBI field office. It would have been even more surprising that a young, female, Vietnamese American agent clad in full combat armor would be parking her car in a lot marked "Official FBI Personnel Only." In fact, the sovereign nation known as "Vietnam" did not even exist when Leon C. Simon was alive. He may have heard about the French colony known as "Indochina," but he never could have conceived that a first-generation Catholic family from the jungles of Southeast Asia would produce an American girl now serving in the United States Department of Justice. On the other hand, Leon C. Simon was himself a descendant of highly motivated German Jewish immigrants fleeing nineteenth-century *Deutscher Bund* persecution, so he might have felt a kinship with Margot. After all, her family had escaped similar oppression at the hands of the Viet Cong when they were air lifted out of war-torn Saigon. Whether he could have imagined Margot's interethnic romance with a German American police officer named Francis Ernst was another question.

Margot was altogether unaware that, in the early 1900s, Leon C. Simon was a principal in the firm of Kohn, Weil & Simon—wholesale purveyors of hats, gloves, and trunks—who initiated the formation of the New Orleans Association of Commerce and served as its first president. At that time, the area where his eponymous boulevard now stretched was an uninhabitable swampland so remote from city boundaries that not even an ambitious businessman like Leon could have imagined such growth. Not only that, Leon could scarcely have imagined that Indochinese immigrants might one day be eligible for government employment. For that matter, Leon could never have imagined that nobody wore hats anymore. Then again, J. Edgar Hoover and his boyfriend wore hats all the time, so maybe Leon could take some credit for the fashion styles adopted by early G-men for so many years. Who's to say?

Despite her ignorance of this improbable history, Margot parked her car and entered FBI headquarters through its front glass doors. She pressed her radio-frequency identification card to the face of the security sensor, waved to the marine sentry, and boarded the elevator for the third floor. Upon arrival, she made her way to her assigned cubicle, stopping only to exchange greetings with other agents and office personnel. She always made it a point to be affable but not too personal, sincere but not too familiar, light but not too flippant.

At her desk area, she hung her utility belt on a stainless-steel hook bolted to the four-foot-high upholstered aluminum cubicle wall, sat in her castered plastic-and-metal chair, and rolled into the cavity beneath the horizontal desk surface that was anchored to the cubicle wall. A gentle nudge of her mouse brought her computer screen to life. She placed her wireless headset in a comfortable position and resumed the monitoring of wiretap recordings of the Phuoc Tho Duong Grocery audio surveillance.

Listening to taped recordings of phone conversations was a tedious assignment no agent ever really enjoyed, but because the target of the investigation was a Vietnamese business, she had been given the responsibility to translate outgoing and incoming calls. The Phuoc Tho Duong Grocery, one of several in the New Orleans East area, was an ordinary American-style convenience store nestled in a strip mall, except that it also catered to a Vietnamese clientele accustomed to Asian merchandise that might be considered exotic in other parts of the city.

Most of the tape recordings involved the quotidian operations of a retail concern, such as delivery schedules and inventory maintenance. There were also arguments over hiring a new security guard to replace the one who had taken a different job. The woman who ran the store wanted to hire a man she referred to as "the funny one," but apparently a woman, who sounded Black and claimed she lived in the neighborhood— was her name Arabella?—kept coming into the store and pestering the owner to hire her. The owner called her "the crazy one." But the owner called a lot of people crazy, including family members.

Margot was fascinated by the bickering among family members, which seemed more frequent than what she'd grown up with. These family arguments were always in Vietnamese, so the job required translation and transcription for the benefit of the English-speaking bureau chiefs— no matter how mundane. Margot accepted the drudgery in stride, all the while hoping she might eventually be given more stimulating assignments. Insofar as the job was fairly mindless and certainly routine, she could drift passively into daydreaming without any professional guilt.

In moments like this, she could relive her dates with Francis and assess the progress of their relationship. They seemed to be interested in the same things, and even if she may not have been interested before, she *became* interested in them. Her willingness to do so was a sign that she had feelings for him. That, she thought, was what lovers do. Funny how that happens: romantic attraction to a prospective mate automatically awakens an enthusiasm for his peculiar interests, whatever they may be. In this instance, Margot and Francis already had a lot in common.

On one recent occasion, they had spent an afternoon at a private firing range they had agreed upon—a neutral site free of other NOPD and FBI officers who might see them and start gossiping. It was an enjoyable bit of recreation for both, not only because their employers encouraged it but because it did not involve alcohol. It was a relief to her that Francis was not much of a drinker, for she considered drinking a character weakness, a danger to her professional goals, and a trespass against her Catholic upbringing. It was a habit she had never developed a taste for anyway.

The firing range, by operation of law, did not permit alcohol on the premises, and any indication of drunkenness on the part of its patrons was grounds for ejection. That was a great relief to Margot. Plus, the range was a perfect setting to demonstrate her less feminine aspect: that is to say, she could convey to him she was no *desmoiselle* handkerchiefing for a male possessor. It was a manner of flirting, to be sure. But she sensed, or hoped she sensed, that Francis would have respect for and be attracted to her natural independence. Her perfume was the smell of burnt gunpowder.

"I like to warm up with the target at about fifteen feet," said Margot as they took their places in adjacent shooting stalls that day. "It's like I do at the driving range. Start with a short iron and gradually move up to my driver." Margot didn't actually play golf, but the analogy spoke the language of sport, customarily the exclusive remit of men.

"Very definitely. I always start with my sidearm. It gives me a chance to warm up without sacrificing accuracy. Don't you think starting up close builds confidence?" he asked in a way that she considered a sign that Francis was not your typical boorish pinhead with a single-shoulder tribal tattoo and bleached teeth. The fact that he would actually solicit her opinion on matters of firearm protocol proved that he was not compensating for some other male inadequacy. On the contrary, Margot viewed the question as a gesture of professional equivalency, an overture from one career law enforcement officer to another.

She answered in kind: "No doubt. I can use all the confidence I can get." It was a self-effacing response, but one that only the self-confident naturally make. She hoped Francis would recognize that in her.

"I'm the same way. I suck in the early going, but I like to think I get better down the stretch." Francis was being retiring, modest, and, above all, generous. She liked that. It was a comfort to her that she was not alone— that they were comrades at arms. They were in sync. They were dancing.

As they took turns blasting at paper targets with life-sized silhouettes of human torsi and faceless heads, Margot noticed a young blonde woman wearing earmuffs and safety glasses in an adjacent shooting stall receiving lessons from a muscular instructor. She was practicing with a .25 caliber Muschi pistol in Penelope pink and a satin aluminum reciprocating slide. Margot recognized the weapon to be a personal-protection firearm manufactured and marketed for women otherwise intimidated by the masculinity of standard gunmetal. She resented that such promotional consumerism was necessary to appeal to women and wanted to distance herself from any female who would surrender her independence to a girlish stereotype—not because she objected to the self-reliance of American women and their entrance into the handgun marketplace, but because the introduction of the color pink would somehow make it more palatable. Or, even worse, stylish. Margot would never be seen carrying a .25 caliber Penelope-pink Muschi pistol.

She looked back at Francis to confirm that he shared her reaction to the silliness. He shook his head slightly and smiled to show that he had already enlisted in the confederacy. Margot knew then that they also shared the same sense of humor. Things were looking better and better.

After their session at the firing range, which included practice with service pistols as well as Remington 700 sniper rifles, they decided to relax at a coffee shop—not a diner or greasy spoon, but one of those designer coffee emporia so popular in contemporary urban America. This one was called Fulgencio Barista, a clever trade name for a local version of the coffee franchises that dominated the market, but one unaffiliated with any national chain. It was crammed into a revitalized 1970s strip mall just off Veteran's Memorial Boulevard in Jefferson Parish.

The interior décor made every effort to disguise its prefabricated, suburban location—furnished, as it was, with lots of blonde wood and curved aluminum tubing—very much like Mardi Gras Mambo!, the scene of their first date. The employees were also recruited from what were considered the more bohemian areas of New Orleans—mostly younger girls with leprosy-white complexions, pierced noses, and Celtic tattoos. They had hair dyed unnatural colors with their heads shaved on the back and sides. One barista had purple bangs that hung down across one side of her face, leaving only one eye capable of unobstructed sight. Her black T-shirt had a white silk-screened silhouette of Pierre-Joseph Proudhon above the caption "PROPERTY IS THEFT." The young male employees were similarly groomed but with heavy hobnailed bracelets and other items of motorcycle couture.

As they approached the counter to place their orders, Francis and Margot tilted their heads upward and searched the menu board for something to drink, something simple enough to pronounce so that they would appear accustomed to the selection and ordering process of a gourmet coffeehouse. Neither one wanted to seem disconcerted by the unusual costumes of the baristas. That would be rude. Margot would have liked to look at Francis and share a giggle, but she was too polite to conscript him for a face-off against the young revolutionaries. It didn't matter that the employees were less restrained about their contempt for people like Margot and Francis, people they viewed as indifferent American conformists who were complicit in the injustices being perpetrated, at that very moment, against the oppressed people of the world. Margot wondered whether it was obvious that she and Francis were cops. She secretly hoped it was. After retrieving their beverages from farther down the made-to-order assembly line, they took a seat at a table in the center of the dining room.

At the next table was a group of college students who were engaged, with great purpose, in some kind of academic project. Margot presumed they were from the University of New Orleans because its lakefront campus was just a few miles from the coffeehouse. These college students, like college students everywhere, often met in groups of eight or ten at nearby cafés to discuss class assignments or campus intrigues that the outside world was largely oblivious to. This particular group appeared to be an extracurricular hobby-club meeting of student-activists. An academic advisor, possibly a graduate assistant, presided over the lively but arch-serious meeting. He was an animated, assertive, and effeminate young man in his late twenties who wore his hair close-cropped, with a pronounced part on the right side of his head that had been set with a razor. He wore a tight-fitting white T-shirt that hugged the flab of his torso and his nippled breasts. His T-shirt had black lettering on the front that read "GENDER ASSIGNMENT IS HATE SPEECH." He wore a single diamond stud on his right earlobe.

The students at the table were all White girls between eighteen and twenty-two years of age. They were crackling at their laptops as their advisor imparted his guidance. Their outfits were casual exercise wear: gym shorts or Lycra yoga pants, some with disposable rubber sandals and others with space-age athletic shoes. Cotton tank tops and black sports bras were the fashion, and small beginner tattoos peeked out from the edges of their garments. One wore a pink T-shirt with the slogan "INTERNATIONALE" under an inkjet photo reproduction of Rosa Luxemburg. Another had a bumper sticker pasted to the back of her laptop computer that read "WHITENESS—GET OVER IT."

The squishy group leader, who sat with one leg tucked under his butt, called the meeting to order: "Okay, people, let's try and turn this battleship around and focus on our paradigm. Allison, have you resourced your entry initiatives? We want to ideate with the Ziskind Housing group to get Best Practices underway. Their housing-crisis manifests are really best-of-breed."

"Um, I've exchanged a couple of emails with Rachael at the Ziskind Center, and she put me in touch with the Fruits of Desire Community Garden," said Allison. "They need volunteers to help lay timber beams for their vegetable plots. I'm trying to schedule a time to look at the area and coordinate facilitation."

"Okay," said the graduate supervisor. "Make sure those beams don't have creosote or other chemical treatments that could be harmful. Those people already live on top of an old landfill that is probably toxic. They don't need produce that's more dangerous than the stuff they are forced to eat from the supermarket. Chelsey, have you gotten anywhere with the Gentilly Terrace rent abatement program?"

"Well, according to the people at Ziskind, the Gentilly Terrace Property Owners Association doesn't want any restrictions on their rental properties," said Chelsey. "They aren't really cooperating. The last meeting I went to got pretty heated."

"Okay," said the supervisor. "Suspend that initiative for the time being and concentrate your efforts on St. Roch. Their neighborhood groups would probably be more interested in rental interventions."

After a series of reports from the rest of the girls, the supervisor exhorted the group to continue its commitment to housing equity: "Lean in on your must-haves, and we'll reconvene next week for debriefing."

The supervisor's *cri de guerre* stimulated more tap-typing among his subordinates, leading Margot to conclude, without trying too hard, that the meeting had something to do with housing for the disadvantaged poor of inner-city New Orleans. Neither Margot nor Francis knew much about local politics or the urgency that rising housing costs presented to Orleans Parish politicians and their disadvantaged constituents, whatever that injustice might be. So, any missionary zeal that the meeting might generate was not going to interfere with her coffee date with Francis. Since neither of them drank coffee, it was really more of an iced tea date. In any event, they would be concentrating on each other for the next hour or so. Margot used an ordinary rubber band to gather her hair into a ponytail. With her hands behind her head and her back arched to complete the process, she considered that her bustline might be emphasized.

Francis swallowed and spoke: "What's the latest on your investigation? I don't even know which investigation it is, so I don't know why I'm asking. I guess you can't really talk about ongoing investigations anyway."

"Oh, it's nothing very sexy," Margot said. "Listening to wiretaps, taking notes, translating. Just paperwork stuff. Pretty routine. To tell you the truth, I'm anxious to get out from behind the desk."

"I wouldn't mind a little office time, myself. Almost all of my shift time is beat work. I sometimes welcome a little office work as a break from the insanity on the streets. I guess the grass is always greener."

"Yeah, you're right. But we both still love our jobs in spite of the . . ."

"Oh, no! I don't mean to say I'm unhappy. I wouldn't change jobs for anything. In fact, I'm actually looking to pick up extra shifts doing security detail work for private businesses. I can make extra money working as a security guard when I'm off-duty. In uniform, of course."

Margot smiled and even laughed a little. His defensiveness was a serious reaction, but it occurred to her that she would have laughed at almost anything Francis said. Still, it struck her as funny. She genuinely enjoyed spending time with him.

As she remembered that coffee shop date with fondness, Margot was satisfied that her courtship with Francis was on schedule. They had not gone on any more dinners or even nighttime dates, so the occasion to sleep together had never presented itself. She did not necessarily have any objection to full-blown sexual intimacy, but she did not feel the need to increase the pace of their relationship. It was moving forward steadily and to her satisfaction. She had kissed him passionately enough, so there was no reason to think the romance would fizzle. The prospect of sex was enough to keep up the momentum of their romance.

Margot's daydream about the man she could *almost* consider her boyfriend was interrupted by an aberration in the wiretapped conversations she was monitoring. It was in English, and that alone broke up what had, up to that point, been conducted mostly in Vietnamese. It was a younger woman's voice speaking in English on an outgoing call to an administrative office at New Orleans City Hall. It was answered by the central assessor's office, a general number that commercial property owners could call when they had questions about taxes imposed by any one of the seven separate city assessors. Because each of the seven assessors had regular jobs in the private sector, the city maintained a central administrative office with a full-time staff to handle inquiries and direct them to the individual assessors as necessary.

The call, of course, originated at the Phuoc Tho Duong Grocery. Margot listened carefully for evidence that the business was engaged in tax avoidance or other irregularities related to a private lottery that the owners were operating off the books and out of the reach of the Internal Revenue Service. She had her doubts that a grocery store in the shadow of Mary Queen of Vietnam Church would be involved in organized criminal activity, but she was in no position to express those doubts to anyone at the FBI. Besides, she didn't want to give the impression that her ethnicity would compromise her objectivity in an investigation that offered a chance at departmental recognition. Still, a private lottery at a grocery store in her old neighborhood seemed unlikely, inasmuch as members of her community were law-abiding citizens without mischievous tendencies.

Margot uncrossed her legs, rolled her chair closer to her computer screen, and turned up the volume on her headset. The younger woman on the recording was speaking to the administrator at the Central Office of Assessor Relations: "Yes, this is Tina Nguyen at Phuoc Tho Duong Grocery on Chef Menteur Highway. I'm calling for my mother. She's the owner, but she doesn't speak very good English."

"May I have your commercial tax identification number and full address, please?"

"Um, yes. The address is one-four-two-oh-one Chef Menteur Highway. And the tax ID number is, hold on, I don't have it in front of me." Margot could hear the young woman speak away from the phone to her mother in Vietnamese and ask impatiently for the paperwork that might contain the necessary details. After a brief pause and some rustling of papers, the young woman returned to her conversation with the administrator and gave him the number.

"Very good. Your assessor is Jerry Sonthonax. Would you like me to leave him a message, or would you like to try and contact him directly?"

"No, I already tried to contact him directly. The number we have has been disconnected. I'm not even sure we have the right number. Anyway, I'd like to speak to someone about—or my mom would like to speak to someone about—the new assessment we got in the mail today on the property. On the grocery store. There seems to be some mistake."

"Okay, we can't really field complaints or assessment appeals over the phone. This is not the right office to file an appeal if you want to challenge your assessment."

The young woman was audibly upset with the less-than-helpful bureaucrat: "Last year we, the building, was assessed at a hundred and eighty-five grand. The letter we got today says the building is being assessed at eight hundred ninety! This can't be right."

"Okay, those numbers don't mean anything to me. I'd be happy to give Mr. Sonthonax a message. Or I can direct you to the official forms you can use to lodge a formal appeal."

"Can you connect me with him directly? I've tried calling him but I don't get an answer—or the phone is disconnected—or there is some kind of a problem. Do *you* have a direct number for him?"

"I'm sorry, I don't. The contact number should be listed on top of the assessment letter you received."

"That's the number I tried! That number's no good! Is there someone there I can speak to about this assessment? I mean, is there someone I could speak to now rather than go through the delays of making a formal appeal?"

"I'm sorry, I can leave him a message. Or you can make an appointment directly with his office. Apart from that, you will have to speak to him personally. We don't handle individual property assessments at this office. What were those numbers, again?"

"I thought you said those numbers didn't mean anything to you!"

"Ma'am, there's no need for you to be disrespectful."

"I'm not trying to be disrespectful." Tina was obviously trying to lower the temperature of the conversation. She didn't want to risk a unilateral termination of the call, however frustrating it may have become. "But it's an increase of almost seven hundred thousand dollars. It might not even be a new assessment. It might just be a clerical error that can be cleared up on somebody's computer. Can you at least check whether or not there is a typographical error that accounts for this increase?"

"I'm sorry, we don't deal with individual assessments at this office. You will have to speak to him directly. Or I can leave him a message. You can always send him an email. Do you have his email address?"

"I've already sent him several emails. I haven't gotten a response. And now I can't get him over the phone."

"Well, the only thing I can tell you is to keep trying. And I can leave him a message. You can try to reach him at his law office, but I don't know if he takes assessor complaints at his law office."

"Oh, I didn't know he had a law office. Do you have that number?"

"No, I'm sorry. I don't have that number."

"Well, do you know the name of his law firm?"

"No, I'm sorry, I don't. The best thing for you to do is leave a message with me, and I'll give it to him when he calls in."

"This is crazy! My mom gets an assessment of eight hundred and ninety thousand dollars, and I can't even contact him to find out if it's a simple error!"

"I'm sorry. I just can't help you at this office. I'll be happy to take a message."

"Um. Okay. Is there any chance I can speak to your . . . *a* supervisor?" Tina had attempted to soften the inquiry with a mid-sentence correction. Even still, she had uttered perhaps the most dangerous words in the English language that a frustrated constituent could say to a bureaucrat: *Can I speak to a supervisor.*

"Ma'am, this is a switchboard. My supervisor's not even in the building. Is there a message for Mr. Sonthonax?"

"Tell him we called from Phuoc Tho Duong. I'm sure this is just a big mistake."

At this point in the recorded conversation, Margot stopped the tape. She made sure she had taken accurate notes because this would be something she had to discuss with her superiors. If Phuoc Tho Duong is running an illegal lottery and suddenly the local assessor raises the assessment value of the building by $700,000, there may be something else going on.

Maybe the local assessor had uncovered information that could be useful to the financial crimes section of the FBI, the branch of the Department of Justice that dealt with money laundering, tax fraud, and avoidance of regulatory oversight. Maybe the local assessor had stumbled upon a commercial real estate transaction involving the grocery store that was hidden from the general public. As far as Margot knew, there were irregularities she might not have even considered. Maybe illegal drugs or pill-mill prescriptions were involved.

Margot was curious to know more about this Jeremiah Sonthonax. She started her research on the city's official website and learned that Sonthonax—who apparently went by "Jerry"—had not been in office very long and that he was also a lawyer. Special FBI clearance allowed her access to personal information maintained by the Department of Justice on all elected officials.

She discovered that Sonthonax was divorced, that he had two kids and a series of judgments pending against him for alimony and child support. He was also under a probation order by the Louisiana Supreme Court and had been flagged by the Louisiana Gaming Commission for reasons not immediately available. This Sonthonax character seemed to be stretched pretty thin. If he was getting tangled up with the fishy business at the Phuoc Tho Duong Grocery, further inquiries would be required. She checked her notes one final time and headed straight to her supervisor's office.

Deputy Assistant Director Kevin Barksdale, a six-year veteran of the United States Navy, was Margot's immediate superior. He was supervising, among several other investigations, the surveillance of the Phuoc Tho Duong grocery store and its questionable business practices.

Margot knew, from past conversations with Barksdale, that the actual target of the investigation was a woman named Binh Nguyen, the registered owner of the business. She was the wife of a man named Chinh Nguyen, who, as far as the FBI could ascertain, was an automobile mechanic and backyard farmer. At the outset of the investigation, the FBI presumed that Mr. Nguyen was the actual head of a possible crime family that was generating undeclared money. It soon became clear that he had nothing whatsoever to do with business operations inasmuch as he never left the family home and mostly busied himself tinkering with lawnmowers. The grocery store, and any side hustle conducted there, was run by his wife.

Although Mr. Nguyen was no doubt aware that the grocery store was generating significant amounts of cash—the driveway of their home was always jam-packed with luxury cars and pleasure boats—it could never be determined that he had any criminal knowledge of the source of those acquisitions. For all he knew, the grocery store was producing the business results he had been told were made possible by the great Land of Opportunity. He didn't speak any English and, to the satisfaction of Barksdale, was an innocent beneficiary of his wife's industriousness.

Having concluded as much, Barksdale had redirected the focus of the inquiry to Chinh's wife, Binh, who spoke enough English to run a grocery store, purchase automobiles, manage an attached gasoline station, and perhaps surreptitiously organize a private lottery system popular with the neighboring Vietnamese community. Barksdale and the FBI knew very well that the Vietnamese were a closed society for the most part, but their cultural family structure was certainly adaptable to the realities of life in America. An English-speaking matriarch could naturally assume command if necessary. Under those circumstances, surveillance of Binh Nguyen would seem to be the investigative tactic from which inculpatory evidence would be best obtained. After all, she spent nearly ten hours a day on the premises presiding over the comings and goings of customers, delivery personnel, and the feckless loiterers that never seemed to leave the store with any merchandise. The Nguyen children (or youngsters the FBI believed to be Nguyen children) also worked at the store when they weren't in school, and they, too, took their instructions from Mama Binh.

Margot tapped lightly on the open door of Kevin Barksdale's office with her notes from the wiretaps in her hands. "We picked up some interesting chatter on the grocery store wiretaps, sir. I thought you might like to take a look at the transcripts."

"What do they say?" Barksdale asked.

"Binh's daughter, Tina, or she represented herself as her daughter, placed a call to the New Orleans assessor's office central number complaining of an inflated assessment on the grocery store building."

"How do you know it's her daughter?"

"Well, she said her 'mom' received the letter raising the assessment. I checked the records we have on family members, and I think the daughter's name is Tina. She spoke perfect English, and she seemed like she was old enough to understand the significance of an assessment, or an inflated assessment, anyway."

Barksdale appeared to be interested in the substance of the conversation: "What did the assessment letter say?"

"According to Tina, or the girl I believe to be Tina, only last year the building—the Phuoc Tho Duong grocery store building—was assessed at one hundred eighty thousand dollars, but the reassessment value jumped up to almost nine hundred grand. She said she had tried to call her district assessor—his name is Jerry Sonthonax . . ."

"Yeah, I know Jerry Sonthonax . . ."

"Anyway, she tried to call Sonthonax to get some answers, but she was unable to reach him . . . She said his phone had been disconnected. And she wanted to speak to someone about the extraordinary increase. I guess she was worried about the increased tax liability."

"Hmmm," murmured Barksdale as he contemplated the significance of this new information. "What do we figure is the basis for this massive increase?"

"I'm not real sure. The real estate has not been for sale in the last ten years, and we have no record that the property has been refinanced. As you know, if you refinance your mortgage, the bank sends an appraiser to value the security. And we don't know of any commercial developers out in New Orleans East who might be snatching up property out there. Quite frankly, the increased assessment might very well be a clerical error, which is what Tina asked about over the phone."

"What did they tell her?"

"They shuffled her off. The usual bureaucratic unhelpfulness."

"What do we know about Jerry Sonthonax?"

"He hasn't been in elected office very long. He's divorced. Has alimony and child support payments to make. He's also a lawyer in private practice, but he's under disciplinary probation by the Louisiana Supreme Court for unauthorized use of client funds. He's never had any serious legal problems, but he seems to be under some financial stress."

"I see. So you think you might be putting the squeeze on the property owners?"

"We don't exactly know," Margot said. "I'm not even sure there's any benefit to him personally if the assessment is raised. So far, he has not been picked up on any of the wiretaps."

"All right. So were you able to get any information on the wiretaps, any Vietnamese-language chatter about the lottery?"

"None whatsoever. But I'm still listening and transcribing. The

Vietnamese stuff is pretty run-of-the-mill. Coordinating deliveries, family discussions, a few phone calls to Mary Queen of Vietnam Catholic Church asking about copies of the church newsletter. Nothing of any consequence."

"Very good," Barksdale said.

"Oh," Margot added, "and an argument over hiring a security guard. A woman called Arabella, I think, who sounds like someone in the community, stopped by several times over the past week. Claimed she'd be perfect because folks in the neighborhood know her. I think I saw this Arabella person on videotape one day, in an NOPD uniform. Short, straight hair, usually pulled back in a ponytail?"

Barksdale raised an eyebrow.

Margot continued. "Mama Binh clearly doesn't like her. She shouted at her, told her to leave, and a couple of times, it sounded like the son had to escort the woman out."

"Maybe it's time you paid them a visit," Barksdale said. "Are you up for a little plainclothes detective work? Just to see firsthand what's going on out there? You don't have to wear a wire or body cam. Just go out there and buy a couple of candy bars and see what you can find out. Don't make a whole day of it. I'm more interested in what we can glean from the wiretaps. But I think it's time to get a better understanding of the grocery store layout and the kind of traffic that comes in and out. Could be they're running a pill mill or even a small-time loan shark operation. And who is this Arabella person? You might even *surveille* the lottery ticket sales procedure."

"They actually sell official Louisiana Lotto tickets and scratch-offs. They have a license, and they're up-to-date on their state lottery remissions. I don't think you want me to ask for a private Vietnamese lottery ticket. Or do you?"

"No, no. Don't make any open lottery inquiries at all just yet. We're not ready to press that hard. We're on the outer edges of our warrant already. Just buy a pack of gum and look around. Take one of our bait cars from the motor pool. And get back on those wiretaps. I'd like to know whether we can pick up anything from Sonthonax."

"Will do. I'll let you know what I find out."

"Oh, and Margot . . . uh, Special Agent Hoang . . . While you're out there, see if you can identify the NOPD cop who recently started a private detail out there—obviously not the woman you've been hearing. We picked this new guy up under photographic surveillance, but we don't know who he is. I didn't want to make inquiries with NOPD. They don't need to know we're interested in the grocery store at these early stages. I don't suppose it's unusual for a convenience store open twenty-four hours with that kinda traffic to need a detail cop for security. But there may be some other reason. Anyway, just figure out who he is, exactly, and we will go from there."

Margot suddenly felt a little sick. Francis had just told her he was trying to pick up extra detail work, and she knew he was assigned to patrol the New Orleans East police district. But it was a big district, and there was no reason to definitively conclude he had been hired by the Phuoc Tho Duong grocery store. It just couldn't be possible that her first real romantic interest in a long time, maybe of any time, could be a part of one of her white-collar crime investigations. It just couldn't be.

9

Jerry Sonthonax arrived at his law office, such as it was, at about 10:15 a.m. He had been avoiding regular office hours for fear that process servers and other messengers of unpleasantness would find him there. He had successfully ducked his responsibilities to courts and creditors for months, and he did not intend to expose himself unnecessarily by spending time at a location publicly listed as his business address. But he needed to retrieve certain documents he had stored in his office filing cabinet that would support, however spuriously, his calculation of real estate values in his assessment district. In addition, there were sure to be regular mail deliveries accumulating on the floor of the office beneath the spring-loaded metal mail slot on the glass entrance door that would be visible from the street. Burglars are attracted by signs of absenteeism like piled-up mail. He didn't plan on staying there any longer than fifteen or twenty minutes.

The earlier part of the morning had been spent feeding his addiction to horse racing. It was part of his breakfast routine to read the racing form, whether he had the cash to place wagers or not. That morning, his handicapping had been less intense than usual because he had something in the works that stood to be far more lucrative: the scheme he and Burton Clayton had devised to squeeze money out of the Phuoc Tho Duong Grocery. Whether or not the first steps of that scheme had been initiated, he could not say. It was up to Burton to determine exactly when Glenn Hornacek would be dispatched on the mission, and Jerry could only wait to hear whether it was, in fact, underway.

As far as Jerry was concerned, it couldn't happen fast enough. The strain of insurmountable debt was such that political extortion, which he, of course, knew was illegal, seemed reasonable. The shakedown of the Phuoc Tho Duong Grocery was—yes—a criminal act punishable by jail time. But it was not a violent street crime or an identity-theft credit card skim. It was an equitable transaction whereby a tax consultation service would be provided in return for a negotiated fee. When Jerry thought of it in those terms, it all seemed so safe.

Besides, Burton had been taking kickbacks for his assessment reductions for a long time. In fact, it was considered a cost of doing business in the CBD. No one, least of all property owners, saw any need to disturb a system that had worked so well for so long. Jerry knew that the Orleans Parish District Attorney's Office, who might have had an interest in prosecuting such matters, would never disrupt a Burton Clayton operation. He was revered by the majority Black voting populace as a successful Black businessman who deserved the forbearance of law enforcement. It was an unspoken immunity enjoyed by certain Black political figures whose iconic status was protected by society's sentimental need for minority heroes in an otherwise racially oppressive New Orleans.

That sense of entitlement belonged to Jerry as well, or so he thought, and he convinced himself that his own smaller version of Burton's business model could be deployed without police interference. But time was not on his side. He could not be sure that Burton understood the exact urgency of his predicament and so could only wait for confirmation that Burton's field operative, namely Glenn Hornacek, would be engaged as promised. It was exactly the same tentative optimism he felt when horses were at the starting gate.

Jerry's law office, which had been provided to him free of charge by a New Orleans East slumlord who cultivated political connections whenever he could, was a lightly refurbished carwash/tire repair facility at the corner of Leon C. Simon Drive and Downman Road near the Lakefront Airport and only minutes from the local FBI headquarters. Vestiges of the former business were evident from the prefabricated architecture, but it had been freshened with minor structural alterations and white paint the landlord hoped would attract a paying commercial tenant. Finding none, it was just as valuable to allow rent-free occupancy to his assessor, Jerry Sonthonax, who could, in turn, provide him with a political accommodation whenever the need arose. The slumlord also paid the utility bills, another emolument Jerry remembered as he pulled his car into the concrete parking area that once served customers with dirty cars and bald tires.

He was surprised and then sickened by the sight of two people standing in front of the commercial glass doors of his makeshift law office: an older Black woman with a cheap wig and a younger Black man. Jerry immediately recognized them as unhappy clients calling, in person, to collect a debt. It was Viola Chavis and her son LeCharles. Because all of his energy had been spent managing the demands of secured creditors, he had completely forgotten about these two relatively minor ones whose ability to put pressure on him was neutralized by simply making himself scarce. He had managed to dodge their phone calls for the past few months, which meant that they could be placed at the bottom of the list of problems he had to solve.

As he stepped out of his car and approached the grumpy faces of the waiting couple, Jerry fumbled with his keys and tried to remember the many excuses he had previously offered for the delay in payment. Of his many creditors—his ex-wife, his bookie, his Supreme Court probation officer, his cellular phone service provider, his kids' grammar school tuition bursar—Mrs. Chavis was not a specter he thought would materialize when he got out of bed that morning.

"Miz Chavis! LeCharles! How are we this morning?" he said, trying to be cheerful while pushing past them to unlock the office door. He made a great show of hustling and fumbling with his keys to give them the impression that their visit was a pleasant surprise. "Come on in! I've been trying to reach you to give you an update on your case."

"We've been trying to get you. I'm not sure Mama wrote down your phone number correctly." LeCharles held the door open for his mother and followed Jerry into a reception area that had the chemical smell of new carpeting mixed with a mustiness that comes with prolonged vacancy.

"Well, we'll make sure to get her the correct number and clear up the confusion," said Jerry, neither asking what number Mrs. Chavis had been dialing nor providing the correct number, which, at any rate, had been cut off for nonpayment. "Come on in, and we'll discuss the latest developments. How have you been? Everybody getting along okay?"

"As well as can be expected," answered LeCharles, less confrontational than what Jerry feared. "We got bills to pay, like everybody else." Up to this point, Mrs. Chavis had remained silent, allowing her son the deference an elderly woman usually gives to a helpful and more experienced son.

The group proceeded to an inner office equipped with a rusted metal desk—the kind you might see in the back room of a hardware store or plumbing supply company—and two stackable metal chairs with brown vinyl upholstery for clients to sit in. Jerry went behind the desk and sat in a larger captain's chair that squeaked when he rolled it toward his older-model dingy-white computer unit. Jerry pretended to consult the computer monitor as if it would reveal all the answers to his clients' concerns. "Let's see what we have here," he said, buying time to choreograph his desperate footwork.

Viola Chavis, as she had explained when she walked into his office six months earlier, was an eighty-seven-year-old retired housemaid who had been injured when struck by a passing car on Chef Menteur Highway. She had taken a city bus from her home closer to the city to do some light shopping at the dollar store. A young man driving a rented car had brushed her with a protruding rearview mirror as she stepped up to the curb. It was not a major collision, but it knocked her down, and she sustained a broken hip. The injury required a two-week hospital stay and several months of home convalescence. The young motorist had been polite and showed concern for the older lady, providing his driver's license and insurance information at the scene. Sometime after that, she and LeCharles asked Jerry to represent them in a lawsuit against the driver's insurance company. She knew Jerry's name from local campaign advertisements, and LeCharles had learned from friends that Jerry was also a personal injury lawyer.

Viola had been born and raised in Paincourtville (pronounced "PANG-core ville"), Louisiana, in Assumption Parish, an hour or so west of New Orleans. She had grown up poor, occasionally working in the sugarcane fields, when she met her husband, who did similar work. They had married and moved to the city in the 1940s when her husband found higher-paying work at the warehouse of Kohn, Weil & Simon, a wholesale hat distributor on Tchoupitoulas Street. In 1952, they took up residence in the gleaming new Desire Housing Project in New Orleans East and raised four children— three boys and one girl. Her oldest son died of an unexpected heart attack in his late twenties, and her second son was in prison for drug distribution. Her third child, a daughter, had married and moved to New Jersey, leaving only LeCharles, the youngest, to care for their mother for the remainder of her widowed life.

Her husband had been killed in an accident at the warehouse when he was crushed by a hydraulic freight elevator manufactured by Kaestner Hecht & Company of Chicago, Illinois. When first told this tragic story, Jerry mused that a valuable lawsuit might have been brought against the elevator manufacturer. But in those days, undereducated Black laborers had limited access to a segregated court system where the civil rights of the Black population were largely unrecognized and often suppressed. Personnel managers at Kohn, Weil & Simon provided Viola with a small amount of money to help her through the difficult circumstances, but she never would have imagined that fifty years later, she would be sitting in a lawyer's office on a street named in honor of one of the principal owners of her husband's employer, namely Leon C. Simon himself.

Her son, LeCharles, age fifty-six, whose responsibility it was to take care of his ailing mother, had been employed by the New Orleans Sewerage and Water Board for the previous twenty years. Starting as an ordinary laborer on a repair crew, he had worked his way up to the position of truck driver assigned to one of the many detachments that provided maintenance to the city's aging drainage system. After twenty years as a driver, LeCharles expected one day to reach the position of crew supervisor—a coveted job title that was almost an emeritus honorarium bestowed upon elder statesmen who rode around on the front seat of the service trucks but who seldom did any physical labor. A typical Sewerage and Water Board crew consisted of shovel men, loaders, tool pushers, one driver, and one supervisor—in reverse order of superiority. None of the workmen did the assigned jobs of any of the others, and none but the designated driver ever drove the truck. The position of supervisor was much desired because he never had to leave the cab of the truck. It took many years to acquire that position, and everybody in the crew understood that the crew supervisor could, by the rules of ancient tradition, remain seated in the air-conditioned truck while the subordinate crew members did the actual repair work. LeCharles, having achieved the status of driver, was only one notch away from that cushy position. Jerry forgave himself for slowpoking the poor lady's car accident recovery by rationalizing that her son's steady job and promising future with the Sewerage and Water Board would sustain them with or without the funds Jerry most certainly owed them.

Shortly after Viola's car accident, Jerry had filed a claim against the young driver's insurance company on her behalf and received a $20,000 settlement check made out to him as Viola's attorney, which he deposited in an escrow account to be distributed to Viola after taking his contingency fee. But that chunk of ready cash, over which Jerry had unilateral access, was just too tempting. He invaded the escrow account and used the proceeds of Viola's lawsuit to satisfy his own consumer debt and the other overdue obligations of his thin-spun life. At the time, he had every intention of reimbursing the escrow account with future income from other sources, but that money never seemed to arrive. So, he still rightly owed Viola $14,000, an amount calculated after his fee had been deducted, and she was there at his office demanding to know when she could expect the funds.

"We received the funds, as agreed, from the insurance company, and they were deposited, as required by law, into your escrow account." Jerry was using as much technical terminology as he could generate so that neither Viola nor LeCharles could challenge the dissembling legalese. "As I told you, that money cannot be made available to you until all the legal appeal delays have run."

This was a lie because the check had been written by the insurance company in final settlement of the claim. No appealable legal judgment had even been rendered, and Jerry's cryptic reference to appeal delays was a deliberately misleading bit of lawyer jargon. Jerry needed time to get his hands on other money sources before there would be enough to distribute to the Chavises. He desperately needed the Phuoc Tho Duong shakedown to produce—and produce it must in the short-term.

"And how long do these delays last?" asked LeCharles. "When does my mama actually get the money?"

"You see," Jerry explained, "those funds remain undisbursable for thirty days from the date of remission. We only got the check last week, so we can't touch that money for at least a month. And then we may have to wait another thirty days in case an appeal is made to the Supreme Court." Jerry was really crawfishing beyond what he thought would be necessary.

"So, we're looking at another sixty days?"

"Not necessarily." Jerry was trying to provide good news to offset the bad news he had dishonestly manufactured. "There may not be a Supreme Court appeal, in which case you only have to wait the one thirty-day period."

"So, when do I get my money?" The sound of Viola's soft voice and her forlorn demeanor brought home to Jerry the perfidy of his behavior. He felt horrible for her, but there was nothing he could do about it at that moment.

"We're gonna get you your money. Don't you worry. It's coming. Just a few more days and you'll have fourteen thousand dollars in your checking account to spend as you please. And it's tax-free! That should make you happy! All yours, free and clear." Jerry was doing his best to end the uncomfortable meeting on a positive note. "I'll tell you what. I will call you in a few days to update you on the appeal status, and we'll go from there. That's the best we can do for now. Does that sound okay?"

At that point, Jerry stood up and smiled, hoping that the overwhelmed couple would understand that the meeting had come to a conclusion. To his great relief, the Chavises gathered themselves and their personal items and rose from their seats to be escorted out of the office. They walked slowly, as if to prolong what was left of the meeting, then left Jerry's office dissatisfied but without any apparent recourse. Jerry waved goodbye and locked the front door as the Chavises walked dejectedly to their car.

He had managed to slough off the Chavises for the time being using every manner of shiftiness and crafty counsels without much resistance from them, though their patience was more attributable to their innocent politeness—they were, after all, good people—and, perhaps, also to their befuddlement. He had abused their ignorance of the law with a despicable cozenage to commit theft. His tongue had cleaved to its palate. It was a regrettable performance he would never have staged had circumstances been less drastic.

Jerry watched and waited impatiently for them to drive away from his office parking lot. Once they were safely out of sight, he unlocked the glass front door, grabbed his mail, locked it back from the outside, and got in his own car. He sat behind the wheel for a minute or so with his eyes closed and tried to pull himself together before his drive downtown. He was scheduled to meet with Burton Clayton and, or so he had been promised, the notorious Glenn Hornacek. This was to be the meeting at which his scheme to extract money from the Phuoc Tho Duong Grocery would be finalized. That was, at least, his expectation.

He pulled out of the parking lot onto Downman Road, heading toward the Mississippi River for the long drive into town. Downman Road had been designed by the area's optimistic developers in the early 1970s as a major commercial thoroughfare to serve the nearby residential communities of New Orleans East. Those dreams of utopian American living had quite obviously not materialized. Downman Road looked more like any other failed experiment at metropolitan expansion that had guessed wrong about the direction of White migration. It had, by that time, become the Eyesore of Peiraeus—a depressing strip of marginal businesses, many of them boarded shut and all of them exhibiting the ravages of low-income urban decay. There were nail salons, wig emporia, beauty shops, massage parlors, boarded-up fried seafood restaurants that had once been national fast food franchises, makeshift car repair garages, urgent care and chiropractic facilities, discount cellular phone outlets, pawnshops, miniature Baptist churches, scattered-site Section 8 apartment complexes, laundromats, and self-service carwash stalls, all interspersed by vacant lots with patches of overgrown weeds that pushed their way through cracks in the concrete. The Downman Road thoroughfare was not going to be placed on the UNESCO World Heritage Site list anytime soon.

At the opposite end of Downman Road, where it intersected with Chef Menteur Highway near the Mississippi River, there were two gentlemen's clubs across the street from one another. One, which was Black-owned and primarily served a Black clientele, was called Thotz, and the other, White-owned and serving primarily a White clientele, was called Thunder Gulch. Jerry was familiar with these strip joints, as he had considered them to be possible targets for tax reassessment. They were, he thought, sure to be profitable cash businesses susceptible to commercial regulation and, therefore, political interference. At the beginning of his elected term, when these thoughts occurred to him, he was too inexperienced to approach the owners with the threat of a shakedown. More than that, it was much too risky to be seen inside such establishments, especially the White one. The Black one, where he might be able to operate in a friendlier environment, was not likely to be impressed by his elected title—he would be perceived as just another low-level political hustler on the make. In any case, he had not, by then, reached the point in his political career where that kind of subtle or not-so-subtle suggestion could be delivered with confidence. People in the business of running strip clubs are not easily intimidated.

With those potential targets set aside for later consideration, he turned onto Chef Menteur Highway and headed west toward town, where cheap architecture and low-brow commerce gave way to more pleasant surroundings. One such place was the campus of Dillard University, a well-known historically Black college with stately buildings designed by New Orleans architect Moise Goldstein in the 1930s. The Gentilly Terrace neighborhood, in which Dillard University sat, was the area of the city where he grew up and went to high school. His fondness for and familiarity with the area imbued him, to some degree, with the confidence he would need for his meeting with Burton Clayton and his trusted myrmidon, Glenn Hornacek

When, at last, he reached Burton's downtown office building, he searched briefly for free street parking but was eventually forced to park in the covered lot attached to the building. Burton, or his secretary, would surely validate his ticket. He could not, in his present circumstances, afford the $20 minimum rate. But all of that, if his scheme was successful, was sure to change.

He emerged from the parking garage elevator onto the ground floor of the office building. The ambient air was much cooler in the elegant reception area. The marble floor and dark wood of the building's concierge desk confirmed for him that money was to be had. The attractive Black woman with relaxed, frosted hair directed him to the twenty-second floor and the appropriate elevator bay. The elevator car was lined with mirrors, but he couldn't bring himself to look at his own reflection. Instead, he cocked his head back, stared at the illuminated floor numerals above the brass doors, made clucking noises with his tongue, and touched the side of his head to make sure his jaw-mounted phone piece was in place, even though it didn't work. He got off the elevator on the twenty-second floor and walked across more marble flooring toward the eight-foot glass entry doors of Burton's office to his left. He had arrived at the crucible of his deliverance.

—

The female receptionist in Burton's office was Black, but light-skinned, with a slender nose, and probably a graduate of the city's parochial Catholic school system, as Jerry was. She was younger than Jerry, but he was certain he knew members of her family. The nameplate on the reception desk read "Lynette," but he dared not call her by that name, even though they came from similar family backgrounds. He spoke to her respectfully but from a position of equivalency and perhaps even solidarity: "Hi. Jerry Sonthonax to see Burton Clayton?"

"Yes, of course. Just a moment." She pressed a button on her over-sized host unit telephone panel and spoke into the microphone of her headset. "Kelly, there's a Mr. Sonthonax to see Mr. Clayton? Great, I'll let him know." She looked up from her desk and spoke directly to Jerry: "Kelly will be out in just a moment to show you in."

"Excellent. Thanks very much." He sat down on a leather sofa in the waiting area and smiled at the receptionist. He considered crossing his legs but thought maybe that was too casual or even disrespectful. He was glad to have put some consideration into his body language when Burton himself appeared from behind a heavy wooden door instead of Kelly.

"Jerry! How are you? Come on in. We're all set up in my office."

Jerry took this greeting to mean that Glenn Hornacek had already arrived. It worried Jerry slightly that the Hornacek fellow had arrived before him because he had hoped to be alone with Burton before the meeting in order to speak informally about the mechanics of the Phuoc Tho Duong shakedown and the risks associated with it. More than that, he would have preferred some time alone with Burton to put himself at ease. No matter. He might as well get down to business.

Burton escorted Jerry into his office, closed another heavy brown wooden door behind them, and began the introductions.

"Jerry Southonax, this is Glenn Hornacek. Jerry is one of my fellow assessors in another district. I'm sure you've heard of him if you haven't met him before. Maybe you even voted for him!"

"Why, yes, of course!" Glenn said, rising from his chair. "I know very well who he is. It's nice to meet you."

Jerry shook Glenn's hand and took a measured look at the gentleman who would actually be administering the extortion plan in the field—that is, of course, should the plan receive the blessing and assistance of the recognized master of these sorts of things, Burton Clayton. Glenn Hornacek, Jerry quickly observed, was a stout White man, somewhat flabby, with an almost bald head and longer dark curls wisping down the back of his neck and brushing against his white shirt collar. He had a starched blue shirt with contrasting white collar and white French cuffs fastened with gold oval cufflinks. His suit coat was draped over the back of his chair, which indicated to Jerry that he had made himself comfortable in Burton's private office. The two of them seemed to have a cozy familiarity that Jerry found unnerving.

Glenn wore his dark leather belt very high, almost to the navel, which exaggerated his waistline and required what Jerry thought would be an extra-long zippered fly. On the outer edges of his bee-sting lips, Glenn had grown a goatee that resembled the food-gathering tendrils that surround the orifice of a beaked mollusk. He bore a resemblance to the baritone of the 1960s singing group The Fifth Dimension, only White.

Burton spoke first from behind his sleek glass-and-aluminum desk: "Jerry has some property owners in his district who might be getting off light on their assessment. He has an obligation to his constituents—actually, an obligation to the city at large—to make sure everybody is paying his fair share. As I'm sure you know, we assessors are elected to determine property values evenly across the board. It's a goal we strive for in my district, which is not always the easiest thing to do. I've always taken the approach that property assessments—and the tax revenues they generate—should take into consideration the income produced by commercial properties in order to ensure an equitable distribution of the tax burden. That, in my opinion, is the fair way. The legal way. You would agree, Glenn?"

"Oh, absolutely. If one property owner is getting a free ride, other property owners who are similarly situated can feel they are being subject to unfair treatment. Arbitrary treatment."

"That's exactly right," said Burton, looking at Jerry but directing his expository comments to Glenn. "Property valuations are a subjective matter. But the city must bring as much scientific certainty to the equation as possible. At the same time, property owners are entitled to challenge our calculations as a check-and-balance to our subjectivity. You would agree with that also, wouldn't you, Glenn?"

"No doubt about it. Property owners are entitled to appeal assessment decisions as a matter of law."

"And in order to safeguard that process, I oftentimes encourage property owners to challenge my assessments, especially where there is room for reasonable minds to differ. You're familiar with that kind of accommodation, aren't you, Glenn?"

"I am." Glenn was responding to Burton but was now directing his scripted lines to Jerry. "I've been helping Burton implement that method of fairness since I've known him. That's why I respect Burton so much— as a politician. Good government begins with an evenly applied tax responsibility."

"Thank you for the testimonial, sir," said Burton. "But my pursuit of good government is not undertaken to help my personal reputation—it's to maintain the fiscal health of the city. Our city. I'm sure Jerry shares those concerns as well."

Jerry took the cue to jump in agreeably: "I do indeed. So much so that I asked Burton for his guidance on assessments in my district. That's basically why I'm here."

The exchange of platitudes about *good government* and *equitable tax burdens* disguised what was really under consideration, almost as if the conversation was being recorded. Jerry nevertheless sensed that the stage-setting had been completed under Burton's expert guidance. He also sensed that the real substance of the meeting would, at last, be taken up.

Burton took command: "Now, as I understand it, Jerry, you have a grocery store out in the East that might be sliding by with an underassessment? An assessment made by your predecessor, not by you. Is that correct?"

"Yes. It has come to my attention that the business is generating quite a bit more income than what the actual, physical property would indicate. It's in the Vietnamese section of my district. And, as you know, it's not always easy to get a handle on commercial activity out there. It's a different kind of culture, a different language even. They've been in business a long time, and it does not appear any property value adjustments or even reevaluations have been made in quite some time. I've actually learned that they may be generating income that is not being reported through the proper channels. My concern is that consumers in that neighborhood—most of whom are my supporters—are being exploited." Jerry took a moment to admire his own subtlety and the sly suggestion that Black constituents were being sucked dry by a Vietnamese business owner who was sandbagging outside of the reach of city regulators.

"And how, exactly, did you come upon this information?" asked Glenn, obviously intent to determine if the matter involved any criminality that might rub off on him.

"I have a friend in the Vietnamese community . . ."

"A racetrack friend?" asked Glenn, interrupting Jerry's explanation and signaling that he already had the drop on him.

For an instant, Jerry considered denying that the inside information might have come from a racetrack acquaintance, so as to disabuse Glenn Hornacek of any suspicion that he had a gambling problem. But there was no point. Glenn seemed much too experienced to be snookered by any flimsy denials Jerry might float.

"Well, yes. My source is a fan of the races." It was a euphemistic restatement of Glenn's blunt question intended to soften his association with a somewhat shady pastime. "But I've actually known him since high school. We've been friends for a while." Jerry was doing his best to deflect attention from horse racing's disreputable image. He soldiered on by changing the subject slightly. "The owner of the grocery appears to be running some kind of illegal lottery. Not the regular state-sponsored lottery—scratch-offs, Powerball, the legal stuff—but a private lottery that flies under the radar. It's pure profit that doesn't get taxed. And it's income that never gets figured into the value of the property. That's why I think I have an obligation to reassess the property in order to accurately establish their obligations to the city."

In any other context, the frank disclosure by an elected official of an illegal lottery would warrant the institution of a criminal investigation by the Louisiana Lottery Commission, if not the attorney general. But that was not the purpose of this meeting. Jerry knew that Glenn understood as much. And Glenn communicated that understanding promptly: "It's not our job to conduct police work for the lottery commission, or any other law enforcement agency, for that matter. I think we—that is to say, you and Burton, as assessors—need only concern yourselves with your sworn legal mandate."

Burton interceded to relieve the tension of this very sensitive area: "I quite agree. Jerry, have you begun the process of reassessment?"

"Well," Jerry replied, "I've made a back-of-the-envelope estimate based on commercial comparables. Nothing firm. More of a discussion draft, so to speak. Something to start the conversation going."

"And have you communicated this estimate—this possible reassessment value—to the property owner yet?" Burton asked.

"I have. I sent a preliminary letter alerting them that the reassessment was under consideration."

"And did you provide a sum certain?"

"I did. Eight hundred ninety thousand. But I was careful to point out that it was only a possible estimate—a possible value that was under consideration by my office."

"And did you send it on your official letterhead?"

"Well, I had to. There wouldn't be much point sending a letter like that under private signature."

"Okay. I think we understand. What I like to do in situations like this is to offer my assistance. Glenn's company has a lot of experience in this field. In order to be helpful, I suggest that property owners—like your Vietnamese grocers—hire Glenn to make an independent evaluation of the property value, emphasizing that his track record—if you'll excuse the racetrack reference—his experience in this area has proved to be very advantageous for property owners who bring challenges to my office. I can certainly recommend his services. And I think you could do the same in good conscience."

"I understand," said Jerry, delighted and relieved to have had his message understood. "And how, exactly, do I get this procedure underway? Should I send another letter recommending Glenn's service to the property owner?"

"No," said Burton. "Contact them and tell them there's a procedure for appeals. Recommend that they retain a consultant to generate a competing or alternate assessment. Explain that a private appraiser can often provide up-to-date market variants that will reduce the value placed on their property as initially reckoned. At that point, you suggest Glenn and his successful results. They'll get the message. Then Glenn can pay them a visit as though it's a matter of customary procedure and provide assurances that his relationship with your office has produced favorable results. They will know then that relief is forthcoming. It's all in the timing. Glenn?"

"Yes. Contact them this morning, and I'll visit them this afternoon. I will handle it from there. I'll pay a visit to the property owner in person and tell him—is it a him or a her?"

"It's a her," said Jerry.

"I'll pay her a visit and express sympathy for her predicament. If all goes well, she'll retain my services, and I'll make a recommendation to you about how her property value should be calculated."

"Okay. I'll call her right after I leave here. Her daughter, who speaks fluent English, has been making inquiries with the central assessor's office and has done so relentlessly."

"I understand," said Glenn reassuringly. "I'll get right on it, and we should have the matter ironed out near-term."

"That sounds excellent," said Jerry.

"Very well," said Burton. "As the song says about fame sometimes coming from indoor sports."

Neither Glenn nor Jerry knew quite what Burton meant, but they both chuckled dutifully at his penchant for referencing obscure songs. Burton smiled proudly at the cleverness of his own witticism, whether his colleagues understood it or not. Nonetheless contented, Burton wrapped up the meeting with his final instructions: "I think we all know what to do. Glenn, why don't you start things on your end, and Jerry and I will visit here briefly about some other matters."

At that point, Glenn rose from his chair, said his goodbyes, lifted his suit jacket from the back of his chair, and disappeared out of Burton's office.

Jerry and Burton were now alone. Burton smiled as if to ask, "Was that meeting satisfactory?" or "Do you now understand how this business works?" Jerry returned the smile and may have even laughed slightly to express his gratitude. But, just then, there was a knock on the door. It was Glenn, who only put his head inside the partially opened door.

"Sorry to interrupt. Just one more thing. Aren't you a lawyer, Jerry? I only ask because I may have a nice referral for you involving a medical malpractice claim. It wouldn't involve much actual litigation. I should think a simple demand letter would secure an easy settlement."

"Yes, I am. And I always appreciate a nice referral."

"Good. I'll be in touch. Thank you, gentlemen. I'll let you get back to the important stuff." Whereupon, Glenn closed the door and left Jerry and Burton to their privacy. Burton smiled at Jerry again as if to say, "I know how to take care of my friends." It occurred to Jerry that Burton and Glenn had danced this dance many times before.

After some brief conversation about family and friends, Jerry thanked Burton and walked out of the office into the reception area, glancing quickly behind to make sure Burton's office door was closed. He spoke to the receptionist in a cheerful whisper that was meant to show he had a simple request unrelated to actual office operations.

"May I use your phone? My headset's not getting good reception in this building for some reason."

She was gracious: "Certainly. Right there on the side table. Just dial nine."

10

After his meeting with the two assessors, Glenn Hornacek boarded the office elevator and congratulated himself on another swell performance, another exhibition of his talent for knowing, without being told, exactly how to synchronize his responses to Burton's promptings whenever one of their business conferences with a third party required subtle political diplomacy. He always felt satisfied after these Burton Clayton meetings, especially when they produced, or stood to produce, a favorable result.

Glenn knew perfectly well he was operating outside the rule of law, but it was fun pretending to be a legitimate businessman conducting legitimate business at a legitimate business office in the heart of the Central Business District.

In a way, he was. After all, he was the president of a consulting firm with embossed stationery, a fancy car, a tight schedule, a harried demeanor (when he wanted to adopt one), a closetful of Super 100s, and a sense that he mattered in a world of serious men. The fact that he was only a parasitic simulacrum of a private-sector business executive did not diminish the thrill of coat-and-tie, office tower appointments involving real money. Nothing beats the intoxication of wheeling and dealing like a real baron of industry.

Such was the euphoria he felt as he descended to the ground floor in the main office elevator. There were no other passengers in the car, so he could admire his reflection in the closed brass doors in the vain way that only solitude allows. It struck him that he looked a bit slimmer than usual, but he was forced to admit that the soft reflection off the brass could be very forgiving. It also occurred to him that maybe his coat sleeves were a bit long, hanging, as they were, almost to the second knuckles of his stubby, hairy thumbs. Even still, it was an acceptable flaw in his physical profile because it gave an artificial length to his arms, which also relieved the horizontal aspect of his waistline. Not to be outdone, his goatee provided some relief to the fleshiness of his round face and the smoothness of his balding skull. All in all, the effect was most pleasing, especially since his business concerns were motoring along smoothly.

So smoothly, in fact, that he could turn his attention to the other matter that had the potential to be even more lucrative than any of the usual single-shot Burton Clayton shakedowns: the referral fee he stood to earn from Caroline Calloway's lawsuit against her North Carolina treatment facility. His meeting at the Phuoc Tho Duong Grocery was not scheduled until later that afternoon, so it gave him at least three hours to meet privately with Caroline. He had arranged to meet her for coffee away from the madness of the AA group and the distractions of fellow-addict meltdowns. She had suggested an organic juice bar called Silverbeet on Magazine Street.

When he made it to his BMW after a short ride in a separate set of garage elevators, he removed his suit coat, folded it neatly on the passenger seat, and slid underneath the steering wheel, which was cocked as high as its tilt setting would allow. With the air conditioner blasting at full capacity against the folds of his white French shirtcuffs, he palmed his smartphone and punched in the query "Silverbeet on Magazine."

The website instantly appeared as "Silverbeet: A Source Cleanse Resistance." That had to be the place. It was a trade name that sent a coded but unmistakable message of solidarity with the maquisards of alternative culture: sustainable-farm costermongers, climate-justice bee-keepers, renewable-energy alchemists, emeritus college professors in

brown corduroy suits and eyebrow dandruff, anguished pet-rescue pros-
elytizers, and every bumper-sticker moralizer who ever sat on a PBS
fundraiser phone bank.

Glenn was familiar with this latest generation of health food dispen-
saries. They always seemed to have a decided political element to them,
a sententious ethos, a socially conscientious gestalt that trumpeted the
sensibilities of its proprietors to attract like-minded customers. In this
instance, Glenn concluded, the name was crafted to convey an association with the titles given to great works of art and literature, like
Middlemarch: A Study of Provincial Life or *Gare Montparnasse: The
Melancholy of Departure.* The intended effect was lost on him, inasmuch
as he thought the name sounded like one of the restaurant chains his parents frequented back in St. Louis, like "Tavernalium: A Gathering Spot"
or "Tony Roma's: A Place for Ribs."

The primary business name, Silverbeet, was sleek and modern without scaring away patrons in search of pumpkin-patch wholesomeness.
The subtitle, A Source Cleanse Resistance, expressed a much more sub-
versive sentiment. "Source" was a shibboleth that frequently appeared
on menus around Glenn's Gentilly neighborhood to signal their loyalty
to the small farmer and his modest but plump harvest. Glenn always
felt reassured that fresh ingredients would be served when he spotted
the word on any menu. The word "Cleanse" in the subtitle conveyed a
slightly more polemical sentiment, as if to say, "Eat here to purge body
and soul of all things toxic, exploitative, colonial, and oppressive." It
was small-business sloganeering that denounced supermarket pesticides
and American agribusiness in general. "Resistance" was positively ten-
dentious, even to Glenn, who considered it a hortatory identity badge
that spoke in sympathy with a labor class wriggling under the jack-
boot of an industrialized, capitalist West. In its totality, the juice bar's
name struck him as a rallying point for the innocent victims of global
profiteering and the urban consumers who sympathized with them. All
of this messaging from a tiny restaurant that offered fresh-squeezed
refreshments at $12.95 a glass.

Glenn parked his car on Magazine Street, walked a short distance to the entrance, and took a seat at a small white Formica table. He had a few minutes before Caroline arrived, so he busied himself with the touchless QR menu code-square that had been printed on a white paper card and slipped into a standing tabletop acrylic displayette. Once he had scanned the digitized image onto his smartphone, he was able to download the full menu and browse. It listed all kinds of tonics, ambrosines, nostrums, elixirs, and purgative electuaries made from blended ingredients like Tunisian rosemary, Madagascar vanilla, Carpathian nutmeg, and Albanian tarragon. The pastry section of the menu had things like house-made sourdough clusters with shingled root flakes and gooseberry barley margarine.

All he wanted was a cup of coffee, but nothing so ordinary was listed. When the waitress came to his table, he took a moment to read the epigram printed in black lettering across the front of her white T-shirt. He read it out loud to show playful agreeability:

"'I'M OK, YOU'RE A FRENCH POST-STRUCTURALIST.' Well," he continued, "and so am I!" He hoped the playful remark would make her laugh. It did not.

After retreating with a nervous cough, he made some happy inquiries and tried to disguise the fact that he was slightly intimidated by the modern juice bar experience. The waitress was in her mid-twenties and wore a single silver-droplet piercing in the tragus of her left ear. There were unreadable glyphs tattooed on the insides of her forearms.

"What do you have in the way of a good ole cuppa coffee?" Now he was being sarcastic, insulting the pretentiousness of the establishment by posing as the aw-shucks simpleton who found the menu to be incomprehensibly silly to someone from his neck of the woods. She softened a little and suggested the closest thing available: a large granite-pressed Garifuna coffee and Burundi chicory. He accepted, and it was soon served to him in an oversized porcelain coffee mug, which he appreciated.

After one sip of the hot concoction, Caroline appeared at the front door of Silverbeet. He waved at her from the table without standing up.

She acknowledged him and made her way between the other tables. By the time she reached him, she seemed a little short of breath. It struck him that she was trying to give the impression that she was a busy professional who had only just managed to squeeze in this appointment by the grace of an unexpected opening in a crazy-tight schedule. She was certainly showing a lot more self-assurance than she had when she was baring her soul at the AA meeting.

He spoke as she sat. "I already ordered a cup of coffee. Do you want something?"

Just then, the waitress returned to their table. Caroline crossed her legs beneath the table, arranged her laptop in the customary way, and greeted the waitress in a tone of easy familiarity.

"Hi, Thisbe. I'll just have a large deep-kale gland flush, one pump of turbinado emulsion, no husks. Thanks."

Thisbe seemed to know exactly what Caroline was talking about and looked at Glenn: "Do you need a refill on your Garifuna?"

"No, thanks, I'm fine. Just put her on my tab, would you?"

Glenn reflected on the cavalier manner in which Caroline had placed such a complicated order. It struck him that she was showing off just a bit, that she and Thisbe were staging a performance piece for his benefit. The qualified affectation—*just a deep kale*—was an off-hand understatement, a routine flippancy that demonstrated her proficiency with the restaurant's exoticism. She was using the secret language of Silverbeet in a curiously everyday way. Caroline was talking to Thisbe, but she meant for the mysterious terminology to stir enough curiosity in Glenn that he would ask questions. It was, Glenn immediately recognized, a technique people often employ to make themselves suddenly, and by design, the sole source of necessary information. Glenn decided to bite.

"*No husks*?" Glenn asked, playing right along as if he were genuinely curious to learn the basics from an old veteran like Caroline. He was willing to flatter her.

"Oh. Sorry about that. Didn't mean to sound so fussy. What I meant was they'll, like, strain the tamarind seeds, so you don't have to deal with the husks. Some people like them. They get caught in my teeth. Most *jugaleñas* know how to strain. A lot of customers request it."

"Hooga . . . what did you say?"

"*Jugaleñas*. They're called *jugaleñas* at a juice bar. *Barristas* at a coffee bar. It's a different training platform."

Glenn tried to seem grateful for her patience with his ignorance, happy enough was he to provide Caroline the opening every expert jumps at: an invitation to dilate on an esoteric subject. Nothing is more appetizing to a graduate assistant than a fawning undergraduate. Soliciting Caroline on matters of juice bar protocol was, he reasoned, a blandishment he hoped would build trust. He would use that to his advantage when pitching the sizzler he had contrived since first hearing the details of her episode in North Carolina.

"I gotcha." Glenn was ready to move on. "Thanks for meeting with me, and thanks for recommending this great spot. I've never heard of this place, but everything looks delicious."

"I come here literally all the time. I actually feel so much better, physically, I mean, eating natural. It makes me feel, like, energized and peaceful at the same time."

"I could use a little of that myself," said Glenn. "And if I'm going to take in calories, it might as well be healthy ones."

"I feel the same way. And I think it dovetails with The Program and what we're trying to accomplish there."

"That's a good point. It all works together. I'm glad you're feeling good. And you're looking good, too." He had to be careful here. He didn't want to give the impression he was on the make, so he quickly changed gears and got to the reason for the meeting. "Listen, I think you need to consider further action after what happened to you in North Carolina. I think you've been victimized, and it's probably important that your assailant, uh, your doctor, be held accountable, not just to you but to prevent future victims. Do you know what I mean?"

"Yes, I know. I hate that guy, and I'd hate to think what might be happening to other patients. I'd at least like to report it to the college. I thought about doing that at the time. I didn't really lodge an official complaint. I guess I lost my nerve. I was in a pretty bad place back then. I mean, you know, a fragile state."

"Oh, I understand completely. It probably wouldn't have been wise to go through with an official complaint while you were still living up there. You know, while you were still in his care. I certainly doubt they'd ever believe you, right in the middle of your treatment. They would have just asked him about it directly, and he would have dismissed it as the frustrations of a young girl—you know, a chemically dependent patient. They pretty much want to keep those things as quiet as possible, like it's for your own good."

"That's exactly the impression I got. By the time I got home, I wanted to tell my parents. When I did, they seemed even less receptive than the people I talked to in North Carolina. Especially my mom."

"Oh, you brought it up with your parents?"

"Yeah, it got pretty ugly. They didn't see any point in reopening old wounds. I thought when I told them about the abortion, they would be more, like, sympathetic. But that seemed to make them more resistant. Especially my mother. My father is much more sympathetic, but he gets bossed around by my mother and doesn't do anything on his own. I actually feel sorry for him. It's a fucked-up relationship, their marriage."

Glenn had almost forgotten that important detail—Caroline had gotten an abortion. She said it was the doctor's, though he could not be certain. People in recovery don't always tell the truth, but he was fairly sure that she was sexually involved with him because that kind of thing had been known to happen in the psychiatric treatment of addicts. Or so he allowed himself to presume in order to capitalize on the opportunity. He thought it prudent to investigate the matter directly with her to determine for himself its validity.

"I have to ask, did the relationship, I mean the sexual relationship, take place the entire time you were under treatment?"

"It started pretty soon after I got into his program. At first, I really liked him. He was so easy to talk to, and he had such genuine concern.

Maybe he still does, I don't know. But pretty soon, I developed feelings for him. I became attracted to him, in spite of his age. He's almost seventy, or maybe more, I don't know."

"So did these encounters, these intimate moments, occur in his office? Or did you take it somewhere more private? Like your dorm room or maybe his house?"

"Oh, it was always at his house. His wife was never there, or maybe he didn't have one. I didn't really know. I didn't really care. I was in such a state that I just wanted to be comforted. The whole affair actually felt good for a while. But it wasn't long before I sensed that he just wanted sex. The therapy talk got less and less clinical towards the end."

"It sounds like he definitely took advantage of you. You were in a very vulnerable place. You became codependent, and you got abused. That's what it sounds like to me, anyway."

"There's no doubt about it. He did send money when I told him I was pregnant. It was enough to cover the cost of the abortion, and then some. I spent the rest on . . . Well, you know, I was in a bad place."

"No, I understand completely. You were traumatized. You can't be expected to act completely rationally under that kind of stress."

Glenn was satisfied that a sexual battery had taken place, or, at a minimum, an act of medical malpractice. It was an opportunity in the conversation to suggest the possibility of civil litigation.

"Caroline, I think you're sitting on a pretty valid lawsuit. As I said, not just for your own benefit but to protect others in the future. In any case, you would have an easy claim against the doctor as well as the college for emotional damages. It wouldn't necessarily involve a lot of publicity. I don't even think you would actually have to file a lawsuit. I think it could be done just with a letter. You would be sending a message to him and his employer—the college—that you aren't going to sit idly by to have this thing swept under the rug. And you could get a nice little settlement for yourself. All your own. Untaxable and independent of what you rely on from your parents. A little financial security that your parents might not even have to know about."

"I already asked them about the possibility of a lawsuit, and they were dead set against it. The problem is my younger sister. She's supposed to be presented at Carnival balls this year. My parents don't want to jeopardize that with a scandal. I don't really want to ruin anything for my sister either. Not that she really cares. I think she's only going through the society bullshit because my parents are making her. She's still in college."

"That's the beauty of a simple letter demand. There would be no actual lawsuit filed, so there would be no publicity. If things go like I expect them to, the lawyer would simply write a letter to the college, and a check would be sent to you in two seconds flat. The college doesn't want the publicity any more than your parents do. It's a perfect setup."

"You know a lawyer who'd be willing to send such a letter?"

Glenn had her locked in. "Oh, very definitely. I have just the guy. He's a friend of mine who will understand the sensitivity of the case and can do exactly as we . . . as you . . . dictate. I'll be there to help you all the way through it. I understand what you're going through. You won't have to do anything. You won't have to go to an interview or testify or any of those uncomfortable things. And best of all, the doctor will be punished for what he did. I'm sure that's what you want more than anything."

"I definitely think he should be punished. I just don't know how I'm going to explain it to my parents."

"You don't have to. They never have to know about it. I'm not trying to put you at odds with your family, but they're probably better off not knowing anyway. Besides, I'm not sure it's any of their business. You're an adult. You don't need their consent to take care of yourself."

"That's true. I need to separate myself from them anyway. I'm convinced my mental state and all the things I've been through are actually their fault. Mainly my mother. She's the real problem."

"Don't mention it to either of them just yet. Let's get the lawyer lined up, and, when the time comes, you can discuss it with your father. If you think it's appropriate. You don't have to, but you might be able to."

Glenn was convinced he had gained Caroline's trust. It didn't matter to him that the prospect of eliminating Dr. Caldwell as a threat to other girls under his care was, by itself, enough to convince Caroline that some sort of a complaint should be filed. But he was not going to take any chances. If he could frame the idea of a lawsuit in a way that also appealed to her desire for financial independence, so much the better. But Glenn was shrewdly aware that it might also appeal to a twentysomething's inclination to be a part of the latest pop culture phenomenon: public disclosure of a buried sexual victimhood. Movie stars and popular music icons were generating publicity with bombshells of this sort.

Though he would never admit that he was serving his own self-interest, Glenn liked to think of himself in that category—an empathetic soldier with the battle scars of substance-abuse recovery to prove it. He was offering Caroline the chance and the means to join a special group of wounded innocents who, by bravely disclosing an embarrassing life event, had become worthy of public admiration. The virtue diploma earned by filing a lawsuit would be, for Caroline, a prestigious item for her résumé. It might be nice for her to feel like a part of the movement. And Glenn could be the person to award the sticker for her lapel, like the ones that read "I Voted" or "I Gave Blood" or "I Returned My Shopping Cart"— like the Shoulder Pharisees of Ancient Israel who wore evidence of their good deeds and agonies-of-piety on their dusty cloaks. An insecure girl like Caroline could use the recognition.

At the same time, Glenn didn't want to seem like he was encouraging her to participate in a fad. If she saw through him, she might suspect that he was motivated by greed or some other selfish dividend. He had to trust that his skills as a salesman were keeping the manipulation hidden. If successful, it would be one of his more brilliant displays of psychological finesse. But he still had to justify his self-interest by holding himself out as a champion of the weak and defenseless. "What we do for charity," his Jesuit instructors always taught, "is between us and God." As Glenn had come to understand things, that was not necessarily the case when it came time to convince Caroline that the proposed lawsuit was worthwhile.

A malpractice settlement—paid by the doctor or the college or both—would yield a sweet referral fee that he could negotiate with Jerry

Sonthonax ahead of time. It would be an amount much greater than the consulting fee he would earn from the grocery store extortion *brioche*. Either way, he would be providing cash to Sonthonax, a desperate politician on rocky financial ground. At the same time, he would be fulfilling his obligations to Burton Clayton as part of their ongoing business relationship.

Things were coming together perfectly. He knew he was exploiting his position as a political insider, as well as his confidential membership in Alcoholics Anonymous, but he was helping other deserving people in the process. Moral justification for opportunism always ratifies a particular course of action, however unscrupulous that course of action might seem. Exitus acta probat.

"Just think about it and call me in the next few days. I have to leave here and go to another appointment, but you can always reach me on my cell phone. Sound good?"

"Yep. I have somewhere to be also. I'll call you later. And thanks very much for helping me. I'm sorry to bother you with all this. I guess it's all part of recovery."

Glenn had managed to make her think she was asking him for help and not the other way around. He tried to reassure her by sounding magnanimous. "You're not bothering me. We're supposed to be helping each other. It's one of the twelve steps. Just call me. I'm sure you'll have questions. But don't sit on this for too long. I don't want it to mess you up. It's probably best if we deal with it as soon as possible."

As they stood from their table to depart, Glenn and Caroline embraced briefly and set off in opposite directions for the rest of their day's affairs. Suddenly, Glenn remembered he had neglected to pay the bill, so he reentered Silverbeet as Caroline disappeared down Magazine Street. He managed to catch Thisbe's attention before she had time to realize that he had run out on the check.

"I'm an idiot. I forgot to pay!" he exclaimed, waving a credit card above his head that he pinched lightly between thumb and forefinger. He wanted to show that he intended to square up in spite of his absent-mindedness.

Thisbe offered a smile of forgiveness and directed him to the front counter, where the transaction could be finalized: "No worries. I'll take you right up here."

After several feeble attempts, Glenn conceded defeat to the credit card swipe device—as well as its chip-touch sensor option—and ultimately welcomed Thisbe's assistance. It struck him that his struggles with computer technology might be a sign that his age had made certain parts of everyday life impossible to conduct without difficulty. It might not be too late to learn how to scan a contactless digital matrix menu code or initialize a credit card chip reader, but his days on the outdoor concert circuit were certainly numbered. He remained confident, however, that his talent for delicate negotiations on behalf of client-politicians was undiminished. Soon enough, he would be relying on that aptitude to convince the owners of the Phuoc Tho Duong Grocery that his influence over Burton Clayton made his tax-relief services indispensable. The possible language barrier was a concern, but everybody understands political blackmail. Vietnamese brigands, he reassured himself without any specific knowledge that such characters existed, had surely visited Mrs. Nguyen with threats of firebombs and other disruptions to her livelihood, if not here in the United States, then perhaps back in her homeland. After all, Mrs. Nguyen had chosen to engage in an illegal enterprise, so she should be accustomed to dealing with the jackals that always appear at the slightest whiff of an extortion opportunity. If the background information provided by Jerry Sonthonax was accurate, Mrs. Nguyen was a veteran of the black-market economics of war-torn Vietnam. The appearance of government thugs with party badges and concealed truncheons was an inevitable part of doing business. In any case, Glenn was sure to get the message across with his customary winking charm.

—

The iDrive GPS navigation system in his BMW X6 SUV plotted a course to the Phuoc Tho Duong Grocery that began on Napoleon Avenue, which at its lake-bound terminus becomes Broad Street and then bends east past the criminal courthouse. From there, the GPS roadmap directed him onto Gentilly Boulevard, past the Fair Grounds Race Course, through Gentilly Terrace and his home neighborhood, and then out to New Orleans East via Chef Menteur Highway. He was surprised to see just how far out the grocery store mission was going to take him. He had never been such a distance on Chef Menteur, but it looked like a straight shot to the Vietnamese section where the grocery stood.

Just as he had begun his drive out to the Far East, his speakerphone rang, and he saw on the Bluetooth dashboard navigation screen that his wife, Strickland, was calling. Always happy when she called, he pressed the "Answer" button on the right side of the multipurpose steering-wheel spoke. Whenever he used the hands-free phone system in his car, he felt it necessary to raise his voice so that it would carry through the ether of the cabin with sufficient force to be heard by the distant recipient.

"Hey!" he enthused with a cheerful familiarity that showed he knew who was calling even before she identified herself.

"Why are you screaming?" she asked in a censorious tone intended to make clear that she was irritated with his habit of shouting into the invisible microphone whenever she called him in his car.

He acknowledged the offense by making the necessary adjustment: "Oh. Sorry. Just trying to make sure you can hear me. What's up?"

"Where are you?"

"I'm in my car headed to an appointment. Everything okay?" He tried to shift the conversation away from the offensiveness of his telephone speaking voice by asking after her as if he was prepared to come to the rescue.

She ignored the mollification: "I just got out of a meeting at the Ziskind Center. They were talking about the constitutional amendment on the assessor's office. Do you know anything about this?"

"Awwww," he began dismissively. "They try that every year. The rest of the state hates New Orleans. It's a racist thing. We're the only city with more than one assessor, and they're trying to dismantle the system now that we have a solid Black majority. I wouldn't worry about it. The thing fails every time."

It was true. The state legislature had for years entertained a variety of bills that would abolish the city's multi-assessor system, but they had all failed in committee. It was just like congressional attempts to confer statehood on the District of Columbia: a lingering sentiment that, for one reason or another, never made it into law. Whenever he was asked about the possibility of assessor consolidation, he would wave it off as the pipe-dream of anti-urban reactionaries.

It was nevertheless troubling that his wife considered the threat of assessor consolidation a matter of concern to him specifically. He wondered whether she had deduced that his livelihood depended on Burton Clayton's stranglehold on the CBD assessor's district. She knew, of course, that he was in the real estate consulting business, but he had never discussed with her the precise reasons behind his political alliance with Burton.

"I don't understand why it would be a racial thing," she persisted with a line of inquiry that was making him uncomfortable. "If the assessor's office was consolidated into one position, it would still be put to a city-wide vote. How is that disruptive to majority-minority rule?"

He didn't really have an answer for that. And he most certainly didn't want to let on that a consolidation of the assessor's office would be fatal to his career as Burton's bag man. So, he sidestepped the question by dismissing it as a matter of strictly academic amusement: "It's a moot point. The House Ways and Means Committee is packed with relatives of sitting assessors. They'll never vote it through to the full House. I don't see why anyone at the Ziskind Center would suddenly have an interest in this." He did not disclose that one of Burton's nephews was on the House Ways and Means Committee alongside other Burton surrogates who owed their seats to his formidable political influence.

She must have felt insulted by the way he so quickly brushed aside the discussions taking place at the Ziskind Center because she gave him the silent treatment. It lasted long enough that he pretended the cellular connection had been broken.

"Hello?" he asked. "Strickland? Did I lose you?"

She didn't fall for it and, instead, continued the uncomfortable conversation by asking an even more difficult question: "Who are you meeting with?"

He considered lying. She was not generally interested in the people he dealt with during business hours, so he had never had to provide those kinds of specifics. In this instance, it couldn't hurt to tell the truth because there was no way for her to draw conclusions about his shady business practices. So, he told her: "Nobody important. Just some folks out in New Orleans East. They're Vietnamese, actually. It's really just a favor I'm doing. I'm not even sure they speak English, so I don't expect the meeting to last too long!" It was another jokey remark intended to downplay the significance of the meeting at Phuoc Tho Duong Grocery.

"I see," she said in a tone of *yeah-right* incredulity. She did not, however, seem inclined to press for a more specific explanation. It was a courtesy he took advantage of by staying silent himself. She was obviously put out by his evasiveness. He could tell because she abruptly ended the phone call: "Okay. My meeting's starting back up. Gotta go."

Before he could say, "Okay. Bye," she had already hung up. The GPS graphic reappeared on the dashboard display of his onboard navigation system, and he resumed his voyage to the mysterious Levant with an unexpected sense of guilt. Whether it was due to the fact that he had not come completely clean with his wife, he could not say. Perhaps it wasn't guilt that he felt at all. It could have been misgivings about the negotiations he had agreed to undertake on behalf of a politician other than Burton Clayton in an assessment district outside his usual sphere of operations.

Either way, his luxury car seat was suddenly feeling uncomfortable.

11

Attendance at the Hiller-Bloch Gallery art opening was mandatory. The Calloway family was in crisis, but Hildy and her obedient husband, Lecky, were not going to give the world reason to talk by altering their social schedule. When life's priority is social standing, it's imperative to maintain a perfect attendance record at all the same parties, balls, openings, and galas they had logged before the Caroline Situation arose. Conspicuous participation in events like the Hiller-Bloch art opening would preserve the appearance that the Calloways were sailing through life in a manner befitting their wealth and status. It was important for their smiling faces to be counted by society registrars.

There had been a time when Lecky enjoyed these occasions. It was once intoxicating to circulate in the foam of the *haute bohème*. But his enthusiasm was flagging. His concerns about Caroline's emotional condition were gradually supplanting his need to be seen with all the right people at all the right places. And, what was more, he was gradually marshalling the courage to break free from his suffocating marriage and, at last, come out of the closet.

It might have been spiteful, but Lecky took pleasure in the fact that his wife's world was under siege and that she didn't even know it. Lecky would be long gone before Hildy had the chance to foil his plans. But for now, it was enough to know that an insurrection of his own design was coming together.

After gathering their keychains and other personal effects from ceramic bowls near the kitchen door, they descended the rear staircase onto the paved surface of the carport. Lecky uncharacteristically, but very deliberately, walked toward the driver's side of his wife's Mercedes-Benz as if he were going to be doing the driving. Though there was no doubt they would be arriving at the gallery opening in Hildy's Mercedes, it was almost unthinkable that Lecky would be driving. Hildy stopped at the bottom of the stairs in disbelief that Lecky would assert himself with such impertinence.

"What's this all about?"

"What's what all about?"

"You seem to be getting in the driver's seat."

"I thought I'd drive us downtown," he said as he opened the driver's-side door, lifted his right leg, and placed his right foot on the floorboard of the Mercedes with such purpose that she scarcely had time to protest.

"The seat and the mirrors are all memory-set to my preferences."

Lecky smiled as if to say, "I can make the necessary adjustments." As a matter of fact, he said as much: "I can make the necessary adjustments. They're not permanent."

"Oh. Well, I suppose. What's the difference." The quick surrender on her part, Lecky concluded, was meant to make his boyish attempt at daddy-takes-charge captaincy seem silly and inconsequential. But he considered it a small victory, especially when she walked directly to the passenger side of the Mercedes and stumbled slightly.

Carpet-clad in yards of beaded damask, she came to berth in the front passenger seat with such mass that the car rolled on its stabilizer springs. The car wobbled again when she pressed her feet against the floorboard and forced her shoulders against the seatback to facilitate the seat belt fastening procedure. Lecky waited patiently for her to get settled before turning the car's ignition key. *Who is this woman, and why am I in the front seat of a Mercedes with her?*

Whoever she was, he had claimed stewardship of the evening's logistics. He backed the Mercedes out of the carport onto Duffossat Street and threw the gear lever into "drive" with an abruptness that caused Hildy's head and shoulders to pitch backward sharply as she was taking an inventory of the contents of her purse. She turned to glare at him for the rudeness of his operation of the luxury car, but he kept his eyes forward to leave no doubt that the coup de maître was underway. She maintained her glare. But Lecky would not give her the satisfaction of knowing that he was aware of it or, even more, that he would be intimidated by it. So confident was he in this realignment of battlefield forces that he brought up the almost unspeakable topic of the Caroline Situation as they drove.

"I've been thinking about this situation, and I'm moving more and more towards the belief that a lawsuit should be filed." He tried to say it in a conclusory way, as if his opinion was actually a contributing part of their joint decision-making process or even that he had authority to decide such things unilaterally. At a minimum, he was hoping to jar his wife just enough to clear a spot for himself at the negotiating table. It had no such effect. Hildy had, by then, returned her attention to the contents of her purse and never looked up to dignify the brazenness of his statement. She was not in the habit of letting on that his opinion on such things really mattered.

Instead, she waved it off on the air. "We both know that's not going to happen." She spoke without any hesitation, as if she had never conceded the smallest fraction of her authority in the first place. "Take St. Charles Avenue all the way to Lee Circle and make a left on Camp."

Lecky knew immediately that it would not be easy to engage her in substantive discussions of the Caroline Situation. He accepted the fact that she was in no mood to renounce her customary place in the relationship. By instructing him to take a specific course to the art gallery, she was trying to beat back his audacity with a shrug. Lecky considered taking an alternate route in defiance of her instructions, but he could not, at that moment, think of another way to get there.

Instead, he raised the subject of Caroline once more: "A lawsuit against Longleaf College would not only be for her benefit—or for our benefit. The college needs to know the score. Who knows how many other girls have been abused by this doctor? There may have been others before, and there are probably more to come. It seems like we have a responsibility to other patients he's treating, or will be treating, who have been abused. It just seems like the responsible thing to do."

This got her attention. She thrust her forearms sharply against the opened edges of her purse, which crumpled under the force of her bone mass. She shifted her body weight onto her left hip to look directly at him. Her mouth opened and remained so for a few seconds before she spoke.

"We have been through all of this. She's as much at fault as he is if what she claims is true—though I have my doubts. And now she wants to throw our lives into a tailspin? What about Ainsley? What are we supposed to tell her? Caroline thinks now is the best time to think only of herself? I'm sorry. I'm not gonna encourage that behavior. And neither are you. You're being just as selfish as she is."

For the first time, Lecky found some satisfaction in the disruptive effect he could introduce to his wife's sense of family orderliness. He had issued the challenge and decided that he would be silent and watch what might flow from the pierced abscess.

"Did you hear what I said?" she asked in a tone most serious and a volume most desperate. "Don't you see a lawsuit would be a disaster? Don't you know that we would be humiliated? Would you stop and think about Ainsley for a minute? She didn't do anything wrong, and now you want to embarrass her just when it's her year."

At that moment, Lecky knew that he'd succeeded in forcing his wife to express her real priorities in life—that she was more concerned about the consequences of a social scandal than she was about the rape of her own daughter. On top of that, she was shrewdly suggesting that Caroline's selfishness was somehow a direct attack on Ainsley, her innocent sister. It was an indignation he saw right through, an accusation she was making to disguise her own social agenda and shallowness.

That was enough turmoil for the time being, so Lecky turned his thoughts and the Mercedes to the Hiller-Bloch Gallery art opening on Julia Street. As he backed the car into a parking spot on Camp Street, both of them remained silent. The silence continued as they made their way to the gallery entrance.

A gallery opening at Hiller-Bloch was always, as it was on this night, a glittering affair. It was not an especially aristocratic event, such as a debutante party, a Carnival ball, or a Christmas celebration at one of the exclusive men's clubs downtown. But it carried social significance nevertheless, more like a museum fundraiser or other charity gala. There would be well-to-do Blacks, immigrant-stock but powerful politicians, wealthy trial lawyers and their taxidermified wives, directors of non-profit outreach organizations, celebrated but impoverished musicians, stylish homosexuals, and *Geldsäcke* Jews—none of the bloodless mandarins that dwelt in the upper echelons of patinated old-family privacy but important, nonetheless, in the parallel universe of *la bonne compagnie*. In a way, it was becoming more important to participate in the celebration of *Art* than it was to maintain the traditional institutions of high-born insularity. Some could do both, and some could do one to the exclusion of the other. Hildy and Lecky Calloway liked to think they possessed the cultivated tastes that would be welcomed in artists' precincts, notwithstanding their Tory political beliefs and aristocratic sympathies. That night's opening at the Hiller-Bloch Gallery was an occasion to demonstrate as much. That was part of the reason their attendance was mandatory.

The artists whose paintings were making their debut were not local. They were transplants who had moved to New Orleans based on a fondness for its perceived cosmopolitan diversity and celebrated appreciation of minority (especially Black) cultural traditions. Episcopalians like Hildy and Lecky Calloway, the natural enemies of socialist provocateurs and uppity ethnic minorities, were always keen to overcome the perception that they were closed-minded by showing support for emerging artists as if they, too, were part of an enlightened class.

It was, perhaps, inconsistent with the exclusionism of the White establishment in which they held a prominent position, but everyone was doing it. Besides, neither the Hiller-Bloch Gallery nor the artists they represented were inclined to refuse cash from slumming bluebloods, no matter what their motivations might be.

Hildy and Lecky Calloway entered the gallery from the Julia Street sidewalk through a flagstone loggia into a bright gallery space with glossy white walls and track lighting. The space was so jam-packed with people that Lecky could not at first see whether any paintings had been hung. The patrons who held champagne flutes and chatted noisily were dressed for the occasion. Nearly all the men wore sport coats without ties. The women's outfits were more varied depending on their age and weight.

Both men and women alike, almost without exception, wore some kind of scarf, each with a special knot: some simply wound the scarf once around the neck and let the ends hang low, some wound them two or three times around their necks in a strangling effect that resembled *Les Incroyables* and *Merveilleuses* of post-revolutionary France. One elderly but tall woman with dyed black hair had wrapped a ribbon of thin gauze around her long neck that resembled the golden choker in Klimt's *Judith and the Head of Holofernes*. One well-dressed gentleman had doubled over the length of his scarf and fed the two ends through a loop created by the fold. Another woman had even fashioned her scarf into a complicated braid that looked like a loaf of challah bread.

The gay men wore loafers and no socks. The older lesbians with long gray hair wore ankle-length denim dresses and flesh-colored sandals with straps that ran horizontally across their metatarsals instead of between the toes. The younger lesbians who had not entirely abandoned their femininity wore creased linen Capri trousers in a variety of pastel colors and matching flat T-strap thong sandals. They seemed to prefer tiny earrings and kept their frosted, razor-cut hair very short. Lecky noticed that they sometimes held hands with one another. The Black or mixed-raced men tended to wear white linen suits. Many of the Black women wore mustard-yellow maxi dresses, colorful tignons, and large hooped earrings of gold.

Lecky, in his worsted-wool suit and printed silk tie, was forced to acknowledge that his style had never graduated from what he had learned in his early years as a lawyer. Still, he wore a gold collar pin beneath the knot of his necktie, which, if not up-to-the-minute, was at least sharp. Hildy wore her usual sleeveless knee-length brocade dress that might be described as *Matron Frump*. Lecky was slightly embarrassed by their hopelessly American mothball mediocrity.

As they made their way deeper into the gallery, Hildy saw someone she knew from the board of directors of an architectural preservation concern and was soon in the vortex of an overanimated conversation. His wife was wiggling her lips like a monkey cleaning shrimp. Lecky took the opportunity to survey on his own the actual artwork on display. The gallery was known for promoting anti-traditional, nonobjective art.

It was looking like, on that night, the gallery was living up to its reputation as a repository of modernist art orthodoxy, but Lecky intended to do his best to appreciate what the Hiller-Bloch Gallery had to offer. The title of the exhibit certainly challenged him to do so:

AVOID THE OBVIOUS. EMBRACE THE ETHEREAL.

The first artist featured was a woman named Sophia Murchison-Merks, a graduate of the Rhode Island School of Design and the recipient of a master of fine arts degree from Boston University. According to her brief biography, she had been raised in Connecticut and spent much of her childhood touring the museums on which her parents served as board members. Lecky immediately concluded that she was a privileged heiress who had the wherewithal for a leisure-class education. Her interests, the biography continued, led her to all parts of the globe and the farthest reaches of human settlement, primitive or otherwise. An avid photographer, she had assembled a collection of images and cultural artifacts that formed the basis of her artistic *œuvre*. The collection of paintings on display was entitled "Distant Climes, Inner Resonance."

Lecky was not entirely sure what that meant, but he could expect that the paintings would be abstract. His personal taste in art, such as it was, tended more toward the figurative, but he understood that deference to Hiller-Bloch's expertise would be required if he were to avoid being lumped in with the philistines.

On a rigid poster board next to the series of hung pieces, the gallery's directors provided an introduction to the artistic stylings of Ms. Murchison-Merks:

> *Calling upon the sub-conscious qua consciousness, Murchison-Merks probes the crevices of intellect for deposits of unreified emotion. Verisimilitude and imposture are consigned to their temporal limits, and the imagination is given voice. The traditional vocabularies of painting give way to more expressive techniques capable of metaphysical discourse.*
>
> *Each of the works in this series employs gesture and tone to the service of poetry. Murchison-Merks says of her process: "I ask the shapes and pigments to reveal themselves as I paint, without preconception or boundary. Though the images originate from my personal experience, they carry a sense of the universal. They are narrative only because they can be heard, like a whimper or a yawp." The primordial freshness of these watercolors at once assaults and caresses the viewer with a sensory communion that is, at first, irresistible and ultimately sublime.*

Moving left to right from this précis, Lecky saw that the Sophia Murchison-Merks paintings were indeed watercolor abstractions. The first piece was entitled *Sense Memory: Iridescence of the Tufted Cloud VII*. He immediately wondered whether he had missed numbers I through VI or whether they might be hung in another part of the gallery. Perhaps they had already been sold. In any case, he supposed it could be appreciated on its own. The painting was 24" x 36" and consisted of soft billows of azure blue against a soft sky-blue background with smaller wisps of butter yellow. He gave himself credit for identifying the "tufted cloud," and it certainly seemed "iridescent." So far, so good.

The second piece was entitled *Persephone's Petals*. This one seemed to be less abstract insofar as it very obviously depicted the swollen female vulva: a *mandorla aureole* with swollen labia, a vesica piscis in varying shades of rose and carnation pink. The painting was also 24" x 36", and the vulva occupied almost the entire picture plane. There was no mistaking the image depicted in this watercolor. Lecky was embarrassed that he felt embarrassed, so he quickly moved on to the next piece in the series.

This one was entitled *Aurora Sensualis: She Softly Beckons*. This one was completely abstract, and Lecky struggled to make the connection between the title of the work and the work itself. The painting was also a suffusion of red shades—amaranth and magenta and solferino and musk-mallow pink—but no discernible shapes or suggestion of shapes were evident. It was color-field painting in its simplest form. Lecky was growing impatient with these mysterious paintings. It was impossible for him to generate an opinion on the statement, artistic or otherwise, they were trying to make. He had seen cake decorators with greater technical proficiency than was evident in the watercolors of Sophia Murchison-Merks. But that was not the point of Abstract Art, and he knew it. Perhaps other works at the exhibit would interest him enough to stimulate a deeper reaction, just in case he was later asked to comment on the exhibit.

The second artist was Rigoberta Palenque, and the exhibit was entitled "Garifuna! Por la Anarquia!" Her biography explained that she was an indigenous Mesoamerican from Belize on the first stop of a world tour. Rigoberta's portrait photograph captured her in traditional Mayan garb and an irascible scowl. Lecky hoped he could catch a glimpse of her in person later on. She figured to be quite a sight. Just as had been provided in the Sophia Murchison-Merks series, there was a poster board setting forth Rigoberta's artistic manifesto:

In this series, Rigoberta Palenque examines the injustices perpetrated against the peasant population of her homeland. In styles that range from the purest color-field abstraction to a glyph-symbolism of her own invention, Palenque harnesses the visual lyricism of her ancestral traditions. Whether juxtaposing shape upon tone or forsaking intelligibility for magical gibberish, Palenque's protestations express a visceral empathy.

The repression of indigenous peoples of color by imperialist interlopers serves as the basis for a body of work that knows only the language of anguish. Historical themes of feminism, racism, and classism pervade these canvases and force contemporary viewers to confront their own complicity and prejudice. Because art is uniquely suited to convey the urgency of human distress, Palenque employs an original artistic formulary to produce political imagery that raises awareness and demands action.

Lecky prepared himself to be disturbed, if he wasn't already. The first painting was called *Impactful Empath*. This was a fairly large canvas, 52" x 48". The framed piece was hung slightly higher than eye level, but the panel had been angled from the surface of the wall so that the beholder had to look up at the painting with his head tilted back. Lecky guessed that there must be some significance to this method, but he couldn't immediately fathom what it could be. For the time being, he would attempt to admire the picture itself, though he wasn't sure exactly where he should stand. It was an oil painting in which the entire surface of the canvas was painted fern green with the exception of a tiny brown circle at the bottom left-hand corner. Lecky had no idea what the title meant or how the work itself related to it, so he moved on to the next one.

It was entitled *Cisgender Patho-Normativity*. It was also positioned on the wall in the same manner as *Impactful Empath*, but there was much more going on. It seemed to be a stylized copy of the Mayan glyphs carved into the temples and reliquaries of Central American pyramids before the arrival of the Spanish. There were seated depictions of befeathered chieftains, crouching panthers, flaming firebirds, and other representative symbols from the Mayan syllabary. All these figures were arranged in a geometric grid that had a most appealing archaeological quality. Lecky had no idea what the figures represented or even spelled, but they were interesting to look at. What their relationship was to "Cisgender Patho-Normativity" Lecky could not say. He was not even sure what "Cisgender Patho-Normativity" meant. If asked later, he would nevertheless be able to discuss his reaction to the figurative aspect of the work.

The next offering from Rigoberta Palenque was entitled *Quintillions Ripen and Quintillions Brown*. This picture, also tilted from the wall, depicted ears of yellow corn exposed above their folded husks, one after another, in a regimental arrangement that filled the entire rectangular surface. Lecky actually enjoyed looking at this and the previous painting. They contained representational imagery that he could recognize. He had developed a certain confidence at this exhibition that he had not expected, and it served to distract him from the war he was waging with his wife.

Just as he moved to view the next painting by the surprisingly intriguing Rigoberta Palenque, he was interrupted by his wife, who seemed hot to make an introduction. Perfect timing, he thought, to discuss his appreciation of the artwork. But the opportunity to panegyrize about the groundbreaking art was almost immediately yanked from him. His wife had lassoed two younger men, probably in their thirties, obviously gay, one with a beautifully manicured beard that carpeted his face evenly in a soft brown pile and another, clean-shaven, whom he recognized immediately. It was Felix Peterbilt, the clothing salesman from Cinch at Nowak's.

Hildy had somehow managed to befriend the one person he had not expected to see that evening. She had already become so friendly with him and his companion that she could introduce the two cosmopolitan curiosities to Lecky as evidence of the easy mixing she could pull off among people other than country club regulars, as if they were souvenirs from an exotic adventure abroad.

"Lecky, this is Felix and his friend . . . I'm so sorry. What was your name again?"

"I'm Sean. I don't think I even told you my name. We were so quickly into our conversation. How are you, Lecky?"

Lecky shook hands with both men, trying not to betray that he was struck with terror. The sight of Felix in a public setting caught him flat-footed. The Cinch at Nowak's blow job was a memory set aside for a rainy day. The day of reckoning had arrived much sooner than expected.

Lecky scrambled for something to say, but he was dumbstruck. He could not gather himself enough to chat casually with his secret lover while his wife stood right next to him. He had, for some time, been building up the gumption to make a dramatic confession and break the news to Hildy that the marriage was over. But that note had not matured. For the moment, it was enough to swear to himself that he would turn his life around.

After the initial shock of seeing Felix had subsided, Lecky started to regain his equanimity. Circumstances were not as drastic as he first thought. It was a gallery opening, for heaven's sake. What better occasion could there be to give—temporarily, at least—his suppressed tendencies some breathing room?

Things were happening quickly. All at once, he was being asked to marvel at the seductive power of pigment, acknowledge his complicity in the repression of Central American peasants, and, on top of that, remain calm in the presence of Felix Peterbilt. It was one thing to absorb the demanding concepts of modern art but quite another to cope with his homosexuality right there on the spot.

He decided to put on a brave face. The time had come for him to make a break from it all: the pointless slog through the *must-be-seen* party circuit, the small-potatoes legal career, and the sexless marriage. He even felt plucky enough to question conventional notions that abstract art was at all impervious to criticism. It would be a sacrilege, a blasphemy, a downright apostasy to even suggest the possibility that modern art was anything less than the penetrating expressions of metaphysical geniuses.

Lecky had done some brief research on the genre so that he could speak knowledgeably with Stuart Whitcomb, the managing partner in his law firm who collected the stuff and whose favor he desperately sought. He had stumbled on a dirty little secret that the *intelligissima* had managed to bury. The New York School—the group of artists responsible for what became known as abstract expressionism, America's first original art movement—was bound together by a quasi-religious belief in the occult. Nobody remembered anymore that the basis for the radical art form was a bizarre sect known as Theosophy, a spiritualist polytheism of dubious origin. It had been invented out of thin air by one Madame Helena Petrovna, a Russian charlatan who claimed she could converse with departed souls from across the millennia and summon mysterious mahatmas by means of astral projection.

Lecky got no enjoyment from the unintelligible fingerpainting, let alone the overwrought politics of it all. He wondered whether the spurious premises of nonfigurative art, if brought to light, would undermine the high-minded snobbery of the art world. In any case, he would no longer have to feel inferior for failing to be moved by it—for missing the message. He had discovered a passageway for his exodus.

As he stood there in the gallery among the art lovers and the objects of their anserine admiration, his hatred for Hildy Thompson Calloway continued to crystallize. Hildy's insensitivity to Caroline's emotional well-being suddenly seemed monstrous. He was feeling certain that he should help his daughter, even if it meant defying his wife's direct orders. Yet, he couldn't let all of this introspection sidetrack him from the immediate reality that he was standing side by side with his wife while he was also face-to-face with his would-be boyfriend.

He was at Felix's mercy. Had Felix seen fit, he could have divulged to Hildy and anyone else at the gallery the details of his sexual encounter in the Cinch at Nowak's dressing room. But Felix seemed to be honoring the unspoken rule that homosexual indiscretions are not to be disclosed to unsuspecting wives. There seemed to be a stronger disinclination to do so when the indiscretion was a homosexual one than there might be if it involved, for example, a floozy secretary who wanted to blackmail her horny boss. But Felix showed no signs that he would abuse Lecky's vulnerability.

Felix's demeanor was so reassuring, in fact, that the initial sensation of fear Lecky experienced when he saw Felix from across the gallery completely disappeared. His attraction to the beautiful clothing sales-man grew even stronger because of that discretion. Felix was a good person, Lecky thought to himself, who understood the predicament of a gay man riding out a straight marriage. The resentment he felt for his wife increased correspondingly.

It was a nice feeling, Lecky thought, to have a romantic prospect, but it was complicated by the fact that Felix was with another man. He could not be certain that they, Felix and Sean, were there at the gallery as an exclusive couple. It was possible that Felix was in a relationship with Sean and that the episode at Nowak's was as much an act of infidelity on Felix's part as it was on Lecky's.

On the other hand, Felix and Sean might only be friends. Lecky accepted the possibility that they were friends in a way that he suspected was common in the gay-male community—that is to say, friends who might enjoy occasional sex without commitment. But Lecky really didn't know how that worked. His understanding of gay life was only guess-work. He had never wanted to be an open part of that culture because his designs on high society could not accommodate the aberration.

But things were beginning to shift in Lecky's worldview. Coveting his wife's money, ingratiating himself to aristocratic gatekeepers, and presenting himself as a healthy and responsible member of traditional American social order all seemed to be fading fast. The sight of Felix and the warmth of his understanding gave Lecky a sense of security and self-confidence. He suddenly had no use for any of the things he had devoted his life to.

Meanwhile, his wife was prattling on to Sean, who politely listened and responded in the spirit of her chitchat. The whole thing would have been horribly awkward had not Felix and Lecky kept cool as they, from time to time, glanced at each other in silence. Hildy continued the giggling badinage as the unknown reality of her husband's secrets swirled around her.

"I'm always delighted for a Hiller-Bloch opening. Always important artists and interesting work. I've bought so much in the past I don't know if I'll have room for anything more! Of course, I'll just have to scoop up some of these pieces. They're irresistible. I just love the colors."

"Oh, I'm sure you could find room in the maisonette," said Sean, trying to be charming with a droll understatement. His patience with Hildy's fatuous conversation was providing cover for Felix and Lecky to smile at one another without anyone, most of all Hildy, suspecting that they shared a secret. Sean kept up the interference: "You'll just have to build a new wing to put the new pieces!"

Hildy laughed at Sean's cleverness like she had seen a donkey eating thistles, even though Sean was teasing her a little bit. It was all in fun, but there was something more serious going on between Lecky and Felix. The fact that Sean was occupying Hildy by humoring her false modesty was confirmation that Sean knew the score, that he was hip to the game being played. He was, in fact, facilitating the secret romance. It also confirmed that Sean and Felix were not an item.

Meanwhile, Hildy's chatter had become even more unbearable: "Oh I don't think we have any more room for expansion after all we've done already. But we can always find room for art in our house. Of course, I leave all those decisions to my husband. Art is his department. I just handle the decorating."

This, of course, was total bullshit. Hildy Calloway wouldn't let a splinter of furniture or a stitch of canvas into the house without her explicit approval.

She went on, trying to leave the impression that at least some aspect of home décor—*fine art* in particular—was Lecky's exclusive province, as if he possessed an expertise that contributed to a balanced marital partnership. While he would never publicly traverse his wife's obvious overstatement, Lecky blanched at her campaign to promote him as the

Bernard Berenson of Uptown New Orleans. Through it all, Sean and Felix maintained polite smiles and gave the impression that they believed the ridiculous notion that Lecky might actually have a say in the acquisition of pieces for the prestigious Calloway Collection. It was the kind of remark she often made to captive acquaintances at cocktail parties, always in his presence and in a manner that came across as incidental but rehearsed, unctuous but dismissive, flattering but just barely tolerant. It was an awkward pantomime, but Lecky could only suffer in silence like a child whose adoring mother has forced him to wear a sailor suit that he has long since outgrown.

Hildy wouldn't stop. "Now, I'm sure the two of you have a similar arrangement at home. Would I be right?"

"Oh no," Sean said. "We don't live together. We're just friends. Of course, Felix could do with some supervision with his furniture. I don't think he cares too much about those sorts of things. Maybe you could help him!"

Hildy picked up the bit. "I'd be happy to! Just give me his credit card, and I'll be back in six months with a fresh image!"

Hildy and Sean laughed at the absurd proposition as Felix and Lecky chuckled on cue. The *plaisanterie* was harmless enough until Lecky remembered the legal assignment given to him by Dale Dutton earlier that day. He had been temporarily disoriented by the convergence of so many surprising assaults on his senses that he had forgotten about the Phuoc Tho Duong lawsuit.

His responsibilities as a lawyer were not a priority even under ordinary circumstances, but he suddenly realized that his relationship with Felix was a clear conflict of interest bordering on malpractice. Felix Peterbilt, the centerpiece of his intended future, was the same guy making a claim against his most important client. Lecky had failed to make the connection at first, but it came to him once he had absorbed the shock of Felix's surprise appearance, the heavy political messages of the artwork, his wife's shameless pandering to the smart set, his inchoate homosexual liberation, and his resolve to render emergency assistance to his troubled daughter.

Lecky found himself in an impossible situation. A lawyer cannot defend a lawsuit brought by his lover, homosexual or otherwise. He would be forced to reconcile his personal life with his legal career sooner than he had planned. If it meant quitting his job, so be it. Furthermore, he was ready to make his father-in-law's college buddy, Dr. Caldwell, pay for the abuse inflicted on Caroline at the drug treatment facility.

He was feeling mighty brave. It might also be time to file for a divorce.

12

FBI field surveillance, at least in Margot Hoang's experience, was the kind of exercise that throws patience against the thwarts of boredom. In most cases, hours could be spent behind the wheel of a parked car with binoculars pressed against her eye sockets while her stiffening legs shifted restlessly in the space underneath a General Motors steering column.

The Phuoc Tho Duong grocery store stakeout figured to be no different except that, in this particular instance, Margot might be making an undercover, on-the-premises visit for a closer look at business operations. She had dressed for the assignment in jeans, a white cap-sleeve, button-up shirt, and a pair of navy-blue Jack Purcell canvas tennis shoes. The outfit was a departure from the cargo pants and lugsoled mid-ankle trail shoes she usually wore to work. She would be leaving her badge, her Glock 19, and her portable two-way radio in the car if and when she received orders to get out of her unmarked car and enter the grocery store. The fifteen-minute drive from FBI headquarters on Leon C. Simon Drive to the target location in New Orleans East would provide the solitude and silence necessary for a field agent's mental preparation. But for Margot, it was an interlude she would use to daydream about Francis Ernst and the courtship that had, almost effortlessly, developed into something serious.

Earlier in the week, she had invited him to her parents' home for a traditional Vietnamese dinner. The time had come, in her estimation, to introduce Francis to the extended family. She was proud enough of her Vietnamese heritage to show off the agreeability and warmth of a traditional Catholic homestead, but it would also serve as a full disclosure of the family baggage. It was to be a critical step in the relationship. Francis could either accept them or be scared away, but she and her family came as an inseparable, packaged set. Margot was falling for him, so a homestyle evening with the whole clan would be a test case to determine whether a long-term commitment was going to work.

She was not as concerned that her parents would approve of him. He was, after all, Catholic and employed. She was much more apprehensive about his reaction to the *foreignness* of her family's Asian appearance and aspect, the ethno-immigrant peculiarities of a Vietnamese way of life that might come as a shock to him. Now that the meeting had taken place, she could enjoy reflecting on the fact that her anxiety had been unfounded.

The gathering had included not only her mother and father but her grandmother, her brother and sister-in-law, and their two girls, ages four and six. She knew a tribal panel of that size might seem imposing to a man who was fundamentally shy—not exactly diffident, but polite and personable, without falling all over himself to make a good impression on people he had never met. In short, he was a happy man—earnest, entirely free of guile and the ginned-up salesman's bonhomie that other suitors might affect on debut. It was the unforced quality of his personality she was attracted to and was falling in love with. She may have dreaded bringing another man, or another type of man, into the core of her family *castrum*, but she had confidence that Francis would meet the mark.

Margot's dreams were coming true. Rather than arriving together, she had asked him to meet her at the family home on Bergerac Place around the corner from Mary Queen of Vietnam Church so she would have time to help her mother and sister-in-law with the cooking. It would also give her some preliminary time to answer any questions the family might have about Francis before he arrived. She figured an hour's worth of background prep would dampen the excitement and smooth over the feverish activity that the anticipation of a special guest can often bring.

When she answered the door, she beheld Francis in his ill-fitting coat and tie, a sight that was endearing by its innocence, just as it was on their first date. As her two young nieces crowded around her in the entrance hall, she smiled at him warmly as a signal that he could relax. It dawned on her that the foreign smells of a Vietnamese home might be offensive to him. Too bad. It was too late to fret about something she wouldn't have been able to ameliorate anyway. He had arrived.

"Welcome to the Hoang home," she said as she offered her hand and cheek. The children fidgeted and tittered around her legs. They were curious to see the new visitor but suddenly shy when the moment of truth arrived. They put their once foreign but now more familiar fingers in their little mouths and clutched the pleats of Margot's white cotton skirt. "These are the munchkins who are very excited to see you!"

"Hello, everyone!" he answered in a tone that tried to match their bib-and-tucker playtime expectation. He turned to Margot and spoke confidentially: "I'm sorry about the coat and tie. Especially the tie. It's department issue. It goes with my dress uniform, and it's really the only tie I have."

"Oh no, you look fine! You didn't need to dress up. Here, let me take your jacket. You'll be more comfortable." She could see he was relieved to ditch the sport coat that she knew was not a regular part of his wardrobe. "Roll up your sleeves if you want. We're a casual bunch."

They walked from the entrance hall into the living room, where her father and brother were seated. The house was a one-story brick suburban ranch house, neat but confusingly cluttered with Oriental bibelots mixed in with ersatz French Rococo furniture and other Louis XV appointments. It was a gallimaufry of ormolu tchotchkes, pastel porcelains, gold picture frames, button-upholstered sofas and chairs with rosewood frames painted white, and wall-to-wall carpeting. On the far wall, there was a giant paper poster print of a Vietnamese fishing-village scene—colonial or precolonial stock characters in rolled trousers and bamboo coolie hats pulling fishing nets up to the beach of a romanti-cized southeast-Asian lagoon. Margot had a vague understanding that the décor was a naïve interpretation of Western affluence by Vietnamese immigrants with newly acquired disposable wealth. But she was not embarrassed by the unrestrained appointments. Certainly not as far as the impression it might make on Francis was concerned. She was proud to welcome him into the family home, in spite of the fact that it would never have occurred to any of her family members that their inexperience in matters of taste was better left shielded from the outside world. Her grandmother, mother, and sister-in-law—blissfully immune from any such possible misgivings—were fussing about in the kitchen adjacent to the living room on the other side of a suburban-style half wall. Her father and brother rose respectfully from their seats in the liv-ing room.

"This is my brother, Charles, and my father, Bao Hoang. You already met my nieces. Over there in the kitchen is my grandmother, we call her Bannie, my mother, Cam Hoang, she goes by Cammie, and my sister-in-law, Celeste. I'm going to go help them for a few. Why don't you sit and talk while we get things ready. I'll bring you an iced tea."

Francis shook hands with Charles and Mr. Hoang and took a seat on a very long sofa upholstered in lime-green velvet jacquard. Margot could observe the men's interaction from the kitchen as she pretended to help the other women with the cooking. She noticed that her mother and sister-in-law would try to steal a glimpse of Francis from time to time, all the while mixing and chopping and stirring. She herself adopted a similar attitude—pretending to be lost in kitchen duty but carefully monitoring the men's club in the living room. The large opening above the half wall between the kitchen and the living room allowed her to eavesdrop on the conversation.

"We've been looking forward to meeting you," said Charles, speaking perfect English. "It's always nice to have a policeman on the premises. It sure brings a sense of security. Okay, kids. That's enough! Francis just got here." The children were running back and forth from their bedrooms to present toys and other treasures for their guest to admire. Francis made a show of amusement with each item of show-and-tell, and Margot could tell he wanted the children to like him. Interacting with the youngsters was an easy way for a bashful candidate like Francis to fill time. It also showed a reciprocal acceptance of her family on his part, which made Margot smile a private smile that she kept to herself by lowering her head as she rinsed a head of iceberg lettuce in a steel colander. If her sister and mother and grandmother witnessed her suppressed moment of happiness, she did not care. But if she had only glanced across the kitchen, she would have seen them enjoying the living room crèche with considerably less restraint than she asked of herself.

She could hear Francis enthuse, "Oh, that's Batman!" or "I know that videogame!" only to be corrected, as children like to do, when Francis was mistaken. Margot watched from the kitchen with growing affection. From time to time, the children would argue over the names or the significance of the items, which would allow him to turn his attention to adult conversation without losing eye contact with the girls long enough for them to think he wanted the game of show-and-tell to conclude. Margot also noticed that Francis never sat back on the sofa or crossed his legs. He maintained something of a hunched position with his elbows resting on his slightly splayed knees and the fingers of each hand interwoven at the knuckles. It was an attitude of humility and perhaps respect that showed he would never presume to treat the Hoang home as his personal sleeping porch.

Francis spoke directly to her brother, Charles: "Margot tells me you work with your father?" He was understandably hesitant to speak directly to Mr. Hoang, given the language barrier. Margot could tell that Francis was going to allow Charles to dictate the extent to which Mr. Hoang would be brought into the conversation. She was impressed with that delicate bit of footwork on Francis's part, and her affection for him expanded.

"I've mostly taken over the business as my father moves closer to retirement. He's worked hard enough over the years. But he still makes all of the important decisions." Charles turned to his father to verify his description of the business arrangement. Mr. Hoang, who understood English better than he could speak it, nodded in agreement and smiled so broadly that his broken and blackened teeth were revealed. Margot's first reaction was to be embarrassed, but her love for her father and his success as a hardworking immigrant put paid to her apprehension.

Besides, she reminded herself, Francis's own grandfather was an immigrant himself who performed the manual labor that economic necessity requires of destitute refugees. Immigrant Vietnamese of the twentieth century, she reassured herself, were not so different from immigrant Germans of the nineteenth century, so she was confident Francis would appreciate their shared heritage of hardscrabble resourcefulness and the difficulties that come with American assimilation. After all, she and Francis had both found their way into law enforcement as ambitious products of those modest but respectable backgrounds.

"What business are you in, exactly?" Francis asked, keen to show an interest. "I know it involves fishing or seafood harvesting of some sort."

"My father started as a commercial fisherman, shrimping mainly. He started with one boat in the seventies and would sell mainly to local groceries. My mother and her sisters would peel the shrimp and also cook for the deckhands. By the early eighties, he had six boats and a couple dozen employees. That's how I got started. I was the oldest son, so it was my responsibility to move into the family business. My brothers and sisters were more educated than me. I'm not complaining, but they're either doctors or engineers or, like Margot, an FBI agent!" Margot pretended not to hear her brother's immodesties, especially when he was referring to her career. Charles was just being sweet, but Margot didn't want to get caught eavesdropping on a conversation about her career success, so she pivoted from the sink and spoke to her mother in Vietnamese while the men continued their discussion.

"Are you still out on the water?" Francis asked. "I do a little shrimping myself, just for relaxation. My father and I have a little skiff we take to the Rigolets."

"Oh no. We don't go out much anymore. Well, actually, never. The business has expanded quite a bit from shrimping. Our main business is seafood distribution. We have warehouses adjacent to the industrial canal and also in Jefferson Parish. I spend most of my time in an office in Metairie. But my father still likes to sit on the docks with the rest of the old-timers. I have an office set up for him, but he never uses it. Do you, Pop?" Charles turned to his father once again for a reaction, however limited it might be. Mr. Hoang smiled again, but this time he made a self-conscious effort to cover his decrepit teeth with a broad upper lip. He took his son's cue to speak:

"I don't like office work," said Mr. Hoang. "That's for Charles."

Francis and Charles and Mr. Hoang and Margot and the kitchen matrons all laughed at the lighthearted irony. Margot saw Francis turn his head toward the kitchen. She looked directly at him and, *oops!*, let slip that the women had been listening in all along. The children, whose game of show-and-tell had been interrupted by the living room levity, also laughed in imitation of the grown-ups. Charles's oldest daughter, a very curious six-year-old, ran between her father's knees and attempted to sit in his lap. She wanted to be part of the fun, even though she didn't exactly understand what the fuss was all about. To Margot's surprise, Charles's four-year-old made a tentative move to copy her sister by taking a step toward Francis as if she might also sit in his lap. The child lost heart, stopped in her tracks, and turned to her mother for a glance across the half wall. Cammie rescued the child from the impulsive copycat conduct by saying, "Go sit in Grampaw's lap."

Francis didn't seem too unsettled by the awkward moment and used the interruption to examine the assortment of framed pictures that her mother had arranged on a side table in the living room. Something had aroused his curiosity and provided a topic of discussion that he could initiate.

"What is that picture on the far right?" asked Francis as he pointed to an 8" x 10" photographic reproduction of an Impressionist painting. "I think I recognize it."

Charles jumped at the chance to explain: "Oh. That's Renoir's *Luncheon of the Boating Party*. You see that man in the bowler hat with his back to the table? The one in the brown suit? That's my ancestor. His name is Baron Raoul Barbier, the mayor of Saigon when Vietnam was a French colony. He had a Vietnamese mistress, and that's who we are descended from."

Margot had heard this stock recitation of the family mythology many times. The younger generation had learned to downplay the illegitimate-birth segment of the family line. But they were always quick to claim a blood relationship with French Second Empire aristocracy. The family wasn't precisely certain which of their female ancestors was Barbier's mistress, and Margot actually had her doubts about the family's claims of a direct connection to famous French colonial administrators.

But it was an oral tradition that had been passed down from one generation to the next. None of it could, by this time, be disproved, so she was in no position to disturb what her family had clung to and repeated for so many decades. It had given the family a slightly elevated status within the Vietnamese community and also carried some degree of cachet in a French Catholic colony like Louisiana. The descendants of European immigrants in New Orleans often made claims to aristocratic, even royal, lineage from France, even if the details were a bit misty. Vietnamese immigrants, she reasoned, could be forgiven for making a similar case for themselves.

"That's very interesting," said Francis. "When I was a child, my grandmother would feed us on TV trays with that exact painting on them. I knew I had seen it before. It must be a very famous painting. But I don't know anything about art."

"I don't either," said Charles as his father rose to take the framed picture off its table and hand it to Francis for a closer inspection. "All I know is that it's supposed to be one of our ancestors. That's what my mother always told me, anyway."

Mr. Hoang returned to his seat, no longer being careful to hide his rotten teeth, so proud was he to provide proof of the family's distinguished origins. Even Josephine Bonaparte, duchess of Navarre and empress consort of the French, whose teeth were blackened and decayed from sucking sugarcane as a child on the island of Martinique, sometimes smiled at court.

Just then, Mrs. Hoang announced that dinner was ready. The men stood politely and walked to the dining room as the children scampered to their customary seats at the table. Margot, her sister-in-law, her mother, and her grandmother began bringing plates and bowls of food to the table in the tradition of communal Vietnamese dining. The women then took their seats, staggered among the other adults and the two little girls, while Margot took a seat beside Francis on one side of the oval table.

"Who wants to say grace?" Margot's mother asked, offering the honor of the benediction to the children. The adults knew that at least one would want the attention. The family joined hands as the six-year-old asked the blessing. Margot slipped her hand into Francis's and interlaced her fingers with his. When the group responded "Amen" in the American Catholic way, Margot turned to Francis and almost leaned to kiss him. They stared at each other for a split second longer than what would be considered courteous regard. The trance was interrupted by her sister-in-law, Celeste, who explained, for Francis's benefit, the individual dishes that had been put out.

"We eat à la Française here at the Hoang home. Let me tell you what we have," said Celeste as she pointed to each dish. The children sat attentively as the descriptions were given. "First, we have cold pickled vegetables, including okra grown by my grandmother in her garden. Traditional Vietnamese soup with beef, shallots, and noodles. Fried shrimp rolls and lobster rolls. Roast pork with spices. Whole redfish and blackened redfish, if you want to avoid the bones. Steamed broccoli and carrots with fresh butter. Sticky rice, the kids' favorite. And grilled tofu with sweet sauce. I'll serve Dad and Grandmother first, since they are the oldest. Then Francis can choose next since he is the guest. I know what the children like, so I'll take care of them. Margot and I will fend for ourselves, as usual." Margot thought her sister-in-law was showing off a bit as if she—a wife and mother of two—was a bit farther along in her womanhood than Margot.

The passing of plates and bowls and sauces commenced in an

orderly but relaxed fashion, and the chatter of casual dinner conversation was exchanged in much the same manner, Margot imagined, as a typical family dinner that Francis would have experienced in his own extended family home.

The children announced their preferences and dislikes but were largely ignored by the adults. Mr. Hoang and Margot's grandmother ate in silence, as they lacked the confidence to speak English the way the younger generations could. Mrs. Hoang, Margot's mother, had no such reservations even though her English was very broken and heavily accented. Francis fumbled with his chopsticks to the delight of the children, who offered their assistance. Margot kept herself from staring at him too obviously, but they managed to share occasional glances as their bond strengthened. As the dinner wore on, Francis put his arm on the back of Margot's chair in mock exhaustion from the feast, and his hand brushed incidentally across Margot's hair. Whether it was a deliberate gesture on his part or not, she blushed.

She may have blushed again while alone in her car headed to the Phuoc Tho Duong Grocery as this memory of their family dinner gave way to her responsibilities as a federal agent investigating possible criminal activity. But it was a nice memory that put a new layer of meaning into her life.

With that pleasant reflection in the back of her mind, Margot turned her attention to law enforcement. She hoped the grocery store surveillance would be completed quickly so that she could call Francis and perhaps have dinner together later that night. It was not like her to look past her official responsibilities in the field, but there was no denying that she wanted to spend as much personal time with him as her job would allow.

The family dinner had been a complete success. Their courtship since then had been nothing but polka dots and moonbeams. Her family had expressed enthusiastic approval, and her mother had even introduced Francis to their parish priest at Mary Queen of Vietnam when they all attended Mass together.

Just as she was about to fall into another daydream about Francis, her thoughts were interrupted by a slew of sirens. She glanced in her rearview mirror to see if she needed to pull over. Sure enough, a fire truck was quickly coming toward her. She pulled aside to let it pass. Just as she pulled back into the main thoroughfare, an ambulance came blaring past her. Then an NOPD cop car. And another.

She thought again of Francis and wondered what he was doing just then. It felt good to think about him, to envision a life with him. As she resumed her trip toward the grocery, she considered that Francis could very well be on patrol somewhere in the district listening to the radio chatter generated by all the police activity.

As the noise of the passing emergency vehicles subsided, she fell into another daydream about Francis. On an earlier Sunday, they had attended Mass at Mary Queen of Vietnam. As the parish children of the Sunflower Choir in traditional Vietnamese silk tunics sang a *Te Deum* in their native language, she and Francis, seated in a nearby pew, held hands discreetly whenever liturgical ritual allowed. From time to time, she could feel Francis looking at her as they sat with the rest of her family. It might be more accurate to say that she could feel Francis looking *upon* her, for she felt *beheld* as if she were an object of adoration. *Ecce Mulier.* She tried very hard not to blush, but she did not know whether it was physiologically possible to suppress. Had they been closer to the initial stages of their love affair, there would have been no way to counteract the effects of adrenaline rushing to her cheeks. But their relationship had, by then, acquired a manner of relaxed familiarity, not least because they were sleeping together. Sexual intercourse, once it becomes an organic feature of a romance, can change the way lovers conduct themselves in public and in one another's presence. It was certainly true in this instance. Margot wondered whether it was noticeable to the members of the church congregation or, most of all, to her family. She presumed that her mother had come to view premarital sex as an accepted part of modern American life and that her father would go along with that decision. For the time being, Margot set aside these concerns in order to concentrate on the surveillance mission assigned to her by Deputy Assistant Director Kevin Barksdale.

As she reached the parking lot of the Phuoc Tho Duong Grocery at the corner of Chef Menteur Highway and Alcée Fortier Boulevard, Agent Margot Hoang came upon quite a bit of commotion, including the flashing lights of police cars and emergency medical vehicles. She even thought she saw yellow crime scene tape stretched across the perimeter of the parking lot. *So that's where those sirens were headed.*

She parked across the street from the strip mall in order to best examine the scene from a tactical vantage point. Through her binoculars, she saw that a stretcher was being deployed from the rear of an ambulance, and she could occasionally hear the shouts of emergency personnel. NOPD detectives were questioning a slim White man in a tight blue suit. Crying Vietnamese women were being comforted by others from that immigrant community. What appeared to be neighborhood regulars, mostly Black, were milling about the outside of yellow crime scene tape. Margot could not be sure whether the incident and possible injuries were related to the grocery store itself. She had not received any notification over her FBI radio that there were problems at the very location she had been sent to surveille. The tumult could have been at the businesses next to the grocery—the nail salon or the cell phone store.

She punched her supervisor's number into her smartphone in order to inform him of the confusing activity and to ask for further instructions.

"I was just about to call you," Deputy Assistant Director Kevin Barksdale said. "We've been monitoring NOPD radio communications. There's been a shooting at the grocery. Your orders are to stand down, keep a safe distance, and . . ."

But Margot tuned out for a moment. She had a terrible feeling she couldn't shake. What if . . . What if Francis . . .

"Okay," she said, trying to sound confident. "I've got my eyes on the parking lot and the entrance to the grocery. I'm not moving till you get here."

"Just sit tight and take note of any comings and goings that might bear on our investigation," her boss said. "Let the cops do their job."

13

As Margot was receiving her surveillance instructions, Jerry Sonthonax was removing a pay-as-you-go burner phone from its cardboard packaging. Without a valid credit card or a liquid checking account to draw funds from, he had no way to reactivate his registered smartphone—the one with the number his ex-wife, his friends, and his professional associates had used for so many years to contact him. But that phone had, of course, been cut off. He had exhausted all of his grace periods, and no amount of inveigling could persuade his cellular service provider to grant even a temporary forbearance. In the past, he had always been able to cajole customer-care representatives with a variety of bullshit assurances and some combination of Western Union wire transfers, high-interest promotional charge-card credit, overdraft protection loans, unauthorized draws from his assessor's office petty cash box, and theft of funds from client escrow accounts. It was an exercise in financial legerdemain, shuffling funds around from one account to another with all the lateral futility of Charlemagne moving the Flemish into Saxony and the Saxons into Flanders. But the phone company's patience had come to an end. His only option was to get his hands on a disposable mobile phone with prepaid connection minutes. Finding a retail establishment that sold these temporary lifelines had not been difficult. Earlier that day, he had come across one of those street-level outlets that open up in rough areas of town—the ones who conscript neighborhood idlers as sandwich-board emissaries to hawk no-contract cellular service. They could be found at almost any stoplight in New Orleans East, where city zoning restrictions would be laughed at if anyone in the area even knew they existed. So, he purchased one with fifty minutes of voice service for $15, a sum he managed to scrape together from the crevices of his couch cushions, and prepared himself for a call to Glenn Hornacek. He was able to retrieve Glenn's number from the contacts page of his old smartphone, even though it could not be used to place outgoing calls. The inactive phone was still good for something.

The problem with using a disposable phone is that people don't ever pick up calls from strange numbers. He had no choice but to leave Glenn a nervous message, the bulk of which consisted of a lame explanation for the new mystery number. This, of course, took up precious connection minutes, but it had to be cleared up if he wanted a return call. The explanation must have served its purpose because Glenn called him back almost immediately. Jerry expected him to ask at least one or two difficult questions about the phone number mix-up, but Glenn was merciful. He suspected that Glenn was accustomed to this kind of fishiness because Glenn was in a fishy business.

"Jerry. Hi, it's Glenn. Can you meet me at Phuoc Tho Duong in, say, twenty minutes or so? I've laid the groundwork for a deal, but a personal appearance by you is going to be critical. I've already spoken to the daughter who speaks English. She'll be there with her mother. They just need to see your face so they can be sure you and I are plugged in. They need to know I'm not some schmuck off the streets without any real connections. Can you do that? We really need to do this to make the deal work."

"Oh, sure. I hear you. I can be there in fifteen minutes if I have to. I'm in my car downtown, headed to my office on Downman Road. But I'll skip that and meet you there straight away."

"Well, don't get there too quickly. I want to be there first. It's better if I'm already there to make the introduction when you arrive. You know what I mean?"

"Absolutely. I'll take my time. So, if I get there in twenty minutes, you'll have plenty of time to get there and set the table, right?"

"Yes. Very good. I'll see you in twenty."

Jerry hoped his tone and willingness to follow instructions had conveyed to Glenn how grateful he was for the assistance. Glenn seemed to have a foolproof aptitude for these things. It also made him happy that his wireless Plantronics Bluetooth earpiece was operating smoothly when paired with his new burner phone. He had been wearing the nonfunctioning earpiece in public, even without a connection, for so long that it was a confidence boost to actually use it for its designed purpose.

And so, he drove down Tulane Avenue, past the criminal courthouse and its bas-relief allegories of Law and Order, took a right on Broad Street past more cellular phone outlets and income tax refund services, took a left turn onto Gentilly Boulevard past the racetrack into Gentilly Terrace, then onto the gentle curve that eventually becomes Chef Menteur Highway. He had it timed out perfectly. Another two or three miles going the speed limit would put him at the Phuoc Tho Duong grocery store at precisely the right time.

As he approached the grocery store, he was met with an unwelcome sight: flashing lights of police units, ambulances, a fire truck, and other emergency vehicles, along with motley scads of onlookers. There were dark-skinned girls in denim hotpants and tank tops, wiry Black men wearing extra-baggy jeans that puddled at the tops of their basketball shoes, and young Vietnamese men and women in similar street garb meant to imitate the rap artists they idolized, in addition to the paramedics rushing around and police officers wearing bulletproof vests. The paramedics were pulling an empty stretcher from the back of a GMC Savana ambulance van. Jerry was close enough to hear the stretcher's collapsible metal struts snap into place and the crunch of its plastic wheels against the asphalt parking lot as the paramedics, one on each end, wheeled it toward the front door of the grocery.

Jerry decided to drive no farther than the perimeter and quickly realized that the meeting with Glenn and the owners of the grocery store was going to be impossible—which was a shame, as Glenn had carefully orchestrated the meeting between Jerry and the store owner and the owner's daughter, who spoke English. As Jerry surveyed the commotion and slowly absorbed the reality that his plans had been scotched, he noticed that Glenn was already on the scene, attempting to make sense of the confusing activity. Glenn seemed to know what he was doing, so Jerry stayed in his car and waited for alternative instructions that would take into account the unexpected change in circumstances.

It made Jerry nervous to see that Glenn was sweating through his shirt. His suit trousers had darkened with dampness as well. From time to time, Glenn would draw the inner sleeve of one arm across his brow to sop up any accumulating perspiration. There was so much of it that he himself seemed disgusted by the spectacle.

After a few more minutes of tense observation, Jerry saw Glenn suspend his discussions with the detectives investigating the scene. Jerry guessed that Glenn had spotted his car and was walking over to provide updates. Watching Glenn's labored approach across the parking lot gave Jerry an unsettled feeling. It was slightly nauseating to watch an overdressed bald man with sweat-soaked clothes move so intently in his direction. The news couldn't be good.

Soon enough, Glenn arrived at the driver's side of Jerry's rental car. Jerry rolled down the window and placed his right wrist on top of the steering wheel in an attempt to look casual. Glenn placed his forearm across the drip rail that ran above the car door and bent slightly so that his fleshy and goateed face filled almost the entire window frame. Jerry heard Glenn's gold cufflinks clink against the metal roof.

Glenn took a few seconds to catch his breath and scan the immediate area circumspectly before he spoke: "There's been a shooting," Glenn said, leaning against the roof of Jerry's car. "The place is crawling with police and internal affairs detectives. We're going to have to suspend the plan for now. Not a good time to talk taxes with the owners. It's best that you get out of here. I'll try and figure out what's going on and call you later. Stay away from your office for the time being. Not that there's any reason for you to be followed, but everything out here is being watched."

"Where should I go?" Jerry asked, hoping for Glenn's veteran guidance. "I guess I'll just drive around until I hear from you."

"I won't be able to call you for a while. It's going to take me some time to get a handle on this. Why don't you lay low at the racetrack OTB? Get lost in the crowd. You'll be close enough there. I'll know where you are in case I need you. But keep your phone on. Is the number you called from earlier the one I should use?"

"Yes," Jerry responded. "This number is good."

The constant changing of phones and phone numbers was certainly indicative of the kind of street-level criminal behavior he was pretending to be above. To hide out at the OTB, as Glenn was suggesting, would not make his deportment any less suspicious. But he didn't see that he had any other options.

It was jarring that Glenn had suggested the racetrack as a layover. Jerry suspected that Burton Clayton had divulged to Glenn more about his gambling problem than he would have liked. His immediate reaction was to protest the insinuation and, in some way, beat back the perception that the racetrack would be a perfect sanctuary for somebody like him. But he saw no point in trying to rehabilitate his reputation at that moment. There wasn't enough time, and it wouldn't have worked anyway. He was sitting in a rental car on the edge of an apparent crime scene, engaged in still another criminal conspiracy of his own design. It was not the time to go into an involved explanation of how he had come to be associated with the sport of horse racing, let alone how unfair it was for such a harmless pastime to be considered disreputable. He had a more pressing problem to deal with.

"Okay. I'll hang there for the time being. You don't think all this stuff will wreck our deal?" asked Jerry.

"I don't know. I don't think so. I need some time to figure out what's going on. Just get outta here and wait for my call. I know some of these detectives. I should be able to get some answers. Don't worry about anything that hasn't happened yet."

Jerry rolled up his window as Glenn returned to the increasingly chaotic scene. As he turned his car onto Chef Menteur, Jerry was able to get a closer look at the individual faces gathered at or near the entrance to the grocery store. There was a well-dressed White man standing in handcuffs, talking to a group of what looked like frumpy detectives. A twentysomething White girl was being placed in the back of a squad car. She appeared to be crying but had not been placed in handcuffs.

There was a slightly built Black woman with straight hair in a short ponytail surrounded by blue-shirted NOPD officers who seemed to know her but who also seemed to be interrogating her like a criminal suspect. She had a blank look on her face and, in spite of the circumstances, was not showing much emotion at all. Then a few TV news vans pulled up nearer to the scene, and several camera operators and well-dressed reporters began unloading equipment. Black children in their bare feet stood quietly behind the yellow police tape and sipped drinks from long red straws as though they were accustomed to police operations in the neighborhood.

As Jerry turned slowly onto Chef Menteur Highway toward the racetrack, he thought briefly about what he could do at the track, given his total lack of funds. How could he kill time at the track if he couldn't put any money on the ponies?

Whether he could get his hands on money for some light wagering or not, the racetrack was his destination. Manny Phan would be there, and Jerry could always touch him up for twenty bucks and a chili dog just to pass the time until Glenn called. Even without an accommodation from Manny, he could always watch the races without actually betting. Or had Manny been part of the setup at the grocery store today?

Zipping down the highway now, Jerry suddenly wondered why Glenn had insisted he avoid his office. Could the shakedown scheme he had hatched with Burton Clayton be somehow mixed up in the police operations taking place now? It appeared to be the scene of a violent crime, the kind that took place almost every day at every convenience store in New Orleans East. But there were more cops at the Phuoc Tho Duong Grocery than he was used to seeing at the usual convenience store armed robbery. He thought he saw at least one federal marshal. Things were spinning out of control.

14

Glenn Hornacek's arrival at the Phuoc Tho Duong Grocery had not been what he'd hoped it would be. Instead, when he arrived that afternoon, he found the entrance to the strip mall parking lot was blocked by police cruisers and ambulances with flashing lights. Yellow crime scene tape had been stretched around the perimeter of the area. Law enforcement personnel were milling about, speaking with one another and clutching their handheld radios. Something was wrong.

Chef Menteur Highway, where the grocery sat, was a dismal thoroughfare lined with one-story retail stores that served low-income consumers from neighboring housing projects and fenced-in light-industrial equipment yards that did not rely on an appealing shopping atmosphere to attract customers. Still, he hoped the Vietnamese owners of a grocery/convenience store would not be surprised by a visit from a government functionary scouring the hinterlands in search of tribute. There was, Glenn thought, plenty of that going on back in Communist Vietnam. And so, he pressed on with his assignment. As he approached Alcée Fortier Boulevard where it intersected with Chef Menteur Highway, he surveyed the strip mall in which the Phuoc Tho Duong building and its appurtenances stood. There were other Vietnamese shops in the same mall, such as an electronics store, a nail salon, a bakery, a noodle house, a pharmacy, a travel agency, and (believe it or not) a video rental store. All of them had signs written in both the *chữ Quốc ngữ* alphabet and in English.

The physical building in which the Nguyens, Glenn had been assured, were conducting their private lottery was like a million other convenience stores he had seen and patronized since he was a boy in the 1970s: a free-standing rectangular bunker constructed of cinder blocks on three sides and part of a fourth that was completed across the front with wire-reinforced glass panes framed in brushed aluminum. The double front doors, also of reinforced glass, were situated toward the right side of the façade. They were equipped with anodized aluminum pull handles so that customers could open them outward and enter beneath another reinforced glass transom.

Almost every square inch of the façade's glass panels was covered by adhesive vinyl advertisements for energy drinks, light beer, menthol cigarettes, phone repair services, fried shrimp plates, and exotic brands of flavored liqueurs. The spaces not covered by those promotional posters were occupied by smaller labels that promised an ATM inside, Western Union cash transfers, a cryptocurrency kiosk, EBT and WIC acceptance, tax docs filing services, electronic bill pay systems, and cannabidiol e-cigs. To the left of the entrance on the exterior of the building stood a freezer holding bagged ice. There was also a propane cylinder exchange locker made of laser-cut ventilated steel. A sign reading "Phuoc Tho Duong Grocery" was fastened to the exterior cornice and rose above the flat roofline. The sign was large enough to be seen from passing cars on Chef Menteur Highway, and, as an added feature, it blocked from sight the HVAC system that hummed away behind it.

These kinds of retail facilities were not meant to be aesthetically pleasing, so it was hard to call them ugly. In fact, this particular building and its strip mall neighbors constituted an improvement over the tire repair service-and-sales establishments that were located on either side of the mall.

He had seen right away that he wouldn't have the kind of cordial first-contact meeting he often conducted with the owners and developers of commercial office towers, in which all parties had an understanding that a personal visit from Glenn meant that their assessor, Burton Clayton, was for sale—and possibly inclined to lower a property assessment in return for a fee.

He needed a moment to figure out how to proceed.

His first reaction was to cut and run, but he had made arrangements to meet Jerry Sonthonax at the grocery, and he could never face Burton again if he abandoned one of his protégés without first offering some assistance. He had been careful to park his BMW SUV outside the police tape so that he could survey the unexpectedly active scene before Sonthonax arrived—a rendezvous scheduled to take place shortly. With all the commotion around the grocery store, there would surely be no way to conduct a calm consultation with the Nguyens.

Glenn looked at his gold watch several times before spotting a gray rental car pulling up nearby. It had to be Sonthonax. Glenn had, by then, made the decision to postpone the mission and send Sonthonax away. In order to do so, he had to walk fifty feet or so to another area outside the police tape where Sonthonax had parked his car. Glenn was able to make the interception and explain to him, through the driver's-side window of a fucking car, that negotiations with the Nguyen family would have to be set aside for another day. Sonthonax was bound to understand.

"I'm not sure what's going on here, my friend. I can't tell whether this has anything to do with our lottery folks, but it'd be hard to get in there even if they're ready to talk to me. It's better if you stay out here while I figure out what's going on. If we have to leave, we'll leave. Just give me a few minutes to ask around."

Jerry seemed willing to follow instructions as Glenn looked up from the car window periodically to make his battlefield assessment. Glenn had been bent over Jerry's car window for so long that the waist belt of his pants had crept up above his naval and was causing his belt buckle to pinch his xiphoid process. In order to relieve the discomfort and resume normal breathing, he slipped his thumbs inside of his waistband and slid it beneath his belly. The exact point of equilibrium he had chosen that morning—and every morning for many years previous—had to be abandoned if he spent any length of time bent at the waist. When, at last, he stood up after sending Jerry away to hide out at the OTB, the tension of his belt was lost, and his pants began to slide down his hips. He managed to catch them just before they fell to the ground. He had prevented the wardrobe malfunction he was often on guard against at his age.

As he watched Jerry put his car in gear and pull slowly away from their meeting spot at the edge of the parking lot, Glenn caught a glimpse of his reflection in the driver's-side rear window. He saw that he had neglected to fasten the lowest button of his shirt front and that his white cotton undershirt had curled up above his deep naval. This created a triangular gap above his waistline, inside of which the skin of his belly and the dark wisps of his stomach hair could be seen by the general public if left uncorrected. He quickly inserted the final button of his shirt into its corresponding buttonhole while holding his pants up at the same time. He retucked his shirttails and returned his beltline to its original position just below his navel. It was then possible for him to turn toward the busy crime scene and plot out a course of action.

He lifted the yellow police tape over his head and walked toward the nearest cluster of law enforcement officers nearer to the entrance of the grocery store. Standing beside a squad car with its lights on was a patrolman he knew from one of his many arrangements with Burton Clayton. He couldn't remember whether he had provided him with complimentary tickets or some other perquisite, but he was certain to be recognized as a police department procurer. As it turned out, it was Officer Tommy Gleason of the NOPD's citywide Violent Crime Task Force. Gleason was writing something in a notebook as he stood next to his squad car with doors open and its blue lights flashing.

"Tommy! Glenn Hornacek. Friend of Burton Clayton. We've met a few times along the way."

Glenn dropped Burton's name with such confidence that Tommy Gleason would have no reason to question his presence within the police cordon or shoo him away from the restricted area. Anyone with connections to Burton Clayton was entitled to preferential treatment.

Glenn tried to strike up a matter-of-fact conversation with Gleason by making an innocent inquiry: "Quite a scene out here. What exactly is going on?"

"Hard to tell from all the radio traffic," Gleason responded. "I pulled into the parking lot to investigate a suspicious hand-to-hand drug deal. Then someone called out a 10-108. I wasn't sure about the exact location, so I tried to secure my drug suspects. By that time, squad cars were screeching in from everywhere. Detectives, shift captains, everybody. Now there's an ambulance. From the looks of it, we've definitely got a 10-108."

"What's a 10-108?"

"Officer down. But there weren't any other police officers—uniformed police officers—in this area when I was cuffing this drug deal. I think there might have been a detail officer inside the grocery store, but I'm not real sure."

Glenn tried to make sense of the crazy scene. The loading doors of the ambulance were open, and its orange lights were flashing, but the unit was stationary. Plainclothes detectives and uniformed officers were milling about the entrance to the grocery store, but no guns were drawn, and no sense of urgency on the part of any law enforcement personnel was evident. Whatever had happened, the scene had been secured.

Glenn turned to Gleason and resumed the soft inquiry: "So you've got somebody detained in the back of this car?"

"Yeah. This girl was out here scoring crack. She's not the type we normally find out here in the East. She's pretty upset. Asked if she could call her father. I haven't had a chance to fully question her yet. She looks like she may be from Uptown trying to score crack from some slick-looking character in a fancy suit. He's not the type of dope dealer we see out here either. A White guy in a coat and tie selling crack to an Uptown White girl in a Chef Menteur parking lot? Fuckin' crazy, but whatever. Eddie's got the dude in handcuffs over there. He doesn't look like any of the gangsters that control this territory."

Glenn stepped sideways to get a better look at the young girl Gleason had placed in the back of his patrol car. She was not handcuffed, but she was crying into her hands. In an instant, Glenn recognized Caroline Calloway.

Glenn stepped back to his original position—face-to-face with Tommy Gleason—and spoke to him discreetly. "I know this girl. She's a client of mine. You mind if I speak to her? I might be able to clear this up. I can at least find out what she's doing out here."

"Go ahead. I'm just waiting for orders from my captain. I'm guessing I'll have to release her anyway if I get called to deal with the shooting."

Glenn moved around Gleason and stood in the open back-door area of the squad car where he could speak to Caroline. He placed his right forearm on the aluminum drip rail at the edge of the roof and bent down to speak. He could feel his belt buckle pinching his xiphoid process again as his waistband rose above his navel. He spoke to her as calmly as possible but still in a tone that would convey to her the seriousness of her situation.

"Caroline," he said. "What are you doing out here? The officer said you were trying to score crack? What the hell's that all about?"

Caroline Calloway looked up with her swollen and bloodshot eyes. Her small pink mouth opened slightly as if she would speak, but no sound came forth. She placed the butts of her hands downward on the rigid plastic seat of the squad car and shifted slightly toward the open door with a pitiful expression on her face that begged for Glenn's intercession.

Glenn asked again: "My God, Caroline. What are you doing? There's nothing but craziness out here." Glenn turned his head briefly away from the back of the squad car and surveyed the activity closer to the grocery store entrance, where most of the emergency personnel had congregated.

When he turned his head back to Caroline, she was ready to speak: "I messed up. I wasn't even thinking about it until my guy said he could hook me up with a little coke. I usually meet him downtown . . ." At that point, she began to whimper as she spoke: "But, for some reason, he told me to meet him out here. I don't know what's going on with all this other stuff. I never even went inside the grocery. Now there's an ambulance and a hundred police officers. You gotta get me out of here!" Her sobs came in convulsions.

"Try and hold it together," Glenn said. "I'm going to get you out of here, one way or another. I'll try and get them to release you to me. I can talk to this officer."

"They wouldn't let me call my dad. They took my phone. Can you call him? I just want to get out of here."

"Let me talk to him."

Glenn stood up from his bent position, secured his peregrinating beltline, and moved away from the back door of the squad car to engage Officer Gleason once again. All the while, he tried to think of action options, some of which were devious. Perhaps there was a way to exploit Caroline's distress for his own benefit by leveraging a commitment from her to make a claim against the North Carolina drug treatment facility.

After all, he had made arrangements for Jerry Sonthonax to represent her. In such a vulnerable condition, Caroline could be persuaded to proceed with the claim, especially if he could somehow engineer her release from police custody. The idea was a selfish one, and it felt a lot like blackmail, but it was an opportunity to solve everyone's problems. Such a sensitive matter required all of the diplomatic skills he had honed over the years as Burton Clayton's bagman.

But the girl needed immediate help, and the best he could do for her at that moment was prove to her that he was trustworthy. The business about the lawsuit could wait. For the time being, he was constrained by matters related to her drug transaction and apparent arrest. All of a sudden, he hit upon a way to secure Caroline's release that seemed plausible:

1) Justify his oddly coincidental presence at the grocery store crime scene by presenting his credentials as a bona fide real estate consultant retained by the Nguyens to review a pending assessment and secure for them concomitant tax relief. This bedrock element of the plan could be corroborated by the Nguyens should the authorities, for any reason, see fit to ask, because Jerry had already told them to expect a visit from him.

2) Establish a cognizable professional association with Caroline by holding her out as an intern in his employ who was at the location to perform an initial evaluation of the property at his behest. This, of course,

was a complete lie, but it could not be challenged unless the authorities got to Caroline before he had the chance to put her wise. He could certainly prevail upon them for a moment alone with his employee simply by playing up his cozy relationship with Burton Clayton. It would require some intricate footwork, but if successful, he could explain that Caroline had been caught at the wrong place at the wrong time and the whole thing was just a stupid misunderstanding.

3) Offer to take Caroline into his custody so that the NOPD could concentrate on the shooting of their fellow police officer. That was a separate and more serious matter that could not have involved a young girl who had no criminal record and who presented no danger to the public. He would be responsible for her and make her available for questioning if, for any reason, the police determined she had any relevant information to provide.

It was a long shot, but he could think of no other way to extricate Caroline from a crime scene getting tighter and tighter by the minute. It was worth a try because he could, if it worked, heroically spirit her away in the isolation of his BMW and use the time to convince her that the lawsuit idea was a good one. But the more he thought about the plan's complex mechanics, the more he doubted he could implement the damn thing without risking his own neck.

It occurred to him that there must be something more serious to the multifaceted police response. For instance, the place might have been under surveillance for a more serious criminal enterprise, in which case wiretaps and video recorders would have been rolling in the hours, even days, before the police arrived that day. Just suppose that his and Jerry's assessment shakedown had been picked up fortuitously, an incidental crime that fell into the lap of law enforcement during the investigation of something bigger?

Glenn could not rule out the possibility that officials monitoring the grocery store for evidence of drug trafficking or other malfeasance had stumbled upon something even more interesting—something involving the bribery of an elected official by means of a civilian intermediary. If that were the case, Glenn's phone call to the Nguyens setting up the consultation could have been recorded. Although it was innocent enough in content, it was made suspiciously close to the time the Nguyens received the Sonthonax assessment hike.

His arrival at the grocery store that day, and his contemporaneous conversation with Sonthonax at the edges of the crime scene, would have been observed by the same surveillance operation. So, absconding from the area with a potential witness in his car would only compound the suspiciousness of his presence there.

But remaining in the area just to look like an innocent onlooker presented its own set of problems. For all he knew, detectives investigating the shooting could have seized the Sonthonax letter. Surely, they had interviewed members of the Nguyen family. No telling what those interviews may have produced.

Glenn was beginning to panic.

According to Tommy Gleason, a police officer may have been shot, a crime that triggers the heaviest possible police intervention and scrutiny. Police officers are not often shot unless major criminal enterprises are at stake, like bank robberies or art heists or other organized crime activities involving large amounts of money. If the Nguyens were indeed running a private lottery, then large amounts of unreported cash would be found on the premises. It was possible that the targeted officer had become entangled in an extensive criminal racket that the police already knew about.

The totality of circumstances was beginning to make sense to him: the police shooting *and* the lottery surveillance were part of the same law enforcement concern.

Glenn's first instinct was to linger in the area and act as if he were simply an innocent businessman making a routine business call, only to find that one of his employees had been mistakenly snagged in an indiscriminate police dragnet. The same instinct, which had been sharpened by years of back-channel chicanery, counseled him to sniff around and collect as much information as he could in order to advise Burton and Jerry.

But that was no longer going to be possible. He had his own well-being to think of. He would have to get the hell out of there. He might even have to leave town.

Glenn always thought that one day the time would come when he would have to leave New Orleans. He had been involved in too many kickback schemes with Burton Clayton to think that the wheeze could continue forever. But it was, up to that moment, only a distant contingency that might never happen. When you make a living on the edges of criminal law, it is wise to have in place options of last resort.

But matters had not deteriorated, just yet, to the point where the rashness of flight was called for. He still had the good faith of Burton Clayton to draw upon. Most of that good faith, it was true, was based on the unspoken threat that he could, at any time, disclose their extortion franchise to the police: in other words, he had the goods on Burton. He did not like to think of himself as a snitch, but it was his only insurance against the prospect that Burton would hang him out to dry. And so, before he packed up his wife, sold his house on Grand Route St. John, and left the festival grounds forever, he would ask Burton to use his political clout to provide some protection.

But a funny feeling had crept up on him, like he had been set up, like people were grabbing their coats and ducking out of a room with a bomb in it that he didn't know about. On any other ordinary day, he could breeze into Burton's office whenever he wanted, with or without notice, and be welcomed by sunny faces and clubby familiarity. But after an objective consideration of recent developments, something felt wrong. It suddenly occurred to him, perhaps too late, that Burton himself might be running for cover. Burton had friends at the highest levels of the NOPD and even had a mole or two at the US attorney's office. If, in fact, Glenn had been caught on surveillance sniffing around the Phuoc Tho Duong grocery store, Burton would know about it immediately. If so, Glenn was radioactive—afflicted with the contagion of criminality. Whatever loyalty Glenn had earned over the years would be forsworn so that Burton could protect himself from criminal prosecution. It made Glenn angry to think that he had become the fall guy in an operation that was Burton's idea to begin with. Under those circumstances, Glenn decided right then to pay his boss, Burton Clayton, an unscheduled visit.

15

ecky Calloway left his downtown law office after discussing with his client, insurance account manager Dale Dutton, the need to conduct a preliminary site inspection of the personal injury accident scene at the Phuoc Tho Duong Grocery. They had agreed that quick action was required in order to avoid an expensive lawsuit. Dale had suggested that Lecky survey the parking lot, locate the metal sign that had buckled and then struck the roof of the victim's car, retrieve any video security footage that might have recorded the incident, and conduct interviews with employees or other possible witnesses who may have been on the premises at the time.

The victim, in this instance, was Felix Peterbilt, the dandy who had fellated him in the dressing room. It was Lecky's usual practice to provide his client with any information that might assist with the overall evaluation of a particular case, but the little matinee knob job at the men's boutique was a detail best withheld. Department store cruising was an underground pastime reserved for closeted gays and their anonymous playmates.

At this stage of the potential litigation, there was no need to confuse the issue with red herrings that had no bearing on the dollar value of the claim. He figured he could continue the representation in good faith until an out-of-court settlement was reached and before Dale Dutton or anyone else got wise to the mildly titillating, but mostly irrelevant, connection. Whether his personal indiscretions created a conflict of interest was a question he would leave for another day. Not that he much cared. The worst that could happen was that he could lose his job at the law firm. For that, he cared even less.

Satisfied that he had temporarily resolved a problem by burying it, Lecky suggested, and Dale agreed, that once the initial assessment of the accident scene had been made, engineering experts should be retained to analyze the condition of the sign and whether it had been maintained properly by the owners as required by the terms of the insurance policy. The point of this inspection was to develop a legal defense that would minimize the company's liability for any injuries related to the sign's collapse.

"Okay, then. I'll get on it right away." Lecky was trying to round off the phone conversation with Dale before his dirty little secret had time to bubble up and force him to make a disclosure he would rather avoid altogether.

Dale seemed to accept, without suspicion, the proposed plan of action as a reason to terminate the phone conversation: "Very good. Off you go. Report back as matters develop."

As Lecky drove down Canal Street and out Chef Menteur Highway for this inspection, he began the mental checklist of investigative items he had relied upon for twenty years when conducting a car-crash analysis. It had become, by that time, a tedious and unfulfilling way to make a living, but it was necessary to maintain the appearance that he had a real job and that he was not coasting through life as a soft appendage to his wife's financial legacy. He was, by that time, convinced that suppressing his dignity for a life of luxury and enviable social status was not worth the humiliation—especially when he had to pretend to have a legitimate legal career. As such, it was hard to concentrate on the items he had discussed with Dale and the tasks he had agreed to complete at the Phuoc Tho Duong grocery store.

Riding alone in his car, he resolved to realign his life's priorities. The routine work a lawyer is trained to conduct at the beginning of any case had become unbearable. On most occasions, it was no more than an irritating errand he could endure without complaint. But on this day, it was to be, for him, like the passing of a bad cramp. What he had come to realize was that his daughter and his emerging homosexuality deserved more of his attention than the stupid lawsuit. But he had made a commitment to Dale, an innocent bit player in this coming-of-age drama, and Lecky wanted to honor that commitment.

The more he mulled it over, the less he cared about his job. Further still, he could draw upon his resentment for his wife to lubricate a personal transformation he had resisted for too long. Her oppressive command of the marriage as a subaltern of her father's fiscal tyranny, combined with his anguish over his daughter's addictions and sexual battery at the hands of her treating psychiatrist—an old college friend of old man Thompson, no less—reduced the significance of his legal career to the point where he could almost abandon his meaningless job and empty marriage without any regrets.

Although perhaps not the best time for him to decide, once and for all, whether to make any such drastic decisions, the journey to the grocery store would give him time, a time when he could reflect on things before the curtain went up, a period of suspended animation he hoped would engender some sense of confidence that his commitment to sovereignty was sound. The time had come, he concluded, to take control of his life one way or another. Though he was not necessarily in love with Felix Peterbilt, Lecky had, at last, acknowledged the primacy of his sexual orientation and his distaste for duplicity. It was as though, in that short drive to the grocery, he was becoming an honorable man.

But the frisk and tingle of his liberation were soon dampened by the frenetic scene he came upon at the grocery store. Emergency yellow-and-black police tape had been stretched around the perimeter of the parking lot. A flashing swarm of NOPD squad cars and other emergency vehicles made it difficult to marshal his thoughts. He found a parking spot on Alcée Fortier Boulevard just a short distance from the plastic police cordon and got out of his car. He placed the crook of an open hand above his eyebrows to block the sunshine and search for answers. Near the entrance to the grocery store were a plainclothes detective and a uniformed patrolman intermittently questioning a well-dressed man and turning out his trouser pockets.

Was that Felix Peterbilt? Before he could get a better look at the man, Lecky heard him call out: "That's my lawyer! Let him through! I know my rights! Let him through!"

It was a crippling body blow to hear his dressing-room lover call out for his legal assistance in what appeared to be a criminal investigation. His first instinct was to act mystified. So, he turned his head left and then right as if the shouting were directed at someone else in his general vicinity. Because there was no one else close enough to deflect attention, he was forced to pretend that he had been mistakenly identified. He couldn't very well walk away. He was stuck, pinned and wriggling, with no other option than to gather himself and face the music.

So, Lecky made a staged show of confidence by slipping beneath the crime scene tape like he belonged there. He took great care to restrain any dainty mannerisms of gait, gesture, and movement that might undercut the self-possessed impression he wanted to make. Over time, he had acquired certain effeminate idiosyncrasies that would blossom if he didn't deliberately suppress them. They were little things—like a gentle tilt of the head, a languorous drape of the hand, a spontaneous *tendu en croix*—that he could not let off the leash at a time like this. Those unmistakable indicators of *gayness* might be safely liberated at exclusively gay or gay-friendly occasions, but they were delicacies of manner the cops would consider evidence of weakness. He simply could not allow them to surface at the very moment he was trying to bluff his way into a restricted crime scene. His tasseled loafers might also be a problem, but he squared his shoulders and pressed on with as much attitude as he could muster.

A nearby patrolman was not impressed by Lecky's stilted bravado: "Get back behind the tape, sir. This is a restricted area. I will stuff you in a police car if I have to."

Lecky protested, never exactly identifying himself as a lawyer, but suggesting that the presumption should be made: "Excuse me, officer. I'm here in an investigative capacity. I represent the owners of this place."

Over the head of the intervening officer, Lecky could see that the plainclothes detective was waving him through. Lecky directed the patrolman's attention to the detective's evidently superior authority: "Look, officer, I believe your colleague is saying that I should be permitted access. I'm not armed. I just want to find out what's going on. I have no intention of interrupting the investigation."

The uniformed patrolman let him pass, and, when he was close enough to Felix and the detective, he spoke calmly but with seriousness: "May I ask what he is being arrested for?"

"He's out here selling crack to young girls," said the plainclothes detective. "We found bindles of crack individually wrapped for sale. We also have a shooting inside the store, and I don't believe in coincidences."

"That's not crack!" Felix pleaded. "Lecky, I'm not selling crack. I'm not a drug dealer. This is just a stupid misunderstanding!"

Lecky tried to stall for time. He had no experience as a criminal lawyer and could only think to ask the detective background questions: "Did you say shooting? What's this man have to do with any shooting? I've never known him to be armed."

The detective shot back: "Wait a minute. Do you represent this man? I thought you said you represent the store owners."

Lecky crawfished: "I represent the owners, but I'm acquainted with him."

"Well, while you're figuring out who you represent, I'll be securing the scene, if you don't mind. One of my men is dead inside that store, and I'm not letting anyone out of my custody until we get this thing figured out. Right now, he's in custody for suspected distribution of narcotics."

Felix interjected: "I didn't have anything to do with any shooting. I never even went inside the store. I just want to get out of here. Lecky, please, tell them to release me! I'm not a violent person!"

"All right. Let's all calm down," said Lecky. "Let the officers do their job. You're not in any danger. Physical danger, anyway."

Just then, Lecky Calloway heard the unmistakable voice of his daughter crying out behind him. When he turned to look in her direction, he saw that Caroline was seated in the back of an idling patrol car with its blue lights flashing some twenty yards away. He abandoned his discussions with Felix and walked urgently toward his daughter. She was pleading for help.

"Dad! Dad! Help me!"

Lecky felt the terror that only a father can feel for an endangered child. He was not even breathing as he squeezed past another police officer who stood between him and the open door of the squad car. He reached into the back seat with both arms and cradled her head against his neck with his right hand beneath the knot of her ponytail. Caroline sobbed and shuddered in his embrace as he tried to console her.

"Shhhh. Shhhh. I'm here, sweetie. Daddy's here. It's okay." Lecky stifled all of the questions he might have asked her if she hadn't been so obviously upset. It would not have been constructive to interrogate her about her wildly unlikely presence at a crime scene in New Orleans East in the back of a squad car. He would have time to satisfy his curiosity later. "We're going to get you out of here." Her tiny torso heaved in swells.

He managed to turn his head far enough to speak to the patrolman without letting go of his daughter. Caroline tightened her grasp.

"Can you release her into my custody, officer? She's my daughter. I don't know what she's done or what she's accused of doing, but I'll take full responsibility. She's never been in trouble, and I'm certain whatever is happening here has nothing to do with her. Please. I'll leave you with all my information, and we can sort this thing out. I'm her father."

At the sight of this pitiful scene, the plainclothes detective who had placed Felix Peterbilt under arrest approached Lecky and Caroline at the open door of the squad car. "This man over here is claiming you're his lawyer. On top of that, you claim to represent the store. I don't know who you are or who you represent, but nobody's going nowhere. The girl is safe in the car with Officer Gleason. You wanna come back over here and talk to this man?"

"Yes, certainly, sir," Lecky said softly and then turned to Caroline. "Just stay here for one second. We're going straight home. Just let me talk to these people."

As he drew near the cluster of police officers and their prisoner, Felix cried out again: "That's him! That's my lawyer! You talk to my lawyer! He'll do the talking now!"

"Well, it's true. I am a lawyer and, yes, I do know this man." Lecky seemed to be directing his remarks to the attending police officers, but he kept his eyes fixed on Felix. The officers stood in a semicircle around Lecky and Felix, waiting for an explanation that would resolve the exact nature of their relationship. The officers remained silent, blinking and turning their heads alternately as each of the two subjects took his cue to speak.

"He is definitely my lawyer," said Felix, as if prompted by Lecky's partial verification. "I don't know why he's denying it. We discussed it at our last meeting. Ask him if he remembers that." Felix was speaking to the officers, but he looked directly at Lecky as if he were calling a bluff. "Or have you forgotten already?"

Lecky broke the stalemate by speaking instead to the plainclothes detective who seemed most likely to be in charge. "It doesn't really matter. I'm here to help him regardless. Can you at least tell me why he's being arrested?"

Felix broke in and spoke directly to Lecky as if they were speaking privately, in spite of the fact that they were standing in a strip mall parking lot surrounded by crime scene vehicles, police officers, curious civilian onlookers, and prison trustees pushing gurneys near the entrance to the grocery store: "They're accusing me of dealing dope! I don't mess with that stuff! They don't got nothing!"

Lecky was stunned to hear Felix revert to the ghetto vulgate of gangsters. Felix had seemed so elegant and refined at the boutique dressing room and later at the art gallery *raôut*. Something about Felix's true personality was leaking out at this moment of great stress. The romantic spell

Lecky was under would have been completely broken if he'd had more time to reflect on the surprising outburst. Lecky was not completely ready to abandon his fantasy of an openly gay relationship with Felix, but suddenly, things did not look promising.

Lecky searched his scrambled mind for something to say, but before he could, Felix broke in again: "Just get Caroline over here and she can tell you! This is not what it looks like."

It was jarring to hear Felix refer to his daughter by name. How in the world would Felix know her name, and how was it possible that she could clarify the circumstances of his arrest?

Lecky would, once again, leave those questions for a later date, at least until such time as he could stabilize the situation. His concern for Felix, whatever it might be, would have to be set aside in favor of a more pressing concern for his daughter.

He decided to buy some time and formulate a new course of action: "Officer, let me get my daughter, and we can ask her to clear up any confusion. She's just over there in that other police car. Give me two seconds. Maybe we can resolve this right here and now." The uniformed police officers and detectives looked amused—like they were watching bumbling amateurs try to untangle a sitcom misunderstanding.

"Okay," said the captain of the command. "Fetch her up." He looked at his fellow officers and chuckled as one of them adjusted his grip on a handcuffed Felix Peterbilt.

Lecky turned smartly and strode toward the other police cruiser a few yards away where Caroline was being detained. When he arrived, he spoke to the policeman in attendance: "The captain said I could escort my daughter over to him to clear up a few things." Lecky gestured to the captain to confirm his permission to carry on. The captain authorized the makeshift plan by summoning father and daughter with an upturned palm and flicking fingers, much as a casino gambler signals a blackjack dealer for another card. "Come with me, Caroline. We're going to talk to the captain. I want you to explain to him what you're doing out here. I need you to tell him the truth, so we can get out of here."

Caroline kept her head down as they approached the larger group assembled around Felix. She stayed silent except for a few sniffles that lingered from an earlier crying jag. Upon their arrival, Felix preempted any plans Lecky may have had to control the conversation.

He spoke directly to Lecky: "Caroline knows you're my lawyer, don't you, Caroline? Tell these officers what we talked about."

Lecky was again put off by the familiarity Felix seemed to have with his daughter. He looked down at Caroline, dreading (but now halfway willing) to hear from her exactly how she and Felix knew each other with such chumminess. The captain and his fellow officers were allowing the awkward caucus to play out.

Caroline kept her eyes downcast and made no response. Lecky drew her closer to his side and spoke to relieve her of any need to respond to Felix's provocation. Lecky realized he had made a mistake placing her into the spotlight, especially since it had been motivated by a selfish desire to help a man he, up until then, had hoped would be in his fledgling gay future. He knew then that he wanted no part of Felix Peterbilt.

At that very moment, there was a burst of commotion near the entrance to the grocery store. Other policemen were placing a slightly built Black woman with chemically straightened hair pulled into a short ponytail under arrest. The woman, dressed in jeans and a zippered sweatshirt, was being subjected to quite a bit of rough handling by the arresting officers.

They yelled for their captain: "Sir! This one's been identified by a witness! You better get over here!"

The captain made a brief assessment of the developing events, turned to Lecky, and spoke: "Arright. I'm gonna release your daughter into your custody." He spoke to the other policemen next: "Release her but get their names. We'll bring 'em in later. Right now, get over to the building and start taking statements. One of ours is down."

The cop holding Felix by the handcuffs asked, "What do you wanna do with him?"

"Keep him here for now. He smells funny to me. Give the girl to her father. Move out."

Lecky didn't want to give the captain time to change his mind: "Come on, baby, let's go home," he said as he started to guide Caroline away from Felix and the arresting officers. Before they could take their first steps, Felix blurted out a desperate protest.

"Why don't you tell Caroline about our little meeting? The one at the shop. The one where I paid you a little, *uh*, retainer to be my lawyer. I could use a little legal representation right about now."

Lecky knew instantly he was being blackmailed. Felix was threatening to reveal that the two of them had had a, *ahem*, special encounter in the dressing rooms in Cinch at Nowak's. It also dawned on him that maybe he had been set up all along. He couldn't quite piece together how that was possible, or even whether Felix could have anticipated that he would use their little tryst to leverage an attorney-client relationship. What was certain was that Felix and Caroline had some kind of association. No doubt drug-related.

It didn't matter to Lecky. Caroline had been released to his custody, and his involvement with Felix Peterbilt was at an end—except, of course, for the immediate threat that Felix would reveal to his daughter (and the amused police officers) that he was gay. The revelation that he was a gay man who disported in the deep sinuses of a men's clothing boutique during business hours would only have complicated the evacuation he was trying to effect.

But things had become clear to him. The things that meant most to him, his children and whatever was left of his integrity, could now be drawn upon to face down the immediate threat of blackmail. At that very moment, he remembered the scene from *Sweet Smell of Success* at Toots Shor's round bar when Sidney Falco attempts to extort a newspaper write-up from showbiz columnist Leo Bartha by divulging to Leo's aging wife his infidelity with a cigarette girl. In that classic film showdown, Leo repulsed Sydney's treachery by admitting the affair directly to his wife, quickly disarming Sydney and earning back his wife's respect. Galvanized by this classic scene, Lecky reached down deep, set his face like flint, and gave Felix Peterbilt a piece of his mind.

"Or what? Or you'll try to humiliate me in front of everybody? I will not be blackmailed." He continued for the edification of the whole group—policemen, Caroline, Felix Peterbilt, everybody: "Hey, everybody, I know this man. It's true enough. I should never have gotten involved with him. It was a case of bad judgment and, what's worse, bad taste." The group remained silent. Using that silence as an opportunity, Lecky continued without ever really disclosing the exact nature of his association with Felix: "It's not some big secret you can squeeze me with. I suspect Caroline already knows, and she doesn't care. And if she does care, it's her problem. I'm sorry. No, I'm not sorry. I'll not be beholden to this man, this creep who thinks he can blackmail me into intervening in this . . . this police action, like I'm his on-call, all-purpose attorney. You guys do what you want with him, but I'm not going to—"

Caroline interrupted him: "Dad! Dad! It's okay! I don't care. I already know it anyway."

Lecky looked at Caroline in a way he had never before, regarding her as someone who had crossed a threshold with him, who had come upon the truth at the same time he had. The two of them had made a connection he had never known was possible, a symbiosis achieved as comrades in arms facing a mutual enemy. The alliance was a miracle of *homophrosyne*. They were a frame of adamant, one in hope and doctrine, marching as to war.

Yet, Felix Peterbilt was not going down easily. He shouted at them both: "Caroline. Maybe you better tell your Dad what you are doing out here in the first place."

"Save it, Felix. He already knows I'm a junk—I'm a user. I'm not your victim anymore."

Lecky beamed at his daughter's defiance of Felix's second blackmail attempt. He felt proud. Happiness is discovering that your child is your friend and not just your responsibility. Felix Peterbilt had been neutralized and dispatched.

Just as Lecky was taking satisfaction in the victory, a police officer came running out of the grocery store. He shouted at the group of police officers who had been observing the strange family drama. Apparently, circumstances had changed.

"Bag his hands!" the officer cried, pointing at Peterbilt. "Bag his hands! We just found more bodies in the freezer!"

16

Margot set down her binoculars—and tried to set aside thoughts of Francis—to answer her cell. It was Barksdale.

"Running late," he said. "Stuck in traffic on I-10. Any more specifics on what's happening at the grocery?"

"It's messy," she said. She put the phone on speaker and put her binoculars to her eyes. "Everyone's still pretty spread out across the parking lot. Several ambulances have arrived now. The EMTs just rolled another stretcher into the target facility."

"Two so far?"

"Maybe one before I got here." She pulled her binoculars away from her eyes for a moment and rolled her shoulders, which were beginning to burn. She replaced her binoculars and looked again at the entrance to the grocery store.

"Can you see anything else apart from the paramedic activity? Is the NOPD conducting inquiries?"

"Yes, sir. Uniform has one subject in custody. Male, early thirties, in a business suit. At least four squad cars with lights flashing. There may be another subject in custody inside one of the cars, or even the store. Detectives in plain clothes are on the scene. There is another Caucasian male who appears to be a civilian milling around the occupied squad car. Mid to late-forties and well-dressed, probably not a detective."

"Can you identify the civilian?"

"No, sir. He has now returned to the squad car. He must know the subject inside. Impossible to identify the occupant from my line of sight."

"Okay. Traffic's moving now. I should be there in ten. Stay in place till I get there."

The EMTs remained inside the store with their gurney.

She then took a wide sweep toward the parking lot exit that led to Chef Menteur Highway and observed a dark-colored Ford sedan, possibly a rental car with commercial stickers on the bumper, waiting for traffic to clear before entering the stream headed downtown. Margot was fairly sure the driver was Jerry Sonthonax, Seventh District assessor and author of the letter that was being disputed in the wiretaps she had transcribed. He was definitely driving away from the area.

Was he trying to avoid the heavy police presence? It was a suspicious retreat, and Margot asked herself whether he could be involved in any of the criminal activity under investigation by the NOPD.

Her first instinct was to put her own car in gear and follow Sonthonax down Chef Menteur Highway, but she was under orders to remain at the scene. The best she could do under the circumstances was to record the rental car's license plate number into her cell phone's notepad and wait for Barksdale's arrival.

She felt the rush of having stumbled upon a confluence of events that was, she believed, more than innocent coincidence.

When she turned her binoculars back to the crime scene, she saw a figure she recognized—the Black woman with short, straight hair, pulled back in a ponytail—being escorted out of the grocery store by two NOPD cops. It looked like Arabella, the woman Margot had seen on surveillance footage loitering around the grocery and the obnoxious off-duty police officer the Nguyens had complained about on the wiretaps. What was she doing—or rather, what had she just done that caused her uniformed colleagues to handle her with such brusqueness?

A few seconds later, the EMTs rolled the stretcher out the door and toward the awaiting ambulance. Margot strained to see who was on that stretcher. All she saw was an arm, but she quickly realized the arm was encased in the same color as the arms of the NOPD cops restraining Arabella—the unmistakable dark blue of a policeman's uniform. The shooting victim must have been a cop. Though she had no reason to imagine this cop could be her beloved Francis, the suspicion overwhelmed her—again. She wanted to open her door, rush to the stretcher, and—

She stopped the thought. It couldn't be Francis. Though he'd mentioned getting work as a uniformed security guard somewhere in the district, it couldn't be the Phuoc Tho Dong Grocery. It was the sketchy job Arabella had wanted, if Margot's interpretation of the surveillance tapes was correct. There had to be more to this story than she could glean from behind her steering wheel. And yet she had been given orders from Barksdale to keep her distance from the fracas. They were, after all, still conducting undercover FBI surveillance. Or she could exit the vehicle, slip quietly into the crowd, and get a closer look. Just as she pulled on the door handle, her phone buzzed. It was Barksdale.

"Margot, I'm two minutes away. Just got confirmation. An NOPD cop is down. Suspect is on premises, Black female, possibly in custody. Apparently, a complication that NOPD isn't revealing."

"And the victim?" Margot asked.

Just then, she saw another stretcher getting wheeled out of the store, this time with a body the size of a child. *Good God. One of the Nguyen children?*

"Ernst," Barksdale said. "Francis Ernst. White male, age—"

But Margot's gasp drowned out the rest of Barksdale's details. She needed to open that door and run to him. As a colleague—as a lover.

"Margot? Agent Hoang, are you all right?"

"I need to—he's—I know him. I—I—need to see him. Is he all right? Where was he shot?"

"Of course, in due time," Barksdale said. "The EMTs will get him to the hospital. For now, orders are to stand down. We can't jeopardize this operation."

Margot's throat was dry, and her heart pounded in her ears. She'd never mentioned their relationship to anyone in her office, let alone her superior officer, Barksdale. But she quickly realized if she'd known Francis was working at the grocery store, she was required to report that to Barksdale, who would have been forced to remove her from the assignment. It was against policy to let FBI officers carry out missions where there could have been the slightest whiff of a conflict of interest.

Now the procedural conflict was subordinate to her personal feelings: Should she disobey orders and rush to Francis's side? Or stay put like the professional she worked so hard to be?

"I'm sorry," Barksdale said.

"Is he all right?" she asked again as she watched crowds push toward the stretcher, blocking her view of the covered victim she feared could be Francis even more. EMTs climbed in behind the stretcher, and the doors were quickly closed.

Just then, another stretcher—the third—came whizzing out the front door and wheeled quickly to a third ambulance. The first ambulance, the one she suspected carried the injured Francis, was already heading out of the parking lot and, siren now blazing, onto the highway.

—

As he drove his car away from the flashing police lights and huddled bystanders in his rearview mirror, Jerry Sonthonax worried he'd been played.

By his own team.

Half an hour before, as he exited a drug store holding his new pay-as-you-go burner phone, he'd phoned Glenn, who asked that Jerry meet him at the Phuoc Tho Duong Grocery—their new target for some easy shakedown funds—in twenty minutes. Jerry was amazed the fellow had even answered his call, considering it came from an unfamiliar number.

Yet, as Jerry drew off from the scene down Chef Menteur Highway toward the racetrack—at Glenn's insistence—he wondered if perhaps the whole police presence had been a setup. Was it possible Glenn had orchestrated something as a way to scare Jerry away so Glenn—and per-haps Burton—could keep the shakedown money to themselves? He barely knew Glenn, and it was clear Glenn was the one in charge today. And what was Jerry going to do at the racetrack anyway, without any cash?

The thought of cash—and how to get it—quickly displaced his worry over Glenn, at least for the moment. He could worry about that later.

He considered checking the balance of one of his many bank accounts but remembered that he could not do so from his disposable phone. The bank websites would not recognize the number, and he would never remem-ber the user IDs and passwords required to gain access. It was unlikely there was any cash to be had anyway. Whether he could get his hands on money for some light wagering or not, the racetrack was his destination.

But things were starting to smell fishy. Glenn warned him against going to his office. Police officers were a heavy presence at the target of their shakedown. People had been injured, possibly shot. The meeting with the Nguyens had to be called off. His only course of action was to retreat from the scene and wait for a phone call from Glenn, which might never come. Glenn's loyalty was to Burton, not him. If they had decided to run for cover, he could very well be left out in the cold. If it wasn't some kind of setup, he had, at the very least, become expendable. Jerry was beginning to panic. In this condition, it was difficult to drive his rental car back down Chef Menteur toward the agreed-upon OTB sanctuary.

When he reached the intersection of Chef Menteur Highway and Read Boulevard, Jerry had second thoughts about killing time at the racetrack. His heart was already beating a little too fast, and he thought it best to stay away from the place that was the source of all his problems. He had a bad feeling about the intense law enforcement presence at the Phuoc Tho Duong grocery store. If he was somehow tangled up in the criminal investigation going on there, it would be wise to avoid the exact place that was to blame for most of his problems. When a man suddenly feels guilty about what his life has become, his natural reaction is to forswear the behavior that put him there in the first place.

Instead of continuing to Gentilly and the Fair Grounds Race Course facility, he turned right on Read Boulevard toward the lake. He knew that the entrance to Joe W. Brown Park was on Read Boulevard. It was a public place with automobile access where he could pass time idly. That's what parks were for. He might even park his car, walk around the greenspace, skip stones across the man-made lagoon, and pretend to lose himself in a little transcendental naturalism—or maybe just smoke a cigarette. He could consider his predicament without being distracted by horse-racing adrenaline.

The park was peaceful enough and usually empty, never having achieved the level of community vitality intended by its benefactor, Joe W. Brown, a man known only to Jerry as an old racetrack personality from the 1950s. He found a parking spot near a lonely children's jungle gym and tried to imagine how a man like Joe W. Brown could become the namesake of a park situated in a remote area like New Orleans East.

Joe W. Brown was well-known in racetrack circles, and Jerry remembered that Brown had his own special section in the Fair Grounds Hall of Fame exhibit on the racetrack premises. Jerry had passed the exhibit many times but had never made the connection with the park that bore his name. Now that he had time to think about it, Jerry began to piece together that Joe W. Brown must have been a man of such respectability that city leaders could accept a charitable donation from him without reservation, even if the donated property had been acquired with the proceeds of a successful horse-racing operation or some other less-than-respectable enterprise.

Maybe it was possible for a guy like Jerry to follow that path and overcome a bad reputation by getting rich off of horse racing and gradually developing a glamorous persona worthy of civic admiration. It might be possible to live down the reputation he had acquired from his bad decisions. As he pulled into a parking spot near the edge of the shallow lake, Jerry tried to think of himself as a modern-day version of Joe W. Brown who just needed a break. Jerry didn't know it at the time, but Joe W. Brown's life story might have given him reason for optimism.

Jerry got out of his car and walked from the parking lot to the edge of the pond, which was really a sump pit left over from the drainage system developers had dug over the years to make the area inhabitable. He drew the disposable phone from his front right pants pocket and made sure there was a strong enough cellular connection to receive calls. He was at the mercy of Glenn Hornacek's further instructions on how to proceed. He would have to wait. He stared blankly across the surface of the filthy water and noticed that the insects created radiating ripples when they touched down to feed. Jerry halfway expected this interlude to bring some peace, or at least a suspension of the guilt he always felt when wasting time instead of working toward a solution to his problems.

No sooner had his shoulders dropped and his lungs expanded than he again became suspicious that he was being set up. It was possible that Burton and Glenn had concocted a plan to suck him into a trap. He had, after all, approached them for assistance in committing a criminal act. Perhaps he had made them uncomfortable, and they needed a fall guy to take away the heat from the criminal operation they had been conducting all those years in Burton Clayton's CBD assessment district. If the FBI or some other law enforcement agency had started sniffing around for evidence of Burton's long-running abuse of power, he could very well have offered to cooperate in a sting to catch Jerry red-handed.

But that didn't make a whole lot of sense. Jerry could not think of a scenario where the Feds would be more interested in him than in Burton, a more experienced politician with a long history of questionable practices in a downtown assessment district full of multimillion-dollar office buildings. If such an investigation were underway, Burton and his notorious bagman, Glenn Hornacek, would have to be the primary targets. Jerry Sonthonax was small potatoes.

On the other hand, if the Feds were after Jerry based on information provided by Burton in a plea deal, he could always turn the tables and give evidence that Burton and Glenn were the real masterminds, the ones who had invented and perfected the assessment shakedown scheme he had only recently—and only once—attempted in his own district.

No, Jerry thought, he was imagining things under the strain of paranoia. Still, there must be some other reason for his anxiety. He could not stop his mind from racing. If detectives were investigating a violent crime at the Phuoc Tho Duong Grocery, they were sure to come across the letter he had sent on Seventh District assessor letterhead threatening an increased tax assessment. If that happened, he could very reasonably expect the cops to come knocking.

Just then, he felt his burner phone vibrating in the front pocket of his khaki trousers. He didn't recognize the number, but since it was a new burner phone, he hadn't had time to program it with the names of his frequent contacts. But nobody, aside from Glenn, knew the number to his burner. It was the call he had been waiting for.

"Hello?" he breathed into the phone, expecting to hear Glenn's reassuring voice. Instead, he heard a different one, but he recognized it immediately: It was his father.

"Jerry? Where the hell are you?"

"Dad? How did you get this number?"

"Have you got yourself in some trouble, boy?" His father did not have a concerned tone. It was an accusatory one, an inflection his father often used with Jerry when he was a child caught misbehaving. It scared him.

"No! No! I'm just out in my district meeting with constituents, doing my job. How did you get this number?" Jerry was trying to piece together what was happening behind the scenes of his own life.

"I got it from Burton. I told him it was a family emergency. Which it might be. I ran into LeCharles Chavis, and he told me you owe his mother money from some lawsuit. I told him I would try and get a hold of you and find out." Jerry knew that his father and Burton were old friends. He had a sinking feeling that Burton had disclosed to his father the extent of his financial distress. "But forget about the Chavises. Burton led me to believe you had bigger problems. He wouldn't tell me what he was talking about, but I got the impression you've gotten yourself tangled up in something more serious. What the hell is going on, son?"

"Nothing! Everything's copacetic. I really can't talk right now. I'm

gonna hafta call you back. Nothin' to be worried about!" Jerry was trying to sound cheerful.

"I don't know what's going on, but you better drop whatever you're
doing and get the hell out of there. People are coming for you. I don't
know who, but you betta watch your ass."

"It's okay, Dad, I've got everything under control. Look, I'm gonna
hafta call you back. I'm expecting an important call. I'll talk to you later."

Jerry pressed the "End Call" button on his burner phone before his
father could protest or, even worse, tease out more information about the
shady activities he was engaged in.

The signs had become clear that Burton was harboring doubts about
their mutual shakedown operation, at least enough to let on to his father
that his position had been compromised. At that point, his only lifeline
was Glenn Hornacek, who had promised to call him with instructions on
how to proceed in light of the intense police presence at the grocery store.

After further reflection, Jerry wondered whether he would trust Glenn,
even if he did call. But he didn't have any other options. Just then, the
phone buzzed in his hand.

It was Glenn, for better or for worse, at last. "Jerry, stay where you
are, wherever you are. I'm heading downtown to find out what's going
on," said Glenn with an urgency that led Jerry to believe he was going to
meet with Burton personally. Before Jerry could ask for some clarification,
Glenn concluded the phone call without waiting for an acknowledgement. "Gotta go."

———

Glenn figured a surprise visit to Burton's office was the only way to catch
his boss flat-footed, to confront him before he had the chance to cut him
off completely. He had every right to show up at Burton's office unan-
nounced, especially because he was indirectly paying for Burton's office
space out of an untraceable slush-fund checking account Glenn maintained with proceeds from their long line of political shakedowns.

Moreover, a surprise visit would be the best way to determine whether Burton was negotiating a separate peace. Glenn was entitled to a face-to-face meeting, and he meant to get one. As he drove downtown toward Burton's office, Glenn felt his distress turn to anger and then thoughts of revenge. He even considered contacting the FBI preemptively.

It might be too soon for that kind of drastic action. What if he was overreacting? What if the whole thing was just a weird, but manageable, coincidence? What if the events at the grocery store were minor, if fatal, street crimes that police encountered every day and were unconnected to a broader investigation of political corruption or organized criminal sophistication?

He couldn't very well leave behind the comfortable and rewarding life he had built without first confirming that his concerns about Burton had a factual basis. His breathing slowed a little, and he loosened his double grip on the steering wheel of his BMW. There was no sense appearing at Burton's office in a frazzled state. Maybe a little *Pock-Ya-Way, Iko-Iko* festival music from his satellite radio would help him relax. Before he could figure out how to tune in to the station that played that kind of music—if there was one—he had reached Burton's office building.

When he pulled into the office garage, Glenn saw Burton's car in its customary reserved parking spot, which meant that there would be no denying, on the part of his staff, that Burton was on the premises. Glenn felt the equanimity he had managed to recapture in the car give way to anxiety as he prepared for what could be a tense showdown.

As he parked his own car in a neighboring spot, Glenn collected himself. It was certainly possible, after all, that he had *not* been picked up on the wiretaps and that he had *not* become a target of law enforcement. If so, Burton would have no reason to avoid him. There was no reason, as a matter of fact, for Burton to suspect that he was making anything other than a customary office visit with his old friend and partner.

Perhaps he was overreacting. Better to keep cool anyway and behave as if there were nothing to be concerned about. The ostensible reason for his visit was merely to elicit guidance on how to advise Jerry Sonthonax.

He went over his opening statement as he rode up the office elevator and rehearsed his delivery: *The Sonthonax operation has become a real pain in the ass. Taking on this project is outside the scope of our trusty system. I realize he's your friend, but there are just too many variables that we can't control. You're gonna have to tell him there's nothing we can do. We need to look out for ourselves.* That was the plan, anyway.

But the affability with which he had been welcomed in the past was not what he encountered when he reached Burton's reception area. He smelled something right from the beginning. Although he breezed in and greeted the receptionist, Lynette, with the usual glad-to-be-here, goofball insouciance, it was stagy and self-conscious. He was trying to behave with her as he had in the past so as not to let on that he had serious doubts about Burton's loyalty.

In the past, he would even flirt with Lynette a little—not in a way that was threatening or creepy, but just enough to show that interracial sexuality was a perfectly acceptable component of his enlightened worldview. Hard as he tried to maintain that same playful mood, he didn't quite pull it off:

"Hello, Lynette! Just popped in for a quick word. Is he in?" Glenn started to amble past the reception desk in his usual cavalier manner but was stopped with an imperiousness he had never faced before.

"Just a minute, Mr. Hornacek. Mr. Clayton is indisposed at the moment. He asked me to tell you that he will call you tomorrow. Whatever you had scheduled will have to be postponed."

Glenn noticed that she called him "Mr. Hornacek." This was a dead giveaway that things had changed. He was being brushed off. It was now clear that Burton had been tipped off and that he wanted no part of Glenn Hornacek. But he knew that Burton was in his office, and he had no intention of being repudiated without due process.

He responded in a demanding tone with a voice that was louder than he intended: "I'll tell you what, Lynette. I didn't come here to be turned away from my own office. I'm gonna speak to him whether he likes it or not." Glenn made certain to call Lynette by her first name if for no other reason than to remind her of their long and easy relationship. It was, at the same time, a test to determine whether she had been instructed by Burton to resist any demonstration of his once puissant authority. "I'm going on in."

As he made his way past her receptionist module, Lynette rolled her chair backward and stood to speak again: "Mr. Hornacek, I must insist. If I were you—"

"If you were me, what? You gonna call security? Have you forgotten who writes your check? I know he's in there. Stay outta this, Lynette. This is way over your head."

He hated to have to insult her. They had been friends for a long time, but she obviously felt a stronger loyalty to Burton than to him. He continued his march to the outer door that led to the interior corridor and the executive office spaces. Just as he reached for the handle, the door unexpectedly swung open. Burton was pushing through from the other side. Glenn was forced to retreat slightly as Burton stepped into the reception area without making any eye contact and spoke directly to Lynette: "Inform Mr. Hornacek that I'm unavailable right now and ask him to leave the premises. If he does not comply, call security, and have them escort him from the premises." Burton remained standing beside the reception desk as he issued this instruction without ever looking directly at Glenn.

Lynette repeated the instructions she had been given: "I'm sorry, but Mr. Clayton—"

"I heard him. No need to repeat him. And there'll be no need to call security. But you might wanna tell him that cowering in his office won't get rid of me forever. If he won't listen to me, there are others who'll be glad to listen to what I have to say." Delivering a message to Burton in the third person was like speaking to a judge in divorce court in the presence of an estranged spouse sitting only a table away.

Threatening Burton with blackmail was a weapon he never thought he would have to use. He hadn't necessarily planned on using it when he came to Burton's office that day, but he had been prepared to do so if he sensed Burton was forsaking him. But he didn't think things would deteriorate so quickly. If Burton was going to initiate divorce proceedings, he expected it to happen in stages. It was sickening to accept the fact that the separation had already happened.

Glenn marched out through the front office doors and into the elevator bay, where he hoped he wouldn't have to wait too long for the next car. He glanced briefly through the front office glass doors to see if Burton had remained in the reception area. He was dejected to see that Burton had disappeared. Lynette was alone at her receptionist desk, carrying on with her office responsibilities through her telephone headset as if nothing had happened.

It was a bleak and disheartening sight. All Glenn could think to do was to call his wife and ask her forgiveness for everything he had ever done in his life. And then, together, they would pack up and leave town—unless he could come up with a better idea.

—

As officers scrambled to secure both Peterbilt and the ponytailed woman outside the grocery, Lecky Calloway took the interruption as an opportunity to spirit Caroline away from the area and into the front seat of his Lexus. He threw the car into gear and drove onto Chef Menteur Highway in the direction of town.

Lecky held off with the probing questions for Caroline and pretended to be preoccupied with the rudiments of driving a car, signaling, merging, and accelerating. It was a forbearance he offered to her as proof of his patience—an act of kindness he hoped would reveal that he was not her mother and that he was not going to demand humiliating explanations the way her mother surely would. Caroline was in distress. What she needed was the mercy and succor that a father is *supposed* to provide his child when she has made a mistake—a mistake she knows was a result of her own bad judgment.

Once they were safely underway, Lecky spoke in a lighthearted and cheerful way to relieve the tension, as if they were two mischief-makers fleeing the scene of an impish prank in the nick of time.

"Whooo-wee! Glad to be getting out of that mess! I think I need a drink." Lecky delivered the witticism with a spontaneity that would be considered reckless by those who walk on eggshells in the presence of recovering addicts. He let it slip off his tongue without any such circumspection as an assurance that no topic would be off-limits in the conversation they were about to have. Caroline almost smiled. She seemed to be grateful that her father had not jumped right into the ugly business of her near arrest, her relationship with Felix Peterbilt, and her presence in the badlands of New Orleans East at an obvious drug buy.

She responded in a similar tone: "That's the first time I've ever been in the back seat of a police car. Don't think I ever wanna do that again. Yikes!"

"Yikes is right. I don't even wanna think about what fluids have puddled in those seats."

"Eeeeww, Dad! That's disgusting! Makes me wanna take a bath!" Caroline laughed a little and cupped both hands over her nose and mouth. Lecky noticed she used the pantomime discreetly to wipe some residual moisture from beneath her swollen eyes. "I guess I should expect things would come to that if I kept fuckin' around with people like Felix. What a scumbag."

She seemed to have opened up, and Lecky desperately wanted to know how, precisely, she had become involved with a guy like Felix Peterbilt. But he was not going to break the spell. Lecky had secrets of his own he wanted to share in the spirit of the transparency they were enjoying together.

"Yeah," he began, "I know Felix. I'm ashamed to say I fell into a moment of weakness with him myself." Lecky was rounding into the subject of his homosexuality with caution, but in an incidental manner that tested the possibility that Caroline was already aware of it. If he could successfully appeal to her sense of pity by means of suggestion, he might avoid the terrible moment of first disclosure that he dreaded. He would be asking for her indulgence by allowing him to skip over the hard part and pretend that the matter was already widely known, an oblique way of inviting her to accept something without the necessity of a formal admittatur. It would require her cooperation. He couldn't be absolutely sure that she already knew, but it might be easier for them both if he jumped into related matters with a baseline understanding that he was gay.

"Yes, well, we all have our moments," said Caroline, reciprocating the mercy that had been extended to her.

To his great relief, she was willing to play along. She could just have easily said, "What are you trying to tell me, Dad?" or worse, "Wait a minute, is this a gay confession?" But she didn't.

They were building on a silent presumption as though it had been proffered, admitted, and established as bedrock fact. Lecky was grateful that she would not insist on the uncushioned shock of a bombshell news break, the kind of climacteric dreaded by a medical student who must tell his parents he has decided to become a poet. Specifically, the difficult and possibly sanguinary ceremony of *coming out*. It was only fair that he show Caroline the same courtesy by suppressing his feelings of shock that his daughter had been caught in a shantytown parking lot buying drugs. He didn't understand how she had arrived there in the first place, let alone how she had become involved with a guy like Felix Peterbilt. None of that really mattered anyway, especially if he was going to pretend that he had already discovered and accepted that information as ancient history.

His next remark was designed to rally a confederacy against a mutual enemy: "I totally misjudged that guy. I should never have trusted him. He's good-looking, but he's from out of town. I guess I thought it would be safer to have an affair with someone outside of our Uptown social group. I'm pretty new to this game, so I suppose I was bound to make a mistake." He was really opening up to Caroline now. But he was leading by example. He had to draw her out somehow in order to maintain what was becoming a constructive discussion.

"I know what you mean," she said. "I met him at my AA meeting. I think dealers like him attend those meetings looking for addicts to prey on. I was stressed out when I called him this morning. Another guy in our group has been after me to file suit against Dr. Caldwell. Says he has a lawyer all lined up. I know Mom's against the whole idea. Every time I think about her, it pisses me off. So, I called Felix. He told me to meet him out here, for some reason. I've never had to buy from him out here—wherever this is. It's usually an easy deal we do after AA meetings Uptown. Anyway, I took an Uber and saw him in the parking lot like he said. I handed him the money, but I never got my shit. Before I could figure out whether he was going to stiff me, all these police cars show up, and I'm sitting in the back of a squad car. Thank God you showed up. How'd you find me out here, anyway?"

"I wasn't even looking for you!" he blurted out in a half laugh, as if they had found themselves in an improbable but happy coincidence. "I came out here for a case! I'm supposed to be representing the grocery store in a minor accident in the parking lot. One of their outdoor signs fell and smacked him in the head. I only found out it was Felix after I was given the case. Well, I shouldn't say that. They told me the injured guy was named Felix Peterbilt, but I wasn't sure it was the same guy I'd met. When I got here, I figured out it was the same guy. That's when I saw you. He tried to blackmail me in front of you. I guess you noticed that."

"Not exactly! I had my mind on other things!" Caroline was laughing like an adventurer who had made a narrow escape and was relaxing in the safety of a rescue helicopter.

Lecky joined in the merriment: "You surely did! The back of that police car didn't look too comfortable."

At that stage of the conversation, he felt he could make some more probing inquiries. He would do so in a matter-of-fact fashion that wouldn't come off as an interrogation but more like he was only satisfying a curiosity: "What the hell was going on with him anyway? It looked like the police were arresting him for more than just a simple drug deal. There were ambulances pulling people out of the grocery store. Did he have something to do with all that?"

"I have no idea. When I got out there, he was talking to a scruffy-looking Black lady who kept going back and forth inside the grocery store. Maybe he was selling to her too, or maybe she's his supplier. I don't really know. It sure seemed like someone was injured inside the store. I'm just glad we got outta there."

"You and me both. In any case, I doubt I'll be kept on the case in any legal capacity. I'm not even sure I'll have a job when all this unravels, not that I want it anymore anyway."

"What are we going to tell Mom?" she asked, formally floating the idea that they were joined in a blood-oath alliance against someone they both feared.

"We don't have to tell her anything. Maybe it's none of her business." He heard himself saying things that had been unthinkable up to that point in their marriage. "As a matter of fact, let's not even go home just yet."

Lecky, who had been driving down Chef Menteur Highway toward town, steered into the left lane and activated his left turn signal as the Lexus approached an intersection where he could make a U-turn. He could feel Caroline staring at him. When he had brought the car to a stop waiting for the traffic to clear for a safe double-back, he turned to her and smiled. "I have an idea. I'm definitely not going back into town. Let's go to Florida. You got any money?"

Caroline smiled back at him. "No. I gave it all to Felix."

He noticed that her eyes had dried, and he was in the mood to make a little joke. At that moment, oncoming traffic broke enough for him to complete the U-turn and accelerate eastward on Chef Menteur Highway— away from the grocery, and away from Hildy.

When they were safely underway in the opposite direction, he turned to her and smiled, this time with an open mouth. "I think we have enough gas to get us to Alabama. We can refuel there and charge it to your mother. We'll be in Florida before she gets the bill. Whaddya say?"

"I like the way that sounds!"

Lecky wanted to move his hand from the gear lever and grasp his daughter's. But he resisted the urge to make any such gesture of affection for fear of seeming sentimental.

17

"She's in the conference room next to your office," said Mildred "Millie" Gamard, one of the special administrative officers the FBI maintained on staff to provide mental health and therapeutic counseling to witnesses, their family members, and even FBI personnel, like Margot, who experienced emotional or psychological trauma related to field operations.

"You left her in there alone?"

"I've been in there with her for an hour. I've just come out to catch you as soon as I heard you were on premises. She's a bit shell-shocked but, all in all, seems to be holding up pretty well."

"How much did she see?" asked Barksdale.

"Well, I know she saw the body being loaded in the ambulance, but I don't think she knew at that point that he was dead. I'm pretty sure she knows that now. I was waiting on you to deliver that confirmation. I haven't been given an official confirmation myself," explained Millie.

"Okay. I'll talk to her. But stick around, would you, in case things take a turn? Once the shock wears off, she's gonna need a shoulder to . . . uh . . . well, I don't want her left alone."

Barksdale did not expect Special Agent Margot Huong to lose her composure. He knew her too well to think that she would ever display any signs of personal vulnerability while on duty. But she was human.

Asking counselor Millie Gamard to remain available was the right thing to do, whether departmental policy called for it or not.

He knocked lightly on the door of the conference room like he was visiting a hospital patient who had just come out of surgery. It was more of a light tap than a knock, with the palm of his hand turned away from the door so that the force of the knuckle strike came only from his first and second fingers rather than a more aggressive knock that started at the elbow. The effect was intended as a request for permission to enter rather than an announcement that entry would be made unilaterally. Though he heard no response from inside, he slowly depressed the metal handle and opened the door just enough to see Margot seated at one of the six castered, mesh-backed chairs around the medium-sized oval table that was just the right scale for the conference room in which it had been placed. She looked up at her superior officer without standing as she might have under ordinary, regimental circumstances.

The room had a large picture window overlooking Lake Pontchartrain, part of a curtain wall of glass that stretched around the exterior of the entire FBI facility. This particular conference room was rarely used, so it did not have a coffee service station or any other office clutter that often got left behind in other, more heavily used, conference rooms.

Barksdale entered the room and spoke softly but deliberately: "I've just received word that the officer Francis Ernst was pronounced dead at 17:50."

Margot closed her eyes. This was the news she'd been dreading. Somehow, she knew it was coming.

He continued: "The NOPD has several people in custody, at least two of them related to the homicide, but others are being questioned as witnesses. We have no reason to believe that Officer Ernst was involved in your, or our, lottery investigation. It appears that he had only this morning been assigned to provide security as part of a private detail for the grocery store."

Margot could feel every muscle in her arms and on the flanks of her torso seize up as she considered some kind of spoken confirmation that she understood Barksdale's synopsis. But she knew that if she tried to say anything more in response to her supervisor that her voice might crack.

Barksdale sensed that Margot would remain silent, so he continued: "I called your brother, and he's on his way now. I'll have Millie sit with you until he gets here. I'm gonna try and get some more information about what happened at the grocery store, but I won't be far. Okay?"

"What do you know so far?" she asked in a whisper. She swiveled slightly in her chair as Barksdale sat down to deliver what he had learned up to that point.

"I've spoken to the Seventh District NOPD commander, and this is what we know so far. The grocery store was, as we suspected, a twenty-four-hour, cash-heavy business. These kinds of places are sitting ducks for drug addicts and armed criminals looking for a quick score. Rumors of a private lottery have been circulating within the NOPD, and apparently in the Chef Menteur neighborhood. The word on the street was the same stuff the IRS Criminal Investigation referred us to. Sounds like the people at Treasury had reason to believe that significant amounts of unreported cash were being laundered through the business. I guess they thought it might be drug-related or some other gambling racket. That was why the intel of a private lottery made sense to them. And that was why we were asked to coordinate a surveillance operation. They figured a private lottery was a reasonable inference on which to base an expanded investigation. The street hustle is often a part of first-generation immigrant communities . . ."

Although she was disquieted by Barksdale's partial acceptance of the suggestion that most immigrant groups resort to the black market by default, she was aware that her old neighborhood was not altogether free from a certain criminal element. But the parishioners of Mary Queen of Vietnam did not deserve to be consigned to that criminal category. Nevertheless, it was not the time to take up the cudgels against racism. She wanted to hear about Francis.

Barksdale continued. "The family that was operating the grocery—the Nguyens—might have been pulling in a lot of cash with that lottery, if they were actually conducting one. We're not altogether sure about that. But with that amount of foot traffic going through the doors, people smell cash in a cash business. For at least a year, the family felt it necessary to hire uniformed NOPD security on a private basis to scare off strong-arm robberies. Convenience stores are already a favorite target of random criminals, and the Phuoc Tho Duong seemed especially inviting."

Margot remained almost motionless. It was hard hearing these details now that she knew what they'd led to.

"At any rate, the security detail assignment had become something of a coveted position within the NOPD, not necessarily for any corrupt reason, even though the previous detail officer had been accepting cash bonuses over and above the hourly rate permitted by NOPD policy."

Margot thought about Arabella—who'd been pestering Mama Nguyen. Maybe she wanted the job.

"But also," Barksdale said, "because it had taken on a certain amount of prestige. Under-the-table payments are often irresistible. So, the NOPD brass didn't want the same officer in place for too long. They like to rotate those assignments from time to time to prevent corruption. That's how your friend, Francis Ernst, got the job. He was a rising star in the department, and the administrators who supervised the private-detail program assigned him the post."

What was it Mrs. Nguyen called the officer—Francis? The "funny" one? The "tall" one? She'd called Arabella the "crazy" one.

Barksdale paused and looked out the window. Then he explained further about how the private-detail NOPD jobs had come under heavy scrutiny lately, especially since more than one officer had gotten caught with his hand in the till. "This had nothing to do with our investigation," he assured Margot, "but the NOPD is always concerned about how things look to the supervising federal judge. I'm telling you this as general background so that you know how Francis ended up in the middle of all of it."

Barksdale continued the précis: "Turns out, another rookie NOPD officer, who actually lived in that neighborhood, had been trying to muscle her way into the plum position by periodically befriending the owners and hinting around to them that she should be given the detail. But apparently, the owners didn't like her—maybe even knew of her reputation in the area. Apparently, she had something of a drug problem that nobody in the NOPD knew about. They would never have assigned the position to her anyway because she was a rookie. So, her efforts to get the position were probably for naught."

Margot nodded. "I know," she said. "I heard this on the tapes. Arabella somebody?"

Barksdale nodded. "Sounds like her addiction took over, and she no longer had patience enough to wait around for the official assignment, which was never coming anyway. As it turns out, her crack dealer was a guy who liked to hang around the parking lot from time to time. He built up quite a little business at that location. From his familiarity with the grocery store—watching the amount of traffic going in and out—he learned pretty quickly that there must be a lot of cash on the premises. I'm sure it was a temptation for him, as well."

Margot was curious enough to break her silence. "Who was this drug dealer? I've noticed a lot of suspicious characters operating out there during my surveillance. Can you tell me which one it was?"

"Well, strange as it may seem, he was more of a regular guy. Not one of the dope dealers we usually come across in that neighborhood. He was actually a salesman at a downtown clothing store. I can get you his name. Felix somebody. Doesn't really matter. It was an alias. We found out he was a con man who bounced around the country under assumed names. I'm told he'd done time for drugs and receiving stolen property before he found his way to New Orleans. It didn't take him long to sniff out Phuoc Tho Duong as a target of criminal opportunity."

"Makes sense," she acknowledged with downcast eyes.

"And when the rookie police officer—or, you think her name was Arabella—was denied the private detail, she set her mind on gettin' the money one way or another. She felt cheated out of what was rightly hers. So, she enlisted the assistance of this Felix character. She agreed to commit the robbery herself but needed a firearm that could not be traced back to her."

Margot winced. The firearm that killed Francis.

"I don't know if she planned the whole thing like this, or if things went wrong at the last minute. But she went in for the cash—and shot the lady who runs the place—"

"Mrs. Nguyen—"

"Mrs. Nguyen, along with two of her children, I should say three of her children—one of them survived—along with the detail officer who was on duty. I'm sorry to say that the detail officer was, in fact, Francis Ernst."

Barksdale paused at this point and looked down at his hands on the conference table, as if he knew Margot needed time to absorb everything. After a few moments, he continued: "He was killed instantly. As were Mrs. Nguyen and two of her children. A third child survived and was able to identify the shooter. The child recognized her as NOPD, a beat cop—I don't know her full name yet, I know you said 'Arabella' someone—who had been to the store often enough that the child could identify her immediately. Apparently, she just walked in there today, in civilian clothes, to get the gun and effect the robbery."

"How do we know this Felix guy provided the weapon?"

"The surviving child. She saw him give it to her just before the incident. She also saw her return the firearm to this Felix fella after everything went down. Apparently, he tossed it into a dumpster. Uniform recovered it there. For some reason, he remained on the scene for almost an hour afterward. Maybe he thought it would look suspicious if he fled. No one's real sure. But—and here's a look inside the mind of a criminal—he took the opportunity to make some other drug deals that he had already arranged. A passing patrolman witnessed some suspicious behavior and detained him."

"What's the girl's name? How old is she?"

"I don't know her name. She's maybe thirteen or fourteen. She and two of her siblings hid in the freezer. They were killed, but she wasn't hit. She stayed in the freezer with the dead bodies until the NOPD found her there."

Margot dropped her head.

"Yes. It must have been horrifying for her. It's the worst tragedy I've seen in a long time. Maybe ever."

Margot sniffled and quickly ran her fingers beneath her eyes in case any tears had dripped onto her cheeks. Barksdale looked around the conference room for a tissue.

"It doesn't really matter, but this Felix guy . . . turns out he has an extensive criminal record. He even claimed to have legal counsel already on site, which was strange, but that turned out to be false. At any rate, no further suspects were identified, and everybody involved in this tragedy— all the perpetrators, anyway—have been arrested. The prosecution should be pretty straightforward. I know that doesn't make it any easier for you, but you should know that the matter is closed, at least for the time being. That includes our investigation of the lottery and any other political malfeasance that had come up on our radar."

Margot thought about the license plate number she'd taken down for the man she'd presumed was Jerry Sonthonax.

"The business will, in all likelihood, be closed down for a while," Barksdale said.

Just then, there was another knock on the door, and Millie Gamard entered. Barksdale excused himself and spoke softly to Millie, but loud enough for Margot to hear: "I already told her everything that I know. Why don't you explain your role and what will happen going forward. I'll be in my office."

Margot and Millie were left alone in the conference room. Millie was one of the agency's crisis intervention counselors commissioned by the Occupational and Mental Health Services Department of the FBI to provide psychological support.

Millie explained her role and how she was there to help in any way Margot needed. "You've been through a terrible trauma and witnessed some things that perhaps your training has not prepared you for. It's important for you to remember that you are a person, not just a federal agent conditioned to control her emotions. As a matter of fact, I've arranged for you to take some personal time away from your duties to be with family, or friends, in order to make some sense of this tragedy, if that's possible. Of course, I want you to consider me a friend who will be available at any time or for any reason."

Margot could hear and understand the words Millie was saying and the refuge she was offering, but she could not muster an intelligible response apart from an almost imperceptible nod.

Millie continued: "I have some literature the bureau provides to help people get through these difficult times. I know you've seen us hand them out many times, so you probably know what they say. I don't think government pamphlets would have anything productive to offer you right now, but they are available. This is my card. Feel free to call me anytime. Until then, I'll let you get out of here. Don't worry about your ongoing case responsibilities. They will be assigned to other agents while you're on leave. Take as long as you want."

After another extended pause, Millie asked, "Do you have any questions for me?"

Margot looked at Millie but could not bring herself to speak. She simply shook her head slightly and stood slowly from her chair as if to signal that she was prepared to begin her recovery elsewhere. Millie stood up as a sign of sympathy and raised one forearm at the elbow without touching Margot in the way that people, mainly cops, do when offering a no-contact escort. Margot again cast her eyes downward and began her exit from the conference room. She turned down the hallway and headed for her desk. She never actually noticed, but she could feel that other agents in the cubicle area were watching her.

Alone for the first time at her desk since watching those bodies on gurneys being rolled into ambulances at the grocery store, Margot took her seat in front of her computer screen and the personal items on her desk: pictures of her parents and her nieces, her academy diplomas, shooting range scorecards, a laminated schedule of the previous year's New

Orleans Saints football schedule, and a color reproduction of Renoir's *Luncheon of the Boating Party* that contained, among the various subjects in the Parisian fête galante, a portrait of her ancestor, Baron Raoul Barbier, the former mayor of colonial Saigon. It was the only item on her desk that might reflect her Vietnamese heritage, however obscure, that she was willing to advertise at the office.

Margot resolved to leave the office before any open crying began. She lifted her duty belt from the hook on the cubicle wall and walked slowly toward the elevator bay. Once aboard the elevator car, she pressed the lobby button and stared at her reflection in the closed brass doors. She wanted to cry but would never allow herself to do so on FBI premises. She could feel the muscles of her stomach and upper back constricting. She managed to make it across the parking lot to her car without bursting into tears. She knew then that she would not know the soft bondage of slumber anytime soon.

Out of the building and into the parking lot, as she approached the driver's-side door of her car, she felt her ability to suppress her emotions weaken. She reached into her pocket and pressed the remote "unlock" button on her key fob. She lifted the car door handle, slid behind the steering wheel, and tossed her duty belt onto the passenger seat. She closed the door, placed both hands on top of the steering wheel, and let her head fall between her outstretched arms. At the moment she felt ready to surrender to grief, her phone rang. It was Barksdale. The luxury of tears was once again suspended because she was determined to demonstrate to her boss that she was maintaining professional decorum. Her voice cracked as she said, "Hello."

"Agent Huong. It's Barksdale. I didn't see you leave. Just wanted to check on you and make sure you were heading home for some rest, you know, that you were safe and sound. I caught your brother on his cell phone and told him to meet you at home instead of coming here. Does that suit you okay?"

"Yes," she managed to squeak into the hands-free microphone mounted at the seam of the cloth headliner where it met the windshield.

"I'm just headed home for some rest." It was the longest sentence she could offer without breaking down.

"Very good. I think that's exactly what you need. Millie told me that she had recommended as much. Get a good night's sleep, and I'll call you in the morning. Don't worry about your caseload for the time being. Things will look better when the sun comes up. Does that sound good?"

"Yes." She was thankful that he had asked a yes/no question. Anything requiring a more substantive response would have been difficult to answer.

"Okay. We'll talk in the morning," said he, politely offering to end a phone call that had completed its usefulness.

"Thank you, sir."

She drew the shift knob one notch toward the back of the gear panel frame and backed out of her space in the parking lot. Once clear of the other parked cars, she proceeded onto Leon C. Simon Drive in the direction of Elysian Fields Avenue. She did not know where to go, but driving was a useful distraction for her anguished condition. The thoroughfare came to an end sooner than she expected, and she found herself at the edge of the French Quarter where Elysian Fields meets the river. Her car seemed to drive itself around a hotel with flags flying from angled flagpoles anchored to a balustered gallery. The car made a gentle 180-degree turn in front of the old US Mint and continued away from the river on Esplanade Avenue. She was traveling away from town on the downriver edge of the French Quarter toward Gentilly and the Fair Grounds Race Course. Just past the interstate overpass but before the entrance to City Park, she no longer felt capable of driving further. She pulled her car over on the side of Esplanade Avenue to allow herself a deep cry that would be horrible and fulfilling at the same time.

She was eyeless in Gaza while all around her was salt and empty earth. Thoughts of suicide flashed across her mind without any real specificity. The only defense she could put against these vague ideas was her Catholic faith and the list of mortal sins she had memorized as a girl from her Baltimore Catechism. Her life, she had been taught, was not hers to take, no matter the magnitude of her unhappiness. But

Margot had become bloodless and friable. Great chunks of her constitution seemed to fall to the floorboards of her little car. She wished only to be abolished, then expire.

Margot fought off these thoughts and allowed herself fifteen minutes of solitary bereavement to try and collect herself. She considered calling her brother, but instead, she decided to call her parents. It had been a long time since she turned to them for emotional support, so she felt that she would not be surrendering too much of her independence to ask for help.

She called but got only their home answering machine. They would, no doubt, be at Mary Queen of Vietnam Church, helping out with preparations for the week's parish activities.

She was, after all that had happened, on her own.

18

After waiting in Joe W. Brown Park for what seemed like an hour, Jerry Sonthonax gave up on the idea that Glenn would be calling. He ripped his earpiece from the side of his head and clipped it onto the body of his latest burner phone. With both devices clutched in his right hand, he walked to the edge of the lake—or the drainage reservoir, whatever it was—and threw the bundle of electronic uselessness into the stagnating water. As it splashed and then sank beneath the surface, he returned to the rental car he had parked nearby.

He had to get moving, to change locations, to go anywhere other than where he was at that moment. Not that he had any particular destination in mind, but he felt impelled to get behind the wheel and drive away. Any kind of physical repositioning would provide relief, even when his geographical situs could not be blamed for the anxiety. Whether the imperative to move made him a fugitive, a refugee, an evacuee, a flight risk, a displaced person, or a nomad, it didn't make much difference. Without Burton or Glenn or his father or anyone at the Ziskind Center or anywhere else as a practicable agency of safe harbor, he really had no place to go. But he had to move.

The rental car was low on gas, and he had no money to fill up. If he were to drive away from town, he stood a good chance of being stranded in the less populated areas along Chef Menteur Highway between Louisiana and Mississippi, possibly surrounded by water or marshland. He chose to drive to friendlier urban territory toward town, through Gentilly Terrace, and past the racetrack, when he found himself on Esplanade Avenue. If he could get close enough to the river, he might be able to lose himself among the gutter punks and grackel brats who busked and panhandled in the French Quarter. What he would do from there, he wasn't entirely certain, but he might be able to scare up a cup of coffee or a beer without seeing anyone he knew.

Before he could get that far, his rental ran out of gas. He was able to coast into a parking spot on Esplanade behind an economy car that appeared to be occupied by a young girl—or, at any rate, a smaller woman with dark hair sitting in the driver's seat with her head down in the idling car—waiting, just waiting, on someone or something to happen by. Jerry remained in his dead car, trying to decide what to do. After a few minutes of indecision, Jerry opened his door and walked toward the woman's car. He approached slowly, but not stealthily, for he didn't want to scare her if his Black man's frame suddenly were to appear from out of nowhere. Taking a position a few steps removed from the driver's-side window of her car, he tried to get her attention by smiling and waving from an unthreatening, but visible, distance. He was relieved, maybe even grateful, that she rolled down the window as if to entertain any overtures he might make.

When she turned her face to ask what he wanted, Jerry could see that she was Asian, with larger eyes than most Asians he was familiar with, but ones that were red from crying. Instead of asking for help with his broken-down car or asking if he could borrow her phone to call for help or deliver some other undeveloped importunity, he seized the opportunity to ask after her well-being, as though he was rendering assistance to a distressed motorist.

"Excuse me, Miss. Is everything okay?"

"Mm-hmm," she said, trying to disabuse him of any idea that she needed help. She brushed her bangs away from her swollen eyes in a casual way meant to reassure Jerry that she was in good shape, in spite of the way things might appear.

"Okay. I was just driving by and saw that you might need some help." Jerry had found himself in a position to show the concern to which he had been refused by his erstwhile allies, Burton and Glenn. "I can go for help or get a message to someone, if you need it."

"No, but thank you for stopping. Everything's under control." She didn't seem nervous about interacting with a complete stranger, a Black man in particular.

"Okay, then. I'll leave you to it," said Jerry.

As he turned to walk back to his own car, unsure exactly where he was going or exactly what he was going to do to solve his own problems, he heard her speak through the car window that she had not rolled back up: "Aren't you Jerry Sonthonax?"

He was surprised but nonetheless flattered by the identification. Getting recognized on the street was one of the benefits of being a politician that he had relished before his personal circumstances had spoiled everything.

"Why yes. Should I count you among my supporters?" he asked, using a stock bit of politician's small talk he had learned from Burton.

"No," she said while offering a consoling smile. "I mean, I'm not in your district. What I mean is, I can't vote for you because I'm registered in another district."

Jerry appreciated her polite demurral and considered that he might have political admirers outside of his voting constituency. He didn't really know how to continue the conversation, but he was certainly enjoying the chit-chat as a respite from the torment of earlier that day and that which surely lay ahead. So, he spoke to show his gratitude for her cordiality: "Okay, well, thanks for your support, anyway, and you have a nice rest of the day!"

He walked back to his car, waved at her one more time, and slumped into the driver's seat of his dead rental. He could see, in the reflection of the compact car's exterior rearview mirror, the driver's-side window glide snugly into the rubber weather stripping of its door.

EPILOGUE

Two years later . . .
The Friday Afternoon Stammtisch at Eberhard Garrison's Steak House

DRAMATIS PERSONAE

Roger Simon: Political Consultant

Dahlia Barton: Columnist for *The Times-Picayune*

Vaughan Wadlington: Former NOPD Spokesman and Security Consultant

Phil Wahoff: Owner of Wahoff Assurance Company and City Hall Insider

Evelyn Martin: Investigative Reporter for WVUE-TV

—

PHIL: The Feds wanted the big fish. They wanted Burton Clayton, the high-profile target. When the FBI interviewed Jerry Sonthonax, he sang like a bird. The US attorney was a Republican, and they wanted to make a major corruption case against an urban Democrat power player like Clayton. They wanted political capital.

VAUGHAN: Sonthonax was small potatoes.

PHIL: Well, they would have prosecuted Sonthonax, but they gave him immunity to build their case against Clayton.

EVELYN: It turned out to be a mistake, to grant Sonthonax immunity, I mean. But they had no idea Clayton was going to die.

VAUGHAN: That's right. He died from esophageal cancer right when they had enough evidence to put him away.

ROGER: It was a bigger fuckup than that because they gave Clayton's bagman, Glenn Hornacek, immunity as well.

PHIL: The Feds thought they were playin' it perfect . . . pickin' off the lower-level conspirators one at a time to get to their main man.

ROGER: It *was* perfect. Sonthonax was completely vulnerable, the weakest link. After the seven assessors were consolidated into one big citywide office, Sonthonax wasn't gonna run for office anyway. He had no shot.

PHIL: Not without the Clayton political machine behind him. Sonthonax knew that HOPE—what's it stand for? Housing Opportunity something something . . .

ROGER: Housing Opportunity Promotes Equity.

PHIL: Whatever it is. The HOPE machine was gearing up to get Clayton elected to the big consolidated assessor's position. Sonthonax would never have gotten the support of HOPE, so all he could do was try to stay out of jail.

EVELYN: Once they got Sonthonax as a cooperating witness, Hornacek saw the writing on the wall. He was already pissed because he thought Clayton had hung him out to dry. When the Feds came a-callin', Hornacek knew Sonthonax had snitched, so he laid out the whole case against Clayton going back years. He wasn't gonna take the fall for Clayton.

ROGER: No way. His wife left him and went back to Virginia. She was some hunt-country type who didn't realize her husband had gotten tangled up in scumbag New Orleans politics. Hornacek just wanted out of the city. There was nothin' left for him here. As soon as he got immunity, he gave up the whole Clayton operation and moved to Arizona, or somewhere out west.

PHIL: I heard he got a job with a big commercial real estate developer.

ROGER: Something like that. Doin' the same thing he was doin' here. Political liaison. He was probably relieved Clayton died. He never had to come back to New Orleans to testify in court. He hasn't been back since.

VAUGHAN: So, the Feds were left with a juicy case against Clayton they could never prosecute. With Clayton dead, they had nothing. All their other conspirators had been granted immunity. What a colossal blunder.

DAHLIA: What's become of the HOPE gang? Don't hear much about them anymore.

VAUGHAN: Oh, it's limping along. With Clayton gone, they've lost their polestar. And their money.

PHIL: The HOPE organization was already on the wane. It was a relic of the civil rights era, based in Gentilly Terrace. Where Clayton's family lived, back in the day. But the old, traditional Black neighborhood ethos has dissipated.

EVELYN: All of those old "alphabet soup" groups, like BOLD, SOUL, and TIPS, have lost their cohesion. And their ability to deliver Black votes. Another result of Black housing displacement.

VAUGHAN: Gentrification. People like Glenn Hornacek movin' into traditionally Black neighborhoods. Showin' they can walk the walk, livin' on the frontier. They're so busy proving their authenticity, they don't realize the Blacks resent their very presence in their old neighborhoods.

EVELYN: Wait a minute! I live in Gentilly Terrace! I get along famously with my neighbors. They don't resent me in the least!

VAUGHAN: They might not say it, but they resent you, believe me.

EVELYN: You don't know what you're talkin' about. It's not like that at all.

VAUGHAN: Well, I can tell you it's the general feeling around the city. You're undermining what they think makes New Orleans so unique. What made it famous.

EVELYN: You're so fulla shit, Vaughan.

VAUGHAN: I know you're tryin' to make yourself feel better, but you're part of the problem. You fail to understand—

EVELYN: (*interrupting*) That's so typical of the way White people think! You don't even live in—

VAUGHAN: (*interrupting*) It doesn't matter where I live! I'm tryin' to help you out here! Whether you realize it or not, there's a suspicion about your motives that—

EVELYN: (*interrupting*) There's no ulterior motive! If anything, I'm boosting their property values!

VAUGHAN: Who's talkin' like a White person now?

PHIL: Hey! Hey! Hey! You two can argue about this later. We were talkin' about the survival of HOPE as a viable political organization. Sheesh!

VAUGHAN: That's exactly my point. Gentilly Terrace is trying to keep HOPE alive, but too many Whites have moved in.

EVELYN: That's not why those groups have lost their viability. It has a lot more to do with the failure of the federal government after Katrina. Anyway, I think Sonthonax still lives there.

VAUGHAN: He does. Moved in with his grandmother, or his grandmother's house, anyway. I think she died.

EVELYN: What's ole Jerry doin' now, does anybody know?

VAUGHAN: Well, he got disbarred. But he never left town. I think he works for the Sewerage and Water Board. Answering phones and fielding complaints. His short-lived political career is probably over, but you never know. Black voters are very forgiving.

EVELYN: He was back in the news briefly when he was listed as a defense witness at the trial.

VAUGHAN: You mean the murder trial of the detail cop?

EVELYN: Yes. Supposedly, he was gonna give testimony for the crack addicts that killed the Vietnamese family out on Chef Menteur Highway. But he was never called. I don't think he knew anything about the murder.

VAUGHAN: That's right. He'd never heard of the girl who actually shot up the place. Arabella something.

EVELYN: Whatever. She had some kinda mental illness. The robbery was totally coincidental with the shakedown Sonthonax was trying to pull on the Vietnamese grocery store.

VAUGHAN: What I could never figure out was, how did Arabella hear there was a stack of cash to be had? I mean, she didn't just show up at the grocery to steal cigarettes.

DAHLIA: Oh, she'd been hanging around that place for a while before. That's where she scored her drugs . . . from that Felix guy who was dealing out there. I forget his last name.

EVELYN: (*interjecting*) Peterbilt.

DAHLIA: That was an alias. His real name was . . . I forget.

EVELYN: Yes. Somebody Google it . . . It was definitely an alias.

DAHLIA: Whatever it was, he told Arabella about the lottery, or what he thought was a secret lottery, and convinced her to rob the place. He's the one who gave her the gun . . . the murder weapon. He didn't tell her the whole Nguyen family would be in there. I'm not even sure he knew. At any rate, he gives her the gun and tells her to grab the lottery stash, and then they could split it. She winds up having to shoot the whole family, only to find out there never was any secret stash. She came away with nothing.

VAUGHAN: Not the whole family. The youngest girl survived. She was covered by her sisters while they all hid in the freezer. They knew what was about to go down. The girl saw the whole thing. She ran into the freezer after she saw the Felix guy supply the gun, and she ducked inside. The mother and the two other kids died on top of their sister. Arabella thought they were hiding the nonexistent cash somewhere inside the freezer. She shot 'em all but didn't kill the youngest one. Big mistake.

ROGER: So, Arabella came away empty?

VAUGHAN: Zero. NOPD narcotics police were there by the time Arabella realized she had been given bad info. They had swarmed into the parking lot to stop a drug deal in progress. Just a regular cop on patrol saw the Felix character selling to one of his regular customers. While they had him in handcuffs, Arabella came sashaying out of the grocery store. That's when the surviving kid ran out of the store, saying that Arabella had killed her family. The patrolmen cuffed her while they tried to figure out what was going on. Went inside and saw Ernst's body. Then they saw bodies in the freezer. By that time, homicide detectives and EMTs were all over the scene.

ROGER: So, Arabella got the death penalty? Murdered that family but never got any money?

DAHLIA: That's right. Zip. Felix, whatever-his-name-is, got life for supplying the gun, and he never got any cash either.

PHIL: (*reading from his phone*) Here it is . . . Peterbilt . . . real name "Wiley Delbert Ropp . . . sentenced to life in prison for conspiracy to commit first-degree murder."

DAHLIA: That's right . . . Wiley Ropp . . . How could I forget that?

VAUGHAN: He was one of those roving sex-manipulator con men who preys on lonely men to finance his drug habit. Like Andrew Cunanan. A real smooth talker.

PHIL: It didn't take him long to get his hooks into Calloway.

ROGER: Well, when you're married to a rich society girl, and you're looking for a secret gay hookup, you're gonna hafta slide into the seedy underground at some point.

DAHLIA: But Peterbilt wasn't exactly an underworld character, was he? I mean, he was a clothing salesman, for chrissake!

ROGER: C'mon! That is pre-*cise*-lee where you find the gateway to the underworld! I buy weed from a car salesman on Tulane Avenue. Those kinda guys bounce around from job to job. They're always on the make.

VAUGHAN: I don't think Calloway knew Peterbilt was dealing drugs. It was only supposed to be his down-low gay playmate. Not drugs.

ROGER: His wife could've forgiven him for the secret gay life. There's no way she was surprised by that part. There's a whole secret coterie of those effete high-society husbands who engage in that lifestyle. Everybody knows about it. It was the drug part that she was scandalized by.

PHIL: Well, she knew about her daughter's drug problem. They had managed to keep that contained. But when the whole thing broke out at the grocery store, she could never have imagined that her daughter, her husband, and his boyfriend would be caught up in the same dragnet. It was too much.

ROGER: Yeah, she had to divorce him after that. Kicked him outta the mansion and paid him a one-time lump sum for his trouble. It was all her money.

PHIL: He gave up the practice of law and moved to the Florida panhandle. Near Rosemary Beach or someplace like that. I think he became a real estate agent.

ROGER: Ahhh, the career of last resorts. Residential real estate sales.

DAHLIA: Or an Uber driver.

PHIL: I heard he's doing okay. He lives there with his daughter. She's a drug rehab counselor. Or some kinda shelter for abused women. Something like that. The other daughter stayed with the mother. And the real money.

ROGER: She knows where her bread is buttered.

PHIL: The quote-unquote Fall of the House of Calloway.

VAUGHAN: And what a fall it was. Once the murder trial was over, they were happy to be done with it.

EVELYN: So was the FBI. The whole thing was a big mess. The lead investigator—the Vietnamese girl—was romantically linked with the dead detail cop. It was a big embarrassment for the bureau.

DAHLIA: I actually tracked her down. I was hoping for an interview, but she wouldn't talk. The FBI must've put a gag order on all their agents. Her name was Margot Hoang. She lives in Nashville now. She's still an FBI agent.

EVELYN: I know the rest of her family is still here. Some kind of seafood processing and transportation company. Her brother runs the family business. It's a big operation. He lives in Metairie now. They got the hell out of New Orleans East, with his wife and kids. And his parents. The whole extended family lives in one of those gated communities off Airline Highway.

PHIL: The Vietnamese population is gradually moving out of New Orleans East. They were grateful for the refuge when they first arrived, but they are under siege from the criminal element out there.

DAHLIA: It only took one generation for them to start producing doctors and lawyers with enough money to move up. And out.

VAUGHAN: The kids go to Catholic high school, make straight As, and then it's off to Princeton and Stanford. Talk about livin' the American Dream!

DAHLIA: Pretty soon, there'll be nothin' left in New Orleans East but welfare traps and convenience stores.

PHIL: It's doomed. To think that the East was once considered the area where suburban settlement would happen! Gentilly Terrace started off as a luxury subdivision.

DAHLIA: You can still see remnants of it on Gentilly Boulevard. When it was first developed, those houses had tennis courts and swimming pools, and croquet courts. The big double and triple lots were all sold off and subdivided for more modest housing.

ROGER: Makes you wonder what happened.

DAHLIA: Metairie happened. White people wanted out of Orleans Parish.

ROGER: It's funny, if you wanna get an idea of what old New Orleans neighborhoods like the Irish Channel and Bywater must have felt like, ya gotta go to Jefferson Parish. The descendants of the Irish and Italian immigrants re-created their old neighborhoods out there. Catholic churches and corner bars everywhere.

DAHLIA: That's true. The classic Yat accents are preserved in those neighborhoods. The accents have all but disappeared in the city limits. White people accents, anyway.

VAUGHAN: Don't forget St. Bernard Parish. Some of those Whites moved farther east into Arabi and Chalmette when they wanted out of Orleans.

DAHLIA: Does anyone know where Arabi got its name? That's always puzzled me.

VAUGHAN: I read about this somewhere. I think when it was first becoming a town—back in the nineteenth century—there was a big fire. At the same time, the Arabs were trying to push the British out of their homeland, and some Arab revolutionary firebombed one of the colonial administrative buildings. When the story hit the papers, the people in St. Bernard read the story and named it Arabi. Or something like that.

DAHLIA: Wow. I did not know that. So, how did Algiers get its name?

ROGER: I don't think anybody really knows the answer to that one!

DAHLIA: What about Gentilly? That sounds French to me.

PHIL: Oh, that's the old Dreux brothers. They were granted that land by the French crown back in the eighteenth century. They named it after their ancestral property. Or so they wanted people to think.

ROGER: O, Gentilly! How false are Thy prophets!

EVELYN: All right, that's enough nostalgia for one day.

VAUGHAN: Yes. I'm hungry. Let's order before they kick us out of here.

THE END

ABOUT THE AUTHOR

Born in New Orleans, Gordon Peter Wilson graduated from Vanderbilt University (BA English) and Tulane University (JD) and practiced law for twenty-five years. His first novel, *Quench the Smoldering Wick*, was published in 2018.